The Stone Necklace

STORY RIVER BOOKS

Pat Conroy, Editor at Large

The Stone Necklace

A NOVEL

...

CARLA DAMRON

Foreword by Patti Callahan Henry

THE UNIVERSITY OF SOUTH CAROLINA PRESS

Published by the University of South Carolina Press
Columbia, South Carolina 29208

www.sc.edu/uscpress

Manufactured in the United States of America

25 24 23 22 21 20 19 18 17 16
10 9 8 7 6 5 4 3 2 1

Library of Congress Cataloging-in-Publication Data
Damron, Carla.
    The stone necklace : a novel / Carla Damron.
      pages ; cm. — (Story River Books)
    ISBN 978-1-61117-619-3 (softcover : acid-free paper) —
    ISBN 978-1-61117-620-9 (ebook)
      I. Title.
      PS3604.A47S76 2016
      813'.6—dc23

                                        2015022501

This book was printed on recycled paper with 30 percent postconsumer waste content.

It takes a village. The people of my village: Rachel Silver, Mary Jane Reynolds, Ashley Warlick, Daniel Mueller, Lauren Groff, Stephanie Thompson, Jane Schwantes, Heather Marshall, Betty Joyce Nash, Shelly Drancik, Sam Morton, Tim Conroy, Jonathan Haupt, Hope Coulter, the Inkplots, and the Queens University M.F.A. program.

Special thanks to Patti Callahan Henry, Pat Conroy, Mary Alice Monroe, Ron Rash, and Lee Smith: writers who are as generous as they are talented. Also to my very, very patient family: Jim Hussey, Katie Damron, Ed Damron, Essie Mae Clark and Pam Knight. Thanks for putting up with me when I enter the crazed writer phase of things.

In memory of Riley, who helped me understand Joe.

The ache for home lives in all of us, the safe place where we can go as we are and not be questioned.

Maya Angelou, *All God's Children*
Need Traveling Shoes, 1986

Foreword

We turn to story to show us how things feel, to understand our larger world, to see truth in fiction, and it is for all of these reasons that readers will turn to, embrace, and dwell in this novel, *The Stone Necklace*.

Carla Damron delves deeply and wholly into the souls of her story's characters. She doesn't just write *about* them, but writes *from* them. She reveres her unlikely mix of protagonists, each representative in her or his way of our larger, shared experiences, as she shows with us with wisdom and grace that there are no absolutes in matters of the heart. When I met Carla, it became so clear to me that her experiences as a clinical social worker grant her uncommon insights about our convoluted journeys in being human, all to the benefit of her characters and ultimately to us as her readers.

At first glance this is a story about suburban wife and mother Lena Hastings, as Lena opens the novel with her poise and charm, but also with her conflicted heart. She's obviously suffered: breast cancer, a doomed affair, a strained homecoming to a daughter who is barely speaking to her, and a husband who is loving, but preoccupied and stressed out. Quickly we realize that this novel is about so much more than just Lena. This is about lives that might appear disparate at first, yet come together in the small crevices of life, the spaces where tragedy meets everydayness, where we must stand by one another or disappear altogether.

Through their unique voices, we meet the other characters whose lives are intersecting in ways they can't imagine. Guided by Carla's skilled storytelling, we are the ones who know, we are the interlopers peeking into minds and hearts. We, as the readers, are the ones who see how the broken characters, most of whom don't yet know each other or fully know themselves, are finding a way to live through illness, addiction, death, loss, and poverty while also coming to know joy and exquisite meaning.

We meet Lena's teen daughter, Becca, and feel her grief and anger over a sudden tragedy, her warring needs to accept and hate her mother. We see her desperate desire for control taking the form of self-harm. Her brothers, whom she misses and loves, come home during the crisis. Her world comes undone and we want to fix it for her, take her aside and tell her "all will be well," but this is Lena's job to do.

Then we meet the young mother, Tonya, who was traveling with her toddler son when a car accident changed the course of her life. After the terrible wreck, which wasn't Tonya's fault, she must come to terms with a world that is nothing of what she'd dreamed.

We unexpectedly come across a homeless man, Joe, who watches this family and these lives while battling his own demons and angels. Is he a madman, a prophet, a hero, a threat? We can't know—until we do know—how his life could possibly have anything to do with the others. A homeless man trying to stay alive and stay sane; where does he fit with these suburban mother-and-child relationships and with the misfortune that unites these families? This is where Carla's story becomes more than a story and takes us into that place where lives overlap in the hidden folds of our world—where the single thread of one life becomes braided with so many others as it helps give form, strength, and vibrancy to the richly layered tapestry of our shared humanity.

The nurse, Sandy, watches over a few of the others while fighting her own battles of addiction and shame. Resisting authentic love, she will have to finally surrender and we feel it, all the way to our bones, when she says, "perhaps, recovery was this: bearing the unbearable moment." Here she speaks for all of us and not just about drugs, not just about shame, but also about living, about returning to life from the brink of anything else.

As the novel unfolds so does our understanding of human conditions, ones we might or might not have lived with or through. I have lived through breast cancer, and although this novel doesn't deal directly with its more vulgar aspects, it does dent the heart of recovery and healing. In this way and so many others, this is a novel about truth, about the caution and compassion needed to know and to be our true selves.

A southern city novel, *The Stone Necklace* also makes a character of its Columbia, South Carolina, setting. When Carla describes the river, "white froth boiled up as the rapids shot between rocks that protruded like smooth gray teeth," we know we are in the hands of a deft storyteller. Carla wields this well-honed skill to tremendous effect throughout her novel. Yet what can prepare us for a line that moves us with emotional truth, a line like "This mourning had so many edges to it, but she'd learned over the days that fighting it gave it strength. Better to surrender. Always surprising to come out on the other side."

And it's the same with *The Stone Necklace*—it is best to surrender, to be surprised, and to come out on the other side.

Patti Callahan Henry

CHAPTER 1

L ena Hastings cupped her husband's cheek to examine a ragged piece of tissue attached to his chin, the perfect blossom of garnet—no, crimson—against the white. "Doing battle with the razor I see."

She lifted the coffee carafe to pour him a cup, but Mitch went straight for the milk in the fridge, a sign that his heartburn had flared up again. She opened the plastic jar of Tums they kept by the sink and rattled two pastel wafers into his hand. He flipped them like coins.

"Sleeping Beauty up yet?" he asked.

"Hope so." She glanced at the ceiling, listening for signs of life from Becca. She'd wait ten more minutes before calling out, hopeful that this morning would go smoother than the others.

Mitch pulled his cell phone from his robe and set it by his place at the table. "I've left a million messages for Phillip. Be nice if he called me back." Mitch often complained about his work. Maybe if he wasn't such a perfectionist. Maybe if he didn't work himself into an anxious knot over every little thing.

Out the window the maple and ginkgo trees, ablaze in reds and golds, shimmied in the autumn breeze. Lena should paint this tantrum of color soon, before the grass dulled completely to cardboard brown. She imagined the feel of the paintbrush, the swirl of shades coming together before she even touched the canvas. It had been eighteen months since she'd allowed herself that luxury, the last piece of normal life she had yet to reclaim.

She returned to the table, a heavy colonial monolith from Mitch's grandmother, surrounded by five sturdy chairs. Once, she had removed two seats and the center leaf, shrinking it from oval to round and freeing space. The change lasted a week. "It doesn't feel right," Mitch had said, and they extended the table again, and replaced the ladder-backs, as though their sons had never grown up and left home, and would bound through the kitchen door any minute to tussle over the last Toaster Strudel.

Mitch tossed back a glassful of milk like it was a shot of tequila, wincing when he lowered it to the counter.

"Honey, if you feel that bad, let Phillip manage things at the office," she said.

"I would if he was in town."

"Where is he this time?" she asked.

"Bermuda."

This was a fight best averted. Mitch's business partner had taken three vacations this year. And Mitch? Just the July beach trip and even then, she'd caught him huddled over work files and answering a dozen calls. She'd removed his wrist watch on day three. On day four, when she seduced him into three rounds of miniature golf, the man finally uncoiled.

He thumped a fist against his chest, his face and bald head flushing pink as the inside of a conch shell. Maybe he really was sick this time, but it was hard to be sure. With Mitch, the sky was often falling.

"You need to eat something. Let me fix you some toast." She spread low-fat margarine on two slices of whole grain bread because it was the one thing Mitch could eat with a turbulent stomach. For their daughter Becca, it was plain yogurt. And for Lena: chicken broth. How many gallons had she consumed last year? Too many, but she had survived both monsters: the cancer that didn't kill her and the chemo that almost did.

Lena heard movement from upstairs and glanced at the clock. Ten until eight. She'd give Becca a few more minutes. Things went smoother if Becca arrived without sounding the alarm.

The vibration of Mitch's cell phone disturbed the cutlery. When he answered, she could tell the caller wasn't Phillip because Mitch didn't say "About damn time" or "Where the hell have you been" in a tone that would be half-playful, half-not. Instead, he spoke in his realtor voice. "I understand. I'm concerned, too. It would help if you'd tell me—" He carried the phone out of the kitchen.

Just as Lena rose to summon her, Becca appeared in the doorway, her jeans hanging from her too-narrow hips. Her long brown hair, still wet from the shower, dripped down her baggy tan sweater. She looked vacantly around the kitchen as if she hadn't entered it a thousand times.

"Morning, sunshine. Want some cereal?" Lena asked like she did every morning.

"I'll get it." Becca hurried to the pantry for the Special K and to the cabinet for a measuring cup. Exactly one-half of a cup made it into her bowl. Lena crossed to the counter for a banana and handed it to Becca, who broke off a third to slice into her cereal.

Lena glanced out the window again. The dappled light through the trees made lace patterns on the patio. Beyond, that one stubborn foxglove, its flowers like droopy lavender bells, stood in defiance of fall. This was what she should paint. The sun would be at the right angle in another hour, so once she got Becca and Mitch out the door, she could unearth her easel from the garage. She would set up beside the crape myrtle. Maybe today she could do it.

Becca poured skim milk into her bowl. No sugar. She took a bite, crunching with her mouth partly open, a drop of milk slithering down her chin, but Lena didn't comment. "Want me to fix you a sandwich for lunch?" Lena asked. "I made chicken salad."

"I'll eat in the cafeteria."

Lena wanted to say, "Make sure to eat your vegetables and finish the milk," but that would prompt a Becca tirade about the "suck-factor" of cafeteria food, and thwart Lena's hope for a drama-free breakfast table.

A few minutes later, Mitch reappeared, the cell phone gripped in his hand. He glanced down at the toast on his plate but didn't touch it.

"Who called?" Lena asked.

"One of Phillip's clients. Annoying bastard's pestered me for two days," Mitch said.

"Try the toast," she said. Maybe Lena would have time to go by the school and get the supplies she'd left in the art studio. Had they kept them after all this time?

"What are your plans for today?" Mitch asked.

She took a deep breath, unsure why she needed courage to say it. "I think . . . I think I may paint."

"Really?" Mitch gave her his most dazzling and private smile.

"Are you going back to school?" Becca's quiet voice contradicted the glare she sent Lena. Maybe the hostility was deserved, but Lena needed no reminders. She wore her sins like a stone necklace. If only Becca had inherited her father's gift for forgiveness, but she was more like Lena—neither would erase the damage done.

"I'm not going back to school," Lena answered. Not even for what she'd left behind.

"Well I think it's great that you're painting again." Mitch squeezed her hand. "About time."

Yes, it was. Had she kept the cadmium blue? The fine-bristled brush?

"Is that all you're having for breakfast?" Mitch asked their daughter. "Want my toast?"

"I'm fine. I'm full. Leave me alone," Becca growled. Fighting over what the child put in her mouth never accomplished anything. They had survived her other phases. This, too, would pass.

"At least finish the banana," he said.

"She can take it to school," Lena said. Once Mitch finished dressing and Becca's ride came, she'd scoot them from the house. A blank canvas awaited her.

• • •

MITCH FOUGHT FOR BREATH as he climbed the stairs to dress. It felt like something hot and furry had climbed inside his chest. Lena didn't take his health problems seriously. Of course, her battle with breast cancer last year had raised the bar on what it meant to be sick. He might feel like a semi ran over him, but how did that stack up against a mastectomy, radiation, and gut-wrenching chemo? Her cancer trivialized everything else. Sometimes, it even trivialized him.

He found more Tums on his dresser and tossed another into his mouth. Spats, Becca's cat, hopped up on the chest and nudged his hand for a stroke. How was it that Spats became his cat? He'd been a gift for his daughter's twelfth birthday, a little black and white blur who chased shadows and slept curled up beside Becca's head. A year later, as Becca busied herself with other interests, Spats had turned his devotion to him, and he'd never liked cats. But Spats was a comfort now. And had been during Lena's illness, those countless days when she was so sick, when there had been nothing he could do to help. Spats would stretch himself across his lap every evening, and Mitch would fold himself into the cat's warmth and purr, as calming as the trickle of a brook. Give Spats a stroke and all was right with the world. Spats didn't ask the impossible of him.

Mitch tucked his shirt into the trousers, straightened his tie—"Republican red" his younger son had called it—and ran a polishing cloth over his Oxford shoes. A final glance in the mirror: an errant eye brow hair he smoothed with a finger. He checked the phone again before easing it into its holster. Phillip had been confident the strip mall deal would go through, that their profits would cover all the recent losses, but the client's escalating calls worried Mitch. They'd sunk too much into this. Of course, it was partly Mitch's fault; he'd been absent from the business during Lena's illness, leaving Phillip without adult supervision. That their future depended on this sketchy deal did not help Mitch's indigestion.

When he went back downstairs, he found Lena and Becca continuing their mother-daughter stalemate expressed by spoons slapped in cereal bowls and itchy silence. At times like this they mirrored each other: the same angular cheekbones, the thin lips pressed tight. Becca had grown into a moody child, but Lena said all teenage girls were like that. Thank God the two boys had been easier: Scouts, then sports, then college. Sims: married, a successful banker, with a kid of his own. Elliott: a jazz guitarist in New York. Good boys. Boys to be proud of.

Lena moved to the window and stared out. "Joe's here."

At first Mitch didn't see him. As big as Joe Booker was, he could almost be invisible standing beside the magnolia tree in the garden, broad shoulders hunched, head down. Mitch had met the homeless man three years before in the graveyard of his church. Joe proved handy with a rake and kept the small cemetery immaculate, so Mitch hired him for yard work. He waved through the window and Joe met him at the back steps.

"Thanks for stopping by. Leaves are getting deep." Mitch didn't get too close—Joe didn't like that—and waited for the sequoia of a man to look up.

The slow lifting of his head made his dreadlocks curtain much of his midnight-dark face. "Gotta get to the breakfast line now. Be back this afternoon."

This could be a problem. Becca returned from school at three, and had an irrational fear of Joe—something he'd told Lena they needed to work on. "Add it to the list," Lena had answered.

"I'll be done before your girl gets home," Joe added.

Relieved, Mitch reached for his wallet and pulled out a twenty.

Joe shook his head. "Too much."

"You always say that." He was lucky to have Joe and not rely on some landscaping crew he could no longer afford. Mitch tucked the bill in the pocket of Joe's pea coat. Joe stiffened at the contact.

"I'll get them weeds around the birdbath, too," Joe said.

"Thanks." He watched Joe shuffle away, noting how his foot bulged over the side of his right shoe. Maybe he'd stop by Goodwill to get him a new pair.

Back inside, he opened his briefcase and removed the small, speckly stone Joe had left for him on a tombstone a few months before. Since then, the strange gift had found its way into Mitch's pocket every morning. Not a good luck talisman—his luck had been atrocious lately—more like a worry stone.

He snapped shut the case and said, "I'm off."

Lena tilted her head up and he bent to kiss her, noticing how her gaze moved from him to the door. Next came Becca, who gave him her most polished adolescent eye roll. He pressed his lips to the top of her head. "See you later, kitten."

5

"What time will you be home?" Lena held the door open for him.

"I'll call you later."

Before climbing in the Lexus, he draped his jacket over the headrest and loosened his tie. He felt hot, like something was searing him from the inside. As he slid behind the wheel he noticed his hands tingling; pressure swelled like bellows in his chest. The inside of the car was starved for oxygen. This felt like more than indigestion. Should he call Dr. Burnside? He was often too quick to make that call.

He opened the window to let in some air. After a few deep breaths, the pain ebbed into a dull ache below his sternum. This was probably just the reflux. He backed out of the garage, careful to miss the leaf bags awaiting pick-up beside the driveway, and eased onto Lakeshore Drive. A few blocks later, he turned onto Forest heading downtown.

And then. "God!" Something hit him in the solar plexus, hit him with the force of a hundred mule kicks. He gasped, releasing the wheel to claw at his shirt like he could claw out the pain. Grayness fogged his eyes. He couldn't breathe; air rejected his lungs. He should brake but his foot slipped.

He could see a dim outline of streets ahead and a smear of red from the traffic light. A silver van coming.

The impact sounded like a bomb. His car door screamed as it crumpled, and the van pushed him sideways across the intersection. Through the empty socket of his window he saw the other driver, a young woman, eyes wide in terror. His mind flashed to a memory of Lena giving birth to Sims, that last horrific moment when she cried that she couldn't push anymore and *please, please, God.*

Off the pavement now. The rush of leaves covered the hood of his car before it crashed into the tree. The airbag knocked him backward, and he closed his eyes against its powdery assault. Pain exploded in his hand where it clutched his chest. He felt remote. Blurred. Why couldn't he breathe? He thought he said Lena's name, to ask her a question. Where was he?

CHAPTER 2

Tonya Ladson tasted blood. Plump red drops fell from her throbbing nose to something white and dusty in her lap. What happened? She could see a cloud, or was it smoke, outside the webby cracks in her windshield. Metal pressed against her side from where the door was bowed in. A car horn blared. She desperately wanted to silence the noise. That's when she noticed her hand on the horn.

"Byron!" Tonya snatched back her hand and spun around to see her two-year-old's car seat tilted sideways from the collision. Byron had almost escaped the contraption just moments before. "Byron?"

She tore at the release for her seatbelt. His corduroyed legs kicked and squirmed; his fingers clutched the strap that held him suspended over the seat. Alive. Her baby was alive.

The skin around her nose burned. Getting to her child took some maneuvering, but she twisted between seatbacks and wrestled Byron's car seat until she had it righted. He whimpered, his tear-streaked face looking up at her like she knew something he didn't. She skimmed a hand over his head to feel for lumps or cuts, wincing as tiny crystals of safety glass sprinkled down from his hair. "Oh baby."

Smoke puffed from the crumpled heap that had been the other car, the Lexus that had run the red light—she was sure her light had been green. She had slammed the brakes but it was too late and she couldn't veer out of the way and it kept coming and oh God.

"Mommy out." Byron reached for her but she hesitated, worried she shouldn't move him. She searched his tiny body for signs of bleeding.

"Shhh," she said, her voice trembling. A buzzing sound erupted. Where? Her cell phone vibrated on the seat beside the driver's.

"Out!" Byron bellowed, feet flailing, a sneaker smacking her in the breast.

"Stop that!" She grabbed his legs but a full-out Byron meltdown was imminent, so she unclicked the strap and let him tumble into her arms.

"You're okay, little man." She begged the words to be true. Byron pressed his face into her shoulder and she held him close, rocking a little, thinking how he almost wasn't here on this earth for her to hold.

"You're fine. Just fine." Moisture warmed her skin from where he'd wet his pants.

The cell phone quieted. She had been calling work when the accident happened. She was explaining that she'd be five minutes (really fifteen) late, and her co-worker said her boss was asking for her. Behind her, Byron was yelling about going potty but she knew she couldn't stop until she got him to daycare and that's when . . . She shouldn't have been on her cell. She knew better. What would her husband say? What if this was her fault? No, her light had been green, she was sure of it. She was.

A man tugged at the Lexus's driver door, others emerging from nearby cars to watch. Tonya breathed in the sickly-sweet odor of gasoline. From her engine? What if it exploded? She scrambled to open the door. An elderly gentleman on the other side reached for her arm and asked if she was injured.

She tried to untwine Byron from her neck but he let out a squeaky cry, like the time he slammed his hand in a drawer and his thumbnail turned blue.

"What's wrong?" Panic boiled up as she scanned his body. "Does your arm hurt?"

He held it awkwardly, elbow pushed into ribs, hand knotted in a fist. Was it broken? Had she made it worse?

The stranger handed her a tissue so she could dab at the blood dripping from her nose. "Did someone call for an ambulance? My little boy needs help." She carried him to the sidewalk, wanting distance between them and the wreckage.

The man told her that help was on its way. They both turned their attention back to the other car. Someone yelled that the door wouldn't open. Two others circled the sedan as a great plume of gray smoke belched out from under the hood. They had to get the driver out before his car burst into flames.

"Help him!" she yelled.

An onlooker smashed the window with a rock and squeezed his hand through to open the door. As they dragged the driver out, a brown shoe snagged on the door frame and slipped from his foot. Tonya fought a mad impulse to run after it like she did a hundred times a day for Byron. They had the man on the ground now. A guy in a gray sweatshirt started CPR. All stilled, no voices, no breeze, no rumble of traffic; everything held its breath as the man tried to revive the victim's heart.

Overhead, a neon green gecko peered down from an insurance billboard. A siren howled in the distance. Tonya rested her head against her son's blond curls as police cars and ambulances halted in front of them. Byron blinked up at the strobing lights. "Pretty," he said.

"Yes they are," she answered. Soon the road teemed with police and EMTs, the quiet replaced with shouts and the clatter of equipment being unloaded. They put the man on a gurney and secured an oxygen mask to his face, which had to mean he was still alive. One EMT made a few muffled comments into a radio as they hoisted him into the back of one of the ambulances.

The EMT who came over to Tonya was mannish, with the uneven cropped hair of someone who'd taken scissors to herself. John would call her a lesbo, but John was not there, thank God.

"I understand your little boy was injured?" she said.

Tonya eased Byron to the ground. He whimpered, eyeing the woman with the skepticism of a terrified two year old. "His arm," Tonya said.

"Was he in a car seat?"

"Yes." But he hadn't been just a moment before, when he'd twisted out of the straps and she had bribed him with the promise of a cookie to get him secured again. "The car seat fell over in the accident."

The woman eyed the inside of the van. "That's probably a good thing."

Good because the Lexus had caved in Byron's door and his fragile little bones stood no chance against the grill of that metal beast. Good because her son might not be alive right now. Tonya closed her eyes against the what-if's swarming her mind.

When a police officer approached and asked for her license and registration, she returned to her car. Her purse was on the passenger seat, and the registration was buried in the repair invoices that stuffed her glove box, which John was always telling her she needed to clean out. As she squeezed back into the van, she noticed her cell phone trembling on the vinyl. She grabbed it with her purse and a fistful of crumpled papers from the glove compartment.

The EMT said, "Okay, buddy, can I take a peek at your tummy?" She lifted Byron's sweater to reveal an angry red stripe bisecting his ribs. He screamed when she touched his shoulder.

"Shhh," Tonya soothed, her hand on his head.

"Could be a collarbone fracture. Best to take him to the hospital and let the docs take a look at him," the EMT said.

Hospital. The word echoed.

The officer held out a hand. Tonya pawed through her purse for her license, but lost her grip on the pile of clutter so that everything hit the sidewalk. The cell phone clacked against the concrete. "Damn it."

9

The creased registration landed on top of a Jiffy Lube invoice, so she gave it to the officer. The EMT had a stethoscope pressed against Byron's chest, which had him distracted. Tonya answered the phone.

"Tonya? Where the hell are you? Jamison's furious," Marion, her office-mate, said.

"I've been in an accident. The car's—the car's a mess. And Byron got hurt and we have to take him to the hospital. And the other driver, I'm not even sure he's going to make it and—" The words exploded from her mouth.

"Oh no," Marion said softly. "Okay, take it easy. Is Byron hurt bad?"

"His arm—just his arm, we think."

"Okay. Want me to meet you at the hospital?"

"No. I'll call John." She would, but not yet.

As she hung up the phone, she heard a tentative "Mommy?" A tearful Byron came to her and as she lifted him, he tucked his head under her chin. When he curved into her like this, when his little body nestled into her flesh, it was like he was secure again in her womb, like they were one creature, sharing blood and oxygen and life.

Nothing made her feel this complete. She wanted to stay in this moment, apart from the police and the crash and the waiting ambulance and the call she had to make to John.

"Ma'am?" the EMT startled her. "Can I take a look at your nose?" She let the woman check her, then answered her questions about the date, the president, and other meaningless stuff. Gentle hands probed her nose and cheekbones, as Byron's head lolled against her breast.

"Okay, Mrs. Ladson, let's get your boy into the ambulance." She didn't remember telling anyone her name. She imagined there might be a lot about this day she wouldn't remember, but some things she'd never, ever forget.

She groped for the phone in her pocket, took a deep breath, and dialed her husband's number.

• • •

BECCA HASTINGS HESITATED ON the stairs leading to her third floor English class so that her best friend Kayla could catch up. "Check out what Amanda Howard has on. Her pants are so tight I can see her butt crack!" Kayla said.

"Gross," Becca answered.

"If I ever look like that, do the humane thing and shoot me." Kayla swiped her lips with petal-pink lip balm.

As if on cue, Amanda Howard pushed past them, her hip-hugging capris riding the waves and valleys of cellulite. Becca slipped her hand down to her own behind, wondering how she might look from this angle.

"I mean it, Becca. Shoot me."

"You don't even have a butt." It annoyed Becca that Kayla wore a size three without trying, that she ate a Snickers bar every single afternoon with her Diet Coke, and her stomach stayed flat as a tabletop.

"I need to make a stop," Becca said.

"Be quick, or Mr. Brunson will write you up."

Becca backed in through the door of the women's room, waving Kayla on to class. She dropped her books on the counter and stood before the mirror, twisting around to take in her own backside view. Still too big, but maybe not as bad as Amanda's. She frowned at the rest of her reflection. She had dieted for seven months. Did the Hip-Hop workout on DVD and ran three miles every single day, yet still so fat.

She lifted her shirt. Maybe a little progress? The ridges of her ribs made a ladder up her chest. Her pants had to be gathered and pinned. Once she lost ten pounds more, she'd pierce her navel and insert a gold ring, like Kayla had, and Dad would completely flip out. She smiled at the idea, seeing Dad's face turn red as a stop sign, hearing Mom rant about the danger of infection. Her parents were so pathetic.

She rested a hand on the pitted, cold porcelain sink and caught a faint whiff of vomit, an odor that no longer bothered her. A bell signaled it was time for English where Mr. Brunson, the artist-in-residence, was making them do poetry. He had long hair and his arms and face had dark freckles like pixels in an out-of-focus picture. Mom's friend Royce had freckles like that but his were reddish orange. Becca had only seen Royce twice but remembered every detail about him: how he was barely taller than Mom. How his two front teeth overlapped like crossed fingers. How his grip squished her knuckles when they met.

"He has an artist's hands," her mom had said.

Becca hoped she never laid eyes on Royce again.

She collected her things and opened the door right into Dylan Dreher, a collision that sent her purse and backpack crashing to the floor.

"Oh, Jeez. I'm sorry." Dylan dropped to his knees to gather her stuff. "Didn't mean to clobber you like that."

"I think I'm the one who did the clobbering." Becca wondered how the fates would pick this particular boy for her to slam into.

11

"You okay?" Dylan gave her that big dimpled grin she'd seen a thousand times from across the arc of desks in Mr. Brunson's class.

"Yeah," she muttered as she tried to think of what else to say.

He handed her the purse and toothpaste tube that had rolled across the floor. Great. He'd think she was some teeth-cleaning nerd. "I should do that, too," he said. "After two years in braces, I should do better with my teeth."

She remembered the braces. They had been blue, like his eyes.

"Looks like we're both late for Brunson's poetry fest. Wish I could cut it," he said.

"I do, too." She leaned against the wall to demonstrate how she was *not* in a hurry to get to class.

"You know, he smokes like a chimney. I caught him outside the cafeteria the other day, doing that chain smoking thing, lighting one cigarette with the burning nub of another."

"You can smell it. And what's with the long hair?" she asked.

Dylan looked away and Becca felt like a complete idiot: Dylan's hair fell in thick curls to his collar. Horrified, she went on, "I mean, long hair is great on guys under thirty, but Brunson's ancient. Maybe he's one of those hippie types from the sixties or something."

Dylan seemed to perk up. "I bet he smokes weed. Doesn't he look like the type?"

"Definitely." Becca didn't know anyone who did weed, except maybe a few musician friends of Elliott's. She'd tried it once and didn't like it.

"There's a teacher at the high school who deals to the students. My brother heard it from one of the ballplayers."

"For real?" Becca couldn't wait to start high school next year. At five foot-seven, Becca towered over half the guys in her grade, but not Dylan. Dylan had an inch on her. She loved his wide shoulders and narrow waist and hoped he didn't plan to play football like his brother.

"Guess we'd better head to class," he said. He started to move but hesitated. "Hey, wanna eat lunch some time?"

"What?" Her mouth dropped open. She probably looked like a guppy. He stepped back, his eyes downcast, and started to turn away.

What a moron she was. Her one chance and—"No, wait!" she yelled. "I'd like to. Sometime."

"Okay, we'll do it sometime." He still wasn't looking at her, and she had a feeling sometime might never happen.

"Tomorrow's good for me," she blurted out, a brave move, a risk, but this might be her only chance. "We could meet outside the cafeteria."

He turned, his dimpled smile as warm as sunlight. "That would be good."

They caught a break in English class because Mr. Brunson wasn't there yet. They both scurried to their seats, Kayla staring wide-eyed at Becca when she saw who she was with. "How'd that happen?" she whispered.

"He wants to have lunch with me tomorrow." She still couldn't believe it. What would she wear? The right outfit would be crucial. Nothing too prim or nerdy, but nothing that made her look fat. If she could just get rid of those last ten pounds.

"Becca Hastings?" Mr. Brunson stepped in the room. "Can I see you for a second?"

"Damn," she muttered, standing. She glanced over at Dylan, who shrugged back. Mr. Brunson held the door, beckoning her into the hall where the principal was standing. She was in trouble this time.

"Becca," the principal said softly. "I'm afraid I have some bad news. It's about your father."

"My father?" She looked at him, wondering what he was talking about. Her dad was fine. She'd just seen him that morning.

"There was an accident. He and your mom are at the hospital right now. Your brother is coming to get you."

"An accident?" No, that wasn't right. It couldn't be. Becca had just seen him. He had kissed her head and—

". . . accident was bad, I'm afraid," Dr. Lowery's lips looked like blubbery worms as he kept talking, but Becca couldn't make sense of what he was saying.

". . . . brother will tell you about it when he arrives."

"Sims is coming?" she interrupted. "When?"

Mr. Brunson laid a gentle hand on her shoulder, and she pulled away from it. "I'm sure your dad will be okay."

"My mom was sick," she said. "Last year she had cancer. She's better now though."

Mr. Brunson and Dr. Lowery exchanged strange looks, like they felt sorry for her. She didn't want their pity. "That's good, Becca. Maybe your dad will be better, too." Mr. Brunson sounded false, like he didn't believe it for a second, and it scared her. She wanted to get away from the two men. Away from the school. Away.

"Let's head to my office. We'll wait for Sam—"

"Sims," she corrected.

"We'll wait for Sims there."

CHAPTER 3

Sandy Albright stood in front of her locker at Mercy General Hospital, relieved to see her name still there; she hadn't been entirely erased. It was her first day back on the job after a twelve-week suspension, and she was more jittery than when she began her career fourteen years before. She wondered how people would treat her. Who on the nursing staff knew.

She found her scrubs, and though the drawstring had to be loosened, the top still fit despite the six pounds she'd gained. She'd walk them off once she got swept away in the chaos on the floor. Sandy was eager to get busy again. Eager to show her nursing supervisor, Marie Hempshall, that she was ready for this. And maybe eager to show herself the same thing.

"Welcome back." Pete Borden draped a hairy arm around her shoulder. He smelled like mint and cigarettes. "Place ain't been the same."

"Really? Didn't we all get big raises? And extra vacation time?" These lines she'd rehearsed, hoping to cut through any tension as she was re-introduced to her job.

Pete laughed. "Yeah, and I won the lottery, and we have a gay Republican in the White House."

"Damn. At least a girl can dream."

He twitched a thumb towards the door. "Ready for PM report?"

Not in the least, she almost said, but she plastered on a grin. "Let's do it."

She survived the meeting by taking copious notes, writing down each patient's name and status, and avoiding the probing eyes of others in the room. Fifteen minutes later, the briefing ended and she sprang to her feet. "Sandy, stick around for a second," Marie Hempshall said. "Pete can handle the first part of rounds."

Here we go, Sandy thought. She twirled the blue NA wristband that her sponsor had given her to read the letters engraved: "TIWBS": *Today I will be sober.* The slogan needed to get her through the hours, the days, the weeks to come.

Marie led her to the small, windowless office that she shared with the third shift supervisor. Marie's face was like a full moon with the nose and eyes squinched close together and a mouth no bigger than a green bean.

She sucked in her stomach to round the desk and drop into her seat. Sandy claimed the other chair, trying not to think about her last visit when Marie tried to fire her.

"You know the situation, right? Probationary status for a year. You have to attend NA meetings the full twelve months. You'll have to maintain a log of your attendance to be signed by the NA group leaders. There will be urine screens. Speaking of which—" Marie pulled a small package from her drawer and ripped open the top. She handed Sandy a cup. "We'll go down to Human Resources."

Sandy stared at the plastic container, swallowing her humiliation. And this was just the beginning. She tucked the cup in her pocket as she pushed out the door, moving fast, Marie's short legs stuttering behind her. Get this over with, she thought. Then get the shift over with, then the day . . . Damn.

She led the way to the administrative offices, through the cube farm that was the billing department, and into the single-stall bathroom beside the HR director's office. When Marie pushed in with her, Sandy realized why they'd come here—no hint of privacy. "I'm not peeing with you staring at me."

"It's policy." Marie snapped on latex gloves. Sandy glared. Marie turned around to face the mirror. "This better?"

Sandy lowered the pants of her scrubs and sat. At first, she wasn't sure she could do it, but she closed her eyes and took a deep breath, which relaxed her enough to fill the cup. She handed it to Marie.

"I've got the testing card right here," Marie said.

"Of course you do." Sandy tied up her scrubs. "Well?"

"We have to give it a minute."

Sandy squirted foamy soap into her palms and turned the faucet on full force, vigorously scrubbing under the torrent of warm water, a comforting hospital ritual. That done, she joined Marie in studying the cup: three ounces of pee that could overturn her life.

Marie removed the card. "You tested clean."

"You sound disappointed. I *am* clean. I've been clean for three months and nine days." Three months, nine days, three hours.

Marie dumped the urine into the toilet. "Okay, here are the rules. You no longer have access to Schedule Two medications. Whoever works the shift with you will have to administer those drugs. You can do vitals and blood draws, change dressings, take care of other medical needs."

"For how long?" Sandy understood the rationale. She'd been caught taking nine Oxycontin tablets from the pharmacy cart, which caused her to be put on probationary status and would have led to prosecution if the hospital administrator hadn't panicked about the publicity. Her current license was probationary. One tiny infraction would implode her fragile nursing career.

"We'll revisit that issue in six months." Marie pursed her small lips. "You think you can do this?"

"Do what?"

"Your job."

Sandy leaned against the counter. "Why are you so pissed?"

"I'm not."

"Take a peek in the mirror, Marie." She gripped the bracelet. *Today I will be sober.*

"You screwed up," Marie said in a rush. "You work in cardiac ICU—you could have hurt somebody. God, Sandy. Someone could have died."

This Sandy knew. Thank God no one had. Her near-miss had happened at the other hospital.

"They never found out about this when you worked up in Charlotte?" Marie asked.

"I didn't use back then." She hadn't needed to, back when she had a life.

"You think the rest of us haven't been tempted?" Marie spoke to her reflection in the mirror. "We work three twelve's in a row, then have to pull a double shift. We're beyond exhausted and desperate for a boost. But the difference is we know it's wrong. That's why we don't do it."

"Guess that makes you stronger than me." Sandy's sarcasm was thinly veiled, but the truth was Marie had a point. She often worked a sixty hour week, covering for nurses who called in. She had no life outside the hospital because there was no room for it. That Marie didn't use drugs was actually kind of admirable.

Sandy said, "The real difference is I couldn't stop with a 'little boost.' A little boost just got me started. I needed ten milligrams of valium to get through some shifts. Eighty of Oxy when I got home."

"Damn." Odd how Marie sounded impressed.

"Yeah. Dug myself quite a hole."

"And you got it all from here?"

"No. You can't take that much without getting caught. Most I got through less reputable channels." She didn't tell Marie how easy it was to buy the stuff, how her dealer worked two floors up from her and supplied at least twenty other hospital staff. Taking from the pharmacy cart had been extraordinarily dumb, something her group therapist had described as Sandy's hitting bottom. Her cry for help. Sandy defined it as her nose-dive off the stupid truck.

16

"Well, I hope you make it. I do. But it's up to you from here on out."

Of course it was up to Sandy. Heaven forbid she should get a little support from her supervisor. "Guess I'll help Pete. I take it he knows my Schedule Two restrictions?"

"Of course. Most of the nursing staff knows."

It felt like a punch. "So that policy about drug treatment being kept confidential was all a load of bull."

"The other nurses have to cover what you can't. But I never told a soul about your being in treatment."

No, of course you didn't. No one would figure it out from the Schedule Two restrictions, would they, Marie? Sandy had been kidding herself—the whole staff probably knew. Welcome back to General Hospital.

She pushed past Marie and fled to the sanctuary of the staff lounge. Did she think her problems would be kept secret? What an idiot she was. She smacked a hand against her locker in frustration.

Thwank.

That sound. The metal resonating, vibrating her fingers, her arms, the nerves running the length of her body. The itch rose inside her. She used to keep her stash in this locker, wrapped in a latex glove and tucked in the toe of one of her Crocs. So easy, open the locker door, make sure you're alone, find the answer. And God, she could use something right now. A few hits of valium would make her smooth as ice cream. She could buy it off the PT assistant on seven; she'd already been screened, no one would know. She groped for the cell phone and pressed the first entry on her speed dial.

Her sponsor's voice said, "Please leave a message . . ."

Sandy didn't leave the message she wanted to: "Real life and sobriety don't mix." She was doomed. On the job less than an hour and ready to undo three months and nine days. Her nerves quivered out of her, stretching for relief. One pill to get her through reentry.

No. She had to get it together. She'd worked too hard. She could weather this. She paced over to the sink and splashed water on her face. As she took in a shuddery breath, she studied her reflection. Brown eyes with new bags beneath them. Dark hair with no shape or luster, the blond highlights remaining on the bottom three inches. A sag behind her chin that hadn't been there a few months before. This wretched sober life touched every part of her. She gripped the bracelet.

Her cell phone rang and she rushed to answer. "Jackie?"

"I saw you'd called. How's it going?" her sponsor's voice was concerned.

"Terrible. I'm about to blow it. I could use some about now."

"This minute?"

"This minute."

"Then take a deep breath and breathe through this minute. Then breathe through the next one."

Sandy was still skeptical about the whole breath-works aspect of recovery but hearing Jackie's voice helped her imagine there might be a future.

"You knew this would be hard. But you can do it."

"Keep telling me that."

"You can do it. You can do it."

The words poked through like sunlight through a blind. "Thanks."

"You said to keep saying it. I'm free till noon. You can do it . . . Hey, want to know a secret?" Jackie asked.

"Sure."

"That bracelet I gave you. What do the initials stand for?"

"Today I will be sober," Sandy recited.

"Yeah, except that's the cleaned up version. What it really stands for is 'Today I won't be a screw-up.'"

Sandy stared down at the purple band. "Oh, hell. That's more like it."

"I thought so."

"Leave your phone on, okay?"

"Absolutely."

Sandy clicked off, but kept a grip on the cell, knowing it would be her lifeline. She would turn it off in the treatment areas but keep it in her pocket, and that would have to do.

At the nurse's station, Sandy grabbed a couple of charts to get familiar with her patients. Cardiac intensive care meant low patient/nurse ratios, but required a special vigilance. She had to anticipate problems, and to do that, she had to check the feel of her floor. Sometimes she had a sixth sense about who to keep a close eye on.

Patient one looked stable. A woman, mid-fifties, recovering from a triple bypass, who'd be moved to a general floor later that day. The second chart told a different story. Mitchell Hastings, admitted yesterday. Fifty-four years old. Massive coronary. Anoxic before resuscitated. Minimal brainwaves, the guy was pretty much dead. Were they keeping him to harvest organs? Or maybe the family hadn't let go. That kind of thing could take time.

"I haven't checked him yet," Pete said, looking over her shoulder. "Would you mind?"

"That's why I'm here." She tucked the chart under her arm, looped the stethoscope around her neck, and headed for room five-fourteen. Mitchell

Hastings might be the perfect first patient for her. Not much there for her to screw up, was there?

Muted lighting at the head of the bed showed a bruised face, intubated respiratory, and half open eyes that saw nothing. Skin on his neck was the color of cigarette ash, streaked red from broken capillaries.

The quiet shoosh and click of oxygen seemed too loud in the thick silence of this man's dying place. Sandy reached out, feeling his cheek with the back of her hand. This was something she always did, making soft physical contact with the patient. Especially patients like this one, caught somewhere between this life and whatever lies beyond. She hoped her touch could reach him.

"What's your name?" A middle-aged woman sat in the shadows, her legs crossed, her bony hands gripping the still fingers of the man in the bed.

"Sorry. I didn't see you there," Sandy said.

"I don't think I've met you," the woman said.

"I'll be his nurse for the PM shift. My name is Sandy Albright."

"I'm Lena." She stood and came to her, moving with a fluid grace. Her yellow sweater had tiny spots of what looked like purple paint on the sleeve. A petite woman, her silver hair had been trimmed at an angle, short in back but chin-length in front. Wrinkles made parentheses around her mouth. "This is my husband, Mitchell."

Sandy opened the chart to record the O2 level and read the other vitals. "He's running a bit of a fever," she said, frowning.

"I know." Mrs. Hastings's fingers fluttered over the back of his wrist. He couldn't feel it. He couldn't feel anything, and Sandy hoped Mrs. Hastings understood that.

"But it doesn't matter," Mrs. Hastings said. "Do you think he knows I'm here? I mean, I know his brain is damaged. I know he can't understand. But maybe, somehow, he knows he's not alone?"

Sandy turned to her, wanting to see her face, to gauge how much denial lingered there. But the woman's weary gray eyes were clear. Honest. "We can see what the brain's doing, so no, he doesn't consciously know you are here. But if you believe in a soul, and I do, then maybe a part of him does know."

Sandy checked the other monitors, moving quietly, unobtrusively, not wanting to interfere. She could be a ghost when that's what the family needed. It was harder when they invited her inside to ride the waves of grief with them. Some nurses managed to detach themselves, but Sandy had never mastered that. Maybe things would have been different if she had.

"I never thought—he was always my rock. I don't think he knew it though," Mrs. Hastings said. "I had breast cancer last year. We weren't sure

I'd make it. Mitch was terrified of my dying. It had been a difficult year, even before." She hesitated, pulling her hand away from him.

"I'm glad you recovered from the cancer."

"It's a miracle, in a way. Think I'm entitled to another?"

Sandy didn't answer. At the hospital, people always wanted a miracle. And some doctors considered themselves deities, hoping to oblige. Her ex-husband, Donald, had that kind of ego. She'd been attracted to his swagger and self-confidence in the beginning, but later on, it had been their undoing.

Mrs. Hastings asked, "How do you do this? I mean, this kind of nursing. It's got to be so hard."

"It has its rewards, too." Sandy reached over to adjust the line attached to the IV, then checked the sink area and small trashcan beside the bed.

"I wish you could have known Mitch. He was a compassionate man. Sensitive. And he could be so funny. He was my high school sweetheart." She let out a loud breath. "I can't believe I'm talking about him in the past tense. It seems wrong."

No, it seemed so right. Sandy looked down at the shell of a man, hoping they'd turn off life support soon. Holding on seemed the cruelest thing. Cruel to the patient who had no quality of life, and to the family holding on to a frayed thread of hope.

"I need to check on some other patients," Sandy said. "But before I go, is there anything I can do for you?"

Mrs. Hastings shook her head. "I'm going to stay a little longer, if that's okay."

"You can stay as long as you like." Sandy exited, closing the door behind her.

• • •

TONYA LADSON STUDIED HER husband in profile as he drove down Washington Street. In the gray haze of twilight, he looked as though he'd been carved from granite: his angled beard, his dark eyes hooded by thick eyebrows. He'd been quiet since they left the doctor's office.

The windshield wipers stuttered against the glass; they should have been replaced weeks ago. She would remind John to do that when he was in a better mood. Impaired visibility could lead to an accident.

Memories from the morning pinballed through Tonya's brain. The white car folded against the tree. The crash of breaking glass and growl of the twisted door. The EMTs working on the other driver, while Tonya prayed, prayed hard, that he would revive. The ambulance blaring as it took the man away.

"Is he asleep?" John asked, eyeing the rearview mirror.

Tonya turned around to check on their son. Byron's head rested against the side of the car seat, his fourth finger dangling from his lips. "Out like a light. Guess the medicine they gave him worked."

"Good."

The broken collar bone couldn't be set, but they'd bound an elastic brace around Byron's torso to keep it in place. She hoped she could remember how to put it on. The doctor said he should wear it during the day for a few weeks. "He was getting out of the straps again," she said. "Right before the accident, he was almost out of that seat. I had just gotten him to sit back down when it happened. If he hadn't . . ." A shiver ran through her, the fear still raw and palpable.

"He's got to learn," John said. "He's got a few more years in that contraption."

"I shouldn't have been on the cell phone," Tonya blurted out. "I was calling work to say I would be late. I shouldn't have been on the cell."

John spun around to face her. "You didn't tell that to the police, did you?"

"It was only a second or two. And my light was green, I'm sure of it."

"Is that what you told the officer?"

"The policewoman at the hospital asked me about it. She said it wasn't illegal to use a cell but I shouldn't, not when I'm driving. She didn't have to say it though. I think I've learned my lesson."

"But you didn't get a ticket. They found him at fault. He ran the light." John's voice was insistent.

"Yes." She wasn't sure why it mattered; the man had been seriously injured. Did he have a family? Children? What was his name? The police officer had told her but now her mind was a complete blank. How could she even check on him if she didn't remember who he was? The accident report, she remembered. She groped for her purse for the rumpled sheets.

"Is that the paperwork from the wreck?" John asked. "You got an address on that guy?"

"Mitchell Hastings. 127 Lakeshore Drive." This was in the older section of town, where the houses stretched across lawns like putting greens. When she was a little girl, she had dreamed of a home like that, with a giant front porch with white rocking chairs and a big horseshoe drive. She'd have three children, two boys and a girl, and a husband who adored her and made enough money for her to be a stay-at-home mom. She didn't envision a two-bedroom bungalow with a postage stamp yard and a mortgage that bled all the money from their account.

But so what if her prince turned out to be a computer software salesman? She and John had built a good life together, though she wished he smiled like he used to. If they could get a handle on the money problems; if they had a little wiggle room at the end of the month. If John's sales would pick up so he wouldn't obsess about every dime they spent.

"Lakeshore. That's in Forest Lake. Bet he had good insurance," John said.

A wave of panic hit her. "Had? Why did you say had?"

"You said they had to do CPR on him. The guy may well have died. Real life isn't like TV. CPR only saves a few."

She stared at him, not wanting to believe. The paramedics had gotten Mr. Hastings' heart going, but she didn't know what had happened after. He could have died on the way to the hospital.

They passed the Methodist church, lit by spotlights from all sides, so bright it glowed. She'd been there once for a funeral. She remembered the sun glittering through stained glass windows, the whispered prayers for the bereaved. She wondered if Mr. Hastings went to church. She hoped he had people to pray for him.

"That man got the ticket, Tonya. Not you. It's his fault this thing happened. Don't you go blaming yourself, okay?" He reached over and squeezed her hand, his gaze softer now.

"It's hard not to. I'm glad Byron's going to be okay." She turned back to her son. His eyes danced behind closed lids. She hoped he was having happy dreams, not frightening ones about car crashes and fire trucks.

"How's the nose?" John asked.

Touching it was a bad idea. The swelling had doubled its size. The doctor had said there was a tiny fracture that didn't need to be set; she'd have two black eyes that would linger for weeks.

"Make sure you keep the bill from the doctor's office. And we'll need to hold on to the rental car invoice. I wonder if we need to hire a lawyer."

"What?"

"A lawyer. The man caused the wreck, he has to pay. That's how this stuff works."

She blinked at him. The man might be dead and John was thinking about getting money from him?

"Does your boss do personal injury suits?" John asked. "Or someone else in the practice?"

"No."

"But maybe he could recommend someone." John patted her leg as he parked the Civic in the lot beside the rental car agency. Her whole torso was one giant bruise. She shouldn't complain, though. She could walk and talk and get back to her life. Mitchell Hastings might not have been so lucky.

"You and the little guy wait here. I'll get the paperwork going." He climbed out, but then turned around and leaned back in. "I'm getting us a four-door. Or maybe an SUV. We're not footing this bill, and we deserve something that will keep us comfortable."

CHAPTER 4

Joe Booker lay still as a gravestone and listened for the Lord's message. Sometimes He came at dawn, his voice a golden warmth in Joe's ear, and whispered instructions. So he began every day like this, motionless on his tattered sleeping bag, tuning out the sounds of traffic, of leaves rustling under raucous squirrels, of beeping garbage trucks emptying dumpsters on Main. Because if the Lord wanted to speak, he was ready to listen.

But lately the Lord had been silent. Joe opened his eyes to see the sun just peeking over the horizon. The headlights from cars on Gervais Street glowed like a string of pearls curling into downtown. He heaved himself up, groaning as his bones tried to awaken, and brushed bits of grass from his jeans and his wool pea coat. The moisture from the morning dew made the ground colder than it had been yesterday or the day before. Days were getting shorter, the icy grip of night holding on into the morning. The fading colors on the trees reminded him that fall was nearly done, and winter would be next, which meant nights in the shelter. He'd postpone that as long as he could.

Joe glanced down at his nest, grateful that he had a place so quiet and secluded. The north wall of the church shielded him from the wind, while the branches of the giant live oak offered some protection from the rain. He leaned against the familiar granite headstone that marked the grave of "Wortham Harden Pinckney, born 1848, died 1901, beloved husband and father, loyal servant of Christ." Mr. Wortham was a good Christian man, letting Joe share his resting place. He felt safe here, like maybe Mr. Wortham looked out for him. That was why the Lord told Joe to seek solace in the tiny old cemetery beside His holy house. Other instructions from the Lord had been slow in coming. Joe knew himself to be unworthy of the Lord's attention, but if He bothered with a man as undeserving as Joe, there had to be a reason. Maybe he had something important he wanted Joe to do. Maybe all the other voices were a test, and Joe had to be ready to hear His voice—the one that mattered—when it came again.

Joe stood and bent down, reaching for the wool blanket and folding it into a square. He shook the plastic sheet he used for ground cover and wrapped it tight around the blanket, then grabbed the knapsack that was his pillow and pulled out the other flannel shirt, the one he wore in the daytime. When it warmed up some, he'd give himself a bath with the garden hose behind the church school building. It got harder to stay clean when the water got cold, but he did his best. Cleanliness was next to godliness, his mama used to say.

What day was it? Different churches served breakfast on different days, and he wasn't sure if today was a Washington Street Methodist Thursday or First Baptist Friday. Reverend Bill had given him a schedule once, but he'd lost it. Nice of the reverend to do that, though. And he never said nothing about Joe sleeping in the graveyard, just seemed to accept it like he belonged there. After being run off from everywhere else, feeling welcomed had come as quite a surprise.

Of course, the Lord told him this was his home. Not with words, but with little gifts left here by his sleeping place. The wool coat appeared last winter. He had thought someone had left it by mistake, but spotted a note safety pinned to it: "For Joe." Socks and gloves came later. And how many brown paper bags had the Lord left? Too many to count. Sandwiches, crackers, peanut butter, cans of soda pop. Tissues, vitamins, and even a toothbrush.

From the angle of the sun, he figured it was breakfast time. Best to start moseying over to the Methodist church, see if that was where the crowd was. He didn't mind getting the last scrapings of eggs, grits, or oatmeal if it meant he didn't have to tangle with the other folks living on the streets. A few he didn't mind, but most he did.

When he saw no line out the door to the big hall at the church, he kept walking. First Baptist was a few blocks away. Last year, they moved the soup kitchen from the big hall with the basketball hoops to a smaller one in the back. They kept building new parts to the church, and it almost filled the city block.

The salty scent of bacon got Joe's stomach rumbling as he positioned himself at the end of the breakfast line. He was careful to not get too close to the skinny woman who always wore layers of tattery skirts she got from the trash behind the thrift store.

"You 'bout missed breakfast." Rag Doll stared at his shirt and at the open door behind him. She never looked anyone in the eye. "They had sausage but it's all gone now. You might get some grits."

So this was Rag Doll's second trip in line. If they caught her, they'd boot her out. "Where you sleeping, Joe?"

She always asked. He never told her. "Around."

25

"They may open the winter shelter sooner than last year. I hope they do, nights are getting cold."

"You up by the river?" he asked. The tent village close to the banks of the Broad was where people who wanted to avoid the police liked to squat. You could get yourself killed real easy if you crossed one of the residents there.

"Some. Last night I was behind the Piggly Wiggly," she said. "Had it all to myself. You should try it."

She rubbed her nose with a dirty hand, a bit of scrambled eggs dangling from her hair. He wondered when Rag Doll had last had a bath. Godliness came hard during cold weather.

"You got any money on you?" She always asked him.

He shook his head, thinking about the twenty Mr. Mitch gave him yesterday. Rag Doll wasn't getting her hands on that.

He inched up to the serving line, not liking the press of bodies as he entered the kitchen area. A woman offered him orange juice, but he shook his head to the offer of eggs and helped himself to two biscuits and a banana. As he reached for a tub of apple sauce, he noticed a big guy wearing a bright red cap stomping up to where the eggs were. Cyphus Lawter, a man full of the devil. Joe hadn't seen Cyphus in months. Rumor was he'd been busted for trying to kill a man, which Joe could believe; he'd once seen Cyphus at the bus station mugging a guy and running off with his wallet.

When Cyphus spotted Joe, he glared at him with eyes black as tar. Joe didn't flinch. A man like Cyphus needed to know he wasn't scared. When the line moved forward, Cyphus took his tray and moved on.

The juice came in a glass. Joe liked it better in a carton or paper cup, because then he could grab the food from his plate and leave. A glass meant sitting down and eating, so he made his way to the farthest table and sat facing the others. You never knew when someone might sneak up on your back. Cyphus Lawter left the dining area with two other men.

"I ain't eaten yet!" The loud voice belonged to Rag Doll who was tangling with one of the servers.

"I know you did. I'm the one who gave you extra grits!" the woman with the spoon said.

"The line's about done, and it ain't like you're running out! What are you going to do with them biscuits?"

The woman slammed the lid on her pot and jabbed a finger towards the door.

"You don't gotta be so mean!" Rag Doll yelled. "You ain't no better than I am!" If she kept that up, they'd call the police, and she wouldn't be back for breakfast anytime soon. She seemed to settle down, though, running a hand down her skirt and stomping into the dining room where she scouted out the tables, looking for leftovers to swipe. When she spotted him, she crossed to his table.

"I could cut that woman's butt," she said.

"You could get yourself tossed in jail," he answered.

A young fella dressed in blue jeans and a USC sweatshirt moved to the center of the room.

"Excuse me, but I have an announcement," he said. He had to yell out twice to get people to quiet down. "Looks like we're in for a very cold night. Temperatures may get in the twenties. So the mayor's decided to open the winter shelter early. We'll open the doors at seven p.m. tonight, and everyone has to clear out by eight a.m., just like last year."

The winter shelter was up by the tracks in what used to be a gymnasium. They set it up like a barracks with cots a few feet apart. No privacy. Smelly, snoring men all around you. But it wasn't the snoring ones you had to worry about—the ones who didn't sleep caused the most trouble.

"Please, please get the word out," the man said. "We don't want anybody freezing because they had nowhere to go."

"I don't think they care a lick if anyone freezes to death," Rag Doll muttered. "'Cept it makes the city look bad."

Joe handed her a biscuit, hoping having something to chew on might keep her mouth shut.

She smiled at the food. "You a good man, Joe. Better than most of the pigs around here."

He wasn't so sure about that. He tried to be good, to do what the Lord wanted. To be the sort of man the Lord could trust to do what He told him to do. Except sometimes there was so much ruckus in his head, he worried he might not hear the instructions. Sometimes—a lot lately—the devil talked to him, too.

Joe slurped down the rest of the juice, shoved the banana in his jacket pocket, and carried his dishes to the little window leading to the kitchen. He hurried out the side door before Rag Doll latched onto him again. Once outside, he again spotted Cyphus in his red hat, standing close to the street like he expected a ride. A pickup truck pulled up, and a skinny guy with a frayed gray pony tail climbed out. Cyphus handed him a bag; he handed Cyphus something back.

Leave it to Lawter to sell drugs in the backyard of God's house.

• • •

"MITCH." LENA'S THUMB stroked the cool flesh on his forehead. She stared at his face, looking for a sign that her husband was in there somewhere. She didn't find it. His skin looked paler than paper. Swelling around his nose and eyes—from the airbag, they told her—seemed to alter his facial structure. When she'd first come to the ER, she had thought it was all a mistake, that this man wasn't her husband. But then she had taken his hand and touched the familiar callus on his thumb from gardening, and the tiny scar where he cut himself carving the turkey one Thanksgiving. Her husband. Her Mitch.

She longed to have that morning back. She would listen when he complained of heartburn. She wouldn't have hurried him from the house, but looked him in the eye and recognized that this was different, and rushed him to the hospital where Dr. Burnside would tell her she got him there just in time.

She would have saved him.

Her hand traced down to where the top of his gown gaped open. The bruises were a collage of bright blue and red from the hands that had pounded and pressed to get Mitchell's heart going again. Nice people, she supposed, trying to give Mitch another chance at life.

"But it didn't work, did it?" She let her fingertips brush over the electrodes taped to his skin. They'd shaved his chest. Mitch would be horrified to see that. She smiled, but it didn't hold up.

How did this happen after so many false alarms? And on his way to work; it was a wonder no one was killed. But then, that wasn't true.

She pulled her hand away, tucking it in her pocket. The ICU room felt arctic. When she'd been admitted here last fall, she could never get warm; the cool air felt like death breathing on her. Mitch had brought her favorite sweater—the purple one her mother had knitted—and wrapped it around her, his gentle fingers buttoning it at her chest where her breast had been. He never flinched, never avoided touching her, even when the bosom that had suckled their children had been sliced from her body. She had loathed seeing herself, the jagged scar, the dent in her puckered flesh, the pale white moon where her nipple had been. How brave Mitch had been to love her in that ugliness when it was the last thing she deserved.

She looked at her wedding ring, at a spot of indigo smeared on the gold from her painting. She had mixed the cadmium blue with the violet, had swirled the colors to that perfect shade, had dipped the tip of the brush and turned to the canvas, that field of waiting white, when the call came. Years ago, but really just a day. She chipped at the paint with her fingernail, wanting to erase it. She'd started wearing the gold band again three months ago. The edema from her chemo had made her fingers so misshapen and grotesque no ring would fit them. And before, there had been that night when she'd torn the ring from her hand and vowed she'd never put it back. How foolish she had been.

She remembered the exact moment she fell in love with Mitch the first time. It was back in high school, an afternoon when Mitch visited her home before baseball practice. They had sat on the front porch, warm air stirred by the lazy blades of a ceiling fan. The iced tea, filled with chunks of lemon, soothed her dry throat. Beside her, Mitch looked uncomfortable on the wooden swing, shifting his legs this way and that, gripping the chain then releasing it. Sweat dotted his chin. The pleasant sweet smell of gardenia wafted over from the neighbor's yard.

Lena pushed with her feet to set the swing in motion, causing Mitch to spill a little of his drink.

"Sorry." Lena was not sorry. She pushed harder, laughing as Mitch downed a third of his beverage to prevent more from splashing out.

"You have a little devilment in you," he said, lowering the glass. "And all this time I thought you were my angel."

"Not an angel. Definitely not." She kicked her feet into the air, her Topsiders dangling from her toes.

Mitch leaned back, sliding his arm behind her. He'd not done that before. Nobody had done that before, not since she was a little girl. She scooted a few inches closer to him.

"This is nice," he said. "I could stay here all day."

"If we stay all day, you'll miss baseball practice." She was counting on Mitch leaving by 6:00. Dad got home at 6:15.

In a bold move, she let her head rest in the crook of his elbow, casting a sideways glance to gauge his reaction. His smile was a faint flickering of lips, but full of promise. He tilted his head so that it touched hers. Warmth spread like fingers in her chest, unexpected and delicious.

"Maybe I should miss it," he whispered.

As he leaned closer, his breath skimming her neck, a new sensation pulsed through her, starting from deep inside, from a place below her stomach. What was happening to her?

Mitch stopped the swing to set his glass on the floor. Lena clutched hers like she needed it for grounding. He turned, brushed knuckles under her chin so she would look at him. And kissed her.

But this was a different kiss from his others. She felt it down through her chest, her abdomen, down between her legs, a stronger pull, like she could reel all of Mitch inside her, and she wanted him there. She needed him there. This was so new, all of it, and it exhilarated her. And terrified her a little.

When his lips released hers, she took in shaky swallows of air, kept her eyes closed, scared and desperately wanting . . . . What? She didn't understand, but she hated for it to end.

"Lena," he whispered. "What you do to me."

She opened her eyes then, to look at him, catching his embarrassed glimpse at his body, at the new bulge straining the pants of his baseball uniform. Kissing her had caused that?

When she took another sip of tea, her hand shook.

He gripped her fingers, their two hands clutching the glass. "I'm going to kiss you again."

She thought it a little funny that he would announce it this way, but she sank against him, pressing her lips harder against his, relishing the concept that this was new to him, too. His tongue flicking into her mouth startled her, but she liked it. Again, that feeling inside, stronger now, like the two of them fit together to become something whole. She could feel the power of Mitch, his hand that could snag a fly ball and fire it to home, his arms forceful enough to bat a pitch out of the park, these ropey muscles quietly holding her like he could keep her still forever.

He pulled back. "Damn. Lena—"

Her name hung in the air like a wisp of smoke. Mitch grabbed the porch swing chains and slid away. She didn't want him to. A half foot between them felt wrong.

The sound of a car pulling into the driveway made her stiffen. Please not Dad. No, it was Abby's bright green Volkswagen. Abby slammed the car door and hurried up the walkway, her dark hair in a long braid down her back, wearing that ridiculous tie-dye tee. When she reached them she paused. "What's going on here?" Abby asked with a suspicious arch of her eyebrows.

"Nothing," Lena said, eyeing the door in a telepathic message for her older sister to leave them alone.

"Doesn't look like nothing." She turned her assessing gaze to Mitch, brows lifting even higher.

"Abby," he said tightly.

She burst out laughing then. "The look on your faces!"

"Shut up," Lena replied, ready to smack her sibling.

Abby moved to the front door. "You might want to wrap things up. Dad's probably on his way."

Lena glanced at her watch.

"Maybe it's time I met your father," Mitch said.

"I don't think so." She leapt from the swing and straightened her blouse.

Mitch pushed the swing back as though he had no reason to budge from it. Lena scanned the street for a sign of Dad's car.

"You're already late for practice," she said, her voice tight.

"I don't care." He patted the seat. "It's still warm. Sit."

Her instinct to sit with him almost overwhelmed her need for him to leave, but Dad was coming, and it was Friday, which meant he'd gotten off work early and headed straight for the Elks Club.

The very slow approach of the Mercury was a bad sign. When drunk, Dad inched along, convinced he wouldn't cause an accident or get spotted by the police. Lena closed her eyes, devastated. There would be no preventing it now. Mitch would meet her Dad. And would run like hell.

"Is that him?" Mitch asked.

She nodded, fighting tears. "You could leave if you hurry."

His foot stopped the swing. "What is it, Lena? Are you ashamed of me?"

Her mouth dropped open. How could he think—she had not told him anything different. Like her mother and Abby, she let nobody see the truth. She looked at Mitch, at the pain reflected in his dark eyes, pain she caused. "No," she whispered. "I'm ashamed of him."

Dad parked, halfway in the drive, halfway on the grass, and emerged from the car. His dark hair, slicked back by Vitalis, looked as it had that morning, but little else did. His unknotted tie hung like a sash down his white shirt. His suit jacket, which had been neat as a pin when he went to work, was now a bundle under his left arm. His venture up the walkway was unsteady, but when he spotted them, he smiled. "How ma girl?" he slurred.

"Fine, Dad." She hurried over to hold on to him as he climbed the steps.

Dad paused in front of Mitch, swaying a little. "Who's this?"

Mitch stood and extended a hand. "I'm Mitch Hastings, Sir."

Dad gripped his fingers and shook. "Ball player?"

"Baseball team, sir."

"Baseball? I play . . . played football. Running back. Fast in mah day."

Lena winced, praying this wouldn't launch into a drunken reminiscence of pretend glory days.

"I'm sure you were, sir."

"Mitch was just leaving. He has to get to practice," she said, taking Mitch by the hand and guiding him away. As she marched him down the brick path to his car, she heard the screen door shut, Dad bellowing for Mom, Abby yelling that she was on the phone. Dad screaming back that she should watch her tone. Typical day for the Parker household.

Mitch stopped at the driver door and turned around to face her. She couldn't look at him. "Lena?" he spoke gently.

"You should get going."

"Lena." With his thumb, he nudged her chin up so she would face him. The tears filling her eyes probably made her look even more pathetic.

"You are so beautiful," he said, and pressed his lips against her forehead. "The most beautiful girl in the world."

Then. That moment, when he knew it all and loved her anyway, she had known she would marry him.

The second time she had fallen in love with him had been last year, during her illness. Strange that such a bond could evolve in that wreckage. It had been a tether for her when the cancer left her adrift, when the monster tried to pull her from this earth.

"You saved me," Lena whispered, again reaching for the cold flesh of his hand. "Why can't I save you?"

She wanted to memorize him. Every curly hair in his eyebrows. Each knuckle on his hand and freckle on his chest. Of course there were no surprises, she knew his body almost like her own, but she hadn't memorized him before, and she had to file these details in a place of permanency in her mind.

What else to place there? The smell of Brace aftershave and Werther's Butterscotch. The feel of heat in their bed, his body like a furnace no matter what the temperature. The way he looked at her like she could fill up all his empty places.

She had to be strong. She would hold Mitch's hand until all three children were here. Until the transplant team arrived, until his liver and corneas could be harvested to maybe change another life or two. She would be here for him the only way she could.

And then would come goodbye.

The door behind her opened a little, a white stripe of light penetrating before she heard a voice. "Mom? Okay if I come in?"

"Of course. You don't have to ask."

Sims entered, ducking his head and knotting his hands in the fold of his jacket. Sometimes he still looked twelve years old to her: the mischievous

32

boy who painted "scumbag" on his younger brother's book bag and shattered her Wedgewood vase with a slingshot. He came to her side and whispered, "Is there anything else you need me to do?"

"Did you reach Abby?"

"I've tried. I left word with the Washington office. Left messages on her satellite cell phone but she hasn't called back."

This was what she expected; her older sister again out of touch. The only real family Lena had, other than Becca and the boys.

"Elliott's flight gets in at three," Sims said. "I'll leave in a little while."

"Take Becca. I think she could use some fresh air." How Lena worried about her youngest. She was far too young for a loss like this.

Sims placed the jacket on the reclining chair next to the window where Lena had spent the night. The nurses had brought a pillow and blanket but there had been no possibility of sleep.

"I called Dad's office too. Margaret said Phillip was due back tomorrow. He still hasn't answered her calls but she said he's bad about forgetting the charger for his phone." Sims offered a little shrug, as if he needed to apologize for Phillip. It was something his father would have done. So much of Sims came from Mitch. His wide shoulders and bald—or in Sims' case, balding—head. The way he fretted about things he couldn't control.

"Anyone else I need to call? Does everyone know . . . who needs to know?" Sims needed to be busy; this had been true even when he was a child. When their second son came, two-year-old Sims became quite a handful, until Lena figured out that he felt important if she let him help. "Mama, I'm a good big brudder," he would say.

"I'm sure there is someone else but I can't think right now." Her voice vibrated, the fatigue leaking out. Sims' head shot up, eyes wide and worried, so she gave him a little smile. "It's okay," she said.

"I was thinking maybe I should take Dad's cell phone," Sims said. "Since Phillip is out of town, someone should take client calls."

"I think it's in that drawer." She pointed to a small table and Sims rushed to open it. The manila envelope contained the phone and Mitch's worn leather wallet.

"Don't turn it on in here," she cautioned.

He nodded, but gripped the thing like it held some important secret message, his lips tightening into a thin, pale line.

"What's wrong?" She moved closer.

"Nothing. Just . . . nothing." He looked like he wanted to say more, but merely pocketed the phone. "Just thinking about Dad's business."

"We can't worry about that now." She smoothed the blanket over Mitch's legs, not wanting the cool breeze from the vent to chill him.

"Guess I'll get going then." Sims shrugged into his jacket and moved to the door. As she watched him leave, she realized that not once had he looked at the man in the bed.

CHAPTER 5

B ecca stared out the passenger window of her oldest brother's Bronco. When Sims had asked her to come with him to pick up Elliott, she had jumped up from the waiting room chair like a Pop Tart, desperate to get away. Away from the creepy antiseptic smell, and having to watch Sims pace around like a cat needing a litter box, and being nice to all the adults who kept stopping by and asking her "how ya doing, hon?"

She looked at the dashboard clock. She had missed having lunch with Dylan, but Kayla would have told him what happened. When Becca went back to school in a few days, she'd bravely approach him and ask, "Is today good?" Or, even more courageously, say, "Meet me in the cafeteria at noon." Maybe he'd smile, kind of nervous, and nod, "yes," and they would sit together and laugh at the school's suck-food lunches. Maybe it would be the first of many hours together. Maybe.

Sims thumped the steering wheel. "Damn traffic."

Blossom Street always had cars backed up, inching along no faster than earthworms, but his bitching about it didn't change a thing.

He waved his hands like a madman at the burgundy Nissan in front of them. "Did you see that! The light was yellow! Why did that idiot stop?" Sims liked to yell at other drivers. Their mom would cluck her tongue and shake her head when a car cut in front of her, but Dad never complained. He drove as slow as a little church lady and, come to think of it, other drivers probably yelled at him.

When would Dad get to drive again?

It would be better once they got him home, back to his own bed, and Becca would bring him meals on a tray, and they'd fend off Spats so he could eat. They would watch TV together, even those awful Matlock reruns if that was what he wanted.

"We're gonna be late," Sims said.

"What time does Elliott's plane get in?" Becca asked.

Sims checked his watch. "In ten minutes, if his flight is on time. But you never know."

Sims floored the accelerator, which was completely unnecessary, then settled into the same speed as the other zillion cars clogging the road. His cell phone rang, but it played "Carolina in My Mind," which was the ringtone she'd downloaded for Dad's cell. Sims pulled it from the pocket of his jacket.

"This is Sims Hastings." He sounded like his name was very important.

"Pull over," she told him. She would not get in a wreck because her stupid brother was on the phone.

He shook his head at her. "No, I'm not Mitch. I'm his son. My father was in an accident."

"Pull over!" She shouted it, and Sims shot her a dirty look before wheeling into a parking spot.

"Yes, Phillip is still out of the country, but he's due back soon. Is there something I can help you with?" Sims said. He mumbled a few "a-huhs" and an "I see" before raising his voice. "What do you mean the deal didn't—"

Becca shook her head at his exasperated tone. Dad never talked like that with his clients. His voice was always calm: "I understand this is a frustrating process," he'd say, his "a-huhs" soothing like warm water.

"I can't help you. I'll have Phillip call you as soon as he returns." Sims ended the call and scowled. "Prick. Like I can miraculously print up some money, or make Phillip appear, or make Dad all better and . . ." He shook his head as he wheeled back into traffic.

Five minutes later they pulled into the Columbia Metro Airport parking garage, and Sims grumbled about the lack of parking spots before squeezing into a space between two other gigantic SUVs. She followed him to the crosswalk connecting the garage to the baggage claim. He stopped at a bench outside.

"We can wait here. Elliott will come out when he gets his luggage. That is, if he brought any." Sims pulled a cigarette out of his pocket and lit it. Big surprise.

"Why wouldn't he have luggage?" Becca asked. Coming all the way from New York, surely he'd need clothes and stuff.

Sims puffed out a plume of smoke. "He probably brought a carry-on because he plans to stay for just a few days. You know Elliott, places to go, people to see."

Becca sat on the bench, in no hurry to leave. Once they had Elliott, they'd go back to the hospital. "Elliott has to stay longer than a few days."

Sims gave her puzzled look. "We'll see. Damn, I should have worn a hat." He lifted his collar as a chilly breeze hit them. His ears and bare scalp always turned as pink as Pepto when he was cold, like Dad's. Elliott wasn't bald at all. He hadn't been home in six months because it was hard to get away when you had gigs to perform, Dad had once explained. One day Elliott would be a famous jazz musician, but you had to pay your dues.

"There he is!" Becca jumped from her seat. Elliott had on a long dark overcoat and a green scarf hanging around his neck. He smiled, dropping the handle to his rolling suitcase so he could wrap his arms around her and lift her into the air.

"How's my girl?" he asked, his breath tickling Becca's neck.

Sims stomped out his cigarette and gave Elliott a hug, holding on a little longer than Becca expected. "Hey Spanky," Sims said.

"Hey yourself," Elliott retorted, slapping his back. Sims pulled away, clearing his throat.

"Any luggage?" Sims asked.

"Nope. Just this."

"You're only staying a few days?" Sims' voice was tight.

Elliott looked down at the bag he'd brought. "I'll be here till Tuesday. Didn't want to have to pay to check luggage. Stupid airlines rip you off however they can."

"So we have you here . . ." Sims made a point of counting finger tips. "Five days?"

Elliott raked a hand through thick curls that were longer than when he came last time. "Is there a problem?"

Becca drew a breath, hoping this didn't escalate. Her big brothers sometimes acted like fifth graders when they were together.

"Still no word from Aunt Abby?" Elliott asked, conflict averted.

"Nope. She's tucked away in some Nicaraguan village. No phones."

"Peru," Becca corrected. She wished Aunt Abby would hurry up and call. She would come once she got the news. She would help them handle things, especially when Dad came home.

"Mom's anxious to see you," Sims said.

"How's she doing? She sounded strange on the phone."

"Strange how?"

"Chipper. Organized. Giving this long list of who had been notified, what has to be done."

"We call that denial," Sims said. "She thinks if she stays busy, she won't have to deal with Dad's dying."

Becca looked up sharply at him. Why did people assume Dad was going to die?

She'd seen *Grey's Anatomy* a thousand times and people sicker than Dad got better. Mom almost died and got better. Dad would, too.

"Sorry," Sims said, dropping down on the bench again.

Elliott stroked his goatee as he regarded their brother. "You okay?"

Sims groped in his pocket for another cigarette, his hand shaking as he lit it. Becca eyed Elliott, waiting for his reaction.

"Stupid," Elliott muttered. "Really stupid. You still smoke? Wasn't what happened to Dad any kind of wake up call for you?"

"Shut up." Sims flashed an awkward smile at a couple hurrying by.

"Damn it, Sims. You have a kid. What's the tobacco doing to her?"

"I never smoke in the house, by the way. Or the car."

Elliott looked at Becca for confirmation. "He's got a tree out back where he keeps an ashtray," she said.

"But smoking still kills you. That's not fair to Connie or Allie. Or to the rest of us." Elliott snapped down the telescoping handle on his suitcase and plopped down beside Sims. His nails were perfectly trimmed because he played guitar. Becca's nails looked like they'd been clipped in a blender.

Sims puffed out smoke away from them and asked, "Did Mom pay for your ticket?"

Elliott replied with an embarrassed shrug. "I didn't have the cash."

"Of course not." Sims studied the glow at the end of his cigarette. "You can't keep going back to that well, little brother."

Elliott shuffled his feet. "What do you mean?"

"I mean they have bills, too. Mom's illness was expensive in more ways than one. And in case you haven't noticed, the real estate business isn't exactly booming."

"You mean . . ." Elliott glanced at Becca like he didn't want her to hear, and it made her want to laugh. Neither brother had a clue. When Dad had taken care of Mom during all those months, she'd heard him arguing with his partner. Mr. Calloway yelling, "properties don't sell themselves" because Dad spent so much time away from work. Once Mom got better, Dad started working six days a week, sometimes staying past dinner time. Maybe that's why he had the heart attack.

"This still seems surreal to me," Sims said. "We had so many false alarms with him. I almost went over there yesterday morning. I came this close—" He held up a hand, index finger an inch from his thumb. "To stopping in for a cup of coffee before work. God, I wish I had."

"I doubt you could have prevented what happened," Elliott said.

Sims snuffed out the cigarette on the sole of his shoe, then spun to face them. "Did you think Mom would die?"

"Didn't you?" Elliott answered.

"Well yeah. But you weren't here. You didn't see how bad it was."

It had been bad. Even Sims didn't know all of it. Besides the surgery and the chemotherapy that took all Mom's hair and made her thin as a drinking straw and left her so weak she could barely leave the bed. Besides Dad's fussing and worrying when things were at their worst and they had to stop her treatment until she got stronger. Sims didn't know how terrible—how fragile—things got. After everything she had done, Dad took care of her and got her well. If Mom got a miracle, then Dad should get one, too.

"It's hard to leave the city," Elliott said. "You give up a few gigs, it can cut you off from future bookings."

"Well you're here now," Sims said, with a hint of sarcasm. "You better prepare yourself. Mom's cancer was just the first act. Dad, well Dad—"

Becca glared at him, daring him to finish the sentence. Dad was going to get well. Period. If her brothers were too stupid to believe it, then the hell with them.

Elliott inched closer, his hand reaching for the back of her neck. "You okay, Bec?"

"We should go." She marched away from them to Sims's car. A few seconds later her brothers followed, and they were headed back to the hospital.

Back to the waiting.

CHAPTER 6

" There's a voice inside you that can guide you to a happier life. You must listen to it. The voice says: Today I will persist until I succeed. I will live in the moment." Dr. Alan Allaway's British accent, like hot chocolate to her ears, resonated from the CD player in Tonya Ladson's small bedroom.

"I will live in the moment," Tonya repeated.

"I will plan my future instead of worrying about it," Dr. Allaway said.

She had turned on Dr. Allaway to get her mind off the nightmare that had played over and over in her sleep. An accident, though not like the real one. Byron pinned inside a yellow truck, screaming for her, but she couldn't get the door open, and she ran barefoot through shattered glass surrounding the vehicle, and then the engine caught fire.

"I choose to act purposefully, with the attitude of a warrior," Dr. Allaway said.

Tonya shook her head to dislodge the dream. Byron was safe and chattering away in the bedroom. She was safe. She would listen to the "You Control Your Own Destiny" CD and not let the car crash take over her life any more. She was a survivor.

She studied her reflection in the bathroom mirror and listened to: "A warrior attacks his day. He does not let others control him."

"A warrior." She forced strength in her voice that she didn't feel, but sometimes acting like you believed led you to believe. Dr. Allaway had taught her that in Lesson One. This was why she had put on the suit. She clipped the tags that dangled from her sleeve and smoothed down the collar. She loved the silky weave of the fabric and the way the tailored jacket hid her remaining baby weight pounds. It made her feel taller. She'd purchased her new "power suit" last week during a hurried lunch hour and hidden it in their closet before John got home. When the Visa bill came, she would bury it and pay off the purchase with money she'd have to save from gas and groceries. John might not notice but if he did, she'd explain that it was an investment in their future.

She stepped closer to the mirror. The butterfly-shaped bruise on her face had deepened to a plum purple, the bottom edge black. From a distance, she suspected, it might look like an abstract painting of a misshapen flower. She usually accented her brown eyes, like small coffee beans, with mascara and eyeliner but hadn't attempted that since the wreck. Maybe she would this morning. Another step toward getting back to normal.

With careful strokes of the cover-up stick, she tried to soften the shade of the bruise, but there was no hiding it. Yet few people asked her what had happened. Marion knew, of course, but nobody else at work had said, "What happened to your face?" Not Peter, the mail guy, or Ruth, the witchy paralegal, or even Mr. Patel, her boss's partner.

"You know why? It's because they think you got punched out by your husband," Marion had explained. "Us southerners don't pry into that kind of domestic matter. We'll ask you where you work or how much you make or who your mama is, but we don't want to know if your husband beats the stuffing out of you when you get home."

Those words sickened Tonya. She wished she had a badge that read, "I was hurt in a car accident," so people would know. And what if John had given her the black eyes? Shouldn't people be concerned about that? Shouldn't someone say, "If your husband did that, you need to get away from him. How can I help?"

She could hear John in the bedroom. She glanced in the trashcan to make sure the price tags were hidden. She was very glad she had the suit. She felt bold, like someone in charge of her life. She was *not* a victim. Tonya Ladson was a warrior.

"Byron dumped his cereal again," John said as he pushed open the door because he'd apparently forgotten how to knock. She glanced down at her outfit, wondering if he'd notice it was brand new. Probably not. He noticed very little about her these days.

"The broom's in the hall closet," she said.

John wedged himself in behind her and reached for his toothbrush. The fruity smell of his aftershave overwhelmed the tiny room. "A broom won't get the milk up. And I've got to get going."

So did Tonya, because she was not going to be late today.

"That bruise gets prettier every day," John commented.

She did not appreciate his sarcasm. The bruise was an ever-present reminder of what she'd been through and survived. She didn't even know if Mr. Hastings had.

John squeezed a perfect pale blue cord of toothpaste onto his brush. She watched from the mirror to see if he'd bother to replace the top. He caught her watching and did.

"Guess I'd better go clean up Byron's mess," she said.

• • •

THIRTY-THREE MINUTES LATER Tonya sipped coffee at her desk, feeling smug that she'd arrived a full seven minutes before she was supposed to. "A warrior must be prompt to the battleground," Dr. Allaway had said. She glanced at the new stack of scrambled notes that Mr. Jamison had left for her to type. If he wasn't such a dinosaur and would use the new six hundred-gig computer that gathered dust on his desk, her job might be tolerable. No, she would not think negative thoughts like that. Not today. She lifted the top sheet and skimmed it. She'd mastered Mr. Jamison's scrawl long ago, so the letter requesting medical files for a worker's comp case should take little time. As she opened the file on her computer, she heard the door creak open behind her. Marion was getting to work on time?

"Tonya? Got a minute?" Not Marion, but Ruth Polinsky, the chief paralegal, dressed in her tweedy brown suit, her hair cut short like a helmet around her head.

Tonya leapt to her feet, fighting a strange urge to salute the woman. "Sure."

Ruth came closer, her wrinkled lips curved into the usual frown. She handed Tonya the pleadings from yesterday. "Did you proof this?"

Tonya scanned the document. Red circles from Ruth's pen scattered the page like buckshot.

"And I don't mean did you proof it on the computer," Ruth continued. "I mean did you print it out and edit it on hardcopy? It's the only way you're going to catch these kind of mistakes."

Tonya swallowed. "I'm sorry. I'll get right—"

"I don't want an apology." Ruth interrupted. "What I'd like to see is fewer errors. A little attention to detail. This is a prestigious law firm. We expect no less than the best from each of our employees."

A prestigious law firm might be a stretch. They handled worker's comp claims, family law, and the occasional pharmaceutical suit, but it wasn't like everybody had heard of the Jamison and Patel firm. Tonya could see Marion watching from the hallway. No way she'd enter the room until Ruth (Marion called her "Ruthless") was long gone.

She thought of a hundred excuses she could make. Heck, half of the errors might have been Mr. Jamison's; the old guy didn't exactly embrace Ruth's "attention to detail" mantra. But excuses weren't the way to go. She looked down. At work for less than twenty minutes and she'd already betrayed the suit. Tonya forced herself to meet Ruth's iron gaze.

"You'll redo this pleading for me?" Ruth asked. No, demanded.

"I will," Tonya replied, doing her best to channel the inner warrior. "I'll bring it to you before lunch."

"Good." Ruth turned to leave, but hesitated. "I was sorry to hear about your accident."

"Thanks," Tonya answered, surprised that Ruth even knew.

"Your little boy was hurt?" Ruth's voice softened the tiniest bit.

"His collarbone. But we were lucky. It could have been much worse," Tonya replied.

"That's a very healthy perspective," Ruth replied, her eyes shifting down to the suit.

Tonya straightened. Warrior.

"I'll look forward to your revisions then."

As soon as Ruth exited, Marion burst in, a Starbucks cup in one hand and her bulging bucket-shaped purse in the other. Her hair sported a pale blond stripe from an unfortunate tinting experiment a few weekends before. Not quite skunk-like, but almost.

"Ruthless ream you out?" Marion asked.

"I need to pay more attention to detail."

"Because if you did, then the paralegals would have *nothing* to do. They get the big bucks, let them do some of the work." Marion plopped into her chair and looked for a space on her chaotic desk to set her coffee.

Tonya glanced at her own work area. She'd lost control of her stacks, too. There was a nine-inch pile of case summaries that needed to be typed and filed. Dictation to be completed. Billing sheets to be formatted and mailed out, not to mention the notes from Mr. Jamison to be typed. She would tackle the clutter today. After finishing the pleading for Ruth, she would launch an attack on pile number one and wouldn't stop until she was done, working through lunch if she needed to. Tomorrow, she would tackle the billing forms, getting them to Ruth before they were due.

"Hey, I have some news for you," Marion said. "I called the hospital to check on that Mr. Hastings guy."

Tonya froze. "How did you get through?"

"My cousin who works there gave me an update. The guy's still in cardiac intensive care. Not conscious though."

"But he's alive."

"Definitely alive."

"Thank God."

Relief flooded her. Maybe her prayers would be answered. Maybe Mr. Hastings would recover. She turned to her computer. She was a warrior, reporting for duty.

• • •

TONYA NARROWED HER EYES against the setting sun as she drove home. After plowing through more work than she'd done in weeks, she'd left work a half hour later than usual, arriving at Byron's daycare minutes before facing the ten dollar fine for late pick-up. Finishing all the reports had exhausted her, so she opted to get Chinese take-out for supper. She'd spent less than ten dollars, which wasn't much for a meal, and she could take the leftovers to work tomorrow.

When her cell phone rang, she glanced down at the number: her mother. She did not answer because of her pledge to not use the device while driving. As soon as she pulled in behind John's car, she dialed back.

"Hey, Mom."

"Tonya? Hadn't heard from you in days. I thought you were dead or something."

Tonya had always hated it when her mother said things like that but this time it cut deeper. She had almost died, hadn't she?

"How's the nose?"

"Blue. No, purple." Tonya touched the tender flesh beside each nostril.

"I still think you should come by the office and let Dr. Padris have a look. You don't want to end up with a crooked nose." Tonya's mother, a registered nurse, worked part time for a plastic surgery practice. In the past two years, she'd had fillers injected in her face, fat removed from her butt, and spider veins erased from her calves. Tonya wondered if her mother even got a paycheck; maybe they paid her in procedures.

"It's fine."

"Guess what Buddy found out today?" Her mother's voice climbed the scale. She would practically sing whatever news she had about her precious youngest child.

"He's got syphilis?"

"Tonya!" A lower pitch to berate the oldest. "No. He got accepted at Wofford. Isn't that grand? He still hasn't heard from Duke but says he'd like to go to Wofford. Of course, his father is grinning like the Cheshire cat, thinking of his son going to his alma mater."

"That's great." Tonya glanced back at her own son snoozing in his car seat, the splint securing his arm to his torso. So far, he'd hardly cried at all about the broken collar bone. Her brave little man.

"Buddy's hoping for a baseball scholarship. Lawrence says he has quite an arm."

"Lawrence says, huh?" Tonya never got to call her stepfather "Dad" or "Daddy." Tonya's parents separated when she was seven. Back then, her mom worked for a gynecological practice and married Dr. Lawrence White days after the divorce. Tonya shuffled between households—her mother's stone and brick five-bedroom castle to her father's stifling two-bedroom apartment —over the next ten years. Neither place felt much like home.

"Does Buddy know what he wants to study? Think he'll go pre-med?" Tonya asked to be polite.

"Wouldn't that be something! Though I wouldn't mind if he pursued nursing. If he got an advanced practice degree, he could work anywhere and make a great living."

Tonya had heard these same words spoken about her before she married John: "Go to nursing school, Tonya. You can write your own ticket then." Of course, there had been no offer to help with tuition.

Tonya spotted John standing in the doorway, undoubtedly wondering why she was still sitting in the rental car. When she waved, he didn't wave back. "I need to get going, Mom."

"Okay. But if you want us to check out that nose—"

"I'll think about it."

John had retreated into the house. Unloading a drowsy toddler, a purse, and a large bag of Chinese takeout took some maneuvering, but motherhood had taught her many skills. As she pushed through the kitchen door she set Byron on the floor. "Daddy's here. Go find him!"

She watched him trot off into the living room and heard John making monster noises that had Byron giggling. The bottom of the takeout bag still felt warm as she placed it on the laminate kitchen counter. The tangy smell of teriyaki did not blend well with the stale odor of the dishes piled in the sink. Tonya needed to become a domestic warrior, too. She'd tackle the kitchen when they finished supper. She would wash all the dishes and put them away, not leave them drying in the strainer. She would clean out the fridge and mop the vinyl floor, which was needed after Byron's cereal mishap that morning. The room would glisten when she was done.

John had Byron sitting on his shoulders when he entered the room. "Take-out again?" he asked.

"I got your favorite."

John stretched his hands around Byron's ribs, lifting him over his head before setting him down.

"I found something I thought was interesting." John placed a crinkled receipt on the table. "One hundred and fifteen dollars? For what? That suit?"

Damn it. She had hidden the tags but must have left the receipt in the bag.

"You think we can afford this?" John's lip curled up in a half sneer.

"I got it on sale."

"Of course you did. It's always on sale, isn't it? The purse you bought last month. The pants and leather belt before that. Being on sale excuses every-thing."

"Daddy?" Byron blinked up at him.

"Come on, big guy. Let's turn on Sesame Street." Tonya herded him to the living room and did what she promised herself she'd never do: turned on the TV to babysit her child. When she returned to the kitchen, John was opening a beer.

"What's our balance on the Visa account now?" He flipped the bottle top into the trash. "I haven't seen the thing in a few months."

"It's not bad. I'll get it paid off, I promise."

"Not bad?" He searched her face as if looking for the edges of the lie.

She almost said "under two hundred" to pacify him, but it took four clicks on the computer to uncover the truth. Nothing pissed off John more than deceit.

"Seven fifty. But I'll pay off the balance in a few months, I promise."

"How do you propose to do that? Jamison giving you a big fat raise because you wore that outfit?" He tilted his head back, the Budweiser rim poised between his teeth, reminding her of Byron when he first learned to manage the bottle on his own.

"It's my problem. I'll figure it out." She busied herself with the food though her appetite had fled. As she spooned out the teriyaki, a plump piece of chicken skimmed across her lapel before landing on the plate. "Damn it!"

She grabbed a paper towel to blot away the sticky sauce.

"Oh, great. You ruined it already." John shook his head as he watched her. "Christ, you spend a fortune and spill sauce down the front."

"It's not ruined." Her hand trembled as she ran warm water on the towel and rubbed the soft fabric. It shouldn't be a big deal, but having John scruti-nize her every move didn't help. Wiping away the last trace of sauce, she said, "There. But I think I'll go change."

"Good idea."

In the bedroom, she slipped off the suit and hung it at the front of their crowded closet. John might be right, she shouldn't have bought it. Of course, if John would forgo a few Friday afternoon happy hours, the Visa bill could be paid much faster, but she didn't see him offering that sacrifice. Not that it mattered, the suit was hers now, and she was glad. She had never felt like she did today when she had it on. Maybe a warrior needed her armor.

Back in the kitchen, John had Byron in his high chair drinking juice from a sippy cup. The food remained on the counter, because apparently John wasn't up to the effort of dishing it out on plates. She divvied up the rice and teriyaki, cutting a few hunks of chicken into Byron-size bites. With his favorite Dora the Explorer spoon, Byron smashed his supper into orange mush before putting any in his mouth. More mess for Mom to clean up.

"I think I may have a solution to the Visa bill problem." John finished the beer and went to the fridge for another one.

"What?" Tonya sat at the tiny table, trying to summon an appetite since she'd paid for this food.

"I talked to this woman I know, Carol Greer. She works for a law firm that does a lot of car wreck cases. I told her about what happened and she had some good ideas about how to handle it with the insurance company."

"Handle what? They pay to get the car fixed. They'll cover our doctor bills, but Byron and I are going to be fine. I don't know why we need an attorney for that."

John shoveled chicken into his mouth. "Okay, but here's the thing. Mr. Hastings is at fault. He's liable for more than our expenses, according to Carol."

Tonya lowered her fork. "You have to be kidding. Mr. Hastings is still in ICU. I think he's been through enough."

"Okay, okay. I get it that you don't want to sue Mr. Hastings. His insurance company will handle the settlement. And don't say you're fine. Byron had two nightmares last night. You broke a bone in your nose and you look like hell."

"Thanks. I appreciate the compliment." This conversation had her craving a beer, too, but she was too tired, and one of them needed to get the little guy bathed, read to, and put to bed.

"I'm just saying it's worth looking into. The lawyer's charges come from the settlement, so it won't cost us anything. And we could sure use the money." He reached over and squeezed her hand, a gesture so unexpected that she stared at him.

"Think about it, honey." His face softened as his thumb stroked her knuckles. She savored the tenderness in this touch. It had been a long time.

"Things are so tight right now," he said. "We could use some help."

John was a hard man to argue with, especially when he was right.

CHAPTER 7

Sandy Albright growled at the coffee pot. Not that she was mad at it. In fact, she had become a caffeine worshipper since abandoning her other addictions. It was the hour that made her groan: five AM. She had to be at work in two hours, but insomnia had her awake since two, sleep deprivation being a fabulous perk to her new sober life. No pills, no zzzzs.

As she interrupted the brewing cycle to pour herself a cup, she felt a warm little body weaving between her ankles. A fuzzy bedroom slipper with legs mewed up at her. Sandy stepped around it to get to the table, but the creature beat her there, jumping onto the table top and nearly toppling over her mug.

"Scoot," she muttered, elbowing the beast out of the way, only to have it cry out again.

"Well aren't we up early?" Her cousin Sean appeared in the doorway, dressed in striped pajama bottoms and a *Wicked* t-shirt, his blond hair standing in chaotic waves atop his head. Even though he'd been her roommate for two years, Sean took some getting used to.

"You know me. Couldn't contain my excitement and all," Sandy replied. At least this was day three back on the job. She'd survived the sucky first two days: the scrutiny and urine dip stick from Marie Hempshall, and the whispers from most of the staff, including housekeeping, for God's sake. She'd gone home tired and hungry and eaten half a large pizza day one, finished it day two. But she had not gotten high.

Day three should be a snap.

Sean opened the refrigerator and rummaged through the shelves, removing a carton of eggs and a pack of sausage. His cat leapt from the table to check what else might be hidden in the fridge.

"Good morning, my precious!" Sean scooped up the creature. Miss Saigon rubbed her whiskers against his.

"Why are you up so early? Do you have a morning shift?" Sandy asked.

"Honey, you know I don't do before noon. Just thought I'd see you off this morning. Now, omelet or scrambled?" He held up the eggs.

"You're cooking me breakfast?" Sandy moved to a stool beside the granite-topped kitchen bar.

"I'm thinking omelet." He returned to the refrigerator for cheese and a green pepper. The bedroom slipper purred.

As Sandy lowered her cup, Sean handed her a slip of paper. "Jesse called, four-thirty. And five-fifteen. S."

Seeing Jesse's name made her catch her breath. She had been desperate for his call that first week in rehab. Her cell phone stayed under her pillow, like she was a pathetic preteen, but she stopped leaving messages when he didn't phone back. She'd come to believe he was a part of that life she'd had to let go. "Why didn't you give this to me last night?"

"I figured you had enough drama going back to the job. Sorry." This from the drama queen of the universe. He cracked eggs into a bowl. Oil sizzled in the pan as she refilled her mug. "Aren't you going to call him?" Sean asked.

"At five A.M.?" She could imagine Jesse's sleep-drunk voice answering. But what if someone else answered? Given Jesse's history—or what she thought was his history, the man loved being so mysterious—it could happen. She didn't need to face that today.

Sean turned to face her, spatula in hand. "So. I . . . uh . . ."

She pressed the mug against her chin. Sean stammered when he was talking about money.

"I know I'm behind in rent," Sean said. "But I'm getting paid tomorrow and I promise I'll have a check for you."

She hadn't realized, when she'd let Sean move in, that she was essentially adopting him. They were both refugees from a family that couldn't accept them, but at least Sandy had grown up. Sean, at thirty-one, still waited tables, took classes at the U, and drove a used and sputtering bright orange Kia. An eternal nineteen-year-old.

Sandy had known her cousin was gay before he had. It wasn't easy being homosexual in South Carolina, but when Sean embraced who he was, he did it with zeal, despite efforts by the rest of their family to shove him back in the closet. Sean's parents hardly spoke to him anymore, and Sandy's father, ever the evangelical preacher, prayed for "Sean's condemned soul."

Sandy wondered if he prayed for her soul, too.

A plate appeared before her, the omelet a plump half-moon edged by a lace of yellow. She took a bite, savoring the warm ooze of cheese and decided that when Sean cooked, she could forgive him almost anything. On the floor beside her, the cat gave her tail an annoyed swish.

Sandy was more of a dog person. She and her ex-husband Don had adopted a greyhound on their honeymoon and named it Chai. She hadn't been sure she could love it; such a quiet, bony creature, a daddy-long-legs with fur, all tired out from his years racing. But he had a gentleness about him, his head balanced on her knee, his soft brown eyes blinking up at her like she was his savior. Don got custody after the divorce. Did Chai have the same adoration for the new wife? She hoped not.

"Don't be cross with me, Miss Saigon," Sean gave the cat a stroke. "No eggs for you. I'm looking out for your girlish figure."

Miss Saigon was nothing like Chai, but Sean adored her. Another concession required to live with her cousin. But Sean was the one who visited during rehab, who rid their home of all alcohol and drugs before her return. Who got up at five A.M. to fix her an omelet.

She finished her breakfast and stood. "I'd better get ready for work."

• • •

A QUICK CHECK OF MR. HASTINGS's chart at the nursing station showed no change in his status, except that the transplant team had been scheduled for later that afternoon. Good. Finally closure for the family.

Outside Mr. Hastings's room stood the youngest child, the daughter, leaning against the corridor wall, her head down, hair screening much of her face. So thin that if she'd worn the same beige as the wall she might not have been noticed. Sandy approached her. "Hey. You're Becca, right?"

The girl looked up at Sandy, eyes squinting like she had a killer headache.

"You okay?" Sandy asked.

"I've seen you before. You're Dad's nurse?"

"Yep. I'm Sandy Albright." She moved to stand beside the girl, her rear against the grainy vinyl wall.

"Dad's had a lot of visitors today," Becca said.

"Lots of people care about him. That says something."

"He's very nice to everybody." Becca squeezed the hem of her jacket between her fingers, curling it up to cover her hands.

"Are you cold?"

"There's this black guy," Becca said, ignoring her question. "He hangs out in the cemetery at our church. Kinda creepy, but Dad's always nice to him. Buys him stuff. Gives him little jobs so he can pay him some money."

"Your dad does sound like a very nice man." Sandy suppressed a sigh. Did this child understand her father was dying? As if this could be understood. She'd had her own experience with incomprehensible loss when she miscarried. After three years of trying to get pregnant, of fertility tests and hormones and, finally, in vitro fertilization, she'd lost her baby in the seventh month. People acted like it shouldn't hurt like the death of a living, breathing child, but it had.

"When I had a sleepover party, Dad ordered us pizza," Becca said. "He let us download a movie to watch, and while we were watching it, he made us cookies."

Her father sounded like a good mother.

"He burned them a little but they weren't bad," Becca said. She had rolled up the bottom of the jacket, her arms tucked inside like a straight jacket.

"Becca, has your mom talked to you about your dad's condition?"

"Everybody talks to me about it," she said, pulling the jacket tighter. "But they don't know him. They don't know how much he . . ." Her words trailed off, her head dropping down.

Sandy leaned to the left so that their shoulders touched. "How much he loves you?"

The girl wasn't crying. Her face wasn't pinched and red; no tears leaked from her eyes. She looked as blank as an empty drawer.

"When I was six, he taught me how to ride a bike," she said. "He made me wear a helmet, knee guards, and a thick sweater, even though it was spring, because he didn't want me to fall and hurt myself. He was always doing stupid stuff like that."

Sandy heard the "was." Good. Maybe she did understand. "He was over-protective?"

"I kept asking about getting a learner's permit to drive and he'd get nervous and say, 'You'll have to ask your mother about that.' Mom said he'd be okay once I showed him how I was a safe driver." A hand snaked out of the fabric. She stuck her thumbnail into her mouth and chomped down on the cuticle.

"Becca, all those people that keep coming to visit today. Do you know why?"

"Apparently, to feed me sandwiches. If one more person asks me if I want something to eat I think I'm gonna kick them." She said this with fire. A red drop of blood oozed from the finger and slid down her knuckle.

"You've nicked your cuticle there," Sandy said, reaching for the hand. A pink flap of flesh opened below the nail, more blood trickling out. "Come on, let's clean that up."

The girl followed her to the family waiting room. Sandy told her to wait there as she went for first aid supplies. When she returned, Becca was standing by the door.

"Let me take care of that finger." Sandy snapped on latex gloves and opened an alcohol pad. "This will sting a little."

Sandy winced at the bleeding hand, dabbing with gentle fingers. She noticed several bruises on the girl's forearm. "What happened here?"

Becca turned her arm over with a jerk. Were the bruises self-administered? Sandy pointed to her thumbnail. "I'm a biter too, you know. Or I used to be. It mainly happened when I was nervous."

"I've tried to stop. I did once." Becca folded her arms against her chest.

"You will again. This is just . . . a stressful time."

"I hate this place," Becca said. "No offense."

Sandy smiled. "You have every right to hate the hospital. But you won't have to hang around much longer."

She snuck a look at the girl's face to see if she understood, but there was no sign of recognition. She'd realize soon enough. Sandy secured a bandage around the thumb as Becca stared out the door.

"I'm going to go check on your dad," Sandy said. "Do you want to come with me?"

"Mom's in there," she answered, as though some invisible gate had been locked.

Sandy started toward the room but hesitated. "Remember my name. If you want to talk, tell the nursing assistants to flag me down."

"I'm fine, Sandy," Becca answered. If only she were.

When Sandy entered the room, she found Lena Hastings by the narrow window, watching the rain. Her posture had changed from the day before; she looked sunken in, like something inside had crumbled.

Mrs. Hastings watched her as she checked vitals but said nothing. Sandy saw that the Stadol drip and saline needed to be replaced. She wasn't sure what Mr. Hastings could feel, but it would not be pain.

"You've been kind to us." Mrs. Hastings' voice was hoarse from fatigue.

Sandy gave her a weak smile. "I was talking to Becca. She's having a tough time."

"She's always been Mitch's kid. I'm not even sure how to help her."

"You'll figure it out."

Mrs. Hastings turned back to the window. Sandy moved closer. She could see the gray swollen sky, the tiny rivers of water rippling down the pane.

"Five days ago, I had my life," Mrs. Hastings said. "We had just rebuilt it, you see, after I had cancer. And before—well, we had a lot to rebuild. But now it's rubble. All of it." She pressed a finger against the glass and slid it down, tracking a trail of rain. She looked wounded, but Sandy recognized something else in Mrs. Hastings' eyes: terror.

Sandy was no stranger to fear. Her first night in rehab, when it felt like her life had been ripped from her, she lay on the hard, narrow bed, fighting tremors and nausea and wanting to die as the drugs leached out of her system. That had been the worst. No, not quite the worst, but close.

"I have these days ahead of me," Mrs. Hastings said. "What am I going to do without him?"

Sandy had read about the seven stages of grief back in school, but for her it had been more like fifty. The telling people who still didn't know about the miscarriage stage. The returning unworn maternity and baby clothes stage. The repainting the nursery stage. The finding out about Donald's pregnant girlfriend stage. The discovery that drugs really, really helped stage, and look where that got her.

Sandy blinked, redirecting her thinking to her patient, busying herself with monitors that didn't need adjusting and drips that she'd already checked.

Lena's fingers swept the glass, down, then around, and up, as though drawing a figure she alone could see. "The transplant team is coming this afternoon. I only have a few more hours with him. This shouldn't be about me."

"But it is about you. You and your kids. And the others who love him." It was always about those left to stumble on. For Sandy, drugs had been the thing that helped her bear it. Or at least, they gave her escape. She prayed Lena didn't fall into a similar trap.

"You're speaking from experience."

Sandy flinched. Maybe she'd said too much, or maybe she wore her pain too close to the surface now.

"Sorry. I'm being intrusive."

"It's okay. Yes, I do speak from experience, but that's not important. What is important is that you take care of yourself during what's to come." Sandy almost added, "the hell you're about to go through" but stopped short of that because Lena would find out soon enough. There would be a day, or even a moment, when the truth would settle over her: this would be her life from then on. This.

And maybe that was where Sandy was, too. No oxy or valium to soften the jagged edges. Just a calendar of days to muddle through.

She felt Lena watching her and made herself meet her gaze.

"I'm scared," Lena said.

Sandy took a step closer. "I'm the last person to give you advice, but . . . You have other roles. You have family. Friends. But most important: you're a mother. Put your energy there. You have the boys and Becca. Don't center your life around what's missing."

"I'll try," Lena answered.

As Sandy exited Mr. Hastings's room, she nearly crashed into a man standing outside the door who didn't look familiar. His skin was tanned the color of bread crust, his eyes a darker brown. A blurry pink stripe accented a high hairline. He lifted his brows at her like he belonged there and she didn't.

"Can I help you?" she asked.

"I'm Phillip Calloway." He glanced down at an iPhone gripped in his hand.

"Okay, Mr. Calloway. Can I help you?"

He scrolled through a few messages, in that oblivious smart phone fog so many people occupied these days.

"You'll have to turn that off," Sandy said. "It causes electromagnetic interference."

"Electro what?"

"Your phone can screw up our equipment."

Said phone decided to ring. That his ringtone was "Carolina Girls" made it even more annoying. "This is Calloway," he said into it.

Calloway and Hastings, Sandy realized. This man was her patient's business partner. His name was on the patient's HIPAA release form. They'd been expecting him to call from somewhere—another country maybe? "Turn it off," she mouthed.

"What the hell are you talking about? We had everything sewn up when I left. What the hell happened?" Mr. Calloway said into the phone.

"Off!" Sandy spoke loud enough that a nursing tech up the hall turned to stare.

"I have to go. I'll call you in ten." With two exaggerated swipes of his finger, he turned off the phone and glared at her. "It was an important call. Important as in make-or-break my business, but hey."

"Go down to the lobby and call back." She started to brush past him, eager to be done with Phillip Calloway and his John Boehner suntan, but he raised a hand to stop her. He smelled spicy sweet, the same cologne her ex-husband used to wear: Bijan, two hundred bucks for a thimbleful.

"What's your name?" he asked.

"Sandy Albright."

He eyed the door. "You've been taking care of my partner?"

55

"Yes."

"Sims told me it was a bad heart attack, but surely something can be done. He's still with us. That has to be good, right? Mitch is a fighter."

Mr. Calloway was new to this drama; it would take a while for it all to sink in. "There was too much damage done." Sandy used a gentler, softer voice.

"Who's his doctor?"

"Dr. Burnside. But he's been seen by our cardiac team. A neurologist. An internist." A half dozen had weighed in, even though his situation had been clear the moment his gurney entered the Emergency Department.

"We need to get him to Duke. Or hell, the Mayo Clinic. Someone up on all the new treatments." He looked at the device in his hand like it was the Batphone and he could summon specialists that would fly in through a window. Was there an app for that?

"There is no specialist who can help him." She gave him a sad smile, and told him the rest. Mr. Hastings' EEG revealed minimal functioning. There was a complete absence of brainstem reflexes. He has no capacity to breathe without the ventilator. Kidneys have shut down. *There is nothing there for you to save.*

He stared at her, eyes hardened, then closed, then a single tear emerging which he brushed away with the heel of his hand.

"He's my best friend." He cleared his throat. "So what? We just wait for him to—"

"We're waiting on the transplant team. His corneas, maybe his liver. It's good of your partner and his family to allow it. Your friend will be helping other people have another chance at life." These were rehearsed lines, spoken often in this corridor. She hoped they offered some relief.

"Mitch is the best man I know. Better than I'll ever be." He shook his head. "Guess I better go talk to Lena."

"She could use a friend." She hoped Mr. Calloway could be someone she might lean on.

He nodded, his face smoothing into an expression of forced calm. He drew a breath and opened the door.

• • •

BECCA SAT IN THE CORNER of the carpeted waiting room—the "family room" it was called—with her fingers wrapped around the cell phone. She had replayed the first message a hundred times already: "Becca? Hey, this is Dylan. Uhh, from school. Hope it's okay that I called." He sounded nervous at first, but then said, "I was sorry to hear about your dad. About the accident and

56

all. And, well, I thought I'd give you the number to my cell. In case, you know, you wanted to call or something. Any time. Day or night." Several other calls had followed; Dylan talking about what happened in school or about Todd, his pet Bearded Dragon. It was nice to hear about a normal day, a normal life. Maybe she could even call him back; she'd programmed Dylan's number into the phone but had not yet been brave enough to dial. Still, she loved having his voice in her pocket, and that felt right.

Nothing else did, though. Everything else felt fragile, like if she moved a millimeter, something horrible would happen. She'd felt that way all day, like there was something gelatinous and unstable in her stomach and any movement, any vibration, would make it capsize. She'd felt like this one other time. Eighteen months ago, sitting in her room, as still as a bedpost, listening to drawers opening and shutting, boxes plopped atop each other, suitcase wheels scraping along the hardwood floors.

"Kitten? Can I come in?" Dad had entered timidly, sitting rigidly beside her on the bed. "You okay?"

She had not answered, not that she meant to be rude but she had no words for how she felt. The phone rang, Mom answering it in the bedroom, chattering about keys and paperwork that she would sign in that new animated voice that arrived after she started school. "I should be there in an hour," she said into the phone.

"It'll just be you and me, kid." Dad spoke like a cartoon, trying to be funny when there was nothing funny about this.

Things had happened so fast. She'd overheard Mom on the phone with Royce, whispering, "It's the right thing. Right for all of us," like she cared about anybody but herself. Mom's talk with Becca came two days later: "I love you more than anything, but things between me and your father have changed. We're separating. I'm going to move out." Mom then described the room Becca would have in her apartment, but there was this new look in her eye, like her life would be plenty full enough without a kid.

"This is not about you, Rebecca." Dad elbowed her. He used her full name when she was in trouble or he needed to say something serious. "This is about your mother and me. We both love you very much."

When his hand reached to squeeze her neck, she could feel it vibrating. "This is new for me. Uncharted territory."

Of course it was uncharted. He loved her mom, worshipped her, which blinded him to so many things about her.

"But listen to me, Bec. I am so grateful that I get to keep you here with me. Of course, you'll get to visit your mom whenever you like."

He had sounded like he *was* grateful, which was something she clung to. At first Dad just needed her company like she needed his, because the house had grown huge and empty, but after a few days, he started talking to her about things. Not personal stuff, thank God, because she didn't want to hear how Mom had stomped all over his heart, but about the news and sports, and his gardening. That first Saturday, she helped him plant annuals around the birdfeeder. When he said, "your mom loves these geraniums," she pondered ripping every plant from the ground.

Next came his on-line banking experiment, when he needed her help because "you're so much better with this computer stuff." She got to see all the bills he paid. Internet and cable cost $120, while Mom's apartment was thirteen hundred a month. She should have moved into a trailer.

Even after Mom came back, Dad remained the parent she could count on, through Mom's sickness and after. He was the one whose love for her never wavered a half-inch and knowing that made her feel—sometimes—worthy of loving.

That was why right now, Becca couldn't move from the cold vinyl chair in the corner of the waiting room. The world might shift, might toss her off balance. It could happen in a blink.

People kept coming in and out of the room. Dad's partner, Mr. Calloway, back from Bermuda, just left. Sandy was there, but there were new faces now. People dressed in scrubs and speaking in hushed voices to her mother and brothers. Elliott kept peering over at her, flashing a strange, barely-there grin but then looking away.

Sims coughed, or at least it sounded like that, but then he was sitting in a chair and Mom was beside him, her arm around his shoulders. Elliott shot her another look and the blob in her stomach starting to shift, making her want to bolt out the door; she could run all the way home if she had to.

The medical people shook Elliott's hand and left, and it was just her family in the room. The clock over the vinyl couch clicked.

When the door opened again it was Reverend Bill from the church. Dad loved Reverend Bill. He was an old guy, with white hair and kind eyes, who always limped a little. Reverend Bill went to Lena, his head bowed, his index finger pressed into the space above his lips. Lena whispered something to him. Then all eyes were on Becca.

"Come over here, sweetie," Reverend Bill said.

She took a few steps towards them and halted, unable to get closer. She looked at her family. Tears streamed from Elliott's eyes. Sims stared at a spot on the carpet. Mom reached out a hand, beckoning her to come, which scared her most of all. Reverend Bill cocked a head towards her and they all approached, making a tiny, imprisoning circle around her.

"The transplant team is here," Mom said. "Do you know what that means?"

Hot. She felt so hot all of a sudden, like someone had lit a fire in the room. Her fingers latched onto a hunk of flesh above her elbow and pinched.

"They're going to operate in thirty minutes. So it's time for us—all of us—to say goodbye."

She tried to back away but they were all around her. Reverend Bill reached for her hand. Too hot. The fire swelled. She squeezed her skin harder, needing the pain.

"Becca, are you all right?" Elliott leaned over to look her dead in the eye.

No, not all right.

"Reverend Bill will be with us," her mom said. "He'll say a few prayers. If you want some time alone with your dad—"

The words swirled around in her mind like a horde of bees. She pinched as hard as she could, grateful for the sting.

Mom's hand touched Becca's hair, a soft stroke that skimmed her ear and neck. Becca dug her nail in deeper.

Her mother turned to Reverend Bill and her sons. "I think we should begin. Becca, come with us. It's important that we're—" she hesitated, her voice breaking. "We need to be together."

CHAPTER 8

Tonya Ladson looked at her naked body in the bathroom mirror. The gray bruise began at her left shoulder, passed over her right breast under the nipple like a zebra stripe. Half moons of purple hung under her eyes; pinkish yellow crossed the bridge of her nose. She looked like she'd gone a round with a cage fighter, but better than five days ago.

Her hand passed to her belly. No bruise there, just that round pooch from when she had Byron. That first year, she tried every exercise she could think of to lose her middle, but the pooch never went away, like her flesh was saving space to get pregnant again. That wasn't likely to happen, not with things like they were. Money problems plagued them. Byron took up so much of their time and energy, which might be why John hadn't touched her in months. Weekends, he'd drink too much beer to get things going in the bedroom and weekdays she was asleep hours before he came to bed. Still, if they worked on their sex life, things might improve; they might find the tie that bound them together five years ago.

"You look like bubblegum." These had been the first words John said to Tonya the moment they met the summer after eleventh grade.

"Bubblegum?" Tonya had raised an eyebrow in a way she hoped looked flirtatious. Her first day as a counselor at Camp Riverwild, she tried to appear confident though inside, she quivered like a jellyfish.

"Your shirt. Could it be any pinker?" John was senior counselor, this being his third tour of duty at the camp. He was wearing his lifeguard shirt, his shoulders bulging like cantaloupes.

"It'll scare away the bears," she answered. It was neon pink, and she hated it, but her little brother had picked it out and presented it to her the morning she was packing to leave. Buddy was a huge pain in her ass, but he had moments of surprising sweetness that made her want to wear a garish pink shirt.

"You're seriously worried about bears?"

"Never know what's going to happen in the woods." Tonya had never been the outdoorsy type, and had not camped a single day in her life, but the promise of nine weeks away from her family was all it took for her to mail a counselor application to the YMCA. So here she was with her clothes, bedroll, five cans of bug repellant and six mystery novels, ready to live in the wild. Except she was sort of worried about bears. And snakes.

"We've never had a bear show up," John said. "Did have a skunk last year. Don't even think about keeping any food in your tent."

This was something she hadn't thought about. Did bug repellent work on skunks?

She slept better the third night in the tent. At least it was on a platform, with a wooden floor, and held a small cot with a mattress no thicker than a marshmallow. The eight kids in her care snoozed in a small arc of tents around hers. The occasional giggles and child-snores comforted her, distracting her from the occasional leaf-rustlings that could be a skunk. Or a bear.

Just as she dozed off, she heard a whisper: "Tonya?"

She peered out the tent flap at a bright moon: John's face, encircled by the beam from a flashlight.

"Tommy Larkin's crying his eyes out. Homesick. I can't calm him down."

She understood. One of her little campers had sobbed in her arms that first night.

"Could you come talk to him?" John asked.

She almost said, "Handle it yourself, senior counselor," but he looked humbled by the problem. She learned later that he had no younger siblings. Tommy Larkin crawled in her lap and told her he'd never been away from his mama for this long and Tonya listened, stroked his pale blond hair, and asked him about his pets. When she launched into a story about "Scruffy, the wonder terrier," who performed heroic acts for her best friend Tommy, and John added the character of Gilda, the flying goldfish, Tommy giggled, then sighed, and fell asleep.

After John carried Tommy back to his bed, Tonya stayed up with him past midnight. They learned that they both loved movies but not romantic comedies and hoped they never turned out like their parents. Soon, they lapsed into silence, the night stretching dark and still around them, except for the call of a distant owl.

Two nights later, John returned to her tent, unprompted by a Tommy-emergency. Their starlit talks became the favorite part of her day. Week two, John held her hand. Week three, their first French kiss. Week five, Tonya decided that she and John fit together like a hose to a spigot, and she wanted nothing more than to feel that glorious cool water connecting them.

Neither dated anyone else, much to the frustration of their parents and step-parents. She married her perfect soul mate when she was twenty-two, bore him the perfect son a year later, and now—now her life was not perfect.

Byron came too soon. She hadn't been as diligent with the birth control pills as she should have been, and if she was honest with herself, she'd admit to missing a few doses on purpose. As much as she'd wanted a kid, she hadn't bargained for how he would change things between them. How much time and energy a little one took. Her grandmother used to say "It's the smallest ones who take the most room."

"Whoa." John came up behind her, wincing at her reflection. She felt even more naked then, grabbing a towel and tying it around her torso.

"Does it still hurt?" He touched her shoulder to turn her around.

"A little." She swallowed, embarrassed about his inspection.

"Maybe some Advil or Tylenol would help." He opened the medicine cabinet and found some Motrin. He put two capsules in her hand.

"Thanks." How strange to have him minister to her like this. A glimpse at the old John, the John she missed. Nice to know he was still in there somewhere. She gave him a grateful smile.

"Mommy!" Byron burst into the tiny bathroom, his good arm outstretched for her. John lifted him, Byron's diapered buttocks nestled in the crook of his arm.

"Hey, little man!" She gave him a peck on his cheek. He wrinkled his nose as he touched her face.

"Ouch," she said.

"Easy, partner." John turned Byron so he faced the mirror and lifted his Elmo tee shirt. Byron's bruises were red slashes at his collarbone and waist.

"Oh, peanut," she said, tears welling in her eyes.

"We were lucky, weren't we?" John's hand flattened on her back. She leaned into it, hungry for this touch.

"Yeah, we were." But maybe not Mitch Hastings. Tonya closed her eyes, chasing that thought away. She was fine. Her baby was fine. And John held on like she mattered to him.

"Here." John handed her son to her. "I have an idea."

Tonya pulled Byron close. She didn't want to go to work today. She didn't want to help Marion with the filing or set up appointments for Mr. Jamison or answer the phone five hundred times, or try to be nice to clients who weren't. What she wanted to do was this: hold her little boy, the two of them whole and able to go on with their lives.

"Okay," John said from behind her. "Turn around. Put the squirt down and drop the towel so I can get a good shot of you."

He held the camera, his finger poised on the button. He wanted to take her picture.

"No," she said.

"Don't say no. We need to get a photo of those bruises. If this thing goes to court, we'll need proof of your injuries."

She put Byron down, not trusting her arms to hold him with the rage simmering inside her.

John scrutinized her through the digital viewer. "I doubt we'll use these, but it's good to have them."

She clutched the towel and held her ground. "No."

"Babe, you're not thinking. They have to cover your medical bills. We need to prove pain and suffering—I was looking on the internet last night. That's what they call the disruption to your life this kind of thing causes."

"The internet?" So he was serious about pursuing this.

He clicked a picture. "It probably won't even make it to court. The insurance company will want to settle, but we need this evidence just in case."

She backed up behind the door. She would not be "evidence." He had no right to her body, to her bruises and swollen nose. They were hers to feel, hers to live with.

"Look." John used a quieter, warmer tone. "Let's not make this harder than it needs to be. Use the towel to hide your breasts, I'll just get that blue stripe above them." He stepped closer, his face softening. "Please, honey?"

She could never fight him when he looked at her like that: the half smile, the crinkled eyes. She positioned the towel over her nipples, cold from the exposure, and recoiled at each click, whir, and flash of the camera.

• • •

SANDY STUDIED THE POSTED list of meetings and tried to summon the courage to go inside the church classroom. Jackie had suggested this meeting because Sandy could attend right after work. The AME church was a mere five minutes from the hospital so she had no real excuse to not attend. Except for the little problem of her feet cemented to the floor and an overwhelming urge to run from the building.

"First time?"

She turned to find a skinny kid with spiky yellow hair and piercing green eyes.

"Yes. Well, no, I've been to meetings, but not here. I mean, this is my first time to this meeting." She blushed at her own stammering but the guy just smiled.

"It's a good one. Can get lively at times."

What did lively mean? Arguments? Fighting? She eyed the exit at the end of the hall.

"Ah," he said, removing a scarf and shoving it in the pocket of his sweatshirt. "First meeting on the outside."

"What?" Was she wearing an invisible sign?

"You have that 'fresh from rehab look.' I'm not being critical—I had the same expression fourteen months ago. The idea of coming here scared the hell out of me." He rubbed a hand across his nose. A tattoo across his knuckles spelled out "VIDA."

"Good guess." She watched a string of people come up the hall to enter the meeting room, but the kid remained.

"I'm Jake."

"Sandy." She almost added "Albright" but this was NA, the land of no last names.

"They won't bite. At least, nobody's gotten bit so far." He cocked a thumb towards the room and she read "LOCA" on the other hand. "VIDA LOCA." Crazy life.

She looked at the odd mixture of men and women in the room. White, black, Hispanic. A guy pushing seventy and this kid in front of her maybe twenty years old. She should go inside. She really should.

"You can sit with me in the back. And you don't have to talk or even introduce yourself if you don't want. Come on."

She eyed the long corridor like an escaping student caught by hall patrol. But the truth was she needed a little shove to get through that door. She took in a deep breath and followed Jake into the meeting. After the mandatory stop at the coffee urn they found seats in the back row of mismatched plastic chairs. She liked the Jesus pictures decorating the room's cinderblock walls; a dark-skinned Christ was much more believable than the blond, blue-eyed version in the fellowship hall at her dad's church. The AME Jesus went with a shepherd motif: in flowing blue robes he smiled his perfect Jesus smile at the lambs, both black and white, gathered around him.

The NA leader started the meeting and invited new members to introduce themselves. Sandy remained quiet while Mark, an old member who hadn't attended in half a year, talked about a career crisis that cost him a ton of money. He was contemplating a move to get away from the pressures of his adrenalin-filled work as an investment manager.

Maybe Sandy should move away, too. Everybody at the hospital seemed to know about her stay in rehab. Some avoided her, while others winked like they shared a secret, something she found troubling. The emotional toll of the job was worse now, like the time she spent with Lena. When she had felt the pain radiating from that woman, it was hard not to absorb it as her own. Would moving again be the solution? Leaving Charlotte hadn't been her choice; she'd screwed up at the hospital and almost killed a patient. She wasn't using drugs when it happened, just depressed and befuddled by the implosion of her life. The hospital administrator let her resign, instead of firing her, saying it was because of what she'd been through, though Sandy suspected it was more a matter of protecting Donald's reputation than hers.

That Mark guy, who kept talking about the economy and how unfair it was that some big deal had fallen through, twitched like a ferret. Dots of sweat covered his bald head. He tapped his foot against the scarred linoleum floor. Crinkled his nose. Coke addict maybe?

When the leader began a discussion on managing addictions during the holidays, Sandy had a terrifying thought: the usual Christmas services at her father's church, followed by a white-linen dinner with her parents, her brother and his perfect Baptist family. She hadn't visited them, un-medicated, in two years. A Christmas Plan B was mandatory if she was to stay sober.

Beside Sandy was one of those annoying water bottle people. Soggy napkins surrounded her sweating one liter container which she kept opening, sipping, replacing the top, then repeating the cycle over and over again like somebody with unresolved weaning issues. Sandy considered snatching the bottle and pouring the water over her head.

A stringy-haired woman brought good news of visitation with her children. She cried as she talked about losing her home and custody of her kids because of crack cocaine. A former interior designer, she now shared a room with two women in a recovery house and tried to get by waiting tables. "But it's a start," she said. "I got two hours with my babies. It's a start."

Sandy glared at the woman. She had kids—how could she do that to them? If Sandy had carried her child to term, had given birth—no way she'd have turned to drugs. She never got that chance. She'd never held her baby. Never nursed her. Never celebrated the first word, the first step. All those months of eager anticipation only to have it stolen from her. Ripped away. And here she was surrounded by a room full of miserable addicts talking about their miserable lives. And there was no relief, because the only life raft she had was snatched away, too.

Twitchy Mark eyed his watch. The foot kept tapping.

"Would you stop all that squirming?" A guy beside Mark said. "You got some place to be or something?"

Mark jumped from his chair. He was wide in the chest and loomed over them. "Maybe I need to get the hell away from all you people. You think you've got it so bad but you don't have a damn clue."

Sandy eyed the picture to see if the black Jesus was covering his ears. "Here we go," Jake whispered.

The group leader stood and took a step forward. "Easy, Mark. We're just concerned."

Mark's gaze doing a bumblebee flight around the room.

"You using?" Jake asked.

Mark spun around as if looking for an assailant.

"You have the look. I mean, I know the look. Real well." There was no accusation in his expression, but calm acceptance.

Mark stared, but Jake just smiled back.

"I slipped. It was stupid. So stupid."

She glanced around at the others. Some flinching, some nodding in calm acceptance.

Mark continued. "But I'm trying to hold it together now. I have too much going on. Real life, you know?"

Nobody spoke for a moment, and Mark took his seat again. "Sorry," he said.

"I'm sorry too, man," the fat guy said. "Real life can suck."

Real life like this new life Sandy never would have planned for herself. Real life without a child or husband or nice home or much reason at all to get up in the morning.

The group sipped their now-cold anemic coffee.

The leader spoke. "I'm glad you came to the meeting, Mark. It wasn't an easy choice, but it was the right one. Every sober day is something to be proud of."

Mark rubbed a palm against his sweaty forehead. "I'm just trying not to crash and burn."

"Ain't we all," said Jake, giving a tight smile to Sandy. "Ain't we all."

• • •

As SANDY PULLED INTO HER DRIVE, she thought she saw movement by the door. Sean? No, he would have let himself inside, unless he lost his keys for the nine millionth time. The shadow looked taller than Sean and very lean. Was somebody breaking in? She reached for her cell as she started backing out, but the figure waved and descended the steps. The ambling gait, the way

66

he buried his hands in the pockets of his leather jacket, the way he stood on the sidewalk, head cocked to the side like a puppy to watch her: Jesse was back.

She turned off the ignition. Strange how the drive to go to him fought the drive to dash away. He gripped the car door when she opened it and climbed out.

"Hey." She knew his arms would be around her before she took a step, and expected a smart ass comment about the weight she had gained, but he said nothing. He smelled the same. Tangy citrus from his aftershave. He felt the same, the supple leather of his jacket, the rough stubble of whiskers on his chin. She had missed him, even when she didn't want to.

"You never called me back," he said. "So I figured I'd better stalk you."

She unlocked the door and let him inside. He surveyed the living room as she switched on lamps and swept Sean's clutter from the coffee table.

"Where's the roomie?" he asked.

"At work."

Jesse sat on the sofa, stretching his long legs out. He wasn't as dark as either parent; Sandy knew this from his family photos. His skin was more the brown of a potato. His hair had thinned on top, like his dad's, and the Rogaine wasn't helping. "Don't suppose you have a beer?" he asked.

"Uh, no." She frowned at the callous question.

"Oh, right. Sorry. I, well, I know alcohol wasn't a problem for you."

She decided to sit across from him, not too close. "I'm not an alcoholic. But if I do drink, I'm more likely to use. It lowers my defenses." Lesson One-A from Brook Pines: know your triggers and avoid them like hell. She hadn't decided if Jesse fit in that category.

He reached for a pillow and started fiddling with the fringe. "Why didn't you call me back?"

"Why didn't you call me back when I was in rehab? Or come see me? Or send a card?" She hadn't meant to blurt it all out but seeing him had her off her game.

"A card? You expected me to send a card?" He flashed a wry smile and tossed the pillow at her.

"No. But something." She flung it back.

"I started to come. They told me visiting day was Sunday. But I thought— hell, I don't know what I thought."

So he had called the center to find out about visiting day, which was something, at least.

"I worried about you," he added. "I wasn't sure how I could help. Thought maybe I was part of the problem."

Maybe he was; she wasn't sure. Everything about life before rehab seemed like one ugly tangle.

"Finishing the program took a lot of guts." Jesse spun the pillow between his hands. Big hands that could palm a basketball.

"Not guts. Desperation. I had to survive rehab or lose everything." At least, that was how it felt. If they took her nursing license, she couldn't work, couldn't pay the mortgage or the car payment, the failures piling on top of her.

"You wouldn't have been destitute. I wouldn't abandon you like that."

"I wasn't about to have you support me." She sounded more bitter than she meant. Jesse sold high-end medical equipment like MRIs and ultrasound machines. His salary was in the six digits, and he traveled all over the southeast. She often wondered if he had a girl in every port. When she asked him, he'd answer, "Trust me, babe." Like that could happen.

"So no beer. Maybe a soda? Coffee? " Jesse asked.

She nodded. He followed her into the kitchen where Miss Saigon purred against his leg like they were lovers reunited. Jesse bent over to scratch her chin. "You are such a flirt," he said.

"Takes after Sean." Sandy opted to make coffee because caffeine might keep her on her toes. Jesse sat in his usual spot at the kitchen table, leaning back, hooking his thumbs around the ladder-back chair. His eyes on her used to be something she enjoyed but now it made her feel exposed. When she placed the cream and Splenda on the placemat, he took her hand.

"What was it like?" he asked.

"Huh?"

"Rehab. What was it like?"

She let her fingers slip away from his and busied herself with cups. She was hungry so she added cheese and crackers to the table.

"You don't want to tell me?" He studied her as if he could see more than she wanted. Jesse was smooth as ice and just as slippery, but this wasn't the kind of conversation they had. They didn't pry. They kept things in the here-and-now.

"Hard as hell. Especially that first night." The agony of withdrawal: uncontrolled shaking. The manic hammering in her heart. The paranoia: the sprinkler head over her bed held a camera. Even after they gave her a tranquilizer she lay awake, trying to hear what the muffled voices outside her room were saying about her.

He stood, ambling over to the coffee maker and pouring cups for both of them. "It got better?"

"Rehab was like another planet. Kind of hard to describe." Sometimes it had been okay, like she was floating in the ocean, cool and peaceful. Then waves came out of nowhere and toppled her into the roiling sea. Drowning had its appeal, even now. She bit into a cracker. A little stale, but tolerable.

"Did anybody come to see you?" he asked.

"Sean did. A lot. He brought me the DVD player and a bunch of movies. My parents came, too." She sipped her coffee.

"Wow. How'd that go?"

"About what you'd expect. I should have sold tickets." Actually much worse than anyone expected. Having them across the glossy black table from her, having Pastor-Dad caress the worn cover of his Bible, having them dare to mention the failure of her marriage. The false condolences and expressions of concern, the subtle gleam in her father's eyes as though he was secretly pleased to witness her failure. After they left, it took two hours of therapy with Dr. Flanders and a mild sedative (too mild) for her to settle down. Dr. Flanders forbade future visits from Reverend and Mrs. Duncan L. Albright.

Then the greeting card came, the crisp white envelope, gold foil inside, the "get well soon" in cursive font and the note from her mother: "we're praying for you every day, Sandy. We're praying for your soul." Don't, she wanted to answer, because she wasn't sure she wanted her soul saved.

"How long had it been since you saw your folks?" Jesse asked.

"Can we not talk about it?" She lowered her coffee, her hand quaking. What a wreck she was.

"Sure, babe. Sure." Jesse tried too hard not to notice her trembling, which humiliated her. She wished she did have beer. Just one, to take the edge off. And a valium. No, that was what Jackie called "stinking thinking."

She glanced up at him and had a fleeting thought of dragging him to the bedroom and undressing him. Sex with Jesse could be mind-blowing and that was one high she was still allowed. But then he'd see her nude, and that new layer of fat around her waist couldn't be ignored. This wretched sober life.

Miss Saigon hopped up in Jesse's lap and swished her tail under his chin.

"What have you been up to?" she asked.

"Same old, same old. Got a new contract down in Orlando. Big facility. They're working me hard."

"Nice to have business in this economy." She wondered if he had a Florida girlfriend yet.

"Always gonna have sick people no matter what Wall Street does. That's why I'm in the biz." Sometimes Jesse took on a hip-hop accent and attitude but he'd just as easily morph into an Ivy-League-grad-stockbroker.

She wished she was more like him. If she could shed her skin and become someone else. She faked it, back when she used drugs. For two and a half years, she had pretended she hadn't lost everything that mattered to her.

Damn it. She had to turn this off. Jesse came over to her and reached for the fists balled at her side, enfolding them in his bear paw of a hand. Touched her face. Kissed her.

She thought about asking him to leave and closing the door on Jesse's part of her life. But his arms came around her, his hips pushing against her, and he felt familiar, the feel of his bristly cheek on hers, the way he mmmmm'ed when their lips touched, the solid warmth of the man. She slid her hands around him.

Finally, *finally,* she stopped thinking.

CHAPTER 9

"Welcome to the bowels of hell." The voice snarled in Joe's ear, and his eyes popped open, half-expecting to see the demon hanging over his nest. But there was nobody there, just the tall limbs of the oak tree waving against the morning sky.

"Bowels of hell," the voice repeated, like Satan's mouth was close enough to eat him alive. Joe jerked up, stiff from the cold air and lack of sleep, and leaned back against Mr. Wortham Pinckney's tombstone. He could hear the rumble of trucks on the road, the nattering of squirrels above him, and that voice of pure darkness speaking on this, God's holy ground. "I'm coming for you, Joe."

He shivered. Sometimes if he ignored the devil, he'd go away, but he was so full of venom now there might be no shaking him. Joe stretched his fingers, trying to get some life into them, his joints tight from the frosted ground. A green van pulled into the church parking lot, beeping as it backed up—one he'd seen before. The driver climbed out and opened the back doors to lift out a ring of white flowers.

Funeralizing flowers.

"I'm coming," Satan said.

Joe was the worst kind of sinner, but had there been one sin, one bad deed in His eyes that caused Him to stop caring? What had it been? Was there some way Joe could make it right?

Other cars came into the church lot. The funeral must be soon, so Joe'd better tidy up his squat. He rolled the jacket he used as a pillow into a tight ball, tying it with a piece of yellow cord he'd found in a dumpster. He brushed away the leaves he'd piled up to sleep on, careful to wipe off Mr. Pinckney's stone so that every letter could be read. The remains of an apple he ate last night had rolled to another grave. When he lifted it, a parade of fire ants stormed up his hand and bit into him.

"Unh!" Joe puffed out at the pain. He hurried to the trash bin and tossed the apple, then swept his hand and wrist to get rid of the swarming ants that didn't want to leave him. Soon both arms felt the stubborn sting.

"He knows what you done," said the devil.

Water would help. He rushed to the church hose beside the east gate, worried that the ants would keep on climbing, maybe get under his clothes and torment all his flesh. He turned on the spigot and the icy water sprayed his arms and calmed the burn. He studied his skin to make sure all the ants were gone. Tiny bumps erupted on his hand. The pain and itch was just another thing he'd deal with that day.

"He knows what you done," repeated the devil.

"What was it?" Joe asked aloud as he lumbered back to his squat. What had he done that the Lord would up and leave him? He'd gotten used to the Lord's little gifts, like socks, or soap, or a brown bag lunch. Sometimes, a jacket or pair of boots. Maybe he hadn't been grateful enough. Maybe he'd forgotten to say a prayer of thanks. Or maybe the Lord realized Joe didn't deserve the things he brought.

Joe winced at the heat on his fingers from the ant bites and considered that maybe the Lord was done with him. Maybe that's why the devil was on him like he was. Joe shouldn't be making a home by His holy house when he wasn't worthy of this sanctuary. The man at the soup kitchen had said they'd opened the winter shelter, but Joe didn't want to stay there. If he had to leave his nest by the church, where else could he go?

Not by the river. People staying there did terrible bad things, people like Cyphus Lawter. The last time Joe had ventured there he'd seen three men beat another half to death over a crack pipe. Cyphus laughed at what they'd done and snatched the pipe for himself.

Rag Doll had talked about a place behind the old Piggly Wiggly grocery store, but if she told him about it, she'd told a number of men. Rag Doll would sell her body for a meal or a pack of cigarettes, and Joe didn't need to be near that kind of carrying on. Not with the Lord already judging him.

Beyond the fence, Reverend Bill parked his big blue car in the usual spot. Joe liked to be gone before Reverend Bill showed up, so the pastor wouldn't think Joe a nuisance. Not that Reverend Bill would ever say something like that, he was always nice to Joe, but Joe didn't want to wear out his welcome. Then again, maybe he already had.

Reverend Bill waved at Joe. He waved back, uncertain what else to do, when he noticed the man walking towards him. Maybe Joe was in trouble. He smoothed down the front of the jacket, praying the pastor would walk on by. The reverend stopped in front of him. "How you doing, Joe?"

"Fine, Reverend. Fine as can be." He kept his face down. It was disrespectful for someone like Joe to look right in the face of a man of God.

"That's good. I hope you weren't too cold last night." He spoke with a soft, gentle voice, like he cared about Joe, like Joe was somebody worth caring for.

"Not too bad, not yet. I still got this nice coat." He fiddled with a wooden button.

"Joe, do you know who left you that jacket?"

He nodded because of course he knew. The Lord left it, back when he wasn't mad at Joe.

"Did he ever say anything to you about it?"

"No," Joe whispered. "He don't say much to me anymore."

Reverend Bill put on this funny expression, like maybe something pinched him inside. "No, I don't imagine he does."

So did Reverend Bill know? Had the Lord told him what had been Joe's sin? Should he ask? "I wish I knew what—I mean, I'm sure there's a good reason."

"Yes, there is." Reverend leaned against the short wall that enclosed the grave yard. "When did you last talk to him?"

Joe thought about how to answer. He talked to the Lord all the time, in his head, but didn't pray out loud much. But the people at this church prayed out loud, he'd heard it. Maybe that was what Reverend Bill was talking about. "Been a while," Joe said.

"I should have told you sooner. I'm so sorry I didn't. But Mitch died. He had a heart attack and—well—he was too sick for the hospital to fix. We're having the funeral in a little while, after morning Communion. We'll bury him here, in the churchyard."

Joe blinked, trying to figure this out. Mitch died, he said. Mr. Mitch? That nice man who sometimes hired Joe to do a bit of yard work? He'd just seen him. He still had the twenty Mr. Mitch had paid him to rake his lawn. He often had jobs for him at his house or in empty buildings that needed some tending to. Joe would pick up trash, cut bushes, mow grass—whatever Mr. Mitch wanted. He paid real good, too. Cash money so Joe didn't have to mess with a bank. Mr. Mitch was dead? "I'm sorry to hear it."

"It's been hard on the family, as you can imagine."

"I sure can." He'd seen Mr. Mitch with his family coming to church some days. They'd be all dressed up, and Joe didn't get too close on days like that. The man's family must miss him.

"Mitch always liked you, Joe." The reverend let out a low sigh and it sounded so sad that Joe started feeling sad, too. It must be hard, working for the Lord like he did. So many souls he had to look out for. So many.

"We're going to put the plaque up later. Mitch will be cremated, and his urn will go in the columbarium. You know where that is?"

Joe shook his head.

"Let me show you." Reverend Bill passed Joe and turned to the south end of the graveyard, where the big stone sculpture had been added. He touched one of the copper plates on the stone. Did he mean Mr. Mitch would be inside that thing?

"You were always important to Mitch. You know that, don't you?"

Joe nodded, because he thought that was what the reverend wanted, but he knew he wasn't important to anyone. Not important like Mr. Mitch's family, or the reverend, or even the people in all those cars driving by. He was just a man who lived in a graveyard and waited for the Lord to tell him what to do. And lately, the Lord had been real quiet.

Reverend Bill looked at the ground around the sculpture. "Leaves keep piling up. I should have tended to them yesterday."

Joe bent over and scooped up as many as he could, twigs scratching his irritated hands. "I'll take care of it."

"That would be great. Don't leave without seeing me first. I want to pay you for your troubles."

"I don't need—" Joe didn't get to finish the sentence because Reverend Bill looked at his watch and then hurried off.

Joe knew where the rake was kept, in the tiny tool room that the church should lock but never did. He grabbed the rake and a pair of gloves, glad to do this task for the reverend. Maybe the Lord would take notice.

• • •

TONYA SLIPPED INTO THE BACK pew of St. Mary's Episcopal Church just as the minister said, "In the name of the Father, the Son, and the Holy Spirit. Amen." She watched him make the sign of the cross in the air, then limp down the aisle, his robe flapping like white wings beside him. A few people had attended the service, which the sign outside described as "Weekday Morning Communion." He shook the hand of each parishioner as they exited, laughing with one, nodding soberly at another. The sign had said his name was Bill Tanner.

She hadn't told John yet about the news. He'd already left for work when she opened the paper and spotted the obituary for Mr. Hastings. A photograph of a smiling bald man topped two columns that detailed a life: a valued member of St. Mary's Episcopal Church, a successful and respected

74

businessman, survived by his wife, Lena, sons Mitchell Sims Jr. and Elliott, daughter-in-law Connie, and daughter Rebecca.

She wished John would be supportive about Mr. Hastings, understand how hard this was for her, but he'd mentioned the attorney again last night. What would he say now that Mitchell Hastings wasn't alive to be sued?

Everyone else had left except the minister, who loosened a rope belt that had a gold fringe. He was watching her, and she was embarrassed. She started to grab her purse and flee, but the man approached, limping up the aisle, and sliding into the pew beside her. He tugged at the collar encircling his throat.

"Dang thing feels like a noose sometimes," he said. The not-very-holy comment came as a surprise.

"I haven't seen you here before. That's the advantage of having a handful of worshippers in these weekday services. I know everybody. To be honest, if it wasn't for the van from the Still Hopes Retirement home, I might be here all by my lonesome. Except today. Today I have you." He smiled at her. His eyes were a milky green, with deep creases surrounding them.

"I missed most of the service. Sorry."

He startled her by unbuttoning the robe where it covered his legs. He reached down and massaged his right knee. "Arthritis," he explained. "Growing old ain't for the faint of heart."

Tonya felt for the purse beside her. She should leave.

"I'm Bill Tanner," he said. "What's your name?"

"Tonya." She almost added, "Ladson," but wanted to stay anonymous.

He pushed harder on the knee, grimacing.

"That must hurt," she said.

"The doctor says if I get a knee replacement it will change my life. But I don't like the thought of someone holding a knife over my leg." He looked at her. "What do you think? Would you let them do it?"

She shrugged. "If it helped I would."

"That's because you're braver than I am." He gave her wink.

"I'm not brave." She wove her fingers through the straps of her purse. She needed to get to the office. Using the excuse of a visit to the office supply store bought her an hour delay, and Ruthless kept an eye on the clock.

"Somehow I doubt that." He leaned back, stretching the leg out into the aisle and wincing. She felt sort of sorry for him.

A door opened beside the giant cross hanging in the front of the church. A man carried in a large wreath of white flowers. "Where you want this?" he yelled.

"Sorry," Reverend Tanner muttered to her. "We have a funeral in a few hours. I'll be right back. Don't move, okay?"

She nodded, though the pull to flee was hard to ignore. He hobbled to the altar rail and instructed the florists to place all the flowers in an arc beside the marble altar. "How many arrangements?" he asked them.

"Twelve so far. The guy was popular," the florist answered.

Tonya lowered her head.

"Put some by the columbarium," Rev. Tanner answered, then turned and walked back to where she waited.

"Are you coming to the funeral?" he asked, settling beside her again.

She shook her head. Hot tears flooded her eyes and she wished she could push them back inside. "I didn't know Mr. Hastings."

He didn't speak, but handed her a thin cotton handkerchief. She felt its frayed corners, and thought about how her grandfather always kept a tattered red kerchief in the back pocket of his overalls.

"I was the one in the wreck with him," she said. "It was my car that hit Mr. Hastings. I didn't see him until it was too late. I tried to slam on my brakes but he came right through the intersection and hit me, and our cars slid together until his bounced off and skidded away and hit a tree. It happened so fast, just a few seconds, and all that damage.

"My light was green. I know it was green. But I keep thinking that I should have done something—swerved or braked or even pulled off the road but I was on my cell and I didn't and Mr. Hastings is dead."

He studied her, his crinkled lips puffing out a sigh. She wished he didn't look so kind.

"Is that how you injured your nose?"

"The airbag. My son was in the car, too. Thank God for his car seat."

"Yes. Thank God."

"Byron's two. He broke his collarbone, but that was all. Except he's gotten real clingy, and he wakes up at night crying. I think he's still scared." She had held his hand when she took him to Little Smiles daycare that morning. He'd ignored his favorite Tonka truck. Rejected the spotted rocking horse. It was when another toddler had teased him with a stuffed octopus that Byron stopped clutching her skirt so she could leave.

She wiped her face again, wincing when her hand touched the bruise. "I feel like I keep reliving those minutes over and over. But at least I'm alive to live them over."

"Tonya." He spoke sternly as though wanting her full attention. "I want to make sure you understand what happened. Mitch had a heart attack before

76

the accident. That's why he ran the light. That's what caused the wreck. None of this is your fault."

She stared at him, desperate to believe. "Before?"

"He had chest pains that morning but the family thought it was reflux. We think the cardiac arrest happened seconds before he went through the light."

It felt as if the room had tilted on its axis. The accident hadn't caused his heart attack. It was the other way around.

"Tonya? You okay?"

"I'm fine. Just surprised." She wiped her face with his handkerchief. "But he didn't die right away. I mean, he was in the hospital for a while."

"Because he was trapped in the car, he went too long without oxygen getting to his brain. Lena—that's his wife—waited until all the family was together before ending life supports."

"So if I hadn't crashed into him, maybe he'd have gotten help sooner. Maybe he would have recovered."

Bill shook his head. "Don't dwell on the what-ifs. Believe me, I've been an expert at that game and it messes with you. Mitch's death wasn't in your control. Thank God you and your little boy weren't more badly hurt."

"I got off easy."

"I don't think you did." He nudged her arm with his elbow. "Do you believe in God, Tonya?"

Oh no. She was not ready for a God speech. She did not want to get on her knees and pray, even if her soul did need saving.

Bill laughed. Another surprise. "Relax. I'm not getting preachy on you. I want to point out that if you do believe in God, you know that sometimes he has plans for us that we don't know about. The accident was a horrible, tragic thing, but maybe something good can come out of it."

"I don't see how."

"No, you can't." He rubbed his knee. "Not yet."

The door behind the altar opened as three more flower arrangements arrived. The thick overripe smell of lilies overwhelmed the sanctuary. "I should get back to work," she said.

He stood and limped into the aisle, letting her out. "I'm glad to have met you, Tonya. I'd love to talk to you again. Anytime."

She nodded. As she pushed past him and moved to the door, she heard him say to the florist, "Take that big pink wreath outside. Stinks like dimestore perfume."

CHAPTER 10

Lena had always hated black. There were women who loved the color for its slimming effect, but she found it morose. Undertakers wore black. Hearses and limousines. Black widow.

So as she stood in her closet searching for clothes to wear to her husband's funeral, she knew she would not wear black. She did not want his service be filled with sadness, she wanted a celebration of Mitch's life, yet that wouldn't happen. Bill Tanner would do his best, but the homily would summarize Mitch in sound bites. The congregation would sing Mitch's favorite hymns and comment on how many friends he had and admire all the flowers and then they'd all go back to their lives. Elliot would leave. Sims wouldn't come around as much. What would Lena and Becca do? This, she couldn't quite grasp. She'd been so busy over the past few days, telling people about Mitch's death, tending to the arrangements. Taking care of her children. There had been a thousand little details to fill her time, but soon would come the day after the funeral, and all the other days, and how would they be spent?

What a funny way to use that word, spent, as if days were currency and eventually she would run out. She had almost run out last year, when her account decreased to mere pocket change. Then came her recovery, her account of days renewed, only to have Mitch's days snatched away.

Her hand trembled as she skimmed through the wall of garments, looking for the right dress, and she felt a flush of panic when she couldn't find it. Then there it was: the tailored purple silk Eileen Fisher that Mitch had bought for their anniversary. As she removed the hanger, she backed into Mitch's clothes, wool itching through her nightgown. She reached for his jacket, the one he had worn the morning of the accident, returned to her at the hospital. She buried her nose in the fabric and breathed in Mitch's cologne. Without thinking, she slipped her hand into the jacket pocket because she always emptied his clothes of mints, Werther's candies, and coins. She found his folded handkerchief, the one he always carried and rarely used, with something hard tucked inside. A grayish stone, as wide as a checker, with specks that shimmered in the light. She skimmed her thumb over its peppery cool skin. Mitch had held it. She imagined his calloused fingers gripping its smooth edge. Her Mitch.

"Mom!" Becca's alarmed cry cut through. She hurried from the closet, almost forgetting the dress, and said, "In here. What is it?"

Becca rushed into the room, wearing a sweatshirt and shorts, her hair damp from the shower. "I can't wear the skirt. Please, Mom, don't make me. I can wear the gray pants and blazer."

"The blue skirt or a dress. You're going to church."

"I saw women in pants last Sunday. Lots of them."

Lena slid the rock into the pocket of her robe and laid the purple dress across her bed. "When I am an old woman, I shall wear purple," the poem went. Mitch's gift had been a joke, reminding Lena she *would* become an old woman now that the cancer was gone.

"Dresses make my legs look fat," Becca said.

So that was what this was about. "Your legs are beautiful. But if you'll be more comfortable in pants, okay."

Becca retreated without another word, drips of water marking her trail in the carpet. Lena returned to the closet. Should she wear a scarf? Was it appropriate to accessorize in widowhood?

The phone rang. There had been many calls, but dutiful Elliot had fielded every one. She heard him answer again, repeating a louder, second "Hello?," then footsteps echoing on the stairs. He came into her room. "It's Aunt Abby. She just got our messages."

Finally, her older sister. Lena took the phone. "Abigail? Where are you?"

"Le-Le? Speak up. I can barely hear you."

"Where are you?" she yelled.

"I've been working in a village five hours from anywhere. No phones. No cell reception. Nothing."

Lena didn't ask why. Surely Abby was on some important mission, rescuing orphans or saving the rainforest, but she hadn't been here when Lena needed her.

"I just heard. My God, Le-Le. My God." Static blurred Abby's words. For fifteen years, Abby had lived in one staticky country or another.

"The funeral is today," Lena said. "I take it you won't be here."

"I'm sorry." Abby's voice quavered. "When did it happen? When did we lose him?"

Lena had to think. She'd been living in this strange contraction and expansion of time, hours like years, days like mere seconds. "The accident was Tuesday. He died on Friday." And today was . . . Monday?

"If only they could have saved him. A world without Mitch? I can't imagine it."

Lena clutched the stone.

"I'm coming, Le-Le. We're trying to book the ticket now."

"It's okay. We're okay. I know you have important work—"

"Don't be ridiculous. I'll call when I have the itinerary worked out. Until then, I'm there. My heart is there with you."

Before Lena could argue, her sister hung up. Abby hadn't come during Lena's cancer. She'd been too tied up with some crisis in Peru to make it to their father's funeral four years ago. Lena had managed all that without her older sister. She could manage this.

"Everything okay?" Elliott stared at her from the doorway.

"She's coming as soon as she can."

"Good." Elliott reached for the phone. "I don't feel right about leaving you and Becca alone here after the funeral."

Don't go then.

"We'll be fine." She gave him a smile that felt fake, but he just nodded and went back downstairs. This would be a long, difficult day. The house, already overflowing with casseroles, would fill with more food. It was an odd southern custom, this ritual of funerals and food, and Lena would play her part.

"A giant basket of fruit just got delivered!" Becca appeared at the doorway again, the gray pants sagging low on her narrow hips. A stiff wind could carry that child away. "What are we supposed to do with all this food?"

"You hardly ate any breakfast. Why not have some?"

Becca's eyes narrowed like Lena had suggested she help herself to a plateful of worms.

Not today, Lena thought, her teeth clenching. Not this battle today. "We'll give some to the food bank. But a lot will get eaten this afternoon. I expect people will stop by after the funeral."

"I don't want to ride in the limousine. Do I have to?"

"I thought you'd want to."

"It's just that, well, everyone will be watching." Becca's hand went to her mouth. At age six she had exchanged thumb-sucking for nail biting.

Lena approached her daughter and frowned. Becca looked so gaunt. Pale. Lost. "You'll be between your brothers. They'll protect you from any onlookers."

"Couldn't I ride with Kayla and her family?"

Why couldn't her child think of someone besides herself? Today of all days. "No. You'll ride with us." She didn't mean to sound so harsh. Becca flinched.

"It's just that we have to be a family right now. We have to be together." Lena moved closer to her, her fingers combing through a strand of Becca's hair and slipping it behind her ear. "Okay?"

Becca nodded as she pulled away. Her untouchable daughter.

How was Lena to fix her?

• • •

SANDY STARED AT THE POPCORNED ceiling over her bed. Jesse had snuck away into the moonlight like a vampire. She'd been awake for two hours, even though today was her first day off. Something to enjoy. Celebrate. Except celebrating meant drugs and she didn't do drugs anymore. This is what defined her now. She was a used-to-be-user, facing an entire day—twenty-four hours—with nothing to do.

A year ago, she would have slept much of the day, rousing herself to get to happy hour with a friend, maybe Jesse. She'd come home later, ready for another kind of altered state. She'd lay out her pills on the table: Oxy, Valium, and Darvocet if she had it. She'd pour a glass of chardonnay as she studied her pharmaceutical options. Valium made her mellow as a tortoise. Oxy sedated, but not too much, and got her high as the North Star if she took enough. Darvocet made her wobbly as a bobble-head doll. After pondering each drug, she chose the Oxy because Oxy always won. She'd take two or three, sip her wine until the drug sizzled inside her. Heaven.

But she wasn't supposed to indulge in stinking thinking. Sandy was due for a meeting today. She'd find one in the afternoon, which would kill an hour. The house needed vacuuming, which would take a good twenty minutes, and balancing her checkbook would take care of another ten. Oh hell, twenty-two hours unaccounted for. Sleep would take five or six because she never slept an entire night un-medicated, which she was now. Woefully unmedicated.

She slid her feet off the bed and found her slippers, ridiculous Wonderwoman fuzzies that Sean had brought to her when she was at Brook Pine, and stumbled out of the room in search of coffee.

"Do not, I repeat, do not go near that litter box!" Sean, wearing plaid flannel pajama bottoms and mismatched socks, skidded across the wood floor to stop in front of Sandy. "I was going to clean it this morning. Promise."

Sandy clutched at her tee shirt to still her heart. "Scare a person why don't you. And yes, you'd better get that stink out of here."

"I was out of cat litter but I got some last night." He grabbed a plastic sack and the pink scooper. Sandy winced at the odor, though it wasn't as bad as some of the hospital rooms at her job. Not her floor, mind you, because she wouldn't allow it.

"You working today?" She hoped she didn't sound too desperate for company.

"I go in at eleven." Sean was a waiter at Prism, an upscale restaurant in the Vista. Daytime, he was a sixth-year senior at the University of South Carolina. Sean was plenty smart but reluctant to grow up. Her personal Peter Pan.

"Adam's coming over," he said. "Maybe you two can go to lunch or something."

"Maybe." Lunch might be safe, Sean's best friend Adam wouldn't order a beer or margarita, and food would distract her for an hour or two.

Sean beat her to the coffee pot and poured two mugs as he hummed, "Oh What a Beautiful Morning." When the doorbell rang, Adam let himself in, wearing his usual khakis and a sweater tied around his shoulders like he was Gatsby himself. He carried a newspaper and a small basket of nectarines, which he placed on the table in front of Sandy. "Fresh fruit is good for your recovery. You need two to four servings every day." He lifted a nectarine. "Is this a serving? What do you think, Sean?"

Sean snagged three and tossed them in the air—two, then one, and then he was juggling them, a circle of peachy-red planets orbiting his head. "I think she can figure out what to eat without our help."

Adam spread the newspaper across the table. "Okay, you gotta see this. I've been waiting all my life for it."

Sandy saw that it was yesterday's edition. Adam was the assistant feature editor for the *Columbia Gazette*.

"I am soooo sending this wedding announcement to Leno." He pointed to a picture of a plump bride in a billowing gown like a tulle-draped Liberty Bell: "Felicity Angel Long to wed Dr. Caldwell Lane Dick."

"Oh my God!" Sean dropped the fruit on the floor, one rolling dangerously close to Miss Saigon, who puffed up like a porcupine.

"That's pretty damn funny," Sandy said.

"I hate editing the wedding page but this makes it all worthwhile," Adam said. "You should see the bulletin board in my cube. I've got the Green-Pease nuptials, the Hogg-Wilde, and my personal favorite, the Wannamaker-High."

"I sure hope she didn't hyphenate."

"Doctor Dick. I'm thinking urologist." Sean tugged the newspaper closer. "Any good obituaries?"

"Not really, though once I got a fax about a man who 'died of natural clauses.'"

Sandy looked over Sean's shoulder at the list of names, finding a familiar one: Mitchell Sims Hastings. "I worked on this guy," she said. "It was a car crash. He'd had a heart attack and was trapped inside. Good Samaritans did CPR and got a pulse but he'd been anoxic too long."

She read the obit, Sean peering over her shoulder, and thought about Lena Hastings, the now-widow, and Becca, the thin, lost child.

"Sims Hastings was in high school with us," Adam said. "Sat in the third row in Mr. Richards' science class. Tall guy. Ball player. The younger brother brought in the obit."

She remembered Elliott, how attentive he had been with his mother.

"What got to me was how fragile he was," Adam said. "He'd handwritten the obituary, listing all the details about Sims and a sister, but had forgotten to include his own name. Freudian slip, I think."

"Poor thing. Is he single?" Sean said, collecting the fruit.

"I felt sorry for him," Adam said. "I rarely have direct contact with the family—usually it's just the funeral home. But this guy was so raw. I wanted the obit to be right. The funeral's at noon."

Sandy closed the paper and carried her cup to the coffee maker for a refill. Outside, clouds like white meringue hovered in a pale blue sky. A pretty day, with so many dreaded hours to fill.

"I'm going to the funeral," Adam said.

"Why? Because the brother is cute?" Sean's voice was half-accusing.

"Because I want to see Sims. And this guy that died—he's very well-connected. The funeral's gonna be big. Can't help but be curious." He looked at Sandy. "Maybe you want to go?"

She surprised herself by not saying no right away. It would be weird to attend. She hadn't known Mitch Hastings. She'd never heard the sound of his voice. She had no clue if he liked chocolate or rock music or Glenn Beck. But she did know Lena Hastings, that proud, terrified woman, and wondered how she was managing. Maybe she would go to the funeral, read this final chapter to Mitch Hasting's life. And, she thought, looking up at the kitchen clock, kill a couple of hours in an endless sober day.

CHAPTER 11

An hour later, Sandy and Adam stood in line behind an elderly couple and a middle-aged man in a tweed Armani suit. They'd come a full forty minutes early because Adam insisted he wanted to watch the guests arrive. Sandy already regretted her decision. She was wearing pantyhose and a skirt for the first time in months, and wished she'd let out the waist button by an inch or two.

They made their way up to the guest book where she wrote her name in an unreadable scrawl. Adam waited for her by the side entrance into the sanctuary. He'd changed into an impeccable gray suit and garnet tie, his goatee a black oval around his lips, and she thought for the hundredth time how unfair it was to single women that Adam was gay. As she glanced around for a program, one was shoved into her hand.

"Here you go." The man had salt and pepper hair, tanned skin, and wore a black suit with a white rosebud pinned to the lapel. Mr. Calloway, the jerk at the hospital who wouldn't get off his phone. She doubted he'd recognize her out of her scrubs. She doubted anyone would, and counted on remaining anonymous.

"You were his nurse," Phillip Calloway said.

"Yes." She gave him a polite smile as she tried to slip by him. He took a step closer, peering down.

"What's your name?" he asked.

"Sandy Albright."

"Sandy Albright," he repeated, as if tasting how the letters came together.

"I'm sorry for your loss." She looked at Adam, whose eyebrows had climbed to the top of his forehead.

"Sorry I was such a pain in the hospital," Phillip said. "I had just found out about Mitch. The news kind of had me in a tailspin."

"I imagine so."

"A week ago, I was stretched out on the pristine sands of Bermuda, beer in hand. Now I'm at my best friend's damn funeral."

She hoped the elderly woman with the white spun hair who was entering the sanctuary hadn't heard Phillip.

"I haven't even been in a church in over a year," he continued. "The last time it was a funeral, too."

"Mine was a wedding. A cousin I don't even like." It had been at a Baptist church, and her father had given the homily. Sandy knew his focus on "till death do us part" was aimed at her because of the divorce.

"I don't like any of my cousins," Phillip said. "Except maybe Marsha. She's my second cousin or first once removed or whatever. In sixth grade she showed me her bra."

Sandy couldn't get a handle on this guy. She barely knew him and wasn't sure why he was confiding in her. "That was kind of her," she said, because she could think of nothing else.

"Hey, no sisters so I didn't have a clue." He nudged her with an elbow.

She looked at the programs in his hand and wondered when he planned to get back to ushering.

"Sorry. I'm rambling." He hesitated, his lips twisting. "I want to thank you for taking care of Mitch. I mean, I know there wasn't much y'all could do but keep him comfortable. But you helped Lena. If you can't help the dying, you help the living, huh?"

She thought that a strange—yet truthful—thing to say. "How is Lena?"

He looked away. "I haven't been by the house. I should have. I have a long list of should-haves when it comes to Mitch, but I couldn't stand the idea of walking in that door without him there. I'm a selfish bastard, if you want to know the truth."

She took a step towards Adam. "I'd better go claim a seat."

"Sure. And I'd better get back to my duties. Thanks for coming, Sandy Albright. I'll make sure Lena knows you were here."

She and Adam sat in a back pew beside a bent old woman who rested a cane against her knees. She wore a black hat, the brim curved up like the crest of a wave, with dangling dark feathers. When the woman smiled at them, wrinkles crinkled out from her gray eyes.

The organ started, a few familiar chords that Sandy thought were from "A Mighty Fortress," but then strange, wheezing sounds erupted. Another off-key groan came from the instrument and Adam squirmed.

"It's the organ," the old lady whispered. "We just desperately need a new one."

Sandy liked the way her voice lilted in that old-south way, hanging on to the first syllable of "desperately" and dropping three pitches as she finished the word.

"Organs are expensive," Adam said.

"Oh, don't I know it!" Her gloved hand clutched a mother-of-pearl button on her chest. "I mentioned it to Reverend Tanner, but he says we don't have the money. I love Anglican music but that—" she pointed in the air as the organ made another wheeze—"sounds like a brood mare in heat."

"I was thinking hyena," Adam whispered conspiratorially.

"A hyena in labor!" The woman chuckled. "My name is Florence Rollison." She extended a hand.

"I'm Adam Montgomery. And this is Sandy Albright." Sandy gave the glove a squeeze, feeling fingers as delicate as her grandmother's crystal.

"I haven't seen you at St. Mary's before. How did you know Mitch?"

"I'm an old friend of Sims's," Adam answered, a bit of a stretch.

"How thoughtful of you to come." She patted his hand, and Adam flashed his most charming smile. "Funerals are hard on the young. Not for me. I've been to hundreds by now. Buried so many of my friends. So many." She shook her head, the tiny black feathers bobbing over her face.

"That must be hard." Sandy said. She couldn't imagine herself as old as Florence. She couldn't see making it to forty, though that was only a few years away.

"Now every time I come, I think about my own funeral. It makes me terribly self-absorbed, but I can't help myself." Again, she clutched the button.

"I understand how it could happen."

"I don't want my funeral to be sad," the woman said. "The world has too much sadness. I'd like it to be a big old party. I want people to toast my departing with champagne." Mrs. Rollison smiled at them, her milky eyes twinkling.

"No, you can't adopt her," Sandy whispered to Adam.

The organ stopped. Muted voices surrounded them as the sanctuary filled with people, mostly well-dressed, well-coiffed, and well-moneyed. Sandy wished she'd worn a more comfortable pair of shoes.

Mrs. Rollison said, "Lena's mother"—she pronounced it "mothah"—"was my closest friend. I watched Lena grow up. Now I get to watch her bury her husband." Her smile quivered a little. She shook her head. "Forgive me. I shouldn't burden you young people with my problems."

Adam squeezed the woman's hand.

"Lena's lucky to have a friend like you," Sandy said.

"Lena has many friends. But she's very private, too. She was brought up to believe you must shoulder your burdens on your own. That came from her fathah. He was a troubled man. Lena's mothah stood by him till the day he died. I think that was hard on Lena and her sister."

Sandy had more in common with Lena Hastings than she realized. They could start a support group: Dysfunctional-Families-R-Us. Lena came out stronger than Sandy, though. At least, Sandy hoped she had. She didn't want to think about hidden vodka bottles or stashes of pills tucked into the drawers of Lena's life.

The organ wailed again. She glanced at her watch: still a half hour before the service started. Then lunch. Then vacuuming.

In every way imaginable, Sandy the addict had an easier gig than sober Sandy.

• • •

BECCA SAT BESIDE ELLIOTT in the rear of the funeral car as it glided along Gervais Street. It had been a slow trip from their house, and it felt like every person in every car they passed stared at them inching along. She'd overdone it with the deodorant. Last Saturday she had snuck into the guest bathroom, the one Dad used for shaving and dressing, and opened his Old Spice antiperspirant so she could sniff Dad's scent: tangy, not too sweet. Yesterday she decided to wear it instead of her Arid Extra Dry. It was stupid to wear a man's deodorant, but she needed to be able to smell him. Just a few more days.

Hot. She felt scorched from the inside, though nobody else looked the least bit warm. Mom sat by the door, cool as a grape popsicle in her dress. Elliott and Sims weren't sweating, though Elliott kept clearing his throat like he was about to give a lecture, which she was glad he didn't give. Even Sims's wife Connie, who was easily two hundred pounds of lard and cellulite and looked like an Easter egg in her yellow polyester dress, didn't have a drop of perspiration on her face. So why did Becca feel like she'd been set afire?

A parking spot was reserved by an ornate metal sign that read "funeral." She could see lots of people lined up to climb the steps to the church: a few of Dad's golf friends, that lady with the wobbly voice who sang in the choir, and a bunch of men in suits, maybe from Dad's work. And there at the door, wearing a white flower in his lapel and dark shades like he was going into a club: Mr. Calloway.

Becca started to climb over Mom to escape the suffocating vehicle but the funeral home guy opened the door and helped Mom out first. Reverend Bill met her on the walkway, taking her hand. Sims and Elliott gathered close and listened to something the minister whispered. Connie leaned against the taillight with her fat arms crossed over her fat boobs, probably mad at being left out of the pre-funeral conference, but Becca was glad to be excluded.

She eased over to the other side of the car and drew a deep breath of cool autumn air, wishing she could disappear without being noticed. She dreaded the service. And the people coming to the house afterwards. And the days and days that followed now that Dad was dead.

The small cemetery was beyond the wrought iron fence. Dad's ashes would go in a column structure in the rear, Mom had said. "That way, he'll always be nearby." Was Becca supposed to find comfort in that?

She wiped the sweat from under her eyes. When she looked up, she spotted a large black man, with long matted hair, moving between tombstones—Joe. He approached the fence, wielding a rake with the prongs overhead, his head bent down. What was he going to do? He'd never been dangerous, according to Dad, but the way he was holding that rake—she glanced at her brothers who were greeting the McAllister family. Mom was still talking to Reverend Bill.

Joe's giant hand gripped the gate as he looked right at Becca. His expression morphed, the crazy-eyed look he wore falling like a mask. His black eyes blinked, his gaze not leaving her. Becca swallowed. He gave her an odd three-fingered wave. Not knowing how to respond, she waved back. Joe lowered his head, as if bowing, then backed away from the gate.

Another figure stood under the live oak that shaded the cemetery, looking at an old tombstone. He was thin, his hands buried in the pockets of his long wool coat, the collar pulled up around his ears. His red hair had been pulled into a ponytail and round wire-rim glasses perched on his nose. He turned, his gaze fixing on Becca and her family. Royce.

What did he want? Had Mom been seeing him? No. Not since she came back home. Becca was sure, wasn't she?

Royce stepped closer and motioned to her. How dare he be here? Becca glanced at her Mom, who was still with Reverend Bill. Becca slid through the gate and stepped in front of him.

"Hi, Becca," he said with a little smile. "It's nice to see you."

"Go away," she answered.

He cocked his head, scrutinizing her. "You're angry."

"You're still here."

He grinned again, flashing his crooked teeth. He swept a hand toward the cemetery. "I was looking at the old gravestones here. Some of the carvings are amazing. Over a hundred years old, but still so vivid. So alive." He accented "alive" with a lift of his shoulders.

"Alive? Seriously? Why are you here?"

"I've been by this church a thousand times and I never once stopped to look at the cemetery," he said, like she was supposed to give a damn about what he thought.

She checked over her shoulder. Mom was still conferring with the reverend and must not have seen him. Her brothers had moved to the edge of the sidewalk.

"How's Lena doing?" Royce lowered his voice like they were sharing a secret.

"She's none of your business," she snarled.

He blinked as though stunned by her words. "Again the anger. Not becoming on you, Becca."

She wanted to kick him in the nuts. To pull that frazzled ponytail from his head.

"Becca?" Elliott waved her to him.

"I have to get back."

He nodded, his eyes softening. "I'm sorry about your dad, Becca."

She looked at the splash of orange freckles across his nose, at the wrinkles pleating his forehead. How had Mom ever loved this man?

Royce laid a hand on her shoulder. "Take care." She jerked away as though scalded and hurried back to her family.

"Who was that?" Elliott asked.

"Nobody." That word seemed perfect. She felt momentary relief to see Royce walking away. Had Mom seen him?

"Ready to go inside?" Sims asked, guiding them toward the sanctuary.

Ten minutes later, Becca sat between her brothers: Sims in his dark blue suit, with Connie on the other side, her arm hooked through his as if he needed an anchor. Elliott was in black, with a narrow tie, and scuffed black Reeboks because he'd forgotten to bring dress shoes.

Her mom was beside him, wearing the pearls Dad gave her on their wedding day. Lena liked to tell Becca that she would get those pearls one day, but she couldn't imagine it. Pearls belonged on people who weren't mutants. That's what Becca was. An alien on earth, because here she was, at her father's funeral, and she couldn't cry. She knew she should, that the loss of a parent was supposed to be so devastating that she should be sobbing on a brother's shoulder, but the tears weren't there. Dad deserved a daughter who would cry over him.

Becca glanced over at Elliott. His eyes were wet, and he kept rubbing his nose with a handkerchief. He must have felt her gaze because he reached over and squeezed her shoulder. He was always doing stuff like that, and sometimes she wished he lived here instead of in New York. Sims was a different kind of brother. Always asking about her grades and complaining about what she wore. He was helpful when she needed math tutoring but otherwise he was the third parent she had never asked for.

At the pulpit, Reverend Bill was talking about Dad in a deep, gentle voice, as if he were talking to them and not a church overflowing with people. He probably thought she should be crying. There were a lot of people who were.

"When I think about Mitch Hastings—the man whose life we are celebrating today—one word comes to mind. That word is *family*."

Beside her, Sims lowered his head. Elliott blew his nose again. Becca couldn't see her mom, but Sims was handing her a tissue.

"He was a quiet man, not one to talk of his own accomplishments. His tireless work on the Homelessness Task force. His dedication to this church. But above all, he valued his family. Ask him about his kids, and he'd talk your ear off. He'd tell you that Sims was a successful banker with a beautiful family. He'd talk about Elliott, the musician wowing audiences in New York City. And he'd describe Becca, his beautiful youngest, almost in high school already. Mitch's pride in his kids could fill this church."

She used to love it when Dad came to her soccer games. They ate ice cream after, and at night, sometimes she'd climb on his lap while he watched TV. But that all changed when she was twelve. She remembered the exact moment: Kayla and Ree Ann came over to spend the night, and they were in the den discussing the Twilight book series, and Dad walked right in, sat down, and joined their conversation. He told the lamest jokes and asked ridiculous questions about the book: "Why does this Bella like the vampire?" and Kayla and Ree Ann rolled their eyes like he was the biggest geek in middle school, trying to fit in where he didn't. Dad, who used to be a spot of sunshine at the end of her day, became an embarrassment.

It had hurt his feelings; she saw it in his eyes. Despite that, he had never given up—every morning came the forehead kiss goodbye. Every night, the "Sleep tight, Kitten," as if she was seven years old. He never gave up on her, and now there was a giant hole where he should be. No matter how hard she tried to walk around it, she kept finding herself at its edge.

"You okay, Bec?" Elliott whispered in her ear. His breath felt warm on her neck, and she was glad. She needed to feel someone alive close by.

"Yeah." Wasn't she? She could see her hands shaking. When had that started?

"This won't be much longer. Be glad we're Episcopalians. Baptist funerals can take days."

Days? She tried to imagine having to spend the night in the sanctuary, then realized Elliott was joking. She found herself smiling, but it occurred to her that she shouldn't be, so she covered her mouth. Once her hand was there, she bit down on the tender meat of her palm. The pain felt right.

"Lena," the minister was saying, "Last year you overcame something no one should have to. Mitch stayed by your side and wished he could share your pain. To be loved so completely is a rare and amazing thing."

Sims nodded. Elliott let out a sigh. Becca bit harder on her hand.

"St. Paul tells us that love never dies. I'm a believer in heaven. I guess that comes with the job." A few mourners chuckled at this.

" . . . and Mitch is there. But he is also here, among us. He is here in Sims's voice. In Becca's beautiful smile."

A thousand eyes fixed on her and she gasped. She jerked her hand from her mouth and stared at the priest. He must have sensed her discomfort because he winked and said, "It's a good thing, Becca. You'll understand when you're older."

A small hand against her back. Mom, reaching behind Elliott. For the first time, Becca looked at her. Her expression was so strange. No tears. Narrowed eyes. Lips flattened against each other. Like every fraction of an inch of her had hardened into cement. Mom must feel like she did, except the hole that Dad left was much larger for her, and it scared Becca to think that it might swallow Mom right up.

The service ended with "A Mighty Fortress is Our God," Dad's favorite hymn. And then they carried the urn down the steps: Mr. Calloway, Dr. Burnside, and four of Dad's golf friends walking beside it. Her dad was in that small shiny box. They were taking him away. They were taking him away and she would never, ever talk to him or feel his kiss on her forehead or hear him say "Night Kitten."

Before she knew it, she opened her mouth and screamed.

CHAPTER 12

After dropping off Mr. Jamison's papers with the court clerk, Tonya listened to her motivational Dr. Allaway CD and tried not to think about Mr. Hastings's funeral. She skipped over "I am Warrior" to part two: "Responsibility Ain't for Sissies."

"Who is in charge of your life?" Dr. Allaway asked. "Let's start with your job. Is your boss in charge? The one who maybe doesn't appreciate you? Is he in control of your work life?"

Tonya hit "pause." Dr. Allaway's words cut deep. Tonya was not appreciated by her boss, even though she'd been trying harder. Even though she got through her assignments and left an empty in-box at the end of the day, Mr. Jamison hadn't noticed. Ruth might have, but she looked for fault in other people, failing to notice when Tonya did something good. Tonya could rescue orphans from a burning building, and Ruth would complain about her getting ashes on the carpet.

Tonya hit play. "It's easy to blame other people when your life isn't what you want it to be. But the blame game accomplishes nothing. Whose life is it, anyway? Yours. You are the captain of your ship. Nobody else. You."

"I am the captain of my ship," she repeated.

"The captain sets the course," said Dr. Allaway. "The captain determines the journey."

"I am the captain of my ship." The words were a lie. She had not set the course for her life. Her parents had decided everything before she got married, then John took control because damned if she didn't hand him the reins. John chose where they would live, which cars to buy. He even selected the jobs she applied for and made her choose the law firm because the pay, such as it was, was better than what she'd been offered at First Citizen's Bank.

"If you give up control of your destiny," Dr. Allaway said, "you don't get to criticize others when things go wrong."

She hit the "stop" button, very annoyed with Dr. Allaway. Everything seemed so easy for him. She had read on the CD that he lived in New York. He probably had a big townhouse by Central Park. Maybe he drove a

Mercedes C class and flew to Paris to shop. Dr. Allaway was the captain of his ship and it was a zillion foot yacht.

As she parked the rental car in front of the office, she spotted Marion by the cigarette urn near the front door, a Salem Long balanced between two garnet-red nails. "FYI," she said as Tonya approached, "Ruthless is on the warpath."

Fighting a knot of anxiety, Tonya eyed the door. Was there something else she was supposed to do?

"Everything has to be drama with that bitch." Marion puffed out smoke with the "b" in bitch.

"What's she mad about?" Tonya asked, waving away the smoke.

"A paralegal called in sick and Ruth has a huge assignment due today. Heaven forbid you get the flu when Ruth needs something." Marion stepped closer. "Bruise is fading some."

Tonya touched her nose without flinching, another sign of healing. A pea-sized bump above her right nostril remained. "Guess I'd better go see if I can help."

"She's in a meeting with Jamison and a new client. They'll be at least an hour."

Good. Tonya wasn't in the mood for a run-in with Ruthless. She leaned back against the door. The sky was blue and crisp, a perfect V of Canadian geese arcing high above. Was the funeral over now? Were they at the grave-side, lowering Mr. Hastings into the ground? Was Mrs. Hastings imagining her life without a husband?

"Guess what!" Marion said. "Dan's invited me to Myrtle Beach for the weekend. He's got a time-share."

"Are you going?" Tonya tried to feign interest.

"Damn right I'm going." Marion flicked ashes off her cigarette. They missed the urn and scattered at her feet.

Marion loved to talk about her latest fling: Dan-the-Man. Which was a lot better than Chuck, who in the waning days of their courtship had morphed into "Upchuck." And who could forget the demise of "My Big Bob-cat" to "Bonehead Bob." Marion went through men like Tonya went through pantyhose.

"I hope the condo is beachfront. I'm gonna need a new bathing suit though."

"Are you nuts? It's November."

"Don't need it for the ocean. Need it for the hot tub." Marion's mouth curled into a lascivious grin.

Tonya didn't need the mental image of bikini-clad Marion—who was easily a size twenty—cuddled up to her balding insurance salesman, though she felt a pang of envy. She hadn't been to the beach in five years. She longed to lie in the sand, listen to the roar of the surf, and let the sun pour over her like honey. Byron would love it, she was sure, though he'd never seen the ocean. The boy was a South Carolinian, and he'd never even *seen* the ocean.

"I think Dan may be a good dancer. Hope he knows how to shag," Marion went on. "Is John?"

"Is John what?"

"A good dancer. Hello. Earth to Tonya."

"Yeah, pretty good. We never shagged though." Tonya wasn't about to admit she didn't know how to shag because if she did, Marion would demonstrate shagging—South Carolina's "state dance"—right there in front of the law firm.

"Think I can leave a little early on Friday?" Marion asked. "Mr. Jamison's in court and Ruthless is leaving town at three."

"Then nobody would notice if you left. I'll cover for you." Tonya couldn't complain; Marion had done the same for her more times than she could count.

Marion ground her cigarette into the kitty litter filling the urn. Tonya eyed the door, knowing she had a pile of work waiting, as Marion lit another Salem.

"I'd better get inside," Tonya said.

Marion ignored her. "Guess what I found out? Janet is getting a raise."

"Who told you that?"

"I was sorting Mr. Jamison's outgoing mail and there was a memo to her. I sort of read it."

"You sort of read it?" Reading correspondence that wasn't addressed to you was forbidden. An unpardonable sin. Ruthless would fire her for less.

"The envelope wasn't sealed. Anyway, Jamison's giving Ms. Cleavage a nice fat paycheck." Marion frowned at the lit end of her Salem.

"Damn." Tonya had never liked Janet Willowsky. She dressed like people on TV: toned legs under her short skirts, boobs bulging out of low cut tops. Mr. Jamison couldn't help but stare whenever Janet was in the room. Her breasts were impressive, and probably expensive, but not worth a raise.

"She's been going to school," Marion said. "Just got her CLA, whatever the hell that is."

"It means Certified Legal Assistant. She must have been going to Tech."

"Janet doesn't do one damn thing that we don't do. It isn't fair. She'll be making over eight hundred dollars a week!"

"No way." Tonya couldn't imagine that sort of salary. She made less than five hundred and hadn't had a raise since she started at the firm three years ago. Janet was in her second year.

"I think Jamison's using the CLA thingie to give her more money. He's awarding the raise to her bosoms," Marion said.

Tonya laughed. It felt good, after her morose morning, but then a tinge of guilt tightened her stomach. The Hastings family wouldn't be laughing any time soon, would they?

"She is not better than you or me. I swear, I'm gonna buy me a push-up bra and wave my girls at Old Man Jamison. See what kind of promotion I get." Marion cupped her breasts the size of honeydews and shook them. Tonya glanced around to make sure they were alone so Marion didn't get herself fired.

Would Janet's job change? She might get assignments to do legal research and client interviews, something Tonya always wanted to do. Just last spring, Ruth got to interview four witnesses to an industrial accident, and had discovered that management had fudged some inspection reports about safety violations. The settlement had been a hundred thousand per plaintiff, thanks to Ruth. Her job had meaning that Tonya envied. You'd think Ruth would be in a better mood.

"If Jamison can give that bottle-blond twinkie forty thousand, then he can give me a raise, too." Marion punctuated her words with the lit end of her cigarette.

"If he knew how you found out he'd fire you."

Marion lifted a shoulder in an exaggerated shrug. "I could find another job."

"You seen the papers? It's not so easy these days."

Of course, the medical section of the help-wanteds had plenty of postings, something Tonya's mother loved to point out. She'd gone to nursing school when Tonya was seven, determined to make a better life for herself. But it meant Tonya went straight from school to the after-school program at a local church. When her mom was late picking her up, the teachers got annoyed, glancing at their watches, donning coats and standing at the doorway waiting for her. Sometimes Tonya worried that her mom wouldn't come, that she had been forgotten. Once her mother finished school and married Dr. Leonard, along came Buddy. Tonya became an afterthought, shuffled between parents. A week at Mom's, a week at Dad's, not belonging in either place.

Byron would never feel that way. If Tonya had a mantra, that would be it. Byron would always, always feel wanted and loved, no matter how broke they were.

"What exactly does it takes to become a CLA?" Marion asked.

"Fifteen months of coursework. Then you have to work for a year and take a test."

"You've looked into it."

"Last Christmas when I was bored to tears from putting mailing labels on Mr. J's Christmas cards." There had been six hundred of them. Six hundred Christmas cards, and Mr. Jamison was Jewish.

The CLA program at Tech had some interesting classes, but she couldn't afford school. And no way she'd have time to study, not with her job, and Byron, and John not being much help at home.

"Maybe we should look into it," Marion said.

"We? Who's this 'we?'" Tonya didn't want to be in any sentence with Marion Whitestone.

Marion crushed the cigarette into the urn. "It won't hurt to look into it. I swear, I'm not staying at this job for that measly salary while someone like Janet gets so much more. It's not acceptable."

Tonya didn't comment as she entered the building. Her work waited for her, and then she had a husband to go home to.

The same could no longer be said of Lena Hastings.

• • •

LENA TIGHTENED THE SCREWS on her smile as she welcomed another guest into her home. The county councilman, she should remember his name. "How lovely of you to come by," she said. She took his hand and felt his dry-lipped kiss on her cheek.

"Councilman Myers!" Sims appeared, intercepting the new visitor. "Let me introduce you to my wife and daughter. Connie? Over here!"

Lena approached the stairs, wondering if she should check on Becca again. She'd never forget that keening cry from her youngest when they carried Mitch's urn from the church, how it had sliced through her. As Elliott gathered Becca in his arms, and he and Sims carried her from the church, Lena had found herself paralyzed by the unbearable sight of her mourning children. She remained in her seat until Phillip Calloway escorted her out, and even now, she tried to block out the echo of Becca's cry.

When they got Becca home, Liam Burnside gave her a Valium "to settle her down." She'd been asleep moments later, tucked under the frayed Saltillo blanket Abby had given her long ago, looking like she was four years old and needed a mother who had all the answers. But Lena had never been that mother, not for Becca. Lena had stayed beside her, watching her daughter sleep, wishing she could do something to help, until the constant ringing of the doorbell pulled her back downstairs. Was Becca okay? No, of course not, but she would be. She had to be.

"Lena?" She turned to find Phillip Calloway by the stairs. He gestured toward a spot beside the hall closet. "I know now's not a good time. But we need to talk about the business. Soon, I think. When you're ready." Phillip crushed a cocktail napkin into a ball.

Why would he bring the business up now? She took a step closer, brows arched, arms folded. "Is something wrong?"

He rolled the cocktail napkin, the size of a plum, between his hands as if starting a fire. "Our business is a complicated . . . affair."

Funny he should use the word "affair." Who had he been in Bermuda with this time?

"I know," she answered. "Mitch lived and breathed the business for thirty years." Given his heart and soul to it. *And what about you, Phillip? What have you given to Calloway and Hastings?*

"I still can't believe—" He fixed his stare on Mitch's leather jacket hanging from its hook in the hallway. "I keep thinking he'll walk through the door any minute."

"He won't. We all have to face that."

He squeezed the napkin even tighter. "When do you want to get together? Probably be good if the boys were here. This week sometime?"

"Sure." She thought it best to get it over with.

"I'll call you." He tucked the ball of paper into a pocket. When he reached for her hand, she felt it trembling.

"Phillip?" She tugged his fingers so he'd look at her. Tears trailed down his whiskered face. He cleared his throat, the way Sims had done earlier.

"I'll see you soon." He turned and walked out.

As Lena returned to her station by the front door, the across-the-street neighbors arrived, bringing the fourth macaroni and cheese, which Elliott collected, thanking them and coaxing them into the living room. Next came Florence Rollison, eighty-years-old and bent over with osteoporosis. She had been Lena's mother's best friend, a warm light in Lena's childhood. "If there's anything I can do," Florence said, huddled over her three-legged cane.

So many others had said the same thing. Lena hoped they had all signed the reception books so she could send cards thanking them.

The bell signaled the arrival of another guest. "How nice to see—" The hand reaching for hers belonged to Bill Tanner, dressed in gray and not wearing his clerical collar. She had never seen him without it before.

"Lena? What are you doing? You shouldn't stand here like a Wal-Mart greeter."

She jerked back as if he had burned her.

"I just mean . . ." Bill shook his head. The noise in the living room swelled, someone chuckling, someone commenting on the pimento cheese sandwiches. Bill pointed at the closed door to Mitch's office. "Can we go somewhere quiet? Just for a moment."

She followed him into the room she'd been avoiding. All was as it should be: the antique claw-foot desk, the floor-to-ceiling book cases, the cracked leather desk chair that Mitch refused to replace because it had been his dad's. She approached the olive green drapes hanging over the window and pulled the cord, letting in light. Outside, the day was ridiculously sunny, the sky absurdly blue.

"How are you doing?" Bill asked, not in the way everyone else had. His eyes searched hers, as if they saw deeper than she wanted.

"I should get back to the guests."

"You don't need to be the hostess right now, Lena. Let the boys greet the company. Stop being so damned Episcopalian."

She escaped his gaze, her own searching the small room. Mitch's books filling the shelves. The computer he'd resisted using until he figured out he could talk to Elliott every day with email. The painting of six-year-old Becca that Lena had done in an acrylics class at the park; "Ah, that's my kitten," Mitch had said when she gave it to him. These memories flooded her. All the drawers and cupboards in her life that Mitch had filled.

"It's my first time in this room," she said.

"Many things will be hard now. Some will surprise you." Bill's voice had a hesitant edge, like he was disclosing something personal. She knew little about him. He was a nice man. A good friend and confidante to her husband who undoubtedly knew more about Lena than she wanted him to know.

"There are surprises every hour," she said. "Like opening the refrigerator and finding half a tuna sub that Mitch had left there last week. He always brought home leftovers but never ate them. Elliott used to call them 'Dad's science experiments.'" She'd even hesitated in throwing it away, though it had long passed the point of being toxic.

"Grief will come in waves. Some will knock you flat over. But stand back up and know you're strong enough to handle every one of them." Bill's knobby fingers gripped the ledge of the desk. "You handled the cancer; you can handle this."

"I had Mitch to get me through that." She shivered, chilled by the cool air squeezing through the panes of the picture window. It needed to be replaced, something Mitch would have tended to in any other room.

"I wish I'd been a better wife." The words tumbled out before she could take them back. She stared down at the floor as if they were still lying there.

"He loved you."

"But I didn't deserve it. You know I didn't."

"There is no deserving that kind of love. It's a gift."

She closed her eyes and prayed, prayed, prayed that Bill didn't start talking about God because she might smack him.

"My point is," he said, "nobody is perfect. But to be loved as you are, warts and all . . . that's an amazing thing."

Lena could picture herself as a wart-ridden witch. She knew her darker side, something her husband had denied even after she'd left him for Royce. She had thrown the marriage away, all but abandoned Becca. She had begun a new life in the loft apartment: Lena the artist. Lena, Royce's lover. Lena the fool.

Sometimes it bothered her that Mitch chose not to see the truth about her betrayal. *Just a folly,* he had said. *We all make mistakes.* But she was relieved, because it made coming home easier when she had so desperately needed to come home.

Becca wasn't blind, though. Looking at the anger in her daughter's eyes was like looking in a mirror. *I know who you really are, Mom. Nobody else may know, but I do.*

What would it be like when it was the two of them? So many things about her daughter terrified her, yet nothing had been more frightening than that howling cry at the funeral. The sound of Becca shattered. How was she, Lena, supposed to piece her back together?

"When does Elliott leave?" Bill asked.

"He called from the limousine and postponed his flight till the end of the week. I'm not sure why. He needs to get back to his life."

"Maybe he needs to be with family more. Sims seems to have a good marriage. Maybe Connie can help him. Becca though," Bill said, stroking the edge of the desk. "She may need some help. Fourteen is such a difficult age, and after all the family has been through—"

"Help," she repeated, tasting the word. A therapist. A psychologist or psychiatrist for her broken child. She had suggested this to Mitch a few months before, but he had insisted this was a phase. "She's still growing into her body." "All girls are self-conscious at her age." Lena had shown him an article about eating disorders. "Our Becca isn't that bad off," he had answered, tossing the magazine aside.

"Once she goes back to school and she's around her friends—maybe things will normalize. When she gets back in her routine she'll be okay." She knew her words to be untrue.

Bill pinched his lip between his finger and thumb and tugged. "That should help. But she's gotten so thin. I just thought—"

Lena stiffened. She wanted no more of this conversation. Not now. Not from her priest. She could hear the doorbell ring, more guests arriving.

"Becca is *my* daughter, Bill. I'll do whatever I have to."

"Of course."

She eyed the door. "I think I'll go check on her now."

Lena wound her way through the guests, found Elliott, and whispered that she'd be upstairs. She moved quickly, ignoring the friends who tried to thwart her, but smiling in that polite way she had perfected as she hurried up the stairs to her daughter's room.

Becca had tossed aside the blanket. She lay sprawled diagonally across the bed, her hair a tangle across the pillow. Dead to the world. Lena switched on the night light that had been there since her daughter was three. She slipped the black loafers from Becca's feet, noting the chipped bright pink polish on her toenails, from the sleepover at Kayla's two weeks ago. Would Becca's feet get cold? Lena replaced the Saltillo spread, tucking in around her ankles, and eased down beside her. She stroked her daughter's hair. Becca's mouth opened a little, emitting a soft sound like an infant's sigh.

Oh, this child. So lost, even before Mitch's death. Lost and a stranger.

Lena glanced around the bedroom that was as familiar to her as her own. The yellow curtains they'd picked out when Becca insisted the pink ones were "Too infantile." The cedar chest, a gift from Mitch for Becca'a thirteenth birthday, hardly visible under the stack of clothes tossed during her panicked dressing that afternoon. The wrinkled *Hunger Games* poster that had replaced the *Twilight* one six months before. On the back of the door, the calorie counting chart, spattered with red circles. Her daughter's obsession.

Fifteen years ago, the news that Lena was pregnant had not been a welcome surprise. The boys had come back-to-back, the mighty diapered-duo darting about the house. They'd tried for a girl a few years later, but nothing happened and Lena concluded that at thirty-three, she was too old; ovaries had a shelf-life, and hers had expired. Then came the missed period and a little blue plus on her Early Pregnancy Test stick. Mitch and the boys had been ecstatic, though Lena couldn't summon the same enthusiasm. She was ready to move on to the next part of her life: art classes or travel to Europe or Africa. A new baby interrupted those plans.

Not that she'd thought of aborting. She couldn't, not with Mitch so happy and the boys bouncing like hungry puppies, proffering potential names for their unborn sibling. The pregnancy was wretched: months of morning sickness and swollen feet and back aches. The resonating clang of bars slamming down on her life.

Becca screamed her way into the world, a red-faced, colicky baby who wouldn't sleep more than two hours and could not be sated. Lena would look at her child and picture a starving baby bird, beak wide open, unquenchable. Lena held Becca, rocked her, sang to her, but never did that child stop crying. Why couldn't Lena feel for her what she had for her boys? Dr. Ryan called it post-partum depression caused by hormones, but the diagnosis did not absolve her. What kind of mother didn't adore her newborn? What kind of mother craved freedom over her own child?

It got better with therapy and medication. Becca grew into a beautiful toddler; a chubby, dimpled critter who loved to waddle around in her father's shoes. Her first word had been "Dada," then "Ehwit." "Mama" came a few weeks before "Simth," but Lena hadn't resented it, not really. At last Lena had become whole, able to smile and hug her little girl.

Becca rolled over, kicking the blanket away.

"Shhh," Lena said.

That their relationship derailed again two years ago was Lena's fault. The separation, the cancer, the return. All the turbulence Lena had caused, and Becca still paid the price for it. Every morning, they battled over cereal. Every evening, Becca compartmentalized her supper into microscopic bits. Every meal, a war of wills.

Becca clutched at her pillow, turning over again. Her eyes blinked open.

"How are you feeling, honey?" Lena had stopped calling her "honey" months ago. She didn't know why.

"Hmmm." Becca scanned the room, trying to get her bearings.

"Dr. Burnside gave you some medicine. You may feel a little muddled."

Becca rubbed her fist against her eye like a pre-schooler. So much of Becca was still so very young. She was still growing. Changing. There was still time to help her. Lena would make sure she ate like she should. Would spend afternoons with her, take her shopping. Help her with homework. Be the mother she needed.

"Are you hungry?" Lena asked.

"A little."

"I can go get you something if you want."

Becca slid her feet off the bed and pulled herself up. "I can get it myself."

Lena eyed the door, wondering if Becca could manage the stairs in her drugged condition. "There are still a lot of people here," Lena said.

"People?" Becca's hands clenched the bedspread, as if she needed it for balance.

"They came by after the funeral." Lena could still hear the clink of glasses, muted voices. Occasional laughter. Becca's clock read 5:15. Two hours since the service had ended. When would the crowd leave?

"You don't want me to go downstairs with all those people there?" Becca's expression tightened, eyes narrowed, watching her.

Maybe Becca didn't remember what happened at the funeral. Maybe the Valium took away the sound of her scream, that horrific cry that might still echo inside the church, but the people downstairs would remember and they would stare at her.

"Is that what you want to do?" Lena asked.

Becca leaned back against her pillows, shaking her head.

"Okay. I'll get you something. Be back in a second."

As Lena stood to leave, Becca said, "Mom?"

"What, honey?"

"Did you see him?"

Lena stilled. "Who?"

"Royce. In the churchyard. Before the service."

Lena gripped the course wood of the jamb. Why would he show up at the funeral? What kind of sick gesture was that? "What . . . what did he say to you?"

Becca gathered the spread to her chest, squeezing it like a child might squeeze a doll. "Are you going to see him again?" Accusation simmered beneath her words.

Lena didn't mean to flinch, to show any sign that Royce's presence in their conversation had any meaning. But she felt raw, unguarded. Unprepared for what felt almost like an assault. She found the smile that had gotten her through the afternoon, a cold flash of teeth. It was all she had left. "You don't need to worry about him."

Becca didn't respond, just looked at her like she could see through skin.

"Let me get you something to eat." As Lena descended the steps to get her some food, she prayed the child would actually eat something.

CHAPTER 13

Becca awakened again to a dark room. She was still in her clothes with the funky wool blanket from her Aunt Abby bunched over her legs. Spats lay beside her, a purring black and white lump. The neon blue numbers from her iPod radio-dock told her it was three fifteen A.M. As she sat up, her head spun as if she'd just come off a roller coaster. There was also a loud grumble from her stomach. When was the last time she had something to eat?

Her mom had brought her cheese and crackers, but she hadn't liked the cheese and had needed something to drink. She had thought about going downstairs, but heard all the people and opted to stay in her room.

The service itself was a blur. So many people, the church suffocatingly hot, the organ coughing like it had TB or something. Reverend Bill preaching about her dad, and everybody looking at her, and Becca watching her mother, until she got out of focus, like her skin had blended into the air, and then they carried Dad away and . . . oh no. Had she screamed? Or was that a dream? Please, please let it be a dream.

Her mouth was drier than sand. At least the house had grown quiet. She could sneak down the stairs and get a glass of water, maybe even a little food.

She untangled herself from the sheets to stand on wobbly legs. The room tilted like it had that time she and Kayla snuck beer from Kayla's house, but it righted itself when she sucked in a few deep breaths. She tiptoed down the steps to the kitchen, careful to skip the creaky fourth step. There should be juice in the refrigerator, but she couldn't find it buried behind all the food people had brought. Her stomach roared again, loud as a grizzly, so she removed trays of deli meats, cheese, fruit, and pastries.

All that food. The swirl of colors—pink ham, purple grapes, pale yellow cheese. She could have a snack. She was entitled, since she'd missed two meals. She started with the ham slices, downing two before moving on to the turkey. Chunks of dotted pepper jack cheese came next. She caught the cinnamony smell of sweet rolls, helping herself to one, then two.

She should stop. She should, but she was still hungry. She found macaroni still cold from the fridge but didn't care. The cake on the table—white frosting topped with chocolate curls—like the one Mom had ordered for Dad's birthday. Mom had joked that all the candles might trigger a fire alarm and Dad had blown out all but one, so Becca helped. She shoved the memory in a closet as she cut herself a wedge of cake, which she inhaled in a few bites. Oatmeal cookies made the next course. Three went down before she even poured the glass of milk.

She took a long swallow and thudded the glass on the table.

Oh God. What had she done? She'd eaten so much. She hadn't meant to, but the food was there and she couldn't stop herself and now—all the calories. In a few stupid minutes, she must have eaten two thousand calories.

A pocket of gas welled inside and a disgusting belch bellowed from her, loud enough to be heard across town.

"Who's there?"

Becca panicked at the sound of Elliot's voice. She rushed to shove the trays back in the fridge, but she dropped the plastic cheese platter with an echoing clunk. Yellow cubes bobbed and danced across the floor.

"Becca? What's up?" He looked sleep tousled, hair standing on ends, one leg of his sweat pants bunched up mid-thigh.

"I just woke up." She dropped to her knees, scooping up cheese and grapes and piling them back on the plate.

Elliot slid the trash can to her. "Mom'll kill you if you put them back in the fridge. She never was one for the five-second rule."

"What?"

"The five-second rule. Sims used to claim that any food that hits the floor can be eaten if you do it within five seconds. But that doesn't work for entire cheese trays."

After taking the plastic plate from her and dumping it in the trash, he moved to the counter. He flicked the foil that had covered the beef and turkey, studying it as if it was a troubling crossword puzzle. Could he tell how much she'd scarfed down?

"You want me to make you a sandwich?" he asked.

"No." She snatched up the meat tray which was now offensive to her and shoved it in the refrigerator.

He moved over to the desserts. Becca hid the Danishes behind a large flower arrangement but noticed Elliot scrutinizing the cookie plate. "I see you've had dessert. Maybe you should eat something healthier?"

"I had a few pieces of cheese." Another huff of gas erupted. She covered her mouth.

"I'm glad that you're eating something." He came closer, meeting her eyes with a look of concerned bewilderment.

"Why is everybody so obsessed with what I eat? Jesus. I wish people would mind their own business." She forced a knife-edge into her voice, but Elliott kept staring.

"Sorry. We're just concerned." He backed up, glancing down at her body. "You're a beautiful girl, Becca. But you're getting too skinny."

Why was he lying to her? She was not thin. Not thin, no matter how hard she tried. *Not* thin, and she just ate a gazillion calories and would have to run a marathon or six to burn them off.

Elliott pulled out a stool and sat, as though he intended to continue this little chat.

"I want to talk to you about the funeral."

"What's there to talk about?" She eyed the door.

"It's just that, well, you got so upset. Do you remember what happened?"

Damn. It hadn't been a dream. She had shrieked like a rabid coyote in front of all those people. She felt heat rising, a flame slithering up her stomach to her throat.

"I want to make sure you're okay, Li'l Sis. That's all." He hadn't called her "Li'l Sis" in years. The fire flushed her skin.

"Why is that your business, anyway?" she answered. "You're about to leave town. Why stick your nose in my life when you're gonna forget all about me when you go back to New York?" Her voice quavered, a sign of weakness. She was furious and felt naked and wanted to flee up the stairs.

"What?" He blinked like she'd hit him. "I don't—just because I'm not here doesn't mean—"

"Doesn't mean you don't care? You're a visitor to this family, Elliott. You come for a few days once a year then vanish. So you don't get to interfere in my life." She spun around and stomped off, determined that he wouldn't see her fall apart.

"Becca—"

She ignored him, taking the stairs two at a time and shutting herself off in her bedroom.

She clutched at her swollen stomach. She'd eaten so fast she hadn't tasted anything. It was revolting. She was revolting. And all that food would turn into lumpy, lardy fat. Tears filled her eyes and tracked down her face. This was the worst part. There was so much to hate when she looked inside.

She cracked open the door and listened. She could hear Elliott puttering around downstairs, putting food away. She inched into the bathroom across the hall and closed and locked the door. Approached the toilet. Just this once. One more time and that was it, she was done with this revolting ritual.

She pulled her hair back and tucked it under her sweater, slipped her sleeves up, and bent over the commode.

Once she had released the food—all of it, and there had been so much— she fell back, sliding down the wall. This was the last time. She'd emptied herself; the calories were erased. She was back in control.

She jumped at the knock on the door.

"Becca? You okay?" Elliott asked.

She pushed the toilet paper against her eyes.

"You're not getting sick, are you?"

"Just a little upset stomach." The lie came easy. It always did.

"Becca—"

"I'm fine. Go on to bed."

• • •

LENA SQUIRTED FANTASTIC on the granite counter and wiped it with a sponge, erasing the red stripe left by the cherry crumble brought by a neighbor. She'd swept up cookie crumbs and bits of cheese, emptied an overflowing trash bin, and tossed a table cloth into the wash. The tile floor could use a good mopping, too, but that could wait till tonight, after Elliott and Becca went to bed. She had hours to fill once they were asleep.

She'd seen neither child since lunch, a quiet, tense meal after Elliott asked Becca how she was feeling and received a curt "fine" in response. No matter. She was relieved to have the house to herself for the afternoon. If one more person asked, "How are you doing?" she was sure she would scream.

She opened the fridge. Trays of food bulged out, much of which needed to be thrown away. She hoped all the names had been recorded on the notebook she'd left by the wine chiller. When should she write thank you notes? Not today, but soon, so she wouldn't forget anyone. Muted piano strains came from her purse hanging on its hook. Her phone. She slid it from its pocket and, when she read the number, nearly dropped the phone.

Royce. How odd to see those numbers she knew so well they might have been tattooed on her heart. Eighteen months ago, this call would have made her smile inside and out. She pressed "Ignore." Her hand quaked as she set down the phone.

What did he want? Now that Mitch was . . . dead, the word still felt foreign in her world . . . Royce thought he should get in touch? Should insert himself back in her life? There was no room for him nor would there ever be. If only she knew how to block his number.

The squeal of the front door opening made her jerk. Voices and thuds followed. "Le-Le? Are you home?"

The voice of her sister, Abigail, bellowed from the living room. Nobody had told her when she would arrive. Lena smoothed the front of her sweater, tucked hair behind her ears, and rushed to meet her. There Abby stood, wearing a nubby fleece jacket, her hair—silver hair now—in a tattered rope of braid. She hurled aside a battered knapsack and reached out her arms.

Lena froze. How long had it been? Three years? Abby looked so different and yet the same. Tall as a tree but fluffier. No makeup. Dressed like she lived in 1975. Abby didn't wait for Lena to budge but came to her, wrapping her arms around her like a warm wooly bear, and Lena fought to catch her breath in the stifling embrace. Abby let go and, holding her at arm's length, said, "Damn you. Still so beautiful."

Elliott laughed behind her. Next came footsteps on the stairs and Becca's voice yelling, "Aunt Abby! You're here!" with more enthusiasm than Lena had heard from her in weeks.

Abby grabbed Lena's youngest and lifted her off her feet. "Becca Bec, you've gone and grown up on me."

"We need to get the guest bed ready for you," Lena said. "I wasn't sure when you'd get here."

"That's my fault. Ell said he'd fetch me. I didn't want you worrying over late flights. I've been in four airports since yesterday. I may smell like it, too."

"I already changed the linens," Becca said.

"Who are you and what have you done with my daughter?"

Becca grabbed Abby's knapsack, hefting it over her bony shoulder. Elliott snagged the the Pullman suitcase. "We'll take these on up."

"Make sure there are towels—" Lena called out as they climbed the stairs.

"Done!" Becca replied.

When they were left alone Abby said, "I'd kill for a glass of wine."

"You must be hungry, too. Go have a seat."

Lena was glad for something to do. She went to the kitchen and loaded a tray with fruit, cheese, and crackers, adding some of Ms. Florence's cheesecake bites for dessert. She opted for the crystal wine glasses, the ones she'd inherited from their grandmother, and found an opened bottle of chardonnay in the fridge. She considered the irony that Abby was here to help her, yet in less than five minutes, she was waiting on her sister. Though to be fair,

Abby looked exhausted. Why had she come? She hadn't come when either parent died or when Lena had cancer. Why now?

Abby sat in the leather La-Z-Boy—Mitch's chair—her legs stretched out, heavy clogs teetering from her feet. Someone had lit the wood piled in the fireplace.

"Damn jet lag has me wacky," Abby said. "But it's nice to speak in English again."

Lena placed the tray on the table and handed her a glass. Abby's voice had changed; her Ls more pronounced, her words slightly more musical. "How long can you stay?" Lena asked.

"As long as you can put up with me. I have an open ticket. And God knows, I have the vacation time." Abby grabbed a cracker and cut off a fat slice of cheese.

Lena hid her apprehension. What did "open ticket" mean? Weeks? Months?

"Okay, Le-Le. Tell me how you're doing."

"I'm managing."

"Of course you're managing. Nothing on earth you can't 'manage.' But Christ, what a blow. You and Mitch—y'all were peanut butter and jelly. I can't even think what this is doing to you." She ate the cheese and cracker in one bite, then finished two more crackers. Crumbs dotted the front of her jacket.

Lena took a sip of wine, her first since this hell began, but she needed fortification for this conversation.

"How was the service?" Abby asked.

"Lovely." Lena sipped again. She thought about the flowers, the wheezing from the organ, the blur of faces. The haunting scream from her youngest.

"Lots of people, I'm sure. Everybody loved Mitch." Abby set her wine on the table and sliced off more cheese. Dancing yellow flames glimmered off the glass.

Becca and Elliott hurried down the stairs. Elliott sat by Lena on the sofa and poured himself a glass of wine. Becca plopped down on the floor beside Abby and leaned back against Abby's knees.

"How's my Becca-Bec?" Abby stroked Becca's hair.

Becca shrugged. "Okay."

"You've grown into such a beauty. Bet you're fighting off the boys every day."

"Ha," Becca said, rolling her eyes. It was such a normal Becca gesture but Lena hadn't seen it in days and it gave her hope.

"Tell us what you're doing now, Aunt Abby." Elliott reached for a cheese-cake bite. "You were off in the jungle somewhere when we called."

"Not a jungle, but pretty far out there. Go to the end of the earth and hang a right—that's where I've been working. It's a small farming community so damn poor and isolated that it's like stepping back in time. But I loved the people there. Well, most of them, anyway." She smiled, but the corners of her mouth faltered.

"What kind of work?" Lena asked. While Abby had worked for the US Agency for International Development since college, Lena had never understood what the job actually was.

"Teaching them about crop rotation. Trying to get a school set up. Trying to keep—" she hesitated, spinning the wine glass by its stem. "It's complicated and I'm too travel-drunk to describe it. Maybe another day."

They all settled back and looked into the fire. Abby's fingers wove through Becca's hair, and Becca didn't pull away. In fact, she scuttled closer to her aunt.

"I still have those dolls you sent me," Becca said. "My favorite is the one from Nicaragua. I named her Soledad."

"Does that mean sunshine?" Elliott asked.

Abby shook her head. "It means solitude."

Amen, Lena thought.

"I love the wooden flute you sent last Christmas," Elliott said. "I've even used it some in gigs. It's got great tone."

"I'm glad. I got it at a local market, but it took a friend with a lot more musical talent than I to pick it out."

Lena wondered about this friend. Abby had been married twice, neither union surviving a year. On her last visit, her companion had been a younger Peruvian man with beautiful bronze skin. Alejandro. Abby described him as a "good friend" though Alejandro told Mitch she was his common-law wife. In subsequent letters, there was no mention of Alejandro.

"How's New York treating you, Ell?"

"It's okay. My band keeps busy. There's a lot of competition." Elliott re-filled his glass.

"I bet none of the competition comes close to you, Ell. You—you have talent." Abby lifted her wine in a toast.

Lena wished Abby would forego the nicknames. Becca Bec. Le-Le. Ell. Like Abby had the right to swoop into town once a decade and rename them.

"Do you have your guitar here? I'd love to hear you play. I mean, if you're up to it," Abby said.

"I keep an old one in my room." He glanced at Lena, as if he wanted permission to bring music into the house.

"God, Elliott. You know there's nothing I love more than listening to you," she said.

He trotted up the stairs and returned, guitar in hand. He didn't bother tuning, which meant he'd done that earlier, but she didn't remember hearing him. Of course he had, though. For Elliott, music was breathing.

He strummed some minor chords and picked a scale up and down three octaves until he settled into a familiar melody: "Autumn in New York." A gentle tune, not too sad, a little sentimental. Becca sat with her knees collected against her chest, staring into the flames. Abby leaned back in the chair, her eyes closed. A roadmap of wrinkles on that so-familiar face. She looked worn, ridden hard by her exotic life.

"Ell?" Abby said. Lena had thought her sister had gone to sleep. "When do you head back to New York?"

"The end of the week."

"You said you were leaving tomorrow," Becca said.

"I changed my flight." Elliott's stare at his sister conveyed something more than his words. Becca responded with a flippant shrug.

"I'm glad you did. I haven't seen you in so long. I want every second I can with all of you. You have no idea how much I've missed you." Abby sighed into the word "missed."

Elliott's fingers danced along the neck of the guitar. Gershwin's "Summertime" glided into Brubeck's "Take Five," notes floating out like bubbles. His eyes squeezed shut like they always did when he concentrated, and Lena pictured a curly-headed five-year-old struggling to spell "dog." Her baby son. She was glad he'd decided to stay longer, though it would make watching him leave more painful.

Abby reached for the wine. Her knuckles were reddened and raw, as if she'd punched someone. She held up the bottle to Lena, who declined. She could already feel the alcohol limbering up her insides. Maybe she'd get some sleep tonight, after all.

CHAPTER 14

Sandy's shift seemed to stretch on for days. All her patients stable, no griping families, two empty beds on the floor with no new admissions in the pipeline. The docs finished their rounds on schedule, leaving nothing for ward staff to complain about. Boring. She wandered back to the staff lounge and went to her locker where she kept the NA meeting schedule. She was already three meetings behind and Marie could check her sign-in journal any time. Even if she didn't think they helped her one iota, she'd better get her butt to twelve sessions. Her job depended on it.

There were two meetings that evening: one a few miles away in Shandon, the other out by the mall. The AME church didn't have another till Saturday. She could hit the one in Shandon, which started a half-hour after her shift, then grab take-out Chinese on her way home.

She latched her locker as Pete Borden dragged in. An L-shaped brown spot covered the left pocket of his scrubs, a coffee mishap. A day-old growth of whiskers dusted his chin—brown sprinkled with white like powdered sugar. His eyes, always droopy on the edges, wore a heavier layer of fatigue.

He plopped onto the metal bench. "Had to pull a double."

"Double eight? Or twelve?"

"Did a twelve the other day. Two eights today." Pete patted his pocket where a square outline bulged, something he often did. Smoking wasn't allowed on the hospital campus but he kept the pack there like Linus's blanket.

Sandy sat beside him. "Are you doing that to yourself on purpose? Or is Marie mad at you?"

"I asked for extra duty after my ex took me back to court. Child support went up to almost eight hundred a month."

Sandy remembered tales of a nasty divorce, the wife hiring a private investigator who caught Pete snuggled up with a respiratory therapist, Pete going after custody when the ex got a DUI.

"How are your kids doing?" she asked.

"Kevin's great. Big-time into soccer. Madison's my younger one. She's having trouble with school. My ex says she has a learning disability. I think she has a mom who doesn't take the time to help with her homework."

"That's gotta be frustrating."

"You have no idea." He hung on to the word "no." "You got an ex?"

"Yep."

"Ever hear from him?"

"He calls sometimes." Sandy never answered when he did.

"Y'all still fighting?"

"We never fought. Just drifted in different directions. Landed on different planets." She wasn't even sure why Donald kept calling. Maybe he'd heard about her drug problems, and she didn't want his condemnation—or worse, his sympathy. Or maybe he'd rub it in how he'd moved on with his life.

"You're lucky. When my ex calls, I reach for the Rolaids. Or a six-pack if I don't have to work." Again, Pete patted the square in his pocket.

She should call Donald back. Avoidance didn't accomplish anything. Maybe it was the what-if's that made it hard. If she'd been able to have the baby they'd fought so hard for, would she and Donald be together? Not that their marriage had ever been perfect. Donald, like every other doctor Sandy knew, required a lot of accommodation. His words in a room had to be listened to, spoons lowered, books closed, tasks interrupted so that he got the attention he expected. If he was late to a planned dinner with friends, a tossed off "had a problem with a patient" was an accepted excuse. The narcissism in Donald grew like a stubborn oak tree; his time became too important for mundane domestic tasks like lawn mowing or taking out the garbage. If Sandy needed to be picked up after taking the car to the shop, she should get a cab. If she asked him to stop at the store to pick up dog food, Donald sighed his consent as though he'd been asked to move a skyscraper.

The miracle of her pregnancy healed them though. Donald was eager to come home to her, happy to shop for cribs and onesies. Something opened deep inside Donald, something warm and pink, like a delicate blossom.

"I get the kids today," Pete said. "Every Wednesday, I pick them up from school and keep them overnight."

She swallowed. "Are you doing something fun?"

"I always try to come up with something. But usually it's me, the kids, and a bunch of other visitation-day fathers at Chucky Cheese's or Cici's Pizza. We look at each other with a sort of shared, 'this sucks' misery."

"Ouch."

"You never had kids?" Pete asked.

She looked at him, her breath quickening. She thought about the lie that she told everyone. Instead, she said, "Almost did. After trying to get pregnant for three and half years I did, then miscarried in the seventh month."

Pete stared at her, mouth agape.

"Yeah." She squirmed under his scrutiny. "I don't like to talk about it."

"No, no. Of course not. I'm . . . I'm sorry though." He scrubbed a hand through his hair. A tiny fleck of dandruff drifted down, landing on his knee. "Is that why you left North Carolina?"

So much for not talking about it. "That's part of it. My marriage fell apart. Then I sort of did."

"Came here for a fresh start?" he asked.

She wondered if she should tell him the rest, if saying it out loud would help. "I had to leave my job at Presbyterian after I screwed up with a patient."

Pete's head shot up, his red-rimmed eyes widening.

"I was working neonatal ICU. Had a preemie with hyperkalemia. I hadn't been sleeping well. Couldn't get my act together." Donald couldn't come to grips with her grief. They should get pregnant right away, he insisted. Idiot. She moved to the guest room. He moved on. "Donald had a new girlfriend and . . ." she paused, drawing in a shaky breath.

"Whoa."

You have no idea, she almost said. She'd come home after a twelve hour shift to be greeted by Donald in the kitchen and his "We have to talk." He'd been seeing her for a few months, he claimed, but he couldn't get her out of his head. "I've never felt like this before," Donald added, as if it justified the betrayal. He moved out the next day.

"I was a wreck. Everything seemed so . . . hard," she went on. "That morning I was preparing a calcium chloride injection for this tiny little newborn. The dosage was one hundred forty milligrams, but I had prepped one point four grams to inject in her IV. Didn't even realize it. I had the syringe in the access port, had started the actual injection when an LPN spotted the error and grabbed my arm. I . . ." Sandy's voice quaked. "I could have killed her. I almost did."

"Damn, Sandy."

She'd never forget the crushing sense of doom when she'd realized what she'd done. A struggling little life that counted on her, and she'd almost killed her. The next twenty-four hours were the hardest of Sandy's life. The child developed an irregular heartbeat. She was already so frail, but somehow, she survived. "They could have fired me. They should have fired me. The administrator said he was sympathetic, given my problems. But I think they were more interested in protecting Donald's reputation. They let me resign. Didn't even report me to the licensing board."

"Were you using then?" Pete asked.

She shook her head. "I took valium at night, but never when on duty. That little nightmare didn't start until after." Had it been the first, or second day with nothing to do, nowhere to go? Their medicine cabinet had been a delicatessen of pharmaceuticals, leftovers from Donald's knee surgery. Her first venture into the Oxy haze had given her exactly what she needed: perfect, delicious escape.

Pete said, "You're clean now though."

She met his gaze. "I am."

He moved over to his locker, opened it, and pulled out a tiny little bottle of some kind of energy shot, which he downed in a single swallow. He turned back to her. "You're no different than any of us. We've all had our screw-ups."

"Yeah, but how many of us almost kill a child?" She swallowed. Facing this bit of her past here in a hospital, unmedicated, was a first.

"Hey, it could happen to any of us. How many medication errors happen every single day?" He shook his head. "What I know is this: you're one of the best nurses I've ever worked with."

She stood. "Pete, nobody here knows about this." She could imagine what would happen if Marie found out.

He gave her a wink. "And they won't hear it from me."

Pete trudged out the door and Sandy returned to her locker where she'd left her phone. Maybe she should call Donald back. What was the point in delaying? Besides, what could he say that would hurt more than she'd already suffered? She dialed his cell but he didn't answer, so she left a message: "It's me. Calling you back from whenever you called. Bye."

She survived the last two hours and seventeen minutes of her shift, changed her clothes, and headed out to the car. Dusk cast the city in a gray, monochrome light. She gathered her jacket tighter around her, realizing with disgust that the button barely reached the hole and she'd need to shop for a larger one. New pants and tops, too, if she continued this body-mass trajectory.

Just as she slid into the driver's seat, her cell phone rang.

"I'd given up on you calling me back." Hearing Donald's voice through the phone, low and confident, churned up memories like tossed dice. Flirting with him at the hospital. Laughing with him during those early dates. The quiet fights when the unspoken words cut the deepest. That last call when she told him she was moving away and he'd answered with an abrupt, "that might be best."

"I wasn't sure I should," she replied, seeing no reason to dance around the truth.

"How are you doing?" he asked.

"It's been a tough few years."

"Yeah, for me, too."

She heard him draw in a breath and wondered if he still had sinus trouble. How many nights had she awakened to the rumble of his snoring? How many times had her elbow nudged him to turn over?

"How's Columbia?"

"Pretty boring." She decided he hadn't heard about the drugs because he wouldn't have avoided the subject. Tact was not Donald's strong suit. "How's Charlotte?"

"Good. I'm on faculty at UNC now, supervising residents. It's kind of fun. Makes me feel younger."

He got to have fun? "I'm working in cardiac ICU," she said. "Not so much fun. I'm thinking about changing to another floor." Or another hospital. Another life.

"Change can be good." He didn't say anything else, and the silence vibrated like a wire between them.

"So you called to catch up?" she asked.

"Yes, and I wanted you to know—we lost Chai." He stumbled over the words.

"What? When?" A knot tangled her stomach.

"Six weeks ago. Cancer. The vet tried everything, but it didn't work."

Tears welled in her eyes, thinking of their bony beast with large, adoring eyes. She had wanted custody, but she'd known it wouldn't be fair. No dog's bladder could wait for twelve hour shifts to end.

"He had a good life, Sandy."

"I know."

"Kelly wants us to get a puppy but I'm not ready for it."

Sandy could not care less what Donald's new wife wanted.

"Besides, we've got our hands full with our son. That kid's a pistol."

She gripped the phone with enough force to shatter it. Donald and his fabulous new life.

"Sandy?"

"What?"

"I'd like to stay in touch. To be able to tell you what's happening with us."

More silence as Sandy sorted through the storm of words that Donald's news had become in her brain. Chai was gone. Donald was happy. He had the child they'd been denied.

"I need to go," Sandy whispered. As she hung up, the edge of anger faded, replaced by a strained hollowness. That was the worst, that black hole unfurling inside. She'd fought it for months but here it was, back again like it belonged. Christ. One thing fixed it. Always fixed it. Just head inside, take the elevator to the seventh floor, score some oxy. So damn easy.

Goodbye, Donald. Enjoy your new life.

She stayed in the car for ten minutes, one hand on the door handle, the other on the steering wheel as she weighed the decision. Her gaze fell on the bracelet: Today I won't be a screw-up. A deep breath. Today.

She started the car and headed to the NA meeting.

Of course it had to be in a Baptist church. The classroom was furnished with a circle of metal folding chairs inserted between upholstered sofas and wing-back seats. She was one of the first to arrive and noted with some anxiety that there was only seating for fifteen. She preferred the anonymity of a larger group, like at the AME church.

She snagged a Styrofoam cup, poured weak coffee from a stainless steel urn, and sat in one of the folding chairs, the metal cool through her pants. Two men in the corner nodded at her before returning to their discussion of a recent football game. She was thankful to be ignored. Within five minutes, the chairs filled. A gray haired man stepped to the blond oak podium and led the group in reciting the twelve steps, his voice a full baritone like a preacher at the pulpit.

The door at the back of the room squeaked open with a late arrival. Sandy recognized him: Jake, her "Vida Loca" friend. He waved at the group, smiled when he spotted Sandy, and came to sit beside her. This brought a sense of relief, like her first day in third grade when she'd been terrified until her friend Kathy plopped down beside her.

A middle-aged woman in a business suit received her thirty day chip. Sandy's had come in rehab and it had made her as proud as getting her nursing license. Thirty days with no drugs. Thirty days in that world with other addicts, all clawing at recovery like drowning children. Holding her chip was like climbing aboard a life raft.

She glanced over at Jake and saw a splint on his right hand, scrapes on his jaw and forehead. He shrugged at her and whispered, "Fell off my bike."

"Yikes."

"A Fed Ex truck caught my rear tire. Guess he couldn't tell I was turning. I'll be glad when I get my license back so I can swap two wheels for four."

Sandy could have had a DUI, too. How many times had she driven high? It was sheer luck that she never got caught. Luckier that she never had an accident and hurt herself or worse, someone else.

The group leader spoke. "An AA buddy told me a story that I thought I'd share with you."

"Uh oh," whispered Jake. "Lame parable alert."

"There was a woman who put three pots on the stove to boil water. In one she put a carrot, in the other an egg, and in the third, she put coffee beans. After ten minutes, the carrot had changed, no longer hard and resilient but soft and pliable."

Maybe he was a preacher, though he didn't have her dad's booming, "I speak God's words" approach. This guy didn't instill fear the way her father did.

The speaker continued: "The egg changed, too; its thin shell had not protected the liquid inside so it hardened into something else." He scanned the room as if taking its temperature. "What happened to the pot that held the coffee beans? The beans remained intact. It was the water around them that had changed."

Sandy looked into her cup, the coffee inside long chilled.

"And now for the punchline," Jake said. "Guy thinks we're his church."

"Which are you?" the leader asked. "Are you a carrot or an egg? You find yourself in hot water, maybe because of your addiction, maybe something else. But it alters you. It makes you weak like the carrot, or hardens you like the egg. Or are you like the coffee bean, when things are at their worse, your best comes out?"

Nobody said anything. Sandy squirmed and her chair squeaked. The lady who'd gotten the chip cleared her throat. Jake played with a fiber at the end of his cast.

A woman with stringy black hair and glasses that hid most of her face spoke. "I may be an egg. I used to be a good person. I used to care a lot about other people—not just family, but friends and people in my church. My house used to be where all the kids in the neighborhood hung out."

Around the room, the other members nodded encouragingly. In her dad's church, someone would have said, "Amen, sister."

"But then I broke my back and needed drugs for the pain. When my back had healed, I still needed the drugs. I needed them more than I needed my family. Anything. My addiction made me selfish and mean. I don't like being so hard inside." Tears fell down her face. A man beside her handed her a handkerchief.

"You don't look so hard right now," the leader said. "Your addiction hasn't changed everything about who you are."

People nodded and offered things they liked about her. Told her she was brave to make the changes she had in her life. Said God and her family were proud that she was tackling her addiction. She wiped her face, smiled, and thanked them.

"How about the rest of you?" the leader asked. "Carrots? Eggs? Or Coffee beans?"

Sandy stared at the floor. Jake raised his casted hand. "Feeling a bit carrot-like."

"At least your head didn't crack like an egg," someone said, and everyone laughed. Sandy faked a laugh, too, though she wasn't sure why. There was so much she still didn't understand about herself.

She pulled the folded NA log attendance sheet from her purse and approached the speaker. He initialed that she'd come and said he hoped to see her again soon.

"You just might," she replied.

• • •

BECCA SAW A FAINT LIGHT on in Dad's office. The housekeeper hadn't been over since the week before last. Mom? She doubted it. Mom was acting too weird, avoiding Dad's chair in the kitchen and Dad's coat hanging on the rack. She probably wasn't ready for Dad's office.

Becca wasn't sure she was, either. She had spent a lot of time in there when Mom left them—helping Dad with computer stuff, or working on her homework across from him while he messed with bills. That all changed when Mom got sick and came home and Dad only entered the office when he had to. Sometimes he'd summon Becca by yelling that the computer had locked up, and she'd come in to reboot it. He'd mutter a distracted "thanks," finish his business, then hurry back upstairs to Mom.

The dim glow was from the computer monitor. She heard clicks, too, and as she stepped inside she saw the familiar chaos of dark curls of her brother bent over the keyboard. She tiptoed in, curious to see if he was emailing someone. Maybe it was that girl in his band, the one he kept calling.

He wasn't in his email account. He had the homepage to Dad's bank open.

"What are you doing?" she asked, sitting on the credenza behind the desk chair, the way she always did back when she was helping Dad. She drew a deep breath to chase that memory away.

Elliott swiveled the squeaky leather chair to face her. He hadn't shaved and stubble made an uneven shadow on his cheeks and chin. "Nothing," he said, rubbing his eyes. "How are you feeling? Stomach better?"

"Yeah." She didn't appreciate the way he stared at her. She pointed to the screen.

"Do you still have money in our bank?" All three of the Hastings kids had bank accounts set up for them by their parents. Becca had five hundred and forty-eight dollars in hers, babysitting money.

"No. I was trying to check on Dad's account."

She narrowed her eyes at him. "Why?"

"Because there are bills to pay. The funeral home. Soon, the hospital. Other stuff. I don't want Mom having to worry about it."

Of course not. Nobody wanted Mom worrying about anything.

"Doesn't matter, though," Elliott continued. "I don't have his password. I've tried guessing but that didn't get me very far."

The screen showed a shimmering photo of the downtown bank at dusk, seven gray stories outlined against a vivid pink sky. Photo-shopped. "I know the password," she said.

His brows climbed up his forehead, as though it was impossible that his stupid little sister knew anything useful.

"Move," she commanded, pointing to the chair.

"Yes, ma'am." He grinned and made a big deal of relinquishing the seat. She propped her feet on the wooden pedestal legs as she spun it back around to face the screen. She clicked in Dad's account number, which she'd memorized, then keyed in the password: Spatz78!.

"Nice," Elliott commented.

"You want checking or savings?"

"Start with checking."

She pulled up the balance info: $853.25. Elliott ran his finger down a long list of withdrawals. "Mortgage is high," he said.

"Dad refinanced it when Mom got sick."

"He never told me."

Her brothers would soon learn a lot that Dad hadn't told them. So would Mom. The second mortgage, the money lost over the past two years. She wasn't sure how much was gone, or how much they'd had before, but it was something Dad always fretted about.

Elliott pointed to another entry. "Over seventeen hundred. What's that? Credit card payment?"

Becca clicked on the "detail" tab. "Oh, right. Mom's hospital bill."

"Really? They have good insurance, don't they?"

"Yeah, but one of her chemo drugs wasn't covered." Becca remembered long arguments over the phone, Dad's face getting redder than his garnet Gamecock shirt, the receiver slammed down so hard it could have cracked. Then she'd helped him type a three page letter appealing the decision that Mom could use a less expensive chemotherapy option. "She's going to use the treatment that's best for her and you're going to pay for it!" Dad had written, though the appeal had been rejected.

At least the new drug had worked. The other treatments had made her so sick they'd had to stop them, but the brand new medication had fewer side effects. And they'd be paying for it for the next hundred years.

"Leave it to big pharma. Bastards." A sheen of perspiration covered Elliott's face, which was weird, because the room was cool.

"What next?" she asked.

"Let's see the balance in savings."

The number surprised Becca. She hadn't seen the account figures in months. Less than seven thousand remained. There had been sixteen thousand the last time she'd helped Dad.

Elliott didn't seem bothered. "Can we access his money market account?"

"What's that?"

"Another form of savings. More long term."

Becca returned to the accounts homepage and clicked the "overview" tab. The money market account had a balance of zero.

"Damn." Elliott dropped onto the credenza, his face blanched. "Does he have money somewhere else? Another bank? A brokerage firm, maybe?"

"I don't think so." She totaled the numbers. Not quite eight thousand. That would cover the mortgage for a few months but there were other bills.

"Damn," Elliott repeated, shaking his head at the screen. He stood, paced over to the book case, then to the window. He carded a hand through his hair so that it stood up in asymmetric lumps around his face.

Would they have to move? Sell this big house? Maybe they'd move into an apartment. But not like the big nice one Mom had leased. What if they wouldn't let them keep Spats? And how would they pay bills? Mom didn't work, so there'd be no money coming in. How long before they were homeless?

Becca joined Elliott at the window and stared out at the bleak autumn day. "Leaves need raking," Elliott said.

Could they even afford to pay Joe Booker now?

"I'll do it in the morning," Elliott said.

She nodded. She could barely make out the fat hydrangea plants that edged Dad's garden. Who would fertilize and mulch it in the spring? Who would plant the annuals and trim the azaleas right after they bloomed? Whose garden would this be after they moved?

"What's going on in here?" Mom's voice made her jolt.

Elliott spun around, looking as guilty as the time he had short-sheeted Sims's bed. "Nothing."

Becca hurried to the computer and powered it down.

"Just reading email," Elliott said.

Mom hovered in the doorway as though scared to step inside. She wore a baggy green sweater without the scarf she put on when she was going out-side. The skin on her neck sagged above her trachea.

She took a step closer to them. "Elliott? You okay?"

"Of course. I'm getting some bookings worked out for when I go back to New York." Elliot's smile quivered at its edges. Lying didn't come easy to him.

"I don't want to think about you leaving," she said. Neither did Becca.

"I may stay a few extra days," he said.

"Good." Mom traced a finger up the oak-stained door jamb. "That's good. It won't cost you any jobs, will it?"

"It'll be fine."

She cast a curious glance at Becca, then turned and left them.

"She's going to have to find out," Becca whispered.

"I know. But not yet." He returned to the credenza and crossed his arms. "Does Sims know?"

She shrugged. "Dad talked to him about most stuff."

"Of course he did." Elliott looked back at the window. "Wait a minute. Dad had to have life insurance. That'll pay. And then there's his business."

"What about it?"

"Dad owns half of it. Gotta be some money there. Hell, five years ago they won that award for being the most successful realty company." He spoke faster now, like a car rolling downhill. "Yeah, it's not so bad. Y'all will be okay."

Becca's gaze returned to the window. A breeze tossed the limbs of the oak tree so that orange and yellow leaves rained down. She wished she could believe Elliott, but somehow, she couldn't.

• • •

JOE BOOKER KEPT MOVING. There was purpose in his step, though he lacked direction. He'd already walked the perimeter of downtown twice, passing over the steel grates puffing out the devil's breath. He cut through the university, climbed up the Capitol steps and down, and looped behind the government buildings on the statehouse grounds. He liked to keep a rhythm in his stride, walk-fast, walk-fast, walk-fast, his wool coat flapping as he moved. People didn't talk to him, not even Pug-eye, the old drunk lying by the statue of Strom Thurmond, and that was how he liked it. The sole voices he heard were the nagging whispers in his head.

He could tell from the angle of the sun that he still had four, five hours before dusk. No matter. Gray clouds hovering west of town might bring some rain or might blow by with nary a drop. In his pocket, he could feel the tin of Vienna sausages that would do for supper and the four dollar bills and two quarters left from what Reverend Bill had given him for cleaning up the graveyard. He felt bad about taking the money. One shouldn't be paid for tending to his own home.

Cold air pushed through the clouds, and Joe buttoned his jacket. The hole in his right shoe had become a bother; his big toe poking through could feel the chill. Tomorrow he'd go behind the Goodwill store and see if they'd tossed out any shoes that would fit. Joe had big, broad feet, even as a child. Feet like a kangaroo, his mama used to say.

Funny the things he remembered. Odd flashes: a wrinkly smile, crust drooping off a slice of pecan pie. A worn baseball glove. A hand swooping towards his face.

Papa couldn't help his temper. He had spirits after him, which Joe didn't understand when he was a child, but he understood now. Best thing was to be away from people, not let the demons' meanness hurt anybody else, which is what Papa should have done, but he didn't know any better. Joe had learned from Papa's mistakes.

He sometimes wondered if Papa had taken to the streets during those months when he'd disappeared. Mama never said. He'd be gone as long as half a year, then show up at the back door like he'd just gone up the road for an Orange Crush. The coming-back times were always happy, Mama so glad to see him, Joe and his brother grabbing on to his knees as he snuck change into their pockets. But weeks, or even days, later the spirits would have their way and Papa'd raise his hand again.

"Joe! Over here! Joe!" Rag Doll had spotted him from up the block. Joe kept moving, but when she had her sights on him there was no getting away. He dipped his fingers in his pocket and wrapped them around the can of Vienna sausages. Rag Doll wasn't getting them from him, no matter what she tried.

"Didn't see you at breakfast," she said, her squat little legs working hard to keep up. "There was a big fight after. Cyphus Lawter took juice and cigarettes off the old white man with no teeth. That old guy went after him like a Chihuahua after a bear. Cyphus Lawter knocked him flat. Split his head open. They had to call an ambulance."

This was another reason Joe stayed away from people. You never knew when you might step into a mess. Cyphus Lawter brought trouble wherever he stepped.

"He don't like you none, does he?" Rag Doll said.

"Cyphus?"

"He don't like you cause you ain't scared of him. You ain't scared of nothing, are you, Joe?"

He didn't answer. There were plenty of things that frightened him, but most were on the inside.

"Where you staying?" Rag Doll asked.

Joe froze. Turned. Stared her down.

"I just want to know, s'all. I ain't gonna bother you or nothin'." She rubbed her nose with the back of her dirty hand. She had blue ribbons tied in her long hair, untidy clumps hanging down past her shoulders. "I got me a good squat. Even has a roof. Not too cold. If you ever want you can stay with me." She shrugged her narrow, bony shoulders. Lots of men had lain with Rag Doll. The offer came with a price.

"You got any money on you, Joe? I just need me a buck or two for some cigarettes."

Joe turned and began to walk. The coins in his pocket clicked against the can.

She fell into step with him. "Or even a case quarter. I go by the river, someone might split a smoke for that."

A gust of wind swept over them, kicking up leaves and a paper sack. A Coke can clattered by, and Rag Doll chased it and snatched it up like she thought Joe was going to fight her for it. He almost smiled at the thought.

Joe picked up his pace, making it hard for Rag Doll to keep up.

"Okay, Joe," Rag Doll said, panting. "I'll see you at breakfast then. Tuesdays are the Catholic Church."

"Maybe." He kept walking, relieved that Rag Doll left him alone. He looped through downtown and approached the church. It was too soon to bed down, but he liked to keep an eye on his squat and quickened his pace when he spotted a man in the graveyard, someone he'd never seen before. He had red hair that fell past his shoulders and was on his knees in front of

124

Mr. Wortham Pinckney's headstone. Joe inched closer, worried when he saw the man scribbling something against the granite. It wasn't right; that grave was a holy thing. Joe wasn't sure he should even sleep on it and knew damn well this man had no business defacing it this way. Joe's hands fisted as he approached.

The man looked up at him. "Hello there."

Joe glared. Up close, he could see that a dark piece of paper had been taped on the granite. Good. The man wasn't writing on the headstone, but scratching something on the paper. But still, why was he here? Did Reverend Bill know?

The man stood and brushed bits of leaves from his brown pants. He wasn't tall, only came up to Joe's neck, with skin as pale as cane sugar. He extended a hand. "I'm Royce Macy," he said.

Joe didn't take his hand. He didn't like touching other people.

Royce Macy lowered his arm. "I was doing a tombstone rubbing. This one has some intricate detail, the way the flowers top his name, the vines winding across the top." He traced the design with his finger. "See this bird? It symbolizes the soul partaking of heavenly food. And the vine itself means God's seeds replanted on the earth. At least, that's what I read."

Joe bent over to look at the sheet. He could just make out Mr. Pinckney's name. "That hurt the marker?" he asked.

"No," Royce Macy said. "I was here for a funeral the other day and spotted this. Never made it into the church though."

Seemed odd he'd come for a funeral and not bother to go inside for it.

Joe heard footsteps in the leaves—he needed to get to raking them—and spotted the Reverend heading their way. Good. Let the Reverend tell Royce Macy to stop messing with Mr. Pinckney's grave. And if he didn't leave, Joe would toss him from the graveyard.

Reverend Bill limped on over to them, wearing his bright white collar like a halo around his neck and a warm smile. "Joe? Who's your friend?"

Joe started to comment that this man was no friend of his when Royce Macy introduced himself, saying he worked at the university and going on about how he liked the vines and stuff on the tombstone.

"Royce Macy?" the Reverend repeated, his grin flattening.

The redheaded man nodded. It looked like his shoulders sunk down, like the two men had had an invisible conversation between them. "Is it okay if I do the rubbing? I'm not hurting the marker."

"Okay, but clean up after yourself. I don't want Joe to have to do it." The reverend's voice took on a different tone than Joe was used to.

The reverend's attention was drawn to someone else walking up the path. Another white man, tall, with dark curly hair, wearing jeans and a scuffed leather jacket, moving with head lowered, like he had to watch every step. "That's Elliott," the Reverend said.

"Hastings?" Royce Macy asked, his eyes widening.

"Yes." Reverend Bill sighed. "He's come to see where his dad has been interred."

Royce Macy looked at the tools gathered around his feet. "Maybe I'd better go."

"That might be best," Reverend Bill said.

As the man scooped up his tools and rolled up the sheet of paper, Reverend Bill walked over to the curly haired man and guided him over to the tall white column with the angel on top. A brass plate had been added that morning: Mitchell Sims Hastings, Sr. March 1, 1960–November 7, 2014. The men who'd added the plaque had left a mess that Joe had cleaned up.

The dark haired man circled the statue, pausing when he got to Mr. Mitch's plate, which he touched with a trembling finger. Mr. Mitch's boy, Joe realized. A few tears trickled down his face. He wiped them with the knuckles of his right hand. Reverend Bill slid an arm around his shoulder and whispered something to him. The young man never spoke, but stood there, as if frozen in his grief. Reverend Bill stood there, too, sharing his pain and offering silent comfort.

Joe knew he shouldn't be watching. He closed his eyes and thought about Mr. Mitch, wondering why the Lord would take someone who had so many people to miss him.

• • •

THE TEXT MESSAGE ON Lena's phone glowed like a beacon in the dark light of early morning. She pulled herself up, propping a pillow behind her shoulders and rubbing her eyes. Another night with so little sleep, a few snatched hours, filled with unsettling dreams. Her arms and legs ached like she had spent hours in the gym but she'd done nothing physical in days. Just carried around what felt like a boulder—this new life of hers. Widowhood.

The phone trembled on the nightstand, wanting her to click the message and read it. She switched on the lamp and lifted the device.

"Can we meet?" from Royce.

The boulder shifted. What did he want, after all this time?

The phone buzzed again. "I just want fifteen minutes."

What about what she wanted? The time for him to reach out was long past. Royce had been a mistake. No, that wasn't quite right. He had been a crucial part of her life two years ago.

They had met when she took his oil and acrylics class at the university, something she'd wanted to try for years but, out of cowardice, never done. Then she'd entered a bleak period in her life when everything grew stale, when her days became long stretches of tedium. The house felt suffocating, her marriage worn out. Every dinner conversation the same: Mitch describing the latest problem with his business, Becca shrugging off their questions, picking at her food, and hurrying from the table as soon as she could. Lena finding herself straining to care, to listen, to not crave something that wasn't there anymore. When the course catalog from the university arrived in her mail, she snatched it up and registered for the class.

She remembered that feeling—the fear, but also the thrill—of preparing for the class. Shopping for campus clothes. Assembling her supplies: easel, paints, canvases. The morning of her first day, changing clothes six times before settling on jeans and a batik top. Feeling absurdly old compared to other students; the perky coeds with rosy skin and slim little bodies and tattoos—she hadn't expected so many tattoos.

Royce had come into the room dressed in chinos, his hair a chaos of red curls that needed trimming. He wasn't tall, but lean and compact, an efficient design in humanhood. He moved manically, rearranging easels to capture the natural light from the tall, rippled glass windows. Handing out supplies. Setting up each student in a work area. He moved Lena's easel near the front.

After an introduction to the class format and syllabus, he assigned the first project: paint a self-portrait. "Take thirty minutes. This is a time for you to be unleashed, not measured. Measured comes later," he said, his voice as animated as his movements.

What the hell did that mean? She wanted to do it right, to impress him, but the way he hurried from student to student, tossing out suggestions, hands fluttering like a bird in flight unnerved her. She remembered portraiture from her undergraduate art degree and started by scaling out proportions, top of head to chin, distance between eyes, establishing the planes of the face with pencil marks on the canvas. So obsessed with these details, she couldn't bring herself to pick up a brush.

"Fifteen more minutes. I don't care about quality. I want to see style. This is a free-paint exercise," Royce said. "Don't over think it. You can't get this wrong."

She managed to paint her hair, blond then, down past her shoulders. Her eyes? Boring, but she got the color and shape right. She sketched the chin and nose, darkened under her cheeks where the shadow would fall, but couldn't begin to get the mouth. A million times she outlined her lips with a liner pencil but she couldn't put it on the canvas no matter how hard she tried.

Royce approached. She said, "This is awful."

"I don't care if it is." He stepped closer to the canvas. "Is realism the technique you always use? Have you tried doing something abstract?"

"No, I—" She hadn't been able to finish her sentence. She felt like she was pretending, like all she would ever be able to do is paint fruit in a bowl or Charleston's Rainbow Row.

When the class ended she asked to take the project home, deciding this had been a huge mistake and she'd never return.

"Let's try an experiment first." Royce put a blank canvas on her easel and told her not to plan or sketch, but "turn the brush loose on the canvas."

It had felt impossible, yet Royce busied himself with his work as though this was a request he made every day. Becca came to her mind; how her daughter would smile to hear that on her very first day, Lena had been kept after class.

She dipped her brush in green and blue, swirling the colors together, and stroked the top of the blank canvas, unwilling to defy his request. A simple curved line was all she managed, but she found she liked the color and shape. Should she try another? She touched a lower section with a broader sweep of brush. It needed more green. This time she pressed the color into the center, swishing right and left. Yes. The texture left by the bristles—yes.

Red. She didn't know why she needed that color but she did and made a dramatic arc that bisected the white space. More. She shimmied the brush down, red sparking the calmer blue and teal. Yellow now, something quiet, a small, secret space atop the red. Next she mixed the red and blue to form a rich, vibrant amethyst that belonged in the very center. She didn't know how much time passed as she explored tints and textures and shapes. Paint spattered her skin but she didn't care, nothing mattered but the painting.

And then she was done. She put down her brush.

It was a mess, but something beautiful was there, in the colors blurring and swirling and bright. Royce approached, giving the canvas a thorough study. He said, "Maybe realism isn't your forte?"

After class time with Royce became a regular event, then extended studio hours. "You have talent, Lena. Just don't let yourself get in the way," he said, the rise and fall of his voice as smooth as water in a stream. One afternoon, after three hours of painting, he suggested a visit to a coffee shop. Over caramel lattes she learned he was divorced, had no children, and was preparing for a gallery show in Charlotte. Coffee became a regular after-studio event, something she enjoyed with an urgency that frightened her. Then came their first dinner at a small restaurant that looked over the river, drinking cabernet by a fireplace as they argued the merits of Paul Klee. She didn't get home until midnight, Mitch rolling over in bed to ask, "Are you okay?" but she didn't feel guilty, just annoyed that she'd had to come home at all. She loved the person she had become when she was with Royce. Someone creative and interesting and passionate.

The phone vibrated again. "Please?" his message read.

Best to put this to rest as soon as possible, she decided. "I'll be at Starbucks at 7."

Dressing proved an interesting endeavor. She wanted something plain, but not black. She refused to be morbid in her widowhood. Jeans and a yellow sweater were her first choice, but she spotted drops of purple paint on the sleeve, and remembered it had been what she wore the day of Mitch's accident. She sat on her bed and fingered the tiny spots and remembered holding Mitch's hand without feeling him there. How that detail had cut through her denial. How she had begged for him to stay, but he was already gone.

She folded the sweater and placed it at the top of her closet. She'd never wear it again but wasn't quite ready to give it away. Maybe she never would be.

After donning a brown top, she ran a comb through her hair and opted not to bother with makeup. She didn't want to look good for Royce.

The parking lot in front of the coffee shop held few cars. She didn't spot his van. As she climbed out of her car, she tugged the scarf up to her ears, surprised by the cold, damp air, like the morning was swollen and ready to burst. A scattering of customers occupied café tables by the window, each huddled over cell phones or laptops. Lena ordered a skinny latte by rote, then changed it to regular. She needed calories for this conversation.

When Royce entered, he headed straight to her table, unwinding the wool coat from around his shoulders and draping it on the chair. "Am I late?"

"No, I was early."

He wore a teal scarf which made his green eyes more piercing. A few strands of silver streaked his red hair, which had grown long enough for the curls to reach his shoulders. More lines etched his forehead than before, but the changes in Royce were nothing compared to hers.

"I'll grab a coffee and be right back. Need anything? Muffin? They have those scones you like."

She shook her head. How did he have any notion of what she liked? It had been almost two years since they'd spent time together. Spent all their time together.

He ordered in that animated way he had, gesturing at the sign and at the muffins in the case, smiling at the multi-pierced coed who took his order. He returned with two pastries that he placed between them. "In case you change your mind."

This was something Mitch might have done, and the too familiar ache bloomed inside once again.

When he sat down, he leaned forward, elbows on the tiny table, and she smelled the musky scent of his aftershave. "How are you doing?"

Had he any clue how loaded that question was for her? She sipped and thought about how to respond. An abrupt "fine," might derail his line of questioning, but would be dishonest. Not that he deserved honesty from her. "I'm doing my best," she said. "I wasn't prepared for something like this to happen."

"How could you be?" He tossed out a hand, then lowered it to the table. "Is there anything you need?"

"From you? No."

He watched her, eyelids narrowing to half-mast. "No, I suppose not." He broke off a piece of scone, studied it, and dropped it back on his plate.

She looked into her coffee, wondering why she had come. She needed to go home. Her children would be awake soon, though Abby would sleep till noon. She was still catching up from the long, difficult journey back to South Carolina

"How was the funeral?" he asked.

"Fine. Difficult." She wasn't sure how much to disclose. Two years ago, she'd have bared her soul to him. "I'm worried about Becca and the boys. Mitch is—was—" still, so hard to use the past tense—"a wonderful father."

He cocked his head at her, then said, "I talked with Becca outside the church. I can see why you're concerned."

What did that mean? How dare he comment on her child? She gripped the cup.

"She looks more and more like you. The shape of her eyes. That long, elegant neck." He lifted a finger, gesturing at her throat.

"Becca has a lot more of Mitch in her," she replied, glancing at her watch. "What did you want, Royce? Why did you call?"

130

"I had to see you. Don't know how else to say it. After all you've been through. After everything—I had to know you were okay." The slightest quiver to his lips was something new.

"Strange that you feel that now. Not when I had cancer. Not when I almost died." She watched as the words hit their mark.

His flinch was hardly perceptible. They had always been gentle together. Loving. Supporting. But he had been neither when she needed it the most.

"I suppose I deserved that," he whispered. "I could tell you I'm sorry. God knows, I am. But I suspect it's too late for that."

She let silence voice her agreement.

"I couldn't handle it. I've never gotten involved with a student before. Hell, it had been years since I'd been connected with anyone like I was with you."

She thought about that, about how an invisible tether had attached each to the other. How those early days together felt, the hunger they had for each other. How it stung when he abandoned her.

He spun his cup on the table. "And then came the lump. Everything had been so perfect. What I felt for you—"

She started to ask what he had felt, and how he could abandon her when she needed him most, but she wasn't sure she wanted the answer.

"I couldn't help you. I couldn't fix it. So I panicked. I'm not proud of it."

"I suppose not." She studied his face over the rim of her latte. He'd lost his swagger, his confidence, but there was a softness behind his eyes she'd missed.

"Are you painting?" he asked.

The question surprised her, though it shouldn't have. Conversation with Royce always circled back to art.

"No. I thought I was ready but . . . it didn't happen."

He let out a loud sigh. "Remember that first project you did in my class? You let so much out that day. You need to paint. It's how you express yourself best. Words have never been your thing, Lena."

It annoyed her that he thought he could diagnose her over latte and uneaten pastries. But maybe he was right, words weren't her "thing." They had been Mitch's though. He could communicate with anyone. It made him a great realtor. He was the one who talked with the kids, explained to them about sex and love, who comforted them when they were hurt or sad. He and Becca had that powerful tie, and now their daughter was left alone with Lena. Lena, who wasn't good with words.

He pushed the plate across the table. "Eat."

131

She lifted a scone and nibbled on a corner. Just the right amount of sweetness, so she took a larger bite. She'd eaten so little over the past week, she wondered how her stomach would handle it, but couldn't stop herself from finishing the pastry.

Royce smiled. "At least I got that right."

She wiped crumbs from her lips and placed the napkin by her cup. What now? She'd heard him apologize, and it changed nothing. Life had taken her down a different path from Royce. Sitting with him here, now, sipping coffee like they used to, felt odd. Out of sync. Wrong. Maybe she didn't hate him, but she didn't want to be here with him.

"What?" he asked. "What's wrong?"

Curious that he could sense the change in her. "I need to get home."

"Of course." He stood, collecting their cups and the plate and hurrying them to the trash. As she put on her jacket he rushed back to hold it for her, the way he used to do, the way Mitch always did, and she thought about how from now on, she'd be donning jackets on her own. Royce walked her to the door but hesitated before opening it.

"I want to see you again," he said, his gaze open, expectant. "I know now is not the right time. I can be patient."

Lena looped the scarf around her neck and breathed in the cold, moist air. "I don't think . . ." she let her words trail behind her as she walked to her car.

• • •

TONYA WRESTLED BYRON FROM the car seat, which was no easy feat because John had parked too close to the curb. Byron's sweatshirt had bunched up under his arms and there was a new purple stain on the sleeve, grape juice from snacks at daycare. His head bumped against her chin when she shut the door.

"Ow."

"Ow," he repeated with a giggle. "Ow, ow."

John checked a slip of paper he'd clipped to a manila folder. "This is the building," he said.

The squat faux-stucco building had a brick walkway like an umbilicus attaching it to the street. A tall fountain gurgled in the tiny yard, water bubbling out of an abstract copper hammer and frothing in a milky pool below. When John had said he'd been talking to an attorney, he hadn't mentioned "Will Hammer and Associates." The Will Hammer TV commercials that played over and over were cheesy and amateurish, always ending with a giant hammer slammed on a judge's desk: "Let Will Hammer hammer out justice for you!"

She still wasn't sure she should pursue this, but Marion had harped about it all during their coffee break. "Damn right, you should talk to a lawyer," she had said. "Somebody has to look out for your interest. And that somebody ain't your husband." Tonya wanted to argue, to say she and John were together in this, but lately there hadn't been much togetherness between them.

Byron squirmed to be put down. She obliged, grabbing his hand before he launched himself into the water. "Me splash!!" he squealed, trying to pull away from her. Me-Splash could be Byron's middle name; the child had come out of her womb with a love for water. She remembered those earliest baths, how his chubby hands splatted the water, how he blinked with happy surprise. How he became a wet little eel when she lifted him from the plastic tub, and she'd been so scared she'd drop him, John waiting with a towel to snuggle him close. Those early, perfect days.

"No splash. It's cold out." John took his groping hand and said, "This shouldn't take long."

Inside the building, a receptionist sat behind an arc of black granite that held a paper thin computer monitor, a phone, and a message pad. The phone rang constantly, but the woman never lost her poise: "Will Hammer and Associates. How can I help you?" Tonya tried to imagine Marion working somewhere like this. After the third call, she'd put everyone on hold and start filing her nails.

While John explained who they were, Tonya wandered into the waiting area and dropped into a chair, a wiggly Byron in her lap. She hoped they didn't have a long wait. John came to sit beside Tonya, the folder tucked beside him, and started thumbing through a golf magazine. Tonya looked around, comparing the lobby to the one at Jamison and Patel's. While the plump leather chairs were comfortable, the plush green carpet was the color of snot. She preferred the plank wood floors at her job, the simple upholstered chairs, and the vinyl office plants that survived despite their neglect.

Byron shimmied down to the table and started rearranging the neat stacks of magazines. She decided to let him have his fun; the poor little guy was no good at waiting, and it was almost dinner time.

"Tonya, can't you control him?" John peered over his magazine.

"He's two. He's hungry and he's bored. Why don't you get one of his books from the car?"

"It shouldn't be much longer." John returned to his reading. Byron batted the table like it was a bongo drum, the vibration sending a NEWSWEEK sliding to the floor.

"Mr. and Mrs. Ladson?" A woman with short, very-blond hair appeared, extending a hand. "I'm Carol Greer, Mr. Hammer's paralegal."

John jumped to his feet. Tonya grabbed her boy, ignoring the disrupted table display. Let Will Hammer's custodial staff straighten things later.

"Nice to meet you," John said. "Though you've been very helpful on the phone."

"That's our job, Mr. Ladson. To help you." The lines sounded rehearsed. She could have been thirty-five or sixty-five. Her skin looked artificially smoothed. Her smile didn't reach her eyes, reminding Tonya of her mother after the Botox experiment: pretty in a mannequin way.

"Let's go to my office," Carol said. She moved fast for such a short woman, her heels clicking down the hall's shiny laminate floor. Byron twisted in Tonya's arms.

"Pretty!" he pointed at a photograph of yellow flowers.

Carol spun around and said, "You like the picture?" in a little girl voice. Byron nodded.

"What a darling boy," Carol commented, leaning into the "darling" before resuming her stride up the hall. Passing door after door, Tonya wondered how many staff Will Hammer had. Carol's cozy office was furnished with a tan wooden desk, two flowered chairs, and a torchiere lamp that Tonya prayed Byron wouldn't climb like a fireman's pole.

"So Mrs. Ladson, how are you feeling these days?" Carol asked, taking a seat behind the desk. "I see you still have some bruising."

"I'm fine."

"Well, she's better now," John rushed to say. "But it's been a difficult few weeks. She has a broken nose, some injured ribs. And little Byron has a fractured collar bone. He's supposed to be wearing a sling."

Tonya cut her eyes at him. "The doctor said he had to wear it when it was hurting him. You can see he isn't in much pain now."

"Good thing kids heal so quickly, isn't it?" Carol asked.

Tonya scanned the surface of the desk but saw no pictures. "Do you have children?"

"Two grown ones. And my beautiful granddaughter, Amelia. She's almost five." Carol pivoted a small desk organizer. A photo of a tow-headed girl on a swing was embedded in the pencil holder.

Tonya had always wanted a girl. In the young days of her marriage, she imagined having four kids two years apart like stair steps: boy-girl-boy-girl. It wouldn't work now to have another kid, not with things so tense with John, and all the money problems, and the hard work required to keep up with Byron, but that didn't stop her from longing for it. A blond girl like Amelia.

"Mrs. Ladson, did you miss work as a result of your injuries?"

"Call me Tonya."

"Just that first day," John said. "I wanted her to stay home longer, but Tonya's very dedicated to her job."

"Dedication is a good thing. Do you have copies of your medical expenses?" Carol asked.

John opened a folder and handed her a neat stack of receipts.

"Our insurance will cover most of it," Tonya said.

"That may be true. But there are things it won't cover, like co-pays. Like the disruption of your life. I'll bet your injuries still hurt—maybe they affect your sleep and your ability to do normal things."

She nodded. She hadn't slept through the night since the wreck, thanks to the nightmares. Her ribs ached, especially when she carried Byron.

"She still takes Tylenol every day," John said.

"Any neck or back pain?" Carol asked.

"A little," Tonya admitted.

"I want you to keep a diary for me. Starting today. Record your pain level every few hours, and every dose of painkillers you need to take. What about your boy? Byron, right?"

"He took medicine the first few days but not since then," Tonya answered.

"Like you said, kids bounce back." John flipped through his file and uncovered the photos. "Here's how he looked the day of the accident. And this is two days later."

Tonya winced at the angry red stripe across her son's chest that seemed brighter in the photo than it had actually looked. The third photo John flipped over was taken from above. It showed Byron wearing the brace, his tear-streaked face looking up at the camera, his bottom lip pooched out in a tragic expression.

"This is a great shot." Carol lifted the picture.

"When did you take it?" Tonya asked. Whenever Byron looked like that, she scooped him up and hugged him. She whispered soothing things in his ear and let him lie against her. Funny that John chose to take a photo instead.

He shrugged. "That first day, I think."

Byron crawled up Tonya's torso and jettisoned himself towards the desk, landing a kick to her chest that made her wince. John slid the folder out of his reach.

Carol opened a desk drawer. "Can he have candy? I have suckers."

"Sure." It might keep her boy occupied for a few minutes, but then they'd have to worry about his sticky fingers. A bright red lollipop appeared, Carol's deft hands removing the plastic so Byron could grab it with a squeal of delight.

"I have pictures of my wife, too," John said.

Tonya wondered why he said "my wife" and not "Tonya." It almost sounded possessive. *His* wife. When the photos emerged, she understood why.

"Don't show her those," she whispered. She hadn't seen the shots before, but remembered every click of the camera when he had snapped them. They looked grainy, the color dulled away, except the bruises on her breasts glowing crimson and black. She studied her own expression, her eyes squeezed shut, her head turned in shame, the towel scarcely covering her nipples. If there had been any "pain and suffering" for Tonya it had been when John took those disgusting pictures.

Carol gazed at the photos before turning them over. Tonya exhaled.

"Have you gotten an estimate on the damage to your van?" Carol asked.

"The body shop says it's totaled, but the insurance company says it's worth eight thousand. We paid close to seventeen for it three years ago," John said with obvious disgust.

She hadn't heard that it was totaled. Did that mean she'd never see it again? She felt a flush of sadness, maybe even grief, that the vehicle that had become an extension of her was gone. Deceased. Dead. Like Mr. Hastings.

"That's often what happens. That's why it's important that you have your legal rights protected."

"Which is what I keep telling Tonya." John reached over and squeezed her hand.

"I understand that the other driver passed away." Carol lowered her voice, looking intently at Tonya.

Tonya nodded. It had only been a few days since the funeral; the wound felt tender.

"It is tragic," Carol said. "And he was the one ticketed?"

"It was absolutely his fault," John said. "He ran the red light and slammed into the van."

"He didn't—" Tonya stammered, furious with her husband. "He had a heart attack. The priest said they think he had it while he was driving. That's why he ran the light. It wasn't his fault."

"What priest?" John glared.

"I went to the church where they were having his funeral. I talked to the priest. He knows the family. He said Mr. Hastings was a wonderful, kind man and they're all devastated by his death." She wanted to leave. To spring from her chair, grab her son, and bolt from the room.

"Mrs. Ladson. Tonya. Listen to me." Carol lifted a pink-nailed finger. "I understand how upsetting his death is for you. His heart attack took his life—and it almost took yours and your son's. He had insurance, and it is his insurance company that will be held accountable." Carol's eyes left Tonya's face. "Perhaps talking to the priest was helpful, but from now on, it's best that you avoid the Hastings family, including their friends."

"Would you have to talk with Mrs. Hastings?" Tonya asked.

"No. Her insurance company will talk with her. If we can settle out of court, there should be minimal disruption to them."

"How much do you think we can get?" John asked.

"We'll need to review the information you've provided before I can give you an estimate. We work on a contingency basis, meaning we don't charge until after the settlement, when we'll deduct a third."

"But what if their insurance tries to low-ball us? What then?" John asked.

"Then we up the ante. In some cases, we go after the personal assets of the ticketed party. For example, if we can prove that Mr. Hastings was impaired when he was driving—given his health issues, maybe he shouldn't have been behind the wheel—then we have a stronger case."

Something clenched in Tonya's stomach. "I don't want to bother the family."

Carol lifted a hand. "And maybe we won't need to." She opened a drawer and pulled out a stack of legal papers. "Tonya, we'd like to represent you. We'll work hard for a prompt settlement. I'll need you to review and sign these forms if you consent."

She glanced over the forms, seven legal-size pages. If she signed them, she may be adding to the troubles of the Hastings family. If she signed them, she and John might get a settlement—enough to pay off the credit cards, and the house insurance which was due next month, and the roof repair they'd been avoiding, and maybe have some left over to put in savings.

"I'd like to have a day to look these over," she said.

"Come on, Tonya. It's just legalese. Sign the papers and be done with it," John muttered, exasperated.

"I work in a law firm. I know how important it is to know what you're signing." She gave Carol a smile as she stood. "You understand."

"Of course." Her tone had lost its warmth as she handed Tonya a business card.

Byron wrapped his arms around her knees. As she lifted him, she said to John, "Ready?"

"I'll meet you at the car in a few," he answered, his voice tight.

CHAPTER 15

When Joe Booker rounded the corner on Main Street, a familiar presence fell in stride with him. The sour smell was familiar, too. Rag Doll, dressed in a stained brown top she must have snagged from the trash behind the Goodwill store, wore a sheen of sweat on her chapped face despite the cold. Her red high-top sneakers had a hole in the right toe.

"Where ya going, Joe?" she asked. "You going to the park?"

He picked up his pace hoping to make it hard for her to keep up.

"Not as cold today," she said. "Bout froze my titties off last night. You stay at the shelter?"

Again, he kept his silence, and tried not to notice when she cupped her saggy breasts to make her point.

"If it gets that cold tonight I'm gonna try to get in," she continued. "Some fat cow run me off from there last time."

He cast a sideways glance at her, wondering what she'd done to get run off. Could have been anything: fighting, stealing stuff, cussing out staff. Why Rag Doll worked so hard to tangle with people he didn't understand, but it seemed something she took pride in.

As he turned the next corner, she stayed at his side. "Hey, you gotta ten you can give me?" she asked.

"No." He put power in the word to shut her up. Rag Doll was always begging. Always. Downtown folks going into their jobs. Mothers coming out of a grocery store. She was good at it, too. Why she was asking Joe for money when she had more than he did was always a puzzle.

"Or a few bucks. I need it." She rubbed at her nose with the back of a dirty hand. "I'll pay you back in a week. I promise."

He paused, arching his brows at her. Her gaze did a dance from his face to the sidewalk to the road ahead, more jittery than normal.

"You owe somebody?" he asked, hoping she hadn't got herself in trouble with a dealer.

"Even a dollar," she persisted. "You got a dollar don't ya?"

He got moving again, Rag Doll a pace behind. Sometimes she was harder to shake than a head cold. Joe tucked his hands in the pockets of his pea coat, glad to have the warm wool between him and the cold breeze stirring up.

After they'd gone a few blocks, she paused, pointing to a brick walkway that led to a tall building. The crisp lawn on either side of the path was too green for this time of year.

"You ever look at that fountain?" Rag Doll jutted her chin towards a strange-looking thing halfway down the walkway: a cement circle around a pool. In the center, a giant hammer made out of some kind of brown metal had water pouring from its head. How the thing didn't get rusted made no sense.

"Sometimes people throw coins in there." She scampered over and sunk her hands into the cold, frothy water. She grimaced as she pulled out a dime and two nickels. "See?"

"That money ain't yours."

"Ain't nobody's." She laughed, pocketing the change. "Till now."

The building had large wooden doors with shimmery glass windows, almost like a church but not quite. When one opened, Joe and Rag Doll stepped away, both knowing they didn't belong there. A woman with a tiny boy came out. The child ran to the fountain and leaned over the edge, worrying Joe. He was about to dash over to stop the little boy when the woman— his mother, Joe guessed—hurried over and grabbed his hand.

"Byron! Be careful!" she scolded. They were white folks, the woman with hair the color of tree bark and the little boy a towhead.

The child giggled. She sat beside him, holding on as she let him touch the water. "It's cold, isn't it?" She spoke in that exaggerated way young mothers did. The boy pounded the surface of the pool, drops sprinkling both of them. As she wiped moisture from her face, Joe noticed a sizable bruise across her nose.

"Byron!" Her tone was half scolding, half laughing.

"Think they got money?" Rag Doll whispered.

Joe frowned.

"This here's one of them TV commercial lawyer places. Everybody comes in and out of here got lots of money." She grinned.

The woman took the boy's hand again and coaxed him away from the fountain and up the sidewalk to the parked cars. A moment later, the big doors opened again and a man and a blond-headed woman emerged. They paused on the steps, the man holding a file, the two huddled close like they were sharing a secret.

"I bet that guy's got cash on him," Rag Doll whispered.

The man leaned in to listen as the blond woman pointed to the papers in his hand. He nodded, and she walked back up the steps towards the entrance, where she hesitated. "John? Talk to her. Then call me later."

He flipped through the pages and answered, "I'll do what I can." He frowned as she returned inside the building.

"Wait here," Rag Doll commanded. She circled the fountain, sizing him up like a house cat cornering a rat. The man's attention remained fixed on what was in his hand.

As he reached the end of the walkway, Rag Doll approached. "'Scuse me sir, but you got a little money you can spare?"

The man's head shot up. He was a youngish fellow, with pale skin like the little boy but darker hair.

"Just a buck or two for some supper. Me and my friend here—" she pointed at Joe. "We're powerful hungry."

Joe's hand squeezed into a fist. He wanted no part of Rag Doll's game.

The man shook his head and pushed past her.

Rag Doll did what she always did: hurried up behind him, nattering away. "Just a dollar then. We can get us some coffee to warm us up."

Joe almost laughed. Rag Doll wouldn't pay nothing for Joe to have coffee. These were lies she told to get her way.

"If you and your friend got yourselves jobs, you could buy your own coffee," the man berated, looking over her head at the cars.

"Ain't so easy to get a job, but I'm trying!" Rag Doll continued. "Don't you got a few bucks to help a woman out?"

The man froze, glaring at her. She stepped closer, smiling, showing him the gap where her front tooth had been knocked out. He turned his head as though repulsed by her. Maybe it was the smell.

"You people are piranha," he said. "Always grabbing for a handout. Some of us freakin' WORK for a living."

Rag Doll's smile flattened. Her eyes narrowed. "You think you better than me? You ain't!"

Joe flinched at the rise in her voice. If she kept getting herself riled up, she'd get herself arrested again.

The man shook her off and started walking.

"You ain't no different from me," she yelled, but then her voice softened. "You ain't nothing special."

He hurried to the car where the young woman and little boy waited, climbed inside, and slammed the door shut. Rag Doll showed him her middle finger as he sped off.

When she returned to Joe, she kept her head down, tendrils of greasy hair hiding her face. Joe got moving, with her a few steps behind, muttering something he didn't care to hear.

"You sure you can't lend me some cash?" This time, her voice sounded weak and young, like a girl was asking, not a woman.

He stopped, turned, and faced her. "Who you owe?"

She looked at him, then away, rubbing her hands against the dirty folds of her skirt. "Nobody," she whispered.

He knew better than to believe her.

• • •

Becca settled into the familiar leather La-Z-Boy, squirming until her butt found the concaved center of the leather cushion that had fit her father perfectly. She felt for the wood handle and tugged, raising the foot stool, and inserted her heels in the two dents that marked where Dad's giant feet used to rest. The remote rested on the narrow table beside his chair. His fingers had been the last to hold it. She sniffed the hard plastic for a trace of him but found none.

He would be watching a football game right now. Maybe the Gamecocks were playing—he never missed his favorite team. Or Clemson, which he'd watch in hopes that they'd lose. He'd have a diet soda beside him, or maybe a beer, and chips in an old plastic bowl. The sound would be turned way up, which would annoy Mom until she'd stick her head into the den and say, "Really, do the neighbors need to hear, too?" to which he'd answer, "I'll bet they're watching the game, too" or "Sit with me, Lena," except she never did. It was all he wanted—all he ever wanted—but she always had something else to do.

Becca turned on the TV and found ESPN where a gold and black team was playing a royal blue team. The score flashed at the bottom of the picture: Vanderbilt losing to Kentucky. Dad hated Kentucky, almost as much as he hated Clemson. He had a long list of hate teams, but thought the South Carolina football coach was a deity to be worshipped.

"Is the game on?" Sims entered the den carrying a large bowl of Doritos. Elliott followed, a beer in each hand. They plopped onto the sofa in their usual spots, Sims on the right end, Elliott on the left, the chips balanced between them. Elliott gave Sims one of the bottles.

"There are probably ten games on," Becca said, not relinquishing the remote.

"Cocks are playing Troy U. Should be a slaughter." Sims mimed pushing the remote.

She scrolled down the channels, pausing on a figure skating event—a couple in red and gold sparkles spinning on the ice. They looked like fire.

"Becca, come on!" Sims said, reaching for the remote.

She held it out of his reach. "Maybe I want to watch this." The female skater leapt into the arms of the twirling male, who lifted her over his head. How much did she weigh? She was tall and thick-muscled, her legs stretched into a perfect split.

"Ouch, that's gotta hurt," Elliott said.

"I'll pay you to change the channel," Sims said. "Figure skating will make my eyes bleed."

"How much will you pay me?" She kept her eyes on the screen like she was mesmerized.

Sims pulled out a wallet. "How much do you charge these days?"

She looked over at the bottle in his hand. "I want a beer."

"No beer for you, squirt," Elliott said.

Tucking the remote beside the cushion under her, she said, "Figure skating it is, then." Balanced on one skate, the woman glided around the man like a sailing ice sculpture. She burned enough calories to eat whatever she wanted.

"A sip of beer," Sims commented. "One sip."

The black remote was exchanged for the Corona bottle. Becca took three quick swallows, the beer bitter and frigid-cold as it slid down her throat. Dad always held the beer to limit her to a mere taste, yet never noticed that time she and Kayla snuck three Amstel Lights from the fridge.

"Here we go." Sims found the game. Gamecocks in garnet and white, Troy in red and silver.

"You're shitting me," Elliott said. "It's the Troy Trojans?"

"Yep. Maybe our Cocks can penetrate the Trojan defense," Sims said.

"Or will the Trojans block the Cocks' drive?" Elliott answered with a laugh.

"Oh . . ." Becca got it. Boy humor didn't change no matter how old the boys were.

Sims's cell phone rang. He frowned at the number displayed and disappeared through the doorway

"We need dip." Elliott hurried off to the kitchen and returned with neon green guacamole which he'd plopped in a pottery bowl. He also carried a glass of orange juice and handed it to Becca. "Since you're not getting any more beer."

She eyed the chips, doing a quick calorie count of her day so far. One hundred forty-three at breakfast because Mom had insisted on the banana on her cereal. Lunch: about two hundred, because she'd eaten half of the chicken salad sandwich and buried the rest in the trash when Mom wasn't looking. The milk—whole milk, because Mom hadn't bought the skim she'd asked for—one fifty. She was almost at five hundred calories for the day!

Sims returned, slipping his phone into his pocket. "That was the insurance company. We may have a problem."

"Dad's insurance?" Elliott asked.

"Yeah. They've been trying to work out a settlement with the other driver. Dad was ticketed, so we have to cover the accident. It looks like the woman in the other car is getting litigious."

"What's litigious?" Becca asked.

"Sue-happy," Sims said. "As in, not settling with what the insurance company has offered. As in, going to one of those shyster TV lawyers so they can squeeze more money out of us."

"We'd have to pay them? Where would we get the money? We have that huge mortgage and everything." Becca heard the panic in her own voice, more than she wanted to give away.

Elliott frowned at his brother. "He doesn't mean our family. He means the insurance company. They'll have to settle this."

Sims nodded. "It's going to be a pain in the ass. If any of the calls come here, make sure you give them my number. We don't want Mom worrying about this."

Of course not. Don't worry Mom: the family mantra.

"What's going to happen with Dad's business?" Elliott asked. "Calloway and Hastings without the Hastings?"

"Damned if I know," Sims answered.

"You and Phillip have gotten to be buds. Has he talked to you about joining the company?"

Sims downed a swallow of beer. "I expect he will, but I dread it."

"Why?"

He shrugged. "I like what I'm doing. I spend my day with numbers. The people I deal with work for me. What Dad does—did—I could never do. There are too many idiots out there and I don't have the patience."

When Elliott scooped a giant glob of guacamole on his tortilla chip and popped it into his mouth, green seeped out the corner of his lips. Guacamole had a ton of calories, even though it was basically a vegetable. She loved it though. And chips—if she ate a couple it would add a few dozen calories. The orange juice was two hundred. She could eat three fistfuls of chips for that. She slid the glass away.

"Don't throw the ball away. Damn it!" Sims waved a hand at the TV like the quarterback needed his guidance. Dad used to yell at him, too, though he loved one of the running backs. "Kid has golden arms," Dad would say.

Their home was so silent now. Even with Mom, Aunt Abby and Elliott puttering around, it seemed like the house was waiting for Dad to speak. This chair molded to him, not her. This room ached for his words, not her brothers'.

Elliott walked over to the wall of shelves and stooped down to look at the long line of record albums, which Dad had filed alphabetically by genre. "Man, I can't believe they kept all these."

"Remember when we bought him the CD player? He complained that CDs didn't sound as good as albums," Sims said.

"He may be right. There's something very authentic about vinyl that gets lost in digital." Elliott pulled out a stack of albums. "I always envied him his Coltrane collection. Think maybe I can take these?"

"No," Becca blurted out.

"Why the hell not?" Sims asked. "You and Mom don't listen to that stuff."

"But it's Dad's," she said, swallowing.

Elliott and Sims both turned to stare at her. She felt like an idiot. Of course she knew Dad wouldn't be listening to any of these albums. Of course she knew he was dead, but that didn't mean they got to paw through his stuff, helping themselves to whatever they wanted.

"You're right. I didn't mean to be insensitive." Elliott replaced the albums and returned to his spot on the sofa. He lifted the bowls of chips and dip, offering them to her. She could almost taste the salty Dorito, the ooze of rich guacamole. She could take another run later to make up for the added calories.

She crammed three into her mouth.

"The dip's delicious." Elliott rested the bowl on the arm of her chair.

He was cruel to put it so close. She skimmed a chip across the surface of green, ten calories. She could afford that many.

The second chip dug deeper and the third worked like a shovel, scooping up a big dollop of avocado.

Elliott's cell played some jazz guitar tune, and he pulled it from his pocket to read the text. He smiled and punched buttons faster than Becca had ever seen—and she knew some texting wizards (Kayla could do it without even looking).

"Who are you talking to?" Sims asked.

"Chloe. A woman in my band."

Sims leaned forward, turning away from the game. "Just a bandmate? Or something more?"

Elliott replied with an evasive shrug.

"Holy crap, you have a girlfriend."

"And you're surprised, why? You think I live like a monk? Or maybe my affections leaned in a different direction?"

"I stopped thinking you were gay after the Megan fiasco."

"Who's Megan?" Becca asked. She moved the bowl of chips to the other side of her brothers, out of reach.

"Freshman year at Carolina. The art student who made collages out of road trash. Had your brother by the gonads for an entire semester," Sims said.

Becca giggled. It made her feel grown up when they talked like this around her.

"I'd argue with you if that wasn't true," Elliott said.

"You almost failed half your classes. I thought Mom was going to have a stroke."

"Really?" Becca couldn't imagine either brother failing anything. Getting As was important in the Hastings household. Bringing home more than two Bs meant restriction and no cell phone.

"Yes really. Elliott and Megan did a lot of reefer back then."

"Sims!" Elliott cautioned, cutting his eyes at Becca like she didn't know about such things. She almost blurted out that she and Kayla tried pot last year, but she didn't like it because she'd eaten an entire sleeve of Fig Newtons.

"Mom and Dad acted like every test score was a direct reflection on them," Elliott said.

Becca knew what Mom and Dad had expected of her, and could recall, in excruciating detail, all the ways she'd let them down. But Elliott and Sims felt the same way?

"Remember when Mom summoned you home?" Sims asked. "You looked like you were facing the guillotine."

"More like the Inquisition. They grilled me for three solid hours because I'd gotten three Cs on midterms."

"But you straightened up after that. After Megan got bored and moved on." Sims lifted his bottle in a mock toast.

"Mom said if I didn't get my grades up, they'd send me to Tech school to study HVAC repair." Elliott scratched at the label on his bottle, his lips pressed into a tight pale line. "Might have been better if they had."

Becca felt a flash of anger. Why did Mom think every little thing reflected on her? Her piano recital in sixth grade: Becca had been terrified during the days leading up to it, how she considered breaking a finger to get out of having to perform. Shaking on the piano stool, lights too hot against her scalp, quiet coughs and foot noises in the audience. Her trembling fingers tripping on the sixteenth notes and her mind forgetting chords she could play in her sleep. Leaving the stage with the piece half-played, horrified, humiliated. Dad hugging her and saying, "It's okay, kitten," but Mom crossing her arms and saying nothing at all. There had been no mention of piano lessons after that disaster.

She reached for the Doritos.

"So Becca, are you making straight As?" Elliott asked, concern in his voice like he was asking if she had a cold or the flu.

"She's AP in all her classes," Sims said. "She's smart as a whip."

"I hate math." Becca didn't like being talked about. "And lately, I hate poetry."

"Lately?" Elliott asked.

"We have a stupid artist-in-residence. He gives me the creeps." She took another handful of chips. She'd eaten too many. Probably three, four hundred calories. She'd need to run three miles to burn them. Of course, there was always the other alternative. She stood, brushing crumbs from her lap.

"Where you going?" Elliott asked, narrowing his eyes at her.

"Upstairs," she answered in a tone that let him know it was none of his business.

As she left the room, she heard Elliott say to Sims, "This is what I was talking about. You know what she's going to do."

Screw him. Screw them both. She pounded up the stairs.

• • •

THE NEXT MORNING, LENA looked up at the clock on the mantle: ten fifteen. Phillip was late, but the man was never on time for anything. Sims and Elliott rattled around in the kitchen getting coffee. She could hear tension in their voices, but couldn't make out the words. They had once been so close. Of course, they had their battles; Sims loved to taunt the more sensitive Elliott, but Elliott would have his revenge. She recalled marshmallow whip oozing out of Sims's baseball glove. A bumper sticker placed on Sims's first car: "I (heart) N Sync," which resulted in a threat of fratricide. But the boys were always quick to defend each other, to compose alibis against accusations from either parent: "I was still up when Elliott came in, just after eleven" or "Sims didn't start it! The third baseman threw the first punch."

They lived such different lives now. Did they talk on the phone other than birthdays and holidays? Surely they emailed or texted each other. She hoped so. She prayed they didn't lose each other to the distance the way she and Abby had. It was hard to get it back once it was gone.

Elliott poked his head through the door. "You want coffee or tea?"

"Coffee would be great."

"You okay?" Elliott came closer, peering at her like she needed assessing.

"I'm fine, honey."

"You look . . . contemplative."

"Phillip's late," she answered. She wasn't only anxious to get the meeting over with, she had a nagging fear that Phillip was bringing bad news. She had never stayed abreast of the business, because Mitch kept details sketchy, but the papers told her that the real estate business had been rocky. Thank God for Mitch's insistence on a safety net. He always kept at least a year's wages in the bank—more after the boys got out of school—his "just in case" fund. So while the business had suffered, she knew they could manage until the market righted itself. There would be life insurance, too; it would help with the mortgage and Becca's education. Still, that niggling worry that there was something she didn't know.

She reached into her pocket and gripped the stone she'd taken from Mitch's jacket. Her rock rosary.

"Why does he want to meet with all of us?" Elliott asked.

"I think he wants you boys to know where things stand," she answered as she squeezed the stone. There was the matter of Phillip, too. Mitch had thought of him as a brother, had since their frat boy days at USC, even though the allegiance wasn't deserved. Could she trust him? His personal life was often in shambles. Several marriages, and he'd cheated on his wives—not that she was one to judge. Come to think of it, his partnership with her husband was the one stable relationship Phillip had.

"Coffee's ready," Sims yelled out.

Lena started to stand but Elliott motioned her to stay seated. "I'll get it."

More commotion as Becca bounded down the stairs, Abby close behind. Becca wore her sweat pants and fleece zip-up, her hair gathered in a ponytail.

"You should have some breakfast before you run," Abby said as they reached the bottom of the steps. Abby wore a bulky cardigan with thick wooden buttons.

"I'll eat later. Don't like to run on a full stomach." Becca tightened the laces on her running shoes.

"But you need energy. You'll run farther if you have a little something."

Lena found it amusing that Abby had assumed her role as food police in this Becca issue. "Please, a Power Bar at least," Lena would often say, and Becca would pretend not to hear. Then Lena would insert herself in front of the door, holding up a banana. Becca would grimace as she broke off a chunk to eat on her way out.

"Back in a few," Becca said and was out the door.

"That child is no bigger around than a twig," Abby commented, hands braced on her ample hips. Lena wasn't ready for this conversation. She had expected the boys to raise the "Becca matter," especially after her outcry at the funeral, but so far, it hadn't surfaced. What would she say when it did?

Elliott carried in the tray, Sims close behind him, and Abby helped herself to coffee cake as she sat in a rocker by the window. She took a large bite, crumbs sprinkling down the front of her sweater like dandruff. Abby didn't look half-starved, or anything close to it, yet she stuffed the pastry into her mouth like it might be snatched away from her.

The doorbell rang.

When Sims answered the door, he pulled Phillip into the corner of the entry hall and whispered something to him. Whatever Phillip answered had Sims shaking his head, his mouth pressed into a grim frown. Something tightened under Lena's sternum. She didn't stand as he came into the living room, carrying a bulging soft leather briefcase in one hand, a steaming Starbucks cup in the other. He wore a gray basket-weave tweed and maroon tie. His steel-colored hair and goatee could use a trim, and would turn a shade darker after a visit to whatever expensive hair salon he used. Mitch had once described an argument he'd had with his partner: "Sixty dollar haircuts are not a business expense."

Abby said, "Phillip! Nice of you to join us. Guess our coffee wasn't good enough for you?"

"Abby," Lena said crisply, but she noticed her boys doing little to hide their grins.

"I couldn't wait for the caffeine," Phillip said, dropping into the sofa and opening the briefcase on the narrow coffee table. He patted his jacket and shirt pockets like he'd lost something, then rummaged through the briefcase for a pen. "Shall we get started?"

Elliott sat beside Lena, his knees bumping against each other, his gaze flitting around the room as if he wasn't sure where he fit in. Sims took Mitch's chair, sitting forward, notebook in hand, eyes fixed on Phillip. She could count on him to ask the right questions. Abby helped herself to another slice of coffeecake. Lena wasn't sure Abby should be there—this was a

Hastings family matter—but Abby might come up with questions Lena never thought of.

"Let me start," Phillip said, "by saying that the business is as solid as it can be in the current market. But we've taken a hit over the past sixteen months. A sizeable one. I've been working on a huge deal since June, one I thought would keep us going until the market improves. Unfortunately, it's not looking good."

"What kind of deal?" Abby asked. "What happened?"

"Commercial. We bought a strip mall when we learned of a large anchor store coming into the northeast section of town. If it happened, the strip mall would have quadrupled in value. It would have saved our butts."

"What kind of store?" Elliott asked.

"Wal-Mart. A stupid Super Wal-Mart." He huffed out a laugh that was too loud and pitched too high. Lena clutched the stone.

Phillip rifled through his papers. "Sorry. The store's going north of Sandhills. So our strip mall is worth . . . pretty much nothing."

"How much did you invest?" Abby asked.

He ignored the question and turned back to Lena. "I wanted to get accurate numbers from the bank in case we were talking about buyout here. To be honest, I wouldn't recommend that, not right now. With the economy like it is, all I can offer is half the value of our assets. And since almost all of our money is tied up in real estate, and the real estate market is in the tank right now—well, you'd be better off letting me build up revenue before I buy out Mitch's side of the business."

Sims looked up from his notebook. "How much capital does the firm have?"

Phillip eyed Sims then Lena. "Right now, we have forty-three thousand in the bank."

"That's all?" Sims stiffened.

"Over a million in investments. At least, they were worth that twenty-six months ago. Now—I don't even want to look into what they're worth. It's too depressing."

"Depressing or not, you sure as hell better look into it!" Abby's voice overwhelmed the room. "And how much did you put in the worthless strip mall?"

"The real estate world is fickle. We may still sell the mall. Any big sale now can make a world of difference."

Abby's scowl made him look away.

"I've got Dad's phone," Sims said. "The son-of-a-bitch you've been dealing with has called a dozen times. Maybe if you'd been around this deal might have happened."

Phillip didn't reply.

"What happens now? What happens to Mom and Becca?" Elliott's voice sounded so young that Lena fought an impulse to pat his leg and assure him everything would be okay. She would not lie. Her sons would be treated like adults.

"What about the reserve fund?" Lena asked. Both sons looked at her. She added, "Mitch always kept a rainy day fund."

"He was always the cautious one," Phillip said with an edge of sadness.

"Then there is more money." Elliott's knees bumped with more vigor.

"Of course," Lena answered, watching Phillip, who was busy looking everywhere but at her.

"This money was in the business account?" Sims asked. "Or personal savings?"

"Business," Phillip replied. "I'm not sure about his personal accounts. Lena has those records. They'll be frozen until they're made into estate accounts."

Lena didn't know how much was in the bank. She didn't want her sons to think her helpless, unable to manage the household finances. Worse would be for her daughter to think she needed a man to take care of her. How had she let this happen?

"What's the situation with the reserve account?" Sims asked.

A taut silence fell between them. Abby stood and walked over to the sofa. "Well? What's the story, Phillip?" she demanded.

He looked at Lena. "The reserve account is nearly dry."

"What the hell happened to it? When was the rainy day?" Abby demanded.

"We've had twenty-six months of rain thanks to the economy but that's not what happened to the account." When he looked at her again she sensed him telepathically trying to tell her something.

"I don't understand," Elliott said. "Dad was always so careful with money."

"Of course he was." Sims looked at her, too. A fist squeezed her lungs.

"My cancer." The truth closed around her. "When I was sick. Mitch stayed home to take care of me. That's when he spent down the account."

"He knew where he needed to be," Phillip said. "Business was slow, so I told him to tap into the reserves. But we had no idea how far down the

151

market would go. Who could have guessed? Things will turn around. That's what we kept saying to each other. We've ridden dips before. Hell, we opened shop in the eighties, things seriously sucked then. But not like these last twenty-six months."

How had Mitch kept that from her? Why had he? She felt dizzy from this new information. What would happen to them?

Phillip flicked the pen as he studied her oldest son. "There's one more thing we can consider here. Mitch used to talk about bringing you into the firm, Sims. He and I both know you're an astute business man. Banking has given you a great foundation, and you work under me until you get your own realtor license. Calloway and Hastings can continue for another generation."

Sims's eyes widened.

"I'm serious. The Hastings name means something in this town, thanks to your father. I can't think of anything that would make your dad happier than to have you pick up where he left off."

Lena stared at her husband's friend, astounded. What kind of game was Phillip playing?

"Is that what you want, Sims?" Abby asked. "Did Mitch ever talk with you about it?"

"A few times. But I'm not the salesman he was. That's not my strength. Or my interest."

"You could learn." Phillip spoke with more energy now. "And Elliott, there's room for you, too. I know you've got that music thing going in New York, but if you ever get tired of it, we have room for you with the company."

Lena heard condescension in his tone when he said, "that music thing."

"You could be a realtor, Ell," Abby said. "You could sell ice cream to Eskimos if that's what you wanted to do. But would you be happy?"

"Absolutely not," Lena said, looking hard at her younger son. "You are a gifted musician. You've worked hard on your career and your dad was very proud of you. Don't even think about giving that up."

"Nobody needs to decide anything right now," Phillip said. "Both of you should give it some thought. And Lena, if you do want me to buy you out, we'll need to set up a meeting with your attorney. Again, now is not a good time to do that."

"I'll need some time to think about all this." Lena stood, eager for this meeting to be over. She had so much to consider. So much to learn. The depletion of the reserve account changed everything. It made them vulnerable in a way she hadn't expected. She needed to review their personal accounts and Mitch's life insurance policy and found herself a little nauseated from this news.

"Okay." Phillip gathered his papers in a stack and handed them to Sims. "You might want to review these financials. Call me if you have any questions. If I don't hear from you, I'll check in at the end of the week."

CHAPTER 16

Becca leaned against the tree, stretching one leg, then the other, eager to start her run. She had seen Mr. Calloway's silver Audi pulling into the drive for the big meeting, which she was glad to miss. They had probably talked about the problems with the real estate company. When was Mom going to find out about the second mortgage on the house? And the other money problems? What was Mom going to do? She didn't work. She was good at spending money, not making it.

Best not to think about that now. Just as she collected her hair in a scrunchy, the cell phone rang: Dylan.

"Hey Becca."

Hearing his voice made something tickle in her chest.

"How are you? You okay?" He spoke fast, like he was nervous, which made her like him even more.

"I'm okay. Getting ready to run."

"Oh, sorry. If it's a bad time—"

"Not a bad time at all. How's school? I don't suppose it burned down while I was out."

"You wish."

"What's been going on?" Becca didn't need to know—Kayla had covered all the relevant gossip on who was dating whom, what stupid assignments she had to finish. But she let Dylan tell her anyway, savoring his concern when he said, "Don't worry about this. It's all crap. When are you coming back?"

"Tomorrow." She plunked down on a patch of bristly grass between the sidewalk and the road. "I can't believe I'm looking forward to it."

"That's . . . weird."

"I just want normal. I can barely remember what normal is," she answered.

He didn't say anything for a few beats, and she wondered if she shouldn't have said that bit about "normal." Dylan never needed to know how far from "normal" she was.

"Sometimes normal is important," he answered. "I'm sure ready for you to get back. You owe me a lunch date."

Becca smiled at the thought of lunch with him. Maybe it would become a daily thing. After, they'd sit under one of the oak trees till the bell rang. It would become their tree.

"Thanks for the card," she said. Elliot had found it stuck in the storm door.

"Hope it wasn't too dorky. I looked through a bunch of them. They all had embossed flowers and crosses and stuff. Didn't seem to fit you."

"No, it was perfect." She smiled that he knew what "fit" her. The card had a yellow dog with its head hanging down and inside it said, "Sometimes life sucks." No other message, except Dylan's name in blue, printed. The D plain, with no elaborate hoops. She'd wedged the card between the frame and the mirror on her dresser.

"When did you bring it over?" she asked.

"Yesterday. Dad never lets me have the car, so I had to do some tricky familial maneuvering."

"Oh yeah? Tell me."

He huffed out another laugh. "No way. You don't want to hear about my family. Trust me."

"I said I wanted normal."

"Normal is not a word you'd use if you knew them."

She imagined walking down the hall at school with Dylan, their hands entwined. He'd kiss her before they went in to class. Every night they would talk on the phone until time to go to sleep. Maybe he would sneak over to her house, throw rocks at her window, and she would tiptoe outside where they'd lie in the grass looking up at the moon.

"Okay, if you really want to know," Dylan said. "Here's how I got the car: Mom was at work, which kind of sucked because she's an easier mark. My brother Dwight was watching wrestling, so I knew he'd be tied up for a while. I saw a light on in the sad little room Dad calls his office. Dad can't stand to be interrupted. He claims it disturbs his work but he's playing on-line poker or checking out porn . . . never mind." Dylan cleared his throat.

Becca grinned at the image of Dylan's face flushing pink. "So your dad was researching exotic photos?"

"Uh, yeah. So I go to the office and cough and the uhm . . . exotic pictures disappear fast."

"That's very respectful of you."

"I ask if I can use the car. Dad looks at me like I've asked permission to blow up the kitchen and says no. It's this stupid game we do. I want something, he holds it out of reach."

Dylan's voice darkened. "He asks me where I'm going. I tell him I want to go to Jim's house to borrow history notes for a test next week."

"You're a good liar. I'll have to remember that."

"Well, it's required in my house. So Dad scratches his chin like he actually cares what the hell I'm doing. Just another part of the game. Am I boring you?"

"No, I like hearing about a screwed up family that isn't mine."

"Then Dad makes some comment about Mr. Whedon having gone to Clemson, and launches into his own stellar scholastic career: two years at Tech in automotive repair. He says he makes twenty thousand more than Jim's dad and I sure don't tell him that Jim's dad is an electrical engineer who drives a BMW."

Becca decided Dylan's dad was an ass. "How did you get the car?"

"I had a brilliant insight. We share one computer, so I tell him I could email Jim, ask him to scan the notes and send them. Of course, the computer is so slow, it'll take a while . . ."

"Which would seriously interfere with his exotic photo research."

"Exactly." He sort of laughed out the word. "He gives me the keys, then I get the one card the CVS had that wasn't filled with Bible verses, and find your house."

She plucked up a blade of brown grass. "Sorry I wasn't home."

"You live in a much nicer area than I do. Your house is very . . . big."

"We may have to move somewhere smaller." She pictured her and her mom alone in the house, and the giant mortgage that would have to be paid.

"Maybe you'll end up on my side of town. Well, I'll let you get back to your running. I'll see you in school tomorrow," he said.

"And we're having lunch," she said with a smile.

Becca felt a warm energy inside as she tucked the phone back in her pocket and resumed her stretches. Her muscles would flex like smooth elastic when she was in shape, but they felt hard as rocks after so many days without exercise. A few more bends and she was off.

Becca could run fast when she had a mind to, and her thoughts about Dylan put bounce in every step. She didn't slow for the bulldog behind the picket fence. She sailed across Forest Drive, passing cars stopped at a red light. She felt like a racehorse, not even feeling her legs underneath her, breath puffing out faster and faster. At the garden shed already—a half mile.

How far would she go today? Maybe she'd keep running. She had no desire to return home.

Yesterday she'd had a slip with the Doritos like the night of the funeral. But with Dad dying and all the confusion, a few mistakes could be forgiven. She was back in control now. She'd run off those calories and start afresh.

The hill on Trenholm Road winded her but she did not slow as she crested it and let the downhill side pull her even faster. She didn't worry about stumbling, about some bump in the sidewalk throwing her off stride. She was reckless. Breathless. Breakneck.

Free.

She made the automatic turn that led to the park, but she wouldn't loop it like she normally did. This time she would shoot like an arrow through the middle, not pausing for a drink of water from the fountain, not circling the playground where the little kids climbed about in the sandbox.

And then it hit. A pain stabbed like a knife in her side. She almost tripped trying to stop, her hand groping at the searing spot under her ribs. A cramp, she'd had them before, only this felt so much worse and she thought she might throw up, and not on purpose.

She found a bench, grabbed the back of it and bent forward, frantic to relieve the pain. It didn't work. Her legs tightened, a spasm lightening up her thighs, and she pulled herself around to collapse on the seat. She gulped in shallow pockets of air. What was happening to her?

All she could do was try to breathe away the pain. She leaned over, her side on the bench now, her hands pressing against her gut. The maple tree towering above her blurred, green slurring into the gray, into the blue of the sky. Cold. She felt cold. Shivering.

• • •

JOE BOOKER TIGHTENED HIS coat against the cold breeze. It had been a long day of walking, of battling the demon. He rounded the corner and eyed the park ahead, the one with the shade trees and the swing set. There was a bench where he liked to sit when the sunset filled the sky with color, and the voices inside weren't too loud. Or times like today, when he could watch a storm roll in. Papa had loved storms, too, though mostly he liked heat lightning. "Flashbulbs going off behind the clouds," he'd say.

Someone was there, on his bench. A small person, tilted over like she was napping. No matter, he'd find another spot if he kept walking. He slowed though, studying the girl and wondering if he should wake her before the police spotted her. The girl had a sweatshirt on, the hood pulled up. Nice running shoes, toes dug into the dirt. A pale hand, a nice watch, strands of hair over her face. Shiny hair, not like Rag Doll's matted mess.

"Help her." The voice spoke in a private whisper.

Joe stumbled back at the sound. After so long, he'd almost forgotten. The voice filled him with fear and wonder and made him want to run but he couldn't.

"Help her."

After all this time, the Lord had called to him. He wanted Joe to help the girl? He had to follow the instructions, do what was asked or else the Lord might give up on him again. He inched closer to the girl and touched her shoulder. Her head shifted, tendrils of hair slipping from her face. Joe leaned over, recognizing the small nose, the pink shivering lips. Mr. Mitch's girl.

"Help her."

He nudged her harder but she wouldn't wake. "Miss? Miss!" The skin on her neck felt cold and trembly. Sick. Mr. Mitch's girl was bad sick.

Panicked, he looked around for someone to help but they were alone, no joggers or dog walkers were anywhere close. He ran to the street and, just as a traffic light turned green, stepped off the curb, waving his long arms at the cars rushing by.

Horns blared. A man yelled, "Get out the way, nigger." A van screeched as it maneuvered around him. Joe waved harder, pointing to the park and saying, "She need help, she need help," but nobody stopped, because it was Joe that was asking.

The church. He could get her to the church and Reverend Bill would help, but that was several miles away. He hurried back to the bench but she hadn't moved. He worried about touching her, but worse was leaving her alone sick like she was. He wiped his hands against his trousers, wishing he could wash them before lifting the fragile child, but he didn't have that kind of time. She didn't weigh more than a sack of turnips. He cradled her against his chest, being so careful, not wanting to jostle her as he crossed the busy street towards the crowded mall. People glared. One man coming from a grocery store yelled, "Hey!" but Joe didn't think he had any intent to be helpful so he kept moving. He could feel the girl's heartbeat, a fast, fluttering thing and it made him grateful. A beating heart meant she was alive.

He glanced at the storefronts. If he carried her inside one, would they help? He'd never been one to trust strangers. He was all alone with his terrifying burden. And instructions from the Lord.

"Miss? Can you hear me, Miss?" He lowered his head to speak into her ear. "I'm gonna get you some help, I promise."

Should he take her to Mr. Mitch's house? That would take a good thirty minutes of walking and what if nobody was there? The hospital? If he moved fast—and he could, even with the child—he'd get there in a half hour. The girl needed doctoring, and the Lord was counting on him.

She shook in his arms. Cold. That sweatshirt wasn't enough with the breeze coming in like it was. He hurried to a bench and placed her there so he could remove his coat and wrap her in it. When he scooped her up again, she wasn't trembling as bad. Still so pale, though. Pale as Mama's bed sheets.

"Hurry." The Lord sounded more urgent now, and Joe obliged. He bore her like a toddler, his coat secure around her, ignoring the stares from people he passed.

He was out of breath when he reached the street in front of the hospital. Sweat poured from his face. He eyed the giant white building, all lit up by floodlights, and saw the bright red "Emergency" sign pointing to a covered entrance. As he hurried to that door, a man stopped him.

"What you got there?" He wore a light blue shirt and cap, his thumbs looped in a creaky leather belt. A cop of some kind, looking at Joe the way cops always did.

"He knows you're a son of a bitch!"

Joe flinched as panic seized him. Satan was right there, in his ear, and he had this child who needed help and a cop not two feet away. The Lord said to help her. That's what he had to do.

Joe side-stepped the cop and tried to push past but he held out an arm, his hand brushing against Mr. Mitch's girl. Joe spun around, out of his grasp.

"I said, what you got there! Is it a girl? Did you hurt someone?" The cop's eyes narrowed.

Joe drew a stuttery breath to calm himself. "It's Mr. Mitch's little girl. I gotta get her help."

"What did you do to her?" When the cop unclipped the Tazer—Joe knew what it was, he'd been buzzed before—attached to his belt, Joe knew what was coming, and no way he'd let the girl get hurt by that thing. He shoved past the man and ran, ran with all he had in him, scrambled between two ambulances, disregarded the shouts from the man and the crackle of his radio as he summoned help. Joe pushed through the glass door, the man at his back, a fierce grip on Joe's shoulder and metal pushed against his ribs. Joe didn't care. He yelled, "Please, please . . . help Mr. Mitch's girl!"

CHAPTER 17

Lena heard squeaks and thuds coming from the laundry room and wondered if it was Elliott. She could do his clothes for him. It might be the distraction she needed after the horrible meeting with Phillip. Soon there would be two of them, her and Becca, and she'd do a few loads a week. How odd to consider the whittling down of her household. For the first time in her whole life, there would be no male in her home. No sons. No husband. She and Becca would have to move into something smaller, given the state of their finances. Where would they go? An apartment? How was she to support them?

"Hope you don't mind that I used the washer." Abby heaved a basket on top of the dryer. "I didn't get to do laundry before I flew out of South America. Pretty tacky of me to bring a suitcase full of dirty clothes."

"Want me to do it for you?" Lena eyed the tangle of sweaters and underwear awaiting its turn in the wash. Abby's underpants were like the briefs they wore as children, except Abby's were wide, with stretched elastic, and a bit yellowed with age. What would it take to get her sister to a lingerie store? The world would end before that happened.

"Hell no. I don't need you to wait on me, Le-Le." Abby pointed to a few pairs of jeans she'd stacked on the washer. "I found some of Becca's stuff in the dryer. I couldn't believe it when I read what size she's wearing. A three. That kid is as tall as I am. If she was a size eleven, she'd be plenty slender enough."

"I know." Lena glanced at her watch. Becca should have returned from her run, but sometimes she stopped at Kayla's instead of coming straight home. No need to worry.

"Have you taken her to a doctor about it?"

"Two years ago she was on the chunky side. Girls go through phases. And we've had a tough few years," Lena said. Becca had suffered through Lena's time with Royce, through Lena's cancer, and now losing her father. "And yes, I worry. I keep hoping she'll outgrow it."

"Well," Abby said, punctuated by a puff of air. "It is a helluva time. I wouldn't be her age again for anything."

Lena felt relieved that the conversation had shifted away from any implied blame about Lena's mothering. She'd had enough crap dealt to her for one day.

"I brewed more coffee. It seems to be my cure for jet lag. Care to join me?" Abby motioned toward the kitchen. Lena followed, approaching the coffee maker with caution. The beverage smelled like scorched firewood.

"We make it strong in South America," Abby said. "You'll like it if you add enough milk."

She poured Lena half a cup, and Lena added a generous portion of half and half. Abby helped herself to Lena's seat, the one closest to the window. "You were a mess when you were Becca's age. You were trying out for cheerleader and you and Sarah Steadmire would practice those damn cheers for hours."

"I'd forgotten that." Lena stepped around Mitch's chair to Becca's place.

"You obsessed about getting the cartwheel exactly right. Watching you practice that over and over got me nauseated. But damn, you were determined. You and Sarah both made the squad. My preppy little sis."

"My hippie big sister," Lena said with a smirk. "Wearing that poncho and braids. Smoking pot behind the shrubs during lunch."

Abby's laugh was pitched low, from the belly. "Eddie Pierce dealt some damn fine weed, but you wouldn't even try it. Goody two shoes. We couldn't have been more different, you and I."

That statement rang more true today than when they were young. Abby living a brave life in another hemisphere. Lena hanging on by fingernails in suburbia South Carolina.

"Why did you quit cheering? You loved it. You especially liked Will Waterson making eyes at you when you wore your cheer outfit on game day."

"He didn't!" Lena covered her mouth, remembering how it felt to be fifteen with dreamy, blue-eyed Will winking at her. Life for her then was all about Fridays, when she'd take more time with her hair and makeup, when she lingered in front of the mirror to make sure the pleats in the cheerleading skirt hung just right. When she hesitated in the halls between classes, sashaying in purple and white. On Fridays, she wasn't anonymous.

"Why did you quit? You cheered for that one year."

"It took up too much time." A partial truth. She had loved so much about cheering: the way it felt to move in perfect harmony with the other girls. Bouncing on her toes and jostling the pom-poms before an eager crowd, smiling at the little girls who tried to mimic her. But getting her to practice and games inconvenienced her parents. After the final football game, when her father came to get her, she smelled alcohol each time he exhaled. He drove slowly, the car weaving between lanes and Lena holding her breath that they'd make it home without wrecking. How horrified she'd been when Will Watterson's red Barracuda pulled up beside their station wagon, Will hanging out the window and asking if everything was okay.

She quit the cheer squad that next day.

"But it got you out of the house," Abby said. "That was the important thing. I had the school newspaper and that part-time job to keep me away from the parental crossfire. But when you gave up cheering, you were stuck." Abby said it so matter-of-factly, digging up the family skeleton and plopping it on the table before them. What was the point, after all these years?

"I wasn't stuck." A lie, of course, because stuck was how she felt. Not that their parents fought often. More frequent were the quiet, icy times, when Mom looked so worn down by her life, when Dad began his trips to the vodka under the sink as soon as he got home. When he was a gregarious drunk, Lena tolerated him. A few slurred words could be overlooked. But when he was angry, those were the difficult nights. Lena remembered closing the door to the bedroom she shared with Abby, and turning on the radio to drown out the drunken diatribe in the living room. Her mother didn't stand a chance.

"I abandoned you when I went off to college. But I couldn't wait to get the hell out of there."

"Was that why you didn't ever come home?" Lena's voice hesitated on that last word as unexpected feelings surfaced. She had felt abandoned. Abby came home a few days for Christmas, a week or so in the summer, but never really connected with the family after she made her college escape, leaving Lena in the rubble of their family.

"Yeah." She looked into her mug of coffee. "Sometimes I think when I left home, I never found a new one. I've lived like a vagabond, haven't I?"

"You live the way you want to live. Your work has been your life." Lena had always used their mother's words in explaining Abby's departure. Abby was doing important things. Noble things. Abby was unique, brave, brilliant. Too big for Columbia or even South Carolina. Other countries needed her and the US government paid Abby to help them. Lena could still picture her mother's glowing smile when talking about her stellar firstborn.

"It used to feel that way. Not so much now." Abby clicked the rim of her cup with a dirty finger nail.

"What are you doing? I never have a handle on that. I always pray you're somewhere safe and happy."

Abby didn't answer. Her eyes, over the rim of her clutched mug, stared at the table. "Safe and happy. Interesting words."

Outside, there was the click and whir of the automatic sprinkler turning on in the back yard. Mitch had installed it a few years ago for his lawn and flowers, but now the grass had died to a dull brown. No periwinkles or confederate roses bloomed anymore, yet Lena had no idea how to shut off the system. She was watering dead things.

"I've been in this remote village in southern Peru. Helping the farmers learn to rotate their crops," Abby said. "And we built a school for their kids. This place is so poor and isolated, and the villagers worked with us, so proud that they would have a school.

"Only it's not there anymore. You have to understand—things are different in that part of the world. Like another universe. We do our best to help, but so many things work against us. So many things." A darkness crept into Abby's voice.

Lena wasn't sure she wanted to know why—the weight of worry for her sister piled onto her other burdens. "What happened?"

"They destroyed the school. Burned it to the ground. See, we'd been working with the farmers to harvest root vegetables rather than coca."

"Chocolate?"

Abby huffed out a laugh. "Not hardly. Coca that they make cocaine from. The traffickers controlling this region wanted to make a point so the farmers would do what they commanded, so they destroyed the school, and any hope that things could change."

Lena had never seen Abby with tears in her eyes. At least, not as an adult.

"We can't go back to rebuild because it's too dangerous. You put in so much hard work and watch it go up in smoke. For nothing. Not one God-damn thing." A knife edge gleamed in her sister's words.

"Can't the police do something?"

"The politics are dirty, Le-Le. The traffickers are linked to a guerilla group that is very powerful. They make a fortune in the drug trade and don't give a rip who they hurt. In Tingo Maria, that's the little village where I've been working, the natives are fine, simple people who still practice the customs of their ancestors. But the coca trade has taken over. They kill and destroy anything that stands in their way. Nobody can stop them." Abby blinked and looked away.

Lena looked away, too, because watching Abby cry disturbed her. Abby was invincible. Abby didn't cry.

"Shit." Abby wiped her eyes with the back of her hand. "I didn't mean to lay that on you."

"No, it's okay." Lena moved to the coffee pot and refilled her mug even though she'd hardly drunk a drop. "How do you stand it? It sounds so dangerous."

She shrugged. "I've gotten good at keeping my head down. It was easier doing the work when I felt like I made a difference. Now . . . I don't know."

"Then why do you stay? Why don't you come back to America?" Knowing Abby's situation made Lena a little angry at her. She could have come home. She could have been a part of Lena's life. How might things be different if her sister had been here?

"I do have a reason. A very good reason." Abby flashed a nervous smile. "I have a new love in my life."

"Really?" Lena heard the impatience in her own voice at the thought of another of Abby's boyfriends.

"It's not what you think," Abby said, rising and taking her cup to the sink. "It's not a man, it's a little boy. His name is Esteban."

Lena heard a different tone in her sister's voice, like she was suddenly years younger. "Esteban," Lena repeated.

"He's only five years old. He's been in an orphanage since he was one. I'm trying to adopt him."

"You're adopting a child?" She tried to picture Abby as a mom. Abby as a fighter, a teacher, an advocate—these roles she could see. But a mother?

"You were the one who played with dolls," Abby said. "I had the Tonka truck collection. I thought the motherhood gene had skipped me. But then I met Esteban. The orphanage was right beside the school we built. He was this scrawny little creature with huge black eyes and knobby limbs, and he would stare at us from the playground. All the other kids would beg us for things—food, money, anything. But not Esteban. He just watched. One day, I brought him a cookie. He didn't take it at first, but finally he did. He broke off a small bit and ate it, all the while staring at me. Then he snapped the cookie in half and gave me part of it. This child is nearly starving but he wants to share his cookie. So we ate, and then he gave me the biggest, most adorable smile I'd ever seen. That did it." Speaking of this made a light shine out of Abby.

"He's half-native, the Jebero tribe," she went on. "The orphanage is underfunded so he didn't get very good care early on. He's developmentally delayed and too thin but they've let me hire help to work with him. He couldn't say but a few words when I met him but he's quite the chatterbox now."

"When will you get him?"

"I'd have gotten him months ago if I could have. There's some legal BS I have to contest. Corruption is everywhere where I live. They've made the red tape more elaborate, which means I have more people I have to bribe. The latest set-back has to do with my age. Some new regulation about nobody over fifty-five adopting, and I'll reach that milestone this year. More bullshit."

"Good thing you're so persistent." Lena tried to picture her sister in this new role. Reading stories at bedtime. Playing Candyland and Go Fish. Attending PTA meetings at his school. These pictures rushed through her mind and she found she could accept them. Abby was a strong, determined woman who could do anything. Maybe motherhood would make her sink roots into the earth.

"For Esteban, I can be as stubborn as hell. I just wish—" she hesitated, her grin uncertain. "It's been a long battle. I wish it was over."

Maybe now Abby would settle down. Maybe not even stay in South America, but come home to the US, to be a part of their lives again. She started to ask about that possibility, but was interrupted by the ringing phone.

CHAPTER 18

How Becca could sleep in the cold, antiseptic hospital room, with nurses and techs in and out, with the light turning off and on, with rattling medication carts out in the hall, baffled Lena. The drugs probably. Needles pressed into Becca's pale arm. Tubes snaking to plastic sacks on a metal pole. At least she didn't have as many machines monitoring her as had been attached to Mitch.

Still. The room. The waiting. The crawl of fear.

Ketoacidosis. This is what Dr. Burnside had called it, the condition that made Lena's daughter collapse on a bench in the park. That almost killed her.

Ketoacidosis happened because her electrolytes were so out of balance that her body turned on itself. It happened because Becca had starved herself. Nearly destroyed herself. Keeping it all a secret—God, there had been too many secrets in their home, and that had to end now.

Slow suicide, Dr. Burnside had said, talking of Becca's anorexia. Lena had thought him cruel to use that word, but knew Liam Burnside wanted to make sure she didn't take this lightly. She didn't, of course. Becca had been drifting away for months, but Lena didn't know how far she had gone, and now she held on to Becca by less than a thread.

"If she stabilizes, you can take her home tomorrow," Liam had said. "I've arranged for a psychiatric consult. I want her to keep seeing Dr. Owens when she gets out."

Tomorrow? It scared Lena to think of taking Becca home, of what might happen. She needed Mitch—Mitch would know what to do.

Her cell phone vibrated in her pocket. Another text from Royce, she was sure. She'd responded to none of them, hoping her silence would send the message. Royce had always been a stubborn man.

The door inched open, letting in a slice of fluorescent light. Elliott entered, followed by Sims. Elliott came to her and slid an arm around her shoulders. Her affectionate boy. Sims stood at the foot of Becca's bed, whiskered and smelling of cigarette smoke. She could see the outline of a pack of Salems in the breast pocket of his shirt.

"Mom?" Elliott's voice was timid. "I need to tell you something."

She pursed her lips at his confessional tone, as though he was seventeen again and had attached his father's Pontiac to the mailbox post.

"The other night, after everybody left, I found Becca in the kitchen eating. It looked like she'd finished a hunk of beef and a dozen cookies. Later I heard her in the bathroom throwing up. She said she had an upset stomach. I think she did the same thing last night. I should have mentioned it to you but you've got enough going on."

Lena had heard the same thing a month or so ago. "Just ate too many fries," Becca had said, and Lena had wanted it to be true. So many little signs: the breakfast battles. The weight loss. When was the last time she'd had to buy feminine products for her daughter? Had menses halted?

"How long has she been pulling this stuff?" Sims asked.

"Dr. Burnside said it's been a while. She may have damage to her teeth." The acid from her daughter's vomit ate away at the enamel, he had told her. Dear God.

"Making herself puke for months? That's revolting," Sims said.

Elliott spun around to face him. "She's sick. She can't help it."

"It's being a teenager," Sims commented. "All the damn pressure. You have to be thin. Wear perfect clothes. Hang out with the popular kids or be treated like scum."

Lena wished it was that simple.

Elliott said, "I know someone with an eating disorder. She used to be in my band."

"So what? She barfed between sets?" Sims's voice was gruff, probably to annoy Elliott.

"No," Elliott answered. "She's in recovery now. But it's been a long road. I think she was a little older than Becca when it started. She's been hospitalized five times. At her worst, she weighed eighty-four pounds."

Lena examined the subtle contours of her daughter under the dull white sheet. Dr. Burnside said she weighed ninety-three.

"Jesus. She almost killed herself to be skinny? To look good in a bikini?" Sims patted his shirt pocket, then retracted his hand.

"I wish you'd quit being a dick." Elliott's voice swelled in the small, sterile room. Lena glared. Elliott shrugged an apology, but only to please her. He glowered at Sims.

Lena thought of Becca as a fifth grader, readying for a ballet recital, the tutu a little snug around her plump belly. Starting middle school, crying in Belk's dressing room because she couldn't squeeze into a size nine pair of jeans. "I'm so fat," she had said between snuffles.

"You're growing. Your body changes every day," Lena had replied.

"What if I get fatter and fatter! I don't want to look like Connie."

"Well, maybe if you tried a little exercise." Lena had just wanted her off the couch, away from the computer and TV. She wanted Becca to eat healthy things, instead of hamburgers, fries, and candy bars, but what if Becca thought she meant something else?

And two summers ago, Becca trying on a bathing suit, her eyes tearing up when Lena suggested a one-piece might be more flattering. That had been their last shopping trip before Lena moved out, got her own apartment and started a new—however brief—life.

Elliott lifted a finger at Sims. "The point isn't trying to be skinny. The point is control. The point is slowly erasing yourself."

His words rumbled through the room, an earthquake.

"I don't want to scare you guys," Elliott said.

"Oh, you don't?" Sims asked.

"I want you to take it seriously."

"She's in a damn hospital. We get it that this is serious," Sims said.

"Boys," Lena cautioned, weary of this endless tension between them. Elliott inched closer to her, head cocked to the side.

"She's going to be okay," Elliott said. "We'll get her in counseling. I'm going to be here more, I promise."

She patted his hand. Elliott would try, but his world was no longer Columbia.

"You're not alone with this, Mom," Sims said. "Connie and I will help however we can."

Her well-meaning boys. They loved Lena, but in truth, they loved who they thought she was.

When Lena had left Mitch, she had taken three suitcases and all her art supplies. The loft apartment was the third she visited, right in the heart of the Vista downtown, close to the river. Natural light poured through the tall windows. Exposed beams on the ceiling would hold hooks for her ferns and purple heart plants. There were two bedrooms, one for her and Royce, the other for Becca. Only it wasn't. Lena placed her easel there, converting it into an art studio, with a futon in the corner that Becca could use on the weekends she stayed over. She never did. She was too angry. The separation lasted six weeks. Elliott never knew about it. Sims chose to believe it was a brief menopausal folly.

Both boys danced around the truth but Becca never learned how. No more secrets though. That was Lena's pledge to Becca. And to Mitch.

"You should go home," Lena said to the boys.

"I can stay," Elliott replied.

"No."

Both sons stared.

"I mean there's nothing you can do here. Sims, drop Elliott by the house. I'll stay the night with Becca."

• • •

JOE BOOKER CIRCLED THE tiny room like a caged leopard. The man had told him to wait, but not given Joe any choice when he locked him inside. Nothing in the room but two chairs and a table. No window, except a tiny one in the door. A magazine had tattered corners and a picture of football players on the cover. Joe had played ball in high school. It was something he was good at doing, but that was a long time ago.

He hated waiting, especially indoors. Worse was not knowing if Mr. Mitch's girl was all right. She was shivering when they took her from him, and cried out when they put her on the gurney. When he tried to follow her, the blue-uniform guy wrenched his arm behind him and shoved him down the hall into this place. The click of the door lock echoed in his head.

"You're getting what's coming to you," the voice snarled in his head.

Joe nodded. He was long overdue for what was coming to him, but please not here. Not in this tiny room.

His stomach grumbled. Supper at the Methodist church was long over. How long had he been here? Nighttime by now. He needed to get to his squat; Mr. Wortham Pinckney would be expecting him. He felt pressure like a stone in his bladder, but there would be no relieving himself in this small space. The gray walls pushed in; he could feel the weight of the ceiling like a giant hand on his head.

"About damn time they lock you up."

No. He couldn't go to jail. Not again. Never ever again. It had happened in the army when he got into a ruckus with a drunk officer. Worse was the time they busted him for trespassing and tussling with two cops. Said they were gonna throw away the key and damned if they didn't. The voices so loud in his mind he couldn't help but yell back at them, which landed him in solitary. A cold bed frame, a piss hole, a sink. No pillow or blanket. No escaping the noise inside of him. Days and nights that bled into each other until time stopped mattering. That was when the Lord spoke to him and said, "Believe."

He did believe. He'd done what the Lord asked and here he was, stuck in this hole.

Not for long though, because when they opened the door he'd jump them. He was big and strong and he could move fast when he had a reason. He'd flee this hellhole before they could stop him.

Different voices now. Not in his head. Outside the door. A woman yelled, "Why is he locked up in here?" like she was mad.

A man answering, "We called the police to question him. They ain't showed yet."

"Let me talk to him," the woman said.

"I don't think—"

"You're holding him illegally. You damn sure will let me in," she demanded.

Someone jiggled the doorknob. Joe itched to run but wasn't going to tackle a woman to do it. He flattened himself against the wall, watching as the lock turned, the knob twisted, and the door cracked open.

"About damn time!" The woman pushed herself into the room. He'd never seen her before.

She was a tall, ample woman with long hair the color of fence wire. She wore dark pants, a cape, and scuffed shoes. When she approached, her gray eyes were chin level to Joe.

"You must be Joe." She spoke quieter now, the mean look on her face sliding off.

He nodded, eyeing the blue uniform man behind her, the Tazer still clipped to his belt.

"Leave us alone, please," she said to the man. It wasn't a request. When the man didn't budge, she pointed at the door like someone used to giving out orders. The man made a reluctant retreat.

"Please, sit." She gestured to a chair. Joe wanted to appease her but the room got so much smaller with two of them in there.

"Just for a minute," she added.

He did as he was told.

"You brought my niece Becca to the hospital."

Niece. Mr. Mitch's girl was this lady's niece?

"Forgive me. I meant to introduce myself. My name is Abigail Parker. Call me Abby." She extended a wide hand with bulging knuckles like a man's. Joe didn't like touching people, but didn't want her mad at him, so he gripped the strong fingers.

"I'm trying to understand what happened. Would you mind helping me?"

"Okay." His voice sounded scratchy. He cleared his throat.

"Where did you find Becca?"

He eyed the door behind her. "In the park. On a bench."

"Did she speak to you?"

"No ma'am. She was lying there like she was asleep but she didn't wake up."

"Could you tell she was sick?"

"She was pale. Shaky like. I tried to get somebody to help but nobody paid no attention."

"The way of the world these days." Miss Abby shook her head. "What did you do next?"

He wasn't sure what to say. Would she be mad that he touched her? Might be madder if he didn't answer. "I carried her—I was real careful—away. I wanted to take her to the church so Reverend Bill could help but that was too far."

"Reverend Bill? Bill Tanner?"

"Mr. Mitch goes to that church. Not no more though."

"You knew Mitch?"

"Yes ma'am. He's been good to me."

"You recognized my niece."

"Yes ma'am."

"What happened after you realized you couldn't make it to the church?"

Joe lowered his head, wondering if he could trust this woman with the truth. No matter, it wasn't his truth to hoard. "I did what the Lord wanted. I brung her here."

"You carried her? That had to be several miles." The woman leaned back, shaking her head.

He didn't reply. He remembered his feet pounding up the street, the girl so pale, quivering in his arms. How frightened he'd been that he was too late.

"I'll tell you what you did, Joe. You saved her life. I can't bear to think what would have happened if you hadn't found her."

Joe asked the question that had been poised on his tongue since he arrived. "Is she gonna be okay?"

The lady's eyes got moist. She stared down at the table, scaring Joe that she had bad news about the girl, but then she looked up and gave him a sad little smile. "We think we can take her home tomorrow. But she's got some . . . problems . . . she's going to need help with. But no matter. We'll make sure she gets what she needs."

All that had him confused, but if Mitch's girl was going home, it had to be good news.

"Where do you live?" she asked.

Why would she want to know that? It wasn't her business. He scratched at his leg but the itch was more inside. He could make it to the door in two steps and be gone.

"I don't mean to pry," she said. "Don't suppose you have to tell me. But I want you to know how . . . incredibly grateful we are. Mr. Mitch's family, I mean. I wish there was some way I could repay you."

He shook his head. His reward was to please the Lord.

She reached in her pocket and pulled out two twenty dollar bills. "This is a little something."

"No ma'am—"

"Take it. I insist. Think of it as a gift from Mr. Mitch."

He looked down at the bills she'd tucked in his fingers. "Take it," said the Lord.

As she stood, she said, "I suppose you're ready to get out of this place, huh?"

Joe sprang to his feet, startling the woman. "I see you are," she said with a low laugh. She opened the door. "Don't worry about that security idiot. He's got no reason to hold you."

When he reached the hall, he wasn't sure which way to go. She pointed left, and he could see an exit sign. He walked, then ran, then pushed through the glass door, taking in a deep breath of cool night air.

Free.

CHAPTER 19

Tonya gripped the cell phone and half-listened as her mother blathered on about Buddy's stellar performance with his high school debate team. "We bought him a suit and a red tie and he looked great. He argued with such passion I almost thought our Buddy gave a rat's ass about expanding oil drilling operations in Alaska." Mom laughed. Tonya rolled her eyes.

Traffic on Gervais Street inched along. Behind her, Byron snoozed in his car seat, having drifted off as soon as she got him from daycare. Dinner would be take-out; John had gone to happy hour after work, though he'd promise to buy draft beer instead of the martinis he'd developed an appreciation for, which would save a little money.

She passed the state capital, the Confederate flag hanging limp on its dark metal pole, two tourists snapping photos of a man dressed like a Rebel soldier beside it. "Heritage, not hate," his sign read. If only it were that simple.

"Maybe Buddy can go into politics after college," her mother said. "Run for a house seat first, then a senate seat, or even governor." She pronounced it "guv-nuh."

"You've given this some thought," Tonya answered with a smirk. Buddy would last approximately seven minutes in a campaign for office. Tonya could picture him being challenged by a TV reporter and screaming, "Go screw yourself," before being bleeped off the screen.

"How's your nose?" her mom asked.

"A little sore's all. Byron's doing okay, too." That morning, John had suggested taking Byron to physical therapy: "Just to make sure he's healing okay." A few clicks of the desktop mouse showed Tonya that John was still emailing Carol the paralegal, who'd suggested the consult. John wanted to make their injuries look worse than they were, treating the car crash like a winning lottery ticket. Tonya still hadn't signed the papers so Carol's firm could represent them, something he brought up again over breakfast.

"Are you still in the rental car?"

"The van was totaled." Tonya missed it. The way the bucket seat molded to her fanny. The purple Sharpie mark on the console from when Byron snuck the marker from her purse. The tiny brown dots on the ceiling left when John flicked the straw out of his chocolate shake. A little room on wheels where she lived part of every day, now a hunk of scrap metal.

"You should get a Volvo," her mom said. "They're very safe."

"A Volvo? Are you kidding me?"

"A Volvo wagon. Safe, sturdy, and quite comfortable."

Tonya swerved into the left lane and squeezed the gas pedal, her fingers coiled tighter around the steering wheel. Sure, a Volvo. Why not a BMW or Mercedes like Mom had?

"Tonya?"

"We cannot afford a Volvo. Christ, Mom. We'll be lucky to buy a used van the same age as the old one. With our mortgage, and Byron's daycare, and our credit card bills we can barely afford groceries so no, we won't be getting a damn Volvo." She eyed her son in the rearview mirror, relieved he was still asleep.

Her mother grew silent. Tonya turned onto Trenholm Road, but pulled off the road when she realized where she was: two blocks from the site of the wreck.

"Tonya—" her mother spoke, shocked and berating.

"And you never helped, Mom," Tonya went on. "Never even offered. Not with school, not with Byron. Buddy is your whole world and I'm not—I'm not anything." Memories of the accident strobed through her brain. The canopy of tree branches, the gentle rise of hill her van had climbed that morning, Byron fussing behind her, Marion on the cell phone telling her she'd better hurry, the Lexus sailing through the intersection, filling her eyes with pearly white, no time to brake or steer away, the crunch and squeal of metal hitting metal, the van spinning in a half-arc off the road, Byron's car seat suspended by seatbelt straps, the place where he'd been sitting eaten away by the front of Mitchell Hastings's car before it hit the tree. All in the length of a breath.

"Are you asking me for money, Tonya?"

She had forgotten the call, captured again in that moment, in the what-could-have-beens.

"No. I'm not asking you for anything." Tonya clicked off the phone. After a quick U-turn, she made a right on Lakeshore, slowing under the live-oaks with branches spanning high over head. She'd passed the house the first time she'd looked for it, but this was her third visit.

She parked in front of the two-story structure made of pale coral brick. Dark green shutters flanked tall windows, a wide tongue of porch led to a front door with gleaming stained glass insets. Four bedrooms? Five? Maybe a fireplace in the den that blazed on winter evenings, Mr. and Mrs. Hastings sipping brandy. At Christmas, was there a towering fir tree laden with lights and glass ornaments? Had they ever had an artificial hand-me-down tree like she and John used?

The Hastings home was twelve blocks from hers but may as well have been in a different country. She and John would never belong here. John's career was not on this path. Maybe he had the drive once but too many disappointments had eroded his ambition. Now it seemed like he worked for the beer at the end of his day rather than their future.

Still, it seemed unfair that the Hastings had so much while they had so little. Just because Mitchell Hastings got his start when the economy was stronger, when hard work was rewarded with a decent income, and years of success led to a brick house with a lush front lawn and a horse-shoe driveway. He probably paid for his kids' college. She and John would never have this.

The paralegal, Carol, had seemed confident they would get money from the wreck. Was it right to profit from Mitchell Hastings's death? It sure wasn't *right* that she and John and Byron struggled to make it to the end of the month. She looked at the big house again, and thought of their tiny two-bedroom box that needed new carpet and a new roof, and the Visa bill she'd yet to pay.

• • •

BECCA AWAKENED TO WHITE. White walls, white sheets, white trim on the narrow window. A white tray poised beside her, holding a covered plate.

"Hey."

The familiar voice came from the left, but turning her head took effort. Her body felt stiff as metal. The woman stood, leaned over, and tucked the sheet around her legs. It was Sandy, the nurse who had taken care of Dad. "How do you feel?" she asked.

"Sore." Images flashed, the emergency room, needles pricking her arms, Dr. Burnside asking a bunch of questions and shaking his head, worried brothers looming close to a blue curtain. None of the family was there now, though, for which Becca was relieved. Sandy pushed a bed table over her and lifted the lid from a tray. The smell of overcooked chicken made Becca want to barf right there on the pristine sheets.

"Lunch time," Sandy said.

"What are you doing here?"

"I work here." Sandy unwrapped a knife and fork and placed them by the plate. "Your mom called my floor and told me what happened. She went down to get a bite to eat."

"And left you to babysit?"

"She didn't want you to be alone."

Great, there'd been another bedside vigil. Lena, the dutiful wife had become Lena the devoted mother. Though that might not be fair, since Mom had looked like she'd been struck by a baseball bat when she arrived at the ER. Becca remembered little else from those moments.

As Becca lifted the fork, the place where the tube attached to the needle tugged at her flesh.

"Careful." Sandy pulled the metal pole a little closer. Becca glared up at the clear plastic bag it held.

"That's food," Sandy said. "Parenteral nutrition to supplement what you eat. But you do need to eat."

This Becca knew, as it had been harped on by every adult she'd seen over the past . . . "How long have I been here?" she asked.

"A little over twenty-four hours. Your numbers are looking good. You're lucky."

"Right." She was many things: fat, ugly, Virgo. But not lucky.

Sandy stood over the bed, her arms crossed. "What you need to do is eat that delicious-looking lunch."

The meal included a small, pale brick of chicken, a puddle of potatoes, and flaccid, overcooked carrots. How could she eat that? Becca held a spoon over the jiggly orange Jell-O that didn't have many calories.

"Okay, that's a start. Looks more edible than the rest of it," Sandy said.

"Can I go home today?"

"I'm not sure. Depends on how you're doing. Your nurses will have to report what you ate." She pointed to the plate.

Becca squished an orange cube and watched it reformulate. "I'm not hungry."

"No, I suppose not." Sandy sat in a vinyl armchair like the one that had been in Dad's room. Becca wondered how long she planned to stay. As soon as she left, Becca could bury the lunch in the trash can and nobody would be the wiser.

"I promised Lena I'd stay till you were done." Sandy was apparently a mind reader. "That's going to be a recurring theme for you over the next few months."

"What do you mean?" Becca felt an uncomfortable flutter in her stomach.

"You've been good at keeping the secret, Becca." The corners of Sandy's lips tightened.

"What secret?" Becca narrowed her eyes, feeling a profound dislike for the smug looking nurse beside her.

"About your weight loss. About your eating disorder."

"I don't—look. I went for a run, and I hadn't eaten much, and I got kind of crampy in the park, and then . . ." her voice trailed off because she had no clue what happened next. She had blurred images of a big dark man who smelled bad and a car honking and being wrapped in something bulky and wool.

"Then you ended up here. But it wasn't just a cramp, was it?"

"My potassium, and electrolytes, blah, blah, blah." Becca punctuated the blahs with thumps on a Jello cube.

"All that stuff tells us what you've been doing to yourself. Believe it or not, that's a good thing. So eat."

Becca stabbed at the wedge of chicken, flaked off a chunk, and put it in her mouth. "Happy now?"

"Ecstatic."

It felt like a dried up worm on her tongue and almost made her gag. Sandy opened a carton of milk—whole milk—and poured it into a glass. "This will help it go down."

Becca reached for the empty plastic cup and held it up. "Could you get me some water?"

As Sandy carried the cup to the pitcher across the room, Becca clawed the chicken and squeezed it in her napkin, an old habit. She'd keep it under the sheet until she could sneak it into the trash. Sandy spun around. "Where'd the chicken go?"

Becca shrugged. "I ate it. Isn't that what you wanted me to do?"

Sandy placed the tumbler on the bed table, pulled back the sheet, and lifted Becca's hand gripping the chicken. "Seriously?"

Busted. Becca threw it on the tray.

Sandy kept a hold of her arm, turning it so the pale underside gleamed in the light. "These little circles of blue. You pinched yourself, didn't you?"

She jerked back her hand, embarrassed and even more pissed off. Sandy needed to mind her own damn business.

"I'll take that as a yes. So for how long have you been on this course?" Sandy asked.

Becca ignored her.

"How long have you been dieting and exercising? Counting every calorie?"

Over a year, yet with barely noticeable results. She had so much further to go, and it would be harder now with everyone watching. "It's not such a big deal." She let out a sigh. How many times would she have this conversation? And who was Sandy to bring it up? She wasn't even Becca's nurse. She didn't know Becca.

Sandy smoothed down her sheet. "How long has it been since you've had a period?"

Becca shifted. "Seven months." It had been weird, but also good, because she didn't have to deal with the mess and the tampons, but then she started to feel freakish.

"You've been seriously underweight for that long and successfully hid it. That wasn't easy. You are highly skilled at being sneaky."

Seriously underweight? Did she look like one of those African kids in the "Feed the Children" commercials? Was she a size one or even a size three? Becca wanted this conversation to end, and Sandy to leave. And most of all, she wanted that disgusting plate of food gone.

Sandy cocked her head as she studied Becca's expression. "You don't believe it, do you? You don't think this is serious. Jesus, Becca."

"Don't you have something else you need to do?" Becca squeezed as much venom as she could into her words.

Sandy shook her head. "You're a lot like me, you know."

The wave of anger swelled again and took hold of Becca's tongue. "I am not. You're fat."

Sandy's brows arched. Becca closed her mind against a tang of guilt and held her gaze, confident that this would get Sandy out of her room. But then, Sandy surprised her. She laughed.

"I guess I am. But that's better than what I was doing to myself before. My problem isn't eating, but it took a similar path to your eating disorder. And yes, that's what you have. An eating disorder."

Becca swallowed, her anger and guilt replaced with something different. Fear.

"I got myself in trouble, too," Sandy went on. "I kept big secrets. I lied to everyone, especially myself." Sandy scrubbed a hand through her hair. "The lie you're living can kill you. You're so damn smart. You can fool your family if you want. Pretend to eat. Sneak into the bathroom to release the food. Hide how much you're exercising."

How did Sandy know about all that?

She went on: "But don't. Don't become a casualty of this disease."

Sandy sure was melodramatic. Becca jiggled the Jell-O again.

"You'll be going to therapy," Sandy said. "I hope they get you somebody good—you'll outsmart anybody who isn't."

This scared Becca. What if people at school found out she was seeing a shrink? What if Kayla or worse—Dylan—knew? Becca had met a psychiatrist that morning. Dr. Owens was young and asked a lot of questions Becca didn't want to answer. Mom said Becca would see her three times a week once she got out. Her punishment. She looked at Sandy. "So you got over your problem?"

A shadow crossed her face. "It's a battle I fight every day. I have people who help me. You'll have help, too."

People like her mom? Not likely. Dr. Owens and all her nosy questions? Know-it-all Elliott?

Sandy eyed the uneaten food on Becca's plate. Becca pierced a carrot with her fork and put it in her mouth, let it moisten her tongue, let sweet juices slide down her throat.

"There you go. That's a start." Sandy reached in her pocket and pulled out a small notepad. She scrawled something down and handed it to Becca. "I'm not supposed to do this, but here's my cell phone number. I have someone I call when things get rough. Maybe I can be that for you for a little while."

CHAPTER 20

Humans were complex creatures, Sandy thought, as she approached the elevator. That girl, with the bruises up and down her arms, with the gnawed cuticles, with ribs and cheekbones protruding like exposed tree roots, deserved a future she might not have. Sandy had violated hospital policy when she gave Becca her phone number, but if there was a way she could help she would. She didn't understand why, but she had to.

"Can I speak with you?" A petite woman with latte-brown skin in a white physician's jacket stepped between Sandy and the opening elevator door. "Just for a moment."

Sandy knew better than to argue with a doctor. She watched the doors slide shut.

"Sandy Albright," the doctor read her name badge. "I'm Lillian Owens. I'm Becca Hastings's doctor. You were in there with her a good while."

"I know the family. Sort of." Sandy offered a little shrug.

Dr. Owens had short hair, styled in a short fro like a black aura around her head, her ears protruding like little handles. New docs looked so young these days. "Tell me your take on her?"

"She's a mess. Really struggling with her dad's death. Some minor self-injury—chewing at her cuticles till they bleed. Little bruises up her arm from pinching herself, but no serious scars that I could see. I think that's been going on a while. But she's not a cutter—at least, not yet."

Dr. Owens nodded. "I didn't pick up on the bruising. Glad you told me."

"The problem is she's so damn shrewd. Hid a chunk of chicken faster than I could catch her." Sandy shook her head. "It's like a game. She doesn't get how serious this is."

"Most don't. Not without treatment. Some even then."

"This is your specialty?"

Dr. Owens nodded.

"Tough gig."

"No kidding. Most psychiatrists avoid working with these kids. It's a lethal illness and the liability is huge. Anything else you can tell me?" Dr. Owens asked.

Sandy thought about her conversations with Lena in her husband's hospital room. The guilt. The secrets. "Every family has its skeletons. I know Lena had breast cancer, and there were problems before that. Becca may have gotten lost in the shuffle."

"She'll be front and center now." Dr. Owens pushed the elevator button for Sandy. "That's how it works."

"She was very close to her dad. Losing him cut deep."

"Thanks for the consult, Sandy. You know your stuff."

Five minutes later, Sandy escaped the hospital, Dr. Owens's compliment putting a new spring in her step. She was a good nurse. A damn good one. Nice for someone to notice.

"I'm surprised you made it back." Nathan Capers appeared beside her, dressed in scrubs and white Nikes, gray hair ponytailed down his back. The very devil himself.

"It wasn't easy." She picked up her pace.

Nathan wore no jacket, his long arm covered with silver hair like cobwebs. A pager blinked in his hand.

"Shouldn't you answer that?" she asked.

"It'll keep."

She wondered if the page was from the physical therapy department, where he worked as an aide, or from one of his drug clients. For three years, Nathan had dealt Sandy and a few dozen other hospital employees whatever pills or recreational substances they wanted. Just hook up in the hospital laundry and all your prayers were answered.

"How was rehab?" he asked.

"A blast." She kept moving to get away from him, but he matched her stride.

"More power to you," he said.

Her car was at the outer edge of the lot. She had thought the exercise of walking the length of the parking area would do her good, but she felt winded, drops of perspiration dampening her forehead. Her prick of a dealer right beside her.

"I admire what you're trying to do here," Nathan said. "Trying to go straight. Ain't nothing harder. Coming back here to work after your rather stellar exit—not sure if that's brave or a little twisted."

He had a point. Coming back to Mercy General was a stupid decision, but she didn't see other options. To reclaim her life, she had to reclaim her career.

"Where the hell were you, anyway?" she spun to face him, ire from that day flaming up. "I wouldn't have taken anything from the med cart if you hadn't disappeared."

He curled a lip back in a smug grin. "Cruising through Scandinavia."

"You might have mentioned you were leaving." That had been the first domino. Her stash, empty. Cash but a missing dealer. Panic and a missing dealer. Desperation and . . . Twenty-four hours later, a single room at Brook Pines. She raged at him those first few days, until another patient noted, "He did you a helluva favor." Sandy wasn't sure, even now, if that was true.

"The cruise was fantastic," he said. "Gotta love the fjords."

Sandy clutched her "Today I Won't be a Screw Up" bracelet.

"I'm gonna leave you alone." Nathan stroked his chin with hairy tan fingers. "It ain't my way to fuck with someone's recovery. But if you need to come back, I'll understand."

"What do you mean?" She froze. She wished she didn't sound so fragile.

"I mean if this doesn't work out the way you want it to. I don't want you ever going to the street for your fix. You have my numbers. You need me, you call. But I ain't coming unless I hear from you." He accented his comment with a wink.

Now she understood her fury. She wanted to hit him. She could picture the son of a bitch's teeth scattered at her feet.

Nathan wasn't looking at her, though. His gaze was fixed on a man approaching from a small cluster of trees. He was large, as dark as midnight, wearing a vivid red cap.

"Friend of yours?" She didn't like the looks of him as he wove through the cars coming towards them.

"Let's just say he's a business associate." Nathan waved the beeper at her as he backed away. "You remember how to reach me? You know, when it's time."

• • •

TONYA PLACED THE LAST of the groceries in the pantry, stacking the fiber bars atop the oatmeal so she could squeeze the Smart Start cereal on the narrow shelf. She needed to clean out the pantry, something that John had mentioned last week. She'd add that to the long list of things-Tonya-needed-to-do according to John. Maybe one day he'd start on the list of chores she had for him, like mowing the front lawn so that the house didn't look abandoned, or fixing the screw on Byron's sliding board, or changing the light bulb in the linen closet or—

No. That was focusing on the negative, and she'd promised herself not to do that. Dr. Allaway had stressed the importance of "putting one's thoughts in light," during lesson four of the self-help podcast she'd just re-listened to.

"Be proactive," Dr. Allaway had said. "Take action. You control your life."

She glanced around the cluttered, unkempt kitchen. The dishes from this morning lay stacked in the sink. A half banana sat on the counter, brown-edged and circled by fruit flies. She spotted three Cheerios from Byron's breakfast on the floor, which was better than yesterday, when she'd found a dozen. Her toddler was getting better at breakfast.

Tonya grabbed the broom, swept up the cereal and crumbs from John's toast, and dumped the mess into the trash. The trash stank. John was supposed to take it out . . . *no*. Tonya could do it. She'd be proactive.

When she hauled the bulging garbage bag out to the trash can, she even took an extra moment to separate the cardboard and beer cans for recycling, something John never bothered to . . .

Thoughts in light. Thoughts in light. She'd set an example for John. Tomorrow night, if he remembered to take the trash to the curb, he'd see she'd used the neglected recycling bin. It might prompt him to do the same.

She returned to the kitchen and glanced at the clock. She had thirty minutes before John and Byron would be home. She could cook dinner. Not some microwaved Swanson entrée, but a real home-cooked meal. She had ground beef and Prego sauce and spaghetti noodles. She had lettuce and to-matoes, and a cuke that might be salvageable if she cut off the withered end. Snagging the pots from under the stove, she put water on to boil and dumped the meat in a pan for browning. John and Byron would come home to the unexpected aroma of supper cooking.

As she waited for the meat to brown, she tackled the dishes. After adding the Prego sauce, she attacked the counters with a sponge and 409. When the water boiled, she added the noodles and a teaspoon of oil. She had ten more minutes before her guys would be home and wouldn't they be surprised.

She glanced into the den. Byron had left a Lego catastrophe in front of the TV, and John's beer stein sat in a puddle on the table. How hard would it be to take the glass into the kitch-

Negative thinking, she chastised herself. She lifted the glass and wiped up the mess, then dropped to her knees to rake up the toys: Legos, Matchbox cars, and puzzle pieces that had scattered under the sofa. She fluffed pillows and stacked newspapers and moved shoes into the bedroom. She ran a dust cloth over the coffee table and stacked the DVDs scattered on the book shelf. She grabbed the vacuum cleaner and went to work on the carpet, sucking up cracker crumbs and smiling at how good everything looked. Dr. Allaway was right, she could see that now.

"What the hell, Tonya?" John's voice boomed from the door way.

She dropped the hose to the vacuum, nearly fell over the coffee table. He turned off the machine with an exaggerated flick of his hand. "You've got red sauce boiling over. There are burned spaghetti noodles stuck to a pan." He dropped their squirming son to the floor then stared at her, his gray eyes cold as granite. "We're minutes away from needing the damn fire dept. Can't you do anything right?"

• • •

Supper was a quiet affair. Or, as quiet as it could be, with Byron chattering away about "Big ball" and eating "Oh Ohs" (Oreos?) at daycare. The spaghetti wasn't a total disaster. Not all the noodles had burned, and the sauce tasted okay. She'd opted to forego the salad. She'd just mess that up too, giving John more ammunition.

After dinner she loaded the dishwasher and let the pans soak in the sink. Dr. Allaway would no doubt want her to get them all clean, replace them in the cabinet, and leave the kitchen a spotless magazine cover-worthy space.

To hell with Dr. Allaway.

Byron scooted into the room from the den pushing his favorite tractor toy and making engine sounds as he ran it along the floor. When he reached her, the tractor bumped up her ankle and leg.

"Hey little man." She lifted him, held him against her, and pressed her lips into his blond hair that held red traces of spaghetti sauce. "Ready for a bath?"

He puckered his lips and made bubble noises, which she took as a yes. Good. Bath time was so much easier with a willing participant.

Once the water reached the right temperature, she added bubbles and wrestled Byron's t-shirt and chinos off. He giggled as she lowered him in the water.

"Me splash!" he said, splatting his hands against the bubbles. Water splattered Tonya's face and chest.

"Byron!" she said, a little sharper than she meant.

His arms froze, his pink face tilting up to search hers, startled.

"It's okay, baby." *Mommy's just tired. Mommy's just frustrated. None of it is your fault.* She nudged his knee with his favorite yellow boat which he submerged under the bubbles. Keeping his hands busy made the task of getting him clean so much easier. She lathered up a cloth and ran it across his neck and down the knobs of his tiny spine. The bruises from the accident made a string of pale green islands across his skin, so much better than the dark purple they had been. He used his arm as though nothing had happened, as though there had been no car crash, no broken collar bone. Thank God he had healed. Maybe she would, too. One day.

She got him clean, let him have five extra minutes to play with ducks and boats, then wrapped a towel around him. Byron leaned in, his sweet eyes all droopy, his hair smelling lemony from the baby shampoo. He didn't fight the pull-up diaper or the pajamas and, when she read *The Little Engine That Could,* he had her repeat it once before drifting off to sleep. Maybe he wouldn't have car crash nightmares tonight.

Downstairs, the TV blared basketball. John most likely had his second beer open. If there was another puddle on the table, he could clean up himself.

Back in the bathroom, she collected toys and made an unexpected decision to take a bath herself. She'd had a long, trying day and after John's blow up, she needed to relax. As she refilled the tub she added Byron's bubble bath, stripped off her clothes, and dimmed the lights. She lowered herself into the water, the foam closing over her like pale hands in prayer.

She recalled John's face when he'd found her vacuuming. The fire in his eyes. The iron set of his jaw. The ice in his words. Did he regret what he'd said? Did he know how it felt, to have him yell at her in front of their child? How four years of marriage seemed so fragile now, like a butterfly wing?

She ducked her head under so that the water could buffer her from the world. How had this become her life? A house they couldn't afford. Credit cards she'd let get out of hand. And a husband who touched her out of obligation—a quick goodbye peck in the morning, a good night kiss as dry as a brown leaf. It seemed when they'd first been married, they kept in constant contact—hands held, shoulders nudging, a knowing smile or wink across the table. When had that died? Did John still love her, even a little?

The gentle knock on the bathroom door surprised her. She swished her arms so that bubbles covered her as John came in. "Hey," he said, closing the toilet and taking a seat, the Coors bottle sweating in his hand.

"Hey." The foam had thinned, the water grown cold. She turned on the hot tap.

"Byron asleep?" he asked.

Like she'd be here in the tub with a toddler on the loose? "Down for the count," she said.

"Good." He picked at the label on the bottle.

She added soap and shimmied her arms for more bubbles, wanting to crawl beneath them and hide.

"Sorry about earlier," he said. "I shouldn't . . . ." he finished the sentence with a shrug.

Shouldn't have acted like he hated her? "I shouldn't have left the kitchen with the pots on the stove," she said mechanically, because apologizing was what she did.

"We all make mistakes." He took a long swallow of beer.

She wondered at the comment. What mistake had he made that he ever admitted to?

"You thought any more about the law suit? The paralegal called today wanting to know." His gaze shifted, skimming her contours in the suds.

"I haven't decided yet." She slid down, the water brushing her chin.

"We could sure use the money. Pay off the credit cards. A down payment on the car. Maybe even buy you some new clothes if you want."

"New clothes?" Did he think this would convince her? That she was so shallow, a new scarf or jacket would make it okay? Mitch Hastings had died. It wasn't her fault but still, the man was dead.

"Or whatever you want. The check will come to you, you know."

Her eyebrows rose at this. "What do you mean?"

"I mean the paralegal thinks they'll settle. You were the driver. The money goes to you."

To her? Not to them. Not to *him*. Something she hadn't considered.

Silver flecks drifted from the beer label to the floor. "When do you think you'll decide?"

She fixed her gaze on the faucet. "I'll decide when I decide."

"Right." He stood, the lid of the tank scraping against the wall. "Do whatever you want, Tonya. Just don't take too long."

He closed the door as he left. She shut her eyes and floated, a log in a river, a seal in the ocean.

• • •

LENA STEPPED THROUGH THE dewy brown grass, clippers in hand. The bush at the edge of Mitch's garden had erupted in blossoms, the lone sign of color in this fall-dreary yard. She scanned the thick green clusters of leaves and selected four perfect flowers: fluttery pink petals around pale golden crowns. As she cut the stems, drops of cold water plopped onto her unsteady fingers. She should have worn gardening gloves. Mitch would have stopped her at the door, gray gloves in hand, but Mitch was gone.

The morning chill crept through her sweater. She hurried back inside and arranged the flowers in a crystal vase, glad that they brightened the kitchen

186

table. This was Becca's first day back to school, and Lena wanted this small celebration: normalcy restored.

She eyed the kitchen clock. Becca was up; she'd heard the shower and the whir of a hair dryer. The scrambled eggs waited in the pan; the turkey bacon was still warm in the microwave. A tall glass of orange juice marked Becca's place at the table. The vitamins, Lena remembered, and moved quickly to spill a fat pink tablet onto Becca's napkin. Dr. Owens had stressed the importance of calcium, iron, and folic acid to rebuilding Becca's bones and strengthening her. Vitamins would help her physical recovery, but the rest would take more than a pill.

"Something sure smells good!" Abby helped herself to Lena's chair at the table. She wore a navy terry robe that she must have found in Sims's dresser. The belt barely closed the opening at her waist and a dull white pajama top bulged out of its V. She groped the crystal vase, twirling it to study the flowers.

"I decided Becca needed a send-off breakfast. Of course, there's plenty." Lena found another plate.

"Hope we can get her to eat."

This was what Lena dreaded. The breakfast table battle that had gone on for months now took a new dimension. Becca almost died. She still might. The weight of this swung like a pendulum over them, over the clean white plates and thin vase of flowers.

Abby pushed back from the table and got herself a cup. Lena expected her to comment on the coffee, which wasn't the way Abby always made it, but she didn't. Abby refilled Lena's mug, but Lena was too edgy for more caffeine. She looked up at the clock again.

"It's so wonderful to have an American breakfast," Abby said. "A little milder than what I'm used to, but delicious."

"What do you eat in South America?"

"Depends on where I am. In Tingo Maria, I was lucky to get some warmed up potatoes and quinoa—which they make into an odd wheat drink. But always plenty of coffee. My blood's probably dark brown by now." She shook her head. "They are a generous people. But so damn poor. It's no wonder they're easy targets for the drug trade."

Lena flashed on an image of Abby fighting gangsters from the back of a llama. She hated to think of her sister in such a dangerous place.

"But some of the food is very good." Abby guided eggs onto her fork with her toast. "I draw the line at cuy, though."

"What's that?"

"Roasted guinea pig." A bit of yellow fell from Abby's mouth to her robe.

"That's . . . disgusting," Lena said, as much about the robe as the food discussion.

"Oh, they delivered my rental car this morning," Abby said, forking a slice of bacon. "Which means I won't have to borrow yours anymore. I know I've been a damn nuisance."

"No you haven't." Lena remembered getting the call about Becca. Here, in this kitchen with her sister, she had gripped the phone, frozen, unable to even take down information. Abby had taken the receiver, talked to the nurse, grabbed their coats, and herded Lena to the car.

"I have a meeting in a little while. An attorney who specializes in international adoptions who may be able to sort through the political bullshit."

"What can he do from here?"

"I'm not sure. I'm willing to try anything if it will help me get Esteban."

Lena had seen the photo of the little boy: dark-skinned with hair cut straight across his forehead. Eyes like obsidian stones and a crooked grin. How her sister melted as she spoke of him. Lena's new nephew, Esteban.

When Becca came into the kitchen, she had on black jeans, a contoured black sweater, and a teal scarf Lena didn't remember seeing before. Usually Becca wore loose clothes to hide her body. And was that eye shadow?

Lena hurried to scoop eggs onto a plate and add the bacon, then whole grain toast. Becca eyed the food like it was the enemy.

"Your mom made you breakfast. You can at least pretend to be grateful," Abby said, helping herself to another piece of bacon. "This is made from turkey, Becca. Very lean."

Becca toyed with the food, segregating the eggs, slicing the toast into triangles and the bacon into micro-bites, the clinking of cutlery on her plate the only sound in the room. Lena kept her head down, watching to see what made it into Becca's mouth. Becca reached for the vase and twirled it.

"What's with the flowers?" Becca asked.

"I thought they were pretty." Lena found herself defensive, like she didn't have a right to bring life to their dull breakfast.

"A bit early for camellias, isn't it?" Abby asked.

"They're sasanquas," Becca said. How did she know? Lena hadn't.

"Dad never picked them because they won't last in the vase." Becca lifted a fork that held a half-tablespoon of egg which she studied like an odd science experiment. Why wouldn't she eat it?

"Please, Becca. Dr. Owens said you needed protein." Lena's words eked out through clenched teeth; Becca lifted her eyebrows at the tone. After an endless moment, she slid the fork into her mouth and Lena exhaled, counting the calories. That was what Becca had done over the past two years, Dr. Owens had told her. Counted every calorie and fat gram that she put in her mouth. After Becca took a few more small bites, Lena braved the next issue. She pointed to the capsule beside Becca's plate. "That's the vitamin that Dr. Owens prescribed."

"It's too big." Becca rolled it with the blade of her knife. Her scrutiny shifted from the vitamin to Lena's face, eyes narrowed like a gunfighter. They were at the OK corral, Lena realized. She wouldn't win this stalemate. She couldn't win any of them, and now her daughter's life might depend on it. What would Mitch say? She couldn't bear to fail either of them.

"Becca, can you help me with something?" Abby pulled a cell phone from her pocket. "I traded my satellite phone in for this thing yesterday. It's called a 'smart phone.' Damn thing's already outsmarted me. It's got all these application things and I don't know what the hell to do with it. I swear, if I could have gotten one with a rotary dial I would have."

Becca turned over the sleek gray cellular. "It's the latest iPhone."

"Maybe you can show me how to use it later?"

Becca nudged the toggle on the bottom and a bright blue screen appeared. A few more strokes across the surface and pictures emerged.

"You're already farther along than I got," Abby said. "Now take that vitamin before your mom's head implodes."

And miracle of miracles, Becca did.

After Becca finished half the food on her plate (not quite two hundred thirty calories), she returned upstairs to finish getting ready for school. Lena wanted to follow, to see if Becca went into the bathroom. Could she hear the sound of retching through the door? But Becca hadn't eaten that much, and if she caught Lena spying . . . .

"I'll check on her." Abby stood. "I can get her to school if you want. It's on my way."

Lena nodded, relieved. She wondered if Becca was nervous about returning to her classes; it had been almost two weeks since Mitch's accident, but Kayla had kept her up-to-date on school assignments and last night, Lena had seen Becca huddled over her history text. Getting back in her usual routine would have to help.

Elliott stumbled into the kitchen, his eyes sleep-crusted. Even as a toddler, he fought waking up. Sims would rouse with a bounce and storm into the day, but Elliott was the groggy, grouchy boy. She'd coax him with: "How about a glass of milk, honey?" or "Sit with your daddy while I get your cereal." And he'd crawl into Mitch's lap, leaning against his chest, eyes at half-mast while Mitch held the sippy-cup for him. How Mitch had cherished those moments.

A wave of raw pain washed through her. The chair where Mitch sat, empty. His place at the table, no longer set. No tender, gravel-voiced "Morning, sweetheart" to start her day.

"Mom?" Elliott peered at her over his mug. "You okay?"

"I'm fine. There's still some scrambled eggs and bacon." She filled a plate with the remaining food and set it at his place at the table, grateful he was still in Columbia. She needed to have "the conversation" with him about Royce, but not yet. He plopped a book on the table and opened it to a dog-eared page. Lena sat across from him and bent to see what he was reading. *The Fundamentals of Commercial Real Estate.* "Where did you get that?" she asked.

"Dad's office. It's a little old. Doesn't take into account the current disastrous state of our economy, but a decent primer."

"Why are you reading it?" she asked.

"Just wanted to understand Dad's business better. After the meeting with Phillip, I figured I should have some clue what he was talking about."

So did Lena. Because of what happened with Becca, she had let what Phillip had said recede from her consciousness, but she couldn't keep hiding from it. The business was in serious jeopardy. Mitch had spent down their reserve fund during her cancer treatments, and now—now she had to find a way to support them. She hadn't held a job since college, and that had been a work-study placement in the school library. She had a B.A. in Art History—oh yes, she was so marketable. Potential employers would be beating down her door. What was she going to do?

"It's not that hard to get a real estate license," Elliott said. "Unless the rules have changed. You need to take a course, then pass a test, then sign on with a broker."

"What kind of course?" she asked.

"You can take it online. Or maybe at the tech school." He thumbed through the book. "It says it can be hard finding a broker but that's one thing Phillip can do for us."

Lena huffed out a noise of disgust. Phillip was useless, yet so much of her future—of their future—depended on him.

Elliott closed the book. "So I was thinking, maybe I'd stick around for a while. Maybe give this real estate gig a try. I know I'll have to buy a couple of suits, and believe me, I shudder at the thought, but otherwise, I think I can make it work."

Lena's hands wrapped around the table edge, knuckles blanching to white. "No."

He speared a bacon slice with his fork. "I knew you'd say that."

"Then why bring it up? You are an artist, Elliott. You are not a business-man. That kind of life—that's not who you're meant to be."

"Can I have some toast?" he asked.

"Of course." It was an unusual request. Elliott was always self-sufficient, tending to his own needs, and lately, trying to tend to hers. She slipped two slices of wheat bread into the toaster. At least breakfast was something she was good at. Maybe she could have a career as a Waffle House waitress.

"You don't know what I was meant to be," Elliott said. "You think you do. You always had plans for me but I'm not sure they're the same ones I have."

She stared at him, and jumped when the toast popped up behind her. She slapped them on his plate.

"I didn't mean to make you mad."

"I'm not angry." They both knew that was a lie. She wasn't even sure what had her so furious, except she had always thought Elliott was happy, that he had what she didn't: the chance to use his talent. To not live the same boring life as everyone else.

"I love my music, but it doesn't have to be my career. To be honest, it kind of sucks as a career. Maybe I need something else. A real job, as Sims likes to say."

"Now you're taking advice from him? After disagreeing with anything he's suggested for twenty-six years?" Of course, this was an exaggeration. El-liott looked up to his elder sibling, wanting his approval. When he had sent them the CD last year, his first question had been, "Did Sims listen to it?"

"I've given New York four and half years, Mom. Four and a half years and I still live in a crappy, bug-infested apartment. I live on credit cards when business is slow. And I'm tired. I'm tired of the whole damn scene." He pushed the plate away, jostling the vase. A pink petal dropped to the table.

She almost scolded him for cursing but her son was an adult. He could use whatever language he wanted. He could make his own decisions about his life, too—if he made them based on his own needs and goals. Still, while she'd love to have him home, she couldn't picture him moving here without it being a defeat.

"We'll talk about this later," she said.

When he took his plate to the sink, he left the book on the table. Lena opened it to the first page.

CHAPTER 21

Two quick bursts of the doorbell sounded three seconds apart, and Sandy wasn't sure if she should answer. The Lean Cuisine in front of her held all the appeal of a jar of expired baby food, and if she opened that door, she'd never hear the end of it. *You're eating that?*

The bell rang again. She scanned the cluttered living room—couldn't Sean have left his books in one stack instead of six? She smoothed her top, gave her hair a finger comb, and answered the door. Jesse had on shades, a slim gray suit, with an indigo necktie swinging loose around his collar. He lifted a large paper bag. "I brought ravioli from Pasta Fresca."

"Guess I'll have to let you in." She backed away, the door yawning open, Jesse marching through like he belonged there. But that was Jesse, he exuded ownership of any place he entered.

He moved to the dining table. "What the hell is that?"

"Pasta Not-Fresca."

"Holy crap. What did rehab do to you?"

"That's a good question."

Jesse lifted the plastic container and took it to the kitchen. She heard it splatter in the trashcan. Next, plates appeared, cutlery, and two glasses of water. Jesse probably wanted a beer, which he wouldn't find here.

"Do you ever think about calling before you show up?" she asked.

He dolloped out spheres of pasta, plump shrimp, and chunks of tomato, the garlicky smell taking command of the room. "Do you ever think about inviting me over?"

"Touché." She wondered why she didn't call. She had tried during rehab; four unreturned voicemails made the nightmare harsher, but they'd been over that.

He sliced his ravioli into tidy little bites, which he ate with his fork upside down, European style. Sandy did her best not to shovel the pasta into her waiting mouth. She couldn't shake her hunger, even when she was full.

"How's work going?" he asked. It seemed an absurdly normal thing to say, like they were an average couple discussing their day. Not the trajectory their conversation usually took.

"Fine," she said, then corrected herself. "No, not fine. I feel like a pariah. I'm pretty sure everyone knows I'm on probation, even though it's supposed be confidential. And yesterday, my dealer found me in the parking lot to remind me he was open for business."

Jesse's fork froze. "Son of a bitch. You should report him to security. Be the best thing for you and his other victims."

"And I'd have his other customers stalking me if I did."

"Give me his name. I'll turn him in."

Sandy pondered this. She'd like to have Nathan out of her world. "I'll think about it."

"Cal Jefferies plays golf with me. I can slip it into conversation."

"You play golf with the CFO of my hospital?" Something else she hadn't known about him. Jesse had his secrets, but tossed one out now and then like a pearl clattering along the floor.

"He can't putt worth a damn. Last time I threatened to take him to miniature golf." He chased a rebel tomato with his fork. "Did talk him into a new radio-surgery high-def beam shaper though."

"How much did you make on that deal?" she asked, knowing he wouldn't say.

He grinned without answering. She grinned back.

"My commission was twenty-three thou."

Her mouth gaped open, both at the enormity of the sum—made during a freaking golf game—and at the disclosure. New waters with Jesse Harper.

"I'm in the wrong business."

"No you're not. Besides, commissions aren't steady. Every day is a gamble. You gotta roll with the lean times and conserve for the fat ones. Only way to have balance in your life."

Balance. She mentally said the word.

"I feel for all the folks lamenting their 401Ks. Took a gamble and they didn't even know it." Jesse held up the restaurant container. "Want more?"

She did, but she shook her head. "Something else weird happened yesterday. I got to know this family when the father was on my unit. First patient I had when I came back. Guy didn't make it. Anyway, the fourteen-year-old daughter was admitted on Peds. The mom asked for me so I visited her."

Jesse sipped his water, watching.

"The girl is an emotional wreck. Anorexic. Hinting at self-injury. She's a desperate, isolated kid and all I can think of is how I'm the worst person she could talk to."

"Why?"

"Why? Because I'm more screwed up than she is." Sweat sheened her face and pooled in her bra.

Jesse poked at another ravioli.

"She looked so . . . lost." She dabbed at her skin with her napkin. "When I was her age, God. I was so miserable. My parents had me nailed down. Controlled every fiber of my life. And the endless hours they held me hostage in that damn church. A service could last three hours, easy. And if there was a baptism or someone getting saved, much longer. I remember profound relief when I woke up on any day that wasn't Sunday or Wednesday."

Memories bubbled up, unbidden. She had been a little younger than Becca when she started asking the wrong questions. Dad avowed the Bible had to be taken literally, but Sandy puzzled over Exodus where it read: *If a man sells his daughter as a female slave, she is not to go free as the male slaves do.*

"So Dad, exactly when are you selling me into slavery?" she had asked.

"Mind your mouth. You're already a slave to your sinning ways."

When she found a Leviticus verse that forbade wearing "a garment upon you of two kinds of material mixed together," she pointed to Dad's polyester jacket. "That one might get you in trouble."

The back of his hand stung her cheek faster than she could blink. She didn't even mind the pain, she'd made her point, one of many that would get her slapped, scolded, and locked in her room over the course of her adolescence. Her therapist had called it abuse but she'd seen real abuse in the hospital. What she went through had been a sucky childhood that molded her into the disaster she was now, but many, many people had been through worse.

Jesse pushed his empty plate away. "Didn't you use to work Peds?"

"That was in my other life." The one she never, ever discussed with Jesse.

"Might be more your forte than you want to admit."

She shook her head. While she loved working with kids—and she had—the memory of her mistake and the infant she'd almost killed—no. She wasn't going back to Pediatrics.

Jesse reached over and took her hand, which for some bizarre reason had started to tremble. Why?

Jesse lifted a napkin and wiped her face. Tears? She was crying? Holy crap. Not in front of him. She shot up from the chair and started clearing away the dishes. Anger at herself helped the tears evaporate, but now her hands were vibrating so hard she was close to shattering the plates. Christ, could she use a hit just then.

Don't. She eyed the cell phone on the counter. Jackie, a speed dial away. She should have gone to an NA meeting after work. Fingers on her neck. Warm, massaging, playing her shoulders like a piano. She let her head fall back, leaning into the touch, and he slid his hands under her sweater, stealth hands, working up her spine, pulsing into her flesh.

She closed her eyes.

Arms around her waist, slowly, gently, turning her around. Pulled against him, the sinewy strength of him, the familiar warm breath on her skin, this one escape she still allowed. His lips on hers, but something troubling . . . the faintest smell, wafting from the collar of his shirt. She tilted her face away from his, buried her nose in his neck.

"Son of a bitch!" She pushed him, hard enough that he lost his balance and caught himself on the kitchen counter.

"What the hell?"

"You smoked pot. I can smell it on you. Did you light up on the way over? Is that what prompted the sudden meal delivery?"

"Shit." Jesse turned as though looking at her was painful.

"You know I can't be around that stuff."

"I didn't bring it with me. I would never—" He had his hands up.

"But you did. Maybe you don't have a joint in your pocket, but I'll bet it's in your car. Christ, Jesse. I can't be around it at all. Just smelling it makes me crazy."

He didn't answer. She did feel crazy. She wanted to charge out to his Lexus and open the glove box where he kept his stash and light up.

"You're saying that if I'm to see you, I need to live like a monk? No beer? No pot, even if I'm away from you? This is getting to be a damned expensive relationship."

"Well I'm sorry if I'm such a huge inconvenience for you." How could he not understand what life was like for her? How she had lost so much and sometimes she was doing good to keep drawing breath in this gray place that was her life.

Jesse returned to the table. He brought the glasses and forks to the sink. Closed the container holding the leftovers and placed them in the refrigerator, his movements fluid like mercury. After placing his napkin in the trash, he said, "Guess I'll be going," and walked out.

• • •

Becca liked Dr. Owens's office. She sank into the buttery leather sofa, the red throw pillow squeezed in her lap, with Dr. Owens across from her in a swivel chair. She wondered about Dr. Owens's earrings: red dangly things that bumped against her neck. Didn't they irritate her? She had unblemished brown skin and a strong jaw, not like Becca's, which was fleshy and undefined. Dr. Owens's eyes were her best feature: big, and the shade of dark chocolate.

Becca's eyes might be pretty if they weren't so close together. There was no fixing that. Her giant hands she'd gotten from Dad. She'd always wished for Mom's delicate, sloped fingers and narrow wrists. Artistic hands, like Elliott had, which was so unfair.

"Something on your mind, Becca?" Dr. Owens asked.

"I like your hair." She clutched at a strand of her own, which was like neither parent's, hanging lifeless as mown hay.

"Thank you," Dr. Owens replied.

"Mine's more like straw."

Dr. Owens frowned. "And what kind of thinking is that?"

"Negative thinking," Becca said by rote. It wasn't like she wanted to think about how ugly she was. She couldn't turn it off like a light switch.

"Have you been keeping your journal?" Dr. Owens asked.

Becca pulled it from her book bag. In the first section she recorded what she ate. It stunned her how much they were making her put into her mouth, but for the first time in forever, she wasn't hungry. The second section of the journal was much harder. Her feeling/thinking section. She was to record each negative thought that interrupted her day and beside it, write down a more positive one, or an affirmation. Becca had recorded ten thoughts, when she'd had well over a gazillion, and labored over each "corrective cognition" she was supposed to write. "I am fat and ugly," replaced with, "I am beautiful just as I am." "I ate too much," supplanted with, "I must nurture and care for my body." It made her want to barf, but she wasn't supposed to do that anymore either.

"Anything you'd like to share?" Dr. Owens asked.

She flipped to the food diary. "Are you sure I need to eat this much? It seems like a lot."

"You've been meeting with the nutritionist. What does she say?"

"That I need the calories to reach a healthy body weight," which Becca did not believe. One hundred twenty-five pounds was a ridiculous goal. She'd have to buy Plus-size jeans and Spanx.

"So, your first day back at school," Dr Owens said. "How did it go?"

"Okay." Becca tugged at the corner of the Band-Aid the nurse had applied after taking blood from her arm. It had hurt the first time, but she was getting used to it. The weighing in, though—and not being allowed to see how much she'd gained—she didn't get that part.

"Okay how?"

"Everybody was nice to me. Even the principal stopped me in the hall to say how sorry he was." She had hated the attention. Her history teacher had approached her desk, stooped down, and said, "I'm so sorry, Rebecca," because she never called Becca by her nickname. Mostly the kids avoided her, except Kayla and Dylan, who'd walked her to class, and sat with her at lunch. Then Amanda had approached her in the bathroom to say, "You are too nice to have something like this happen."

"Was it uncomfortable, being back?" Dr. Owens asked.

Becca reached in her purse and pulled out the card that Mr. Brunson had given her. It was creamy white, with hand printing:

The Curfew tolls the knell of parting day, The lowing herd winds slowly o'er the lea,

The ploughman homeward plods his weary way, And leaves the world to darkness and to me. Thomas Gray, 1716–1771

"Who gave it to you?" Dr. Owens asked.

"My stupid poetry teacher. Only somebody else wrote it."

Dr. Owens handed it back. "What do you think it means?"

"I don't know. I never know what that man is talking about." She stared down at the last line. She had read those words a dozen times over the course of the afternoon.

"What?" Dr. Owens asked.

Becca glanced up at her.

"You had a different expression. A flicker of something. Do you know what?"

She traced the word "darkness" on the card. She didn't feel her grief like darkness, more like a steady, unyielding gray. "It's nothing." She stuck the card back in her purse.

Dr. Owens thumped a pen against the pad of paper she always held. "What's going on, Becca?"

Becca shifted, pushing herself deeper into the sofa cushions. She wished she could tuck herself inside it like a pearl hidden within an oyster.

"Kayla asked me why I was leaving school early."

"To come here," Dr. Owens clarified. "Did you tell her?"

"I don't want her to know." If Becca had her way, nobody would know she was seeing Dr. Owens. She'd wear a raincoat and mask every time she set foot in this building.

"Are you embarrassed?"

This was a trap. If Becca said she was embarrassed or ashamed, it would have to go down in the negative cognition column.

Dr. Owens cocked her head to the side the way Spats used to do when he was a kitten. "It's important that we're honest with each other, Becca."

Holy crap. She could. Not. Win. "Maybe I'm a little embarrassed. I shouldn't be."

Dr. Owens smiled. "Let's try that again. You don't want Kayla to know because you're worried she'll judge you?"

Becca gripped the journal, remembering the ugly things Kayla always said about Amanda who couldn't help that she was built like a panda bear. "Of course she judges me. She judges everybody. It's sort of her job as chief diva of Woodland Middle School."

Dr. Owens gave her a knowing nod. "It's very hard to be your age."

"It's hard to have friends who have perfect bodies and all the boys like them but they say crappy things about everybody behind their backs."

Kayla might tell everyone. Becca would become Crazy Becca like Amber was Psycho Amber after she took an overdose. The thought of this secret taking flight made panic flutter in Becca's chest.

"It's important that you have support for your recovery somewhere other than at home," Dr. Owens said.

Becca looked at the bronze clock perched on the edge of Dr. Owens's desk, its long slim arms gesturing that she still had twenty minutes to go. Time moved a lot slower in Dr. Owens's office.

"Mom says we've got bad money problems. She may not be able to afford for me to keep seeing you," Becca said, changing strategy.

"You have good insurance. If she can't manage the co-pay, we'll set up a monthly plan." Dr. Owens crossed her legs. "Are you worried about the financial situation?"

"Dad had to spend a lot of money when she was sick, then things tanked with his business." Sims had used the word "tanked." She liked it.

"It's been a tough time for lots of people."

"What if there's no money for me to go to college?" She shot forward, out of the safe folds of the couch. College had been how Sims and Elliott escaped. What if she didn't get her chance?

"That's something you plan on, then. Going to college." Dr. Owens wrote something on her pad.

"Uhmmmm, Yes." Becca said it slowly, because she was thinking maybe Dr. Owens wasn't very bright. Wasn't it obvious that she planned to go to school? But what if she couldn't? What if she was stuck living at home, working in the McDonald's drive-thru to help pay the bills?

"I like it that you have a plan. That you have a future you want to get to," Dr. Owens said.

"Doesn't everybody?" It seemed like they'd be on one track then Dr. Owens would veer off somewhere else.

"No. Some girls with eating disorders don't allow themselves to see a future." Dr. Owens paused, then added, "Some even plan to die."

Die. She hated hearing that word. Die had fresh, gritty meaning for Becca now that Dad was dead. "Not me," she said.

"But you understand that if we don't get a handle on your disease, it could happen?"

Becca clutched the pillow and considered throwing it at Dr. Owens. Did everyone have to beat that drum to death? "I get it. I got it at the hospital from Dr. Burnside. At home from Elliott. Mom. Aunt Abby. I'm pretty sure the Fed Ex guy wants to discuss it, too."

Dr. Owens grinned. "I love your sense of humor. So back to going to college. How are your grades?"

"I do okay in school."

"I'll bet you do better than okay. What did you get on your last report card?"

"A b-minus in algebra." It still pissed her off. She'd studied her ass off for that exam and screwed up a stupid multiplication.

"And As in all your other subjects, right?"

"Mom told you?"

"Nope. She didn't have to. I have a sneaking suspicion that you're a bit of a perfectionist. So As would be the way you'd go."

"It's kind of mandatory in our family."

"It's what your Mom expects?"

"We're 'special.' At least, that's what Mom used to tell us. 'We expect more from you.' 'You're brighter than most kids.' I thought I was the one that felt bad about it, but Elliott and Sims said it was hard on them, too. Only maybe not as hard as I get."

"Why?"

"Sims is really, really smart. He always got straight A's, which was often pointed out to me. Elliott is a gifted musician. He never froze on stage during a stupid recital or anything. They both gave my parents what they expected."

"You're often compared to your brothers?" Dr. Owens liked to ask questions. At the end of the day, if you tallied all the sentences she'd spoken, probably seventy-five percent ended with a question mark.

"Well, yes. That's not unusual. Most families do that." Becca twisted pillow fringe around her finger.

"Your brothers grew up in a different home than you. So comparisons might not be fair."

"No they didn't. We've always lived in that house."

"They weren't living there when your mom left. They weren't there when she came back and had breast cancer. The home where you live is very different from the one they grew up in."

Becca wrapped a tassel around her knuckle and pulled it taut. Dr. Owens was right. Things altered when Elliott went to college. She remembered watching him pack up his room. How he rolled up the Beck poster and placed it in a big box. How he scratched his head at the schoolbus-yellow sheets Mom had bought for his dorm room bed, but didn't say anything because he didn't want to hurt her feelings.

"What are you thinking about?"

"When Elliott moved into the dorm. It got weird then." She had gone to his room the next day and found a note on his bed: "Squirt, You can make this your room if you want, but it doesn't smell as good as yours." She didn't move in, because things could change, he could decide to move back, except he didn't. Like Sims, he never looked back.

"Weird how?"

"Everything changed after he left." Even before Royce and the cancer, things had shifted in their home. Mom stopped pretending she was always happy. Dad worried more and more about his health: the reflux, then the ulcer, then his headaches. Mom acting annoyed at his complaints. She would say the right things, "Why don't you lie down, hon?" while her eyes said something entirely different.

"Your mom told me about the separation from your dad. You were twelve?"

She nodded.

"Did you know there were problems between your parents?"

She nodded again, gathering the pillow to her chest, which felt hollow like a cave.

"Did they fight?" Dr. Owens asked.

"No. They didn't talk much to each other. Dinner time got weird." They always ate in the dining room, with Mom at one end of the table and Dad at the other, Becca the bridge between them. Dad would ask about school. She didn't have much to say. Mom would ask Dad about his day. He wouldn't have much to say.

"Things were especially tense then?"

"Yes." After a while, Dad would pour bourbon in a squat glass. The ice would clink.

"Did it affect your eating?"

She pulled the pillow away to look down at herself. The question was strange, and her answer even stranger, but so very true. "It made me hungry."

• • •

"How did your session with Dr. Owens go?" Lena turned on the windshield wipers. A sputtering rain had started, enough to make the wipers smear damp grit across the glass.

"Fine." Becca buttoned her jacket. Lena turned the heat on.

"Can I get a little more than 'fine?'" She glanced over at her daughter, expecting a petulant shrug.

Becca dropped her leg and turned to the window. The rain had picked up speed, angled fat drops splattering the windshield, thunder cracking in the gray clouds above. Lena turned up the wipers.

"Fine. What I say in there is supposed to be confidential."

"Of course. I just wanted to know if she thought it was helping."

Becca shrugged. If Lena had a dime for every time her child did that, they'd have no financial problems.

"She said I was doing good. The nutritionist said I was on track with gaining weight."

"I'm glad to hear that."

Becca frowned.

"What? You're not glad?"

Becca cut her eyes at Lena. "I suppose."

"That was convincing." Lena gripped the wheel. "Please don't tell me what I want to hear. Tell me the truth."

Becca inserted her finger in her mouth to chew on the cuticle. It would be bleeding soon, and she'd hide it by cramming her hand in her pocket. Lena would have to clean the blood from the pocket lining.

She pulled out of traffic into a parking lot. She wasn't sure what the business was—a dry cleaner or tax place, the storm obscured the sign.

"Why are we stopping?"

"So you can answer my question." She switched off the ignition. The rain sounded like pebbles against the roof of the car. Was it too much to want a future for her daughter? To watch her grow up, go to college—she'd find some way to afford it—maybe get married? For Lena, there were promised moments for her to witness: Becca becoming a mother herself, nursing a baby, changing diapers, walking a little one down the sidewalk. Becca attending piano recitals, only she would do it right, she wouldn't care if her child froze on stage. Sure, Becca would make her own mistakes, but she wasn't destined to repeat Lena's, and there was comfort in that.

"You have so much of your dad in you," Lena said. "I see it all the time. His intelligence. His way of finding humor in the world." Or at least, Becca used to. There wasn't much humor in her now.

Becca moved on to a different cuticle.

"Mitch was always wound tight. Anxious. I think maybe you got that from him, too." She watched the wipers slapping against the glass. In the distance, lightning zipped across the sky.

"Are you blaming my problems on Dad?" Becca's voice held a dark edge.

"No. I'm not blaming anybody except myself. I know I've messed up with you. I was selfish and didn't see that my actions hurt you. I'm so sorry." She could feel Becca's gaze probing her face but she kept her eyes on the rain as it splashed off the hood. "Your father forgave me for leaving him. I didn't deserve it—you and I both know that. But he did."

"You came back because you were sick," Becca said.

"I came back because I needed to be home. Mitch was my home. You were my home. But then my sickness filled up the house and once again, I was neglecting you." There had been signs even then—subtle ones, like the way Becca wore out her running shoes, and her willingness to clean the bathroom—but Lena didn't have the energy to see them for what they were.

"What about Royce?"

The question startled Lena. The name sounded foreign after all they'd been through.

"What about him?"

"Do you still—are you going back to him?" Becca sounded seven years old, scared by the weight of the question.

Lena turned to look at her. "No. Never. Royce is very much behind me. When I left your father—and you—it was because I was very unhappy. I needed to be more than a mother and a wife. I thought I loved Royce, but it wasn't real love."

"It was just sex then?" Becca arched her brows, issuing a dare.

Lena felt a sudden impulse to slap her. This kid always, always brought out the worst in her. "Why do you make everything so hard?"

Becca's head snapped around to face the window. Lena wanted to take the words back as much as she didn't. The rain was like a faucet now. Mitch would be grateful for it. He'd comment how it would help his garden, how his camellias and pansies thirsted for a good soaking. How a wet autumn nurtured the plants that would bloom in spring. If she could channel Mitch, she might know what to say to their child.

"Do you remember when your Dad and I went to Edisto Beach?" Lena spoke softer, remembering that delicious time. Mitch, Lena, a blue dome of sky and a stormy gray ocean. "It was that weekend last spring when you stayed with Kayla."

The back of Becca's head nodded.

"It was my first trip out of town since the chemo." Mitch had rented a cottage right on the beach. From the porch, they peered over rippling sea grass at the shifting gray and green shades of the ocean.

"We took slow walks on the beach—slow because I still didn't have much strength. Mitch collected shells for me and carried them in that green fishing hat he always wore."

Becca shifted, her stare now fixed on her cuticle-reddened hands.

"We were lucky there were so few people. We had the beach to ourselves. Mitch told me he wanted us to renew our vows. He didn't say what he could have—that we should renew them because I'd broken the old ones. Instead, he wanted to celebrate the rebirth of our marriage. He was right, it had been reborn." They had stood ankle-deep in the chilly surf, watching two pelicans skim the ocean surface. The breeze blew her scarf from her naked scalp and she didn't put it back. Mitch kissed her forehead where eyebrows were beginning to return.

"I told him we didn't need a ceremony. We could say our vows right there, at Edisto. So that's what we did. Mitch had his prayer book in the car so the following morning, just as the sun nudged up over the ocean, we vowed to love, honor and cherish each other, 'Til death do us part'. I hadn't thought death would come this soon." Lena felt something spreading in her chest, like wings unfurled. Her eyes filled with tears.

The sky loomed an ominous gray above them. As Lena wiped her eyes, her daughter scrambled in the glove box for a small packet of tissues and gave her one.

"Thanks," Lena said. "What I want you to understand is this: at that time at the beach, we were perfect. We've always fit together but this was something more. I don't know how else to say it. Now your father's gone, and I can't imagine anything will be perfect again."

"Nothing is perfect," Becca said.

Lena looked at her, expecting to see the surly expression again but it wasn't there. "Nothing stays that way, but sometimes you're blessed with these moments. We got to perfect, and not many couples can say that." She knew things with Mitch couldn't stay that way. Marriage was like a living breathing thing. Sometimes it thrived, sometimes it faltered, but she would have stayed with him forever.

She studied her daughter's face, the hills of her cheekbones, the chapped, full lips. Lena reached in her pocket and pulled out the stone. She handed it to Becca.

"You have a rock?"

"Yep. I've carried it since the day of the funeral. I found it in his jacket pocket. I have no idea why it was there. But his was the last hand to touch it. And when I curl my fingers around it, it's like I'm touching a part of him that's still here." She shook her head. "Sounds silly, doesn't it?"

"No." Becca turned the stone over, her fingers brushing the surface. "I've been wearing his deodorant. I wanted to smell him a little longer."

A profound wave of sadness swept through Lena as she looked at her girl. She'd been through so much. Lena had put her through so much. Yet here she was, holding on, going to therapy. Wearing her father's deodorant.

"I want to get better," Becca said. "But it's hard to eat, Mom. Especially with you and Elliott and Aunt Abby watching every bite I put in my mouth. My stomach isn't used to food; it hurts if I eat too much."

"We're being over-cautious because we're scared for you. But I know you're trying." Lena reached a tentative hand to Becca's shoulder and was grateful that Becca didn't rebuff her.

Becca swiped at her eyes. "Dr. Owens says I have to change my thinking. But what if I can't? What if I'm in therapy for years and still can't?"

Lena stroked her daughter's hair, just like she had the night of the funeral. "You can. You're smart and you can do it."

"It's not about being smart. It's about . . . it's about wanting to be something else. Someone else."

Someone who liked herself in the mirror. Someone who knew she was loved every second of every day.

Someone whose mother didn't leave.

Lena's fingers combed through her hair, grateful her daughter would allow this touch when she didn't deserve it. "I wouldn't have you any other way. You are the Becca that Mitch and I created. You have his eyes and his intellect and my . . ." she hesitated, unsure how to finish. What had she given Becca?

What had come from her? But then it came to her. "You have my resilience. Except I think maybe you're stronger than I am."

Becca looked at her, as if searching for some hidden truth. As a girl, Lena would look at her own mother the same way, seeking a sign of resolve or bravery, something that would promise their lives would be different. She never got it. Becca deserved a whole lot more.

"I'm very proud of you, Becca. Mitch would be—Mitch is, too."

The rain slackened, smaller drops misting the windshield. She could see trees beyond the gray building. Tall naked oaks, autumn having taken every leaf.

Becca handed her the stone. She slid it back in her pocket.

CHAPTER 22

J oe Booker felt like an old, old man. His bones creaked like rusty hinges as he walked through the park. Hunger gnawed at him. He hadn't eaten anything since—since when? A day or so ago. He had those two twenty dollar bills the lady at the hospital gave him, but he wasn't a man to go into a restaurant and order a sandwich. Too many whispers of judgment.

He passed the Baptist church, then remembered the Salvation Army served lunch some days and it was three blocks away. As he rounded the corner, he could see the line forming outside the new brick dining room they'd built last year. He limped to the end.

A young man in jeans and a red sweater carried a clipboard as he counted the people in line. Joe hoped he wasn't asking for names. Joe didn't want to be on anybody's list.

The young man approached him. "I don't think I've met you here before. My name's Carl. I'm one of the shelter volunteers," he said. He couldn't have been more than twenty years old, smooth-skinned, with eyes that hadn't seen very much. "What's your name?"

"Joe," he said, hoping that would suffice.

"Glad to meet you, Joe." He pulled a pamphlet from the back of his clipboard.

Joe took a step closer to the kitchen, the line inching along no faster than a caterpillar.

"Here's a brochure that has our hours, the rules, et cetera. We have new cots in the shelter, and a local women's group donated some blankets. So you have a place to stay here, if you want."

Joe took the pamphlet and scanned the long list of rules. Nobody admitted after 6 PM. Must clear the metal detector. No fighting, profanity, or theft tolerated. Must leave shelter by 8 AM. It didn't matter. He wouldn't stay in the shelter until he had to. He'd seen how the bunks lined up—forty or more to a room. Being closed in was one thing, but being shut up with a bunch of men he didn't know was something else entirely.

About ten feet ahead of him a young woman held the hand of a little girl. When the woman turned, he could see her belly full and round like a basketball. Soon, she'd have another mouth to feed, her nothing more than a child herself.

"Do families stay here?" Joe asked, worried for the young woman.

"We use a hotel," Carl said, eyeing the young mother.

Joe remembered those times when Papa left the family, how Joe's mama had a tough time keeping the family fed and clothed, but they never were without a home. They made do with a kerosene heater in winter, all sleeping in the same room, and when they couldn't afford electricity Mama would build a campfire in the back yard to heat up soup. They'd bundle up in blankets and sometimes she'd tell them ghost stories, until the kids were all droopy-eyed and they'd go inside to sleep. Maybe they were hard times, but not to Joe. He had his mama and brothers, and sooner or later Papa would come back, and until the demons started up, things would be good.

The line moved forward. Up at the kitchen door stood Rag Doll, wearing a frayed straw hat with faded ribbons hanging down, tray in hand, looking skittery like she was trying to dodge the police. She carried her food to the furthest table, sitting so she could watch everything, the way Joe liked to.

A voice boomed from inside the kitchen: "That all the fried potatoes I get?"

Joe didn't want any ruckus. He wanted to fill his stomach in peace.

"Damn place always cheap with the food." The man's voice echoed as he pushed himself through the swinging door, tray in hand. Big as a sycamore and nearly as dark, Cyphus Lawter held the tray like a weapon, staring down the whole dining room before making his way to an empty table. Joe lowered his head, not wanting to be noticed. He didn't want any fuss with Cyphus Lawter. Once he got to the serving area, he'd get his food and leave. He'd be long gone before Lawter got into a fight with whoever looked at him the wrong way.

"Just the burger, ma'am," Joe said to the plump woman who tried to put French fries on his plate.

"How about an apple?" she asked.

"Yes ma'am, that'd be fine." The apple would fit in his pocket, the bottled water and sandwich in his hands. As he exited into the dining room, he looked for the young mother, and was relieved to spot her on the opposite side of the room from Cyphus Lawter. Rag Doll had vanished, which was what Joe intended to do, too. He slipped through the side door and up the street.

Once in the park, he found a bench under a towering magnolia to have his lunch. A few crows pecked at the ground around the tree, fat shiny scavengers feasting on bread crumbs left by a picnicker. Overhead, a squirrel leapt branch-to-branch, quivering the heavy leaves on each limb. The burger went down in three hasty bites but he took his time with the apple, savoring its tarty-sweetness, letting the juice slide down his chin. He leaned back, very sleepy. Since no cops were around, maybe he could take a nap. He let his heavy eyelids close and drifted off.

He awoke to a loud whir-scrape-whir-scrape sound: two kids on skateboards careening down the sidewalk, balancing like they were riding a wave. Joe stood, testing his creaky knees. Not as bad as earlier, and a walk would get the blood flowing again. The plastic bottle from lunch bulged in his pocket, so he decided to head deeper into the park and find a water fountain to refill it. Then he'd start thinking about supper.

About five minutes down the narrow walkway he spotted a familiar hat lying in the grass like a napping creature: the ratty straw thing Rag Doll had worn at lunch. She usually took better care of her things, didn't just let them blow away. He snatched it up, thinking he might bump into her sometime later, and continued down the path.

"Stop it!" The voice was muffled. Joe wasn't sure if it was human or demon or even the Lord. He paused, listening.

"Please! You don't got no—" It was not the Lord. The Lord never talked like that. And Satan didn't plead. This was not Joe's business, so he resumed his walk.

"Help!" A woman's voice, familiar like the hat in his hand: Rag Doll. He scanned the wide thicket of bushes, knowing there was a hollow behind them where the crack smokers sometimes hid. He inched in closer, parting the branches, and peered in.

Rag Doll lay on the ground with a man in a bright red hat towering over her. Cyphus Lawter, his fist drawn back, his face hard as flagstone.

"Joe!" Rag Doll's shirt was torn apart to reveal white scratched flesh. Tears streaked her face. "Help me."

"Joe Booker, this ain't none of your business." Cyphus Lawter was ten years younger than Joe and packed with muscle like an ironworker. He straddled Rag Doll, a noticeable bulge in the crotch of his dungarees.

"Leave her be," Joe hollered.

"This ain't your affair," Lawter growled. "She owes me. She know she owe me."

Joe looked at Rag Doll, wondering what idiotic bargain she had struck with this beast of a man.

"I don't, Joe. I borrowed money, but—but I'll pay him back. As soon as

I got the cash. I will." She was always the fast talker, though Cyphus Lawter wasn't letting her talk her way out of this.

Lawter jerked open his belt buckle and clawed his pants down till they were bunched around his knees. "I'll take what you owe in trade."

"You should know better than to deal with a man like him," Joe said to Rag Doll, but his eyes fixed on Lawter. Rag Doll would lie with a man for money—everybody knew that. So why was she begging for help? His gaze skimmed the contours of her splayed body. The torn shirt. The way she cradled her arm against her. The spark of fear in her wide, dark eyes.

"Please Joe," she whispered.

"Please Joe," Lawter mocked, lowering his massive body on top of her. "Please Joe, stay and watch. See how a real man gets it done."

Joe wanted to walk away, to leave Rag Doll to this mess she'd made for herself, but she looked pale and fragile lying there. He thought of Mama and the darker days with Papa, the days when the devil pumped venom into his fists, when he'd seen bruises and fear on Mama's face.

Joe stepped into the thicket. "She don't want you doing her."

Lawter laughed, his teeth white as sandwich paper against his dark skin. "Even better."

"Get off her." Joe could feel his pulse pounding against his skull as his fingers curled into fists.

Lawter pulled up, hands flat against the ground, his junk riding the length of Rag Doll's shin.

"Off her!" Joe shoved him hard, Lawter landing in a heap beside Rag Doll, who scurried back, clutching her torn shirt.

Lawter bolted up. His narrowed eyes glared like they could sear skin. "You a dead man, Joe Booker."

Joe positioned himself between Rag Doll and Cyphus, who jerked his pants up as best he could. "Dead man," Lawter repeated, and lunged.

The elbow caught Joe like a spear right under his ribs. Joe lost his balance, toppling into the shrub. He sprang up, but Lawter was ready, his fist knuckling into Joe's chin. Pain exploded like fireworks but Joe pushed through it. He grabbed Cyphus's arm and swept a leg behind him, knocking him to the ground. Once on top of him, Joe pummeled his face with an angry fist. Blood spurted from Lawter's nose but Joe kept on.

"Kill him!" the devil said.

A trail of red streamed down Cyphus's cheek. The devil was working inside Joe and Joe couldn't stop. "Kill him!"

"Joe," Rag Doll said. "Joe!"

The voice cut through. Joe froze.

Lawter bucked and Joe climbed off him. His hand shook as he pulled one of the twenties from his pocket and threw it to the ground. "You got your money."

Joe grabbed Rag Doll by the elbow, and huffed his way out of the bushes and up the sidewalk.

"Dead man, Booker!" Lawter yelled after them. "Dead man."

As they hurried away, Joe tried to slow his breathing and the steam still building inside. They made it to the bench by the fountain, and Joe dropped down, knotting his hands between his knees to still them. Rag Doll tied up her shirt, wiped her eyes, and took the hat Joe had kept for her.

"He's a mean bastard. I wasn't sure what he'd do to me." She spoke quietly, her voice trembling.

"Stay away from him."

"You, too. You got the better of him. Cyphus Lawter ain't likely to forget." Joe knew this. "Dead man, Joe Booker!" Cyphus's threat rang in his ear.

"I'll pay that twenty back," Rag Doll said, replacing the hat on her head. "I promise. You know I'm good for it."

He watched as she limped off, knowing he'd never live to see that money. He'd be lucky if he lived to see spring.

• • •

LENA HAD PROMISED THERE would be no more secrets. It was a silent vow to her daughter asleep in the hospital room, to her husband, up in heaven (if there was one), and Lena would honor it, starting with her sons. So she told Elliott everything. About her separation from Mitch and her affair with Royce, dancing over the details about the distance that had claimed her marriage long before her cancer. Elliott had been understanding, even forgiving, but that he couldn't look her in the eye, that he'd left the room as though scurrying from a house fire had pierced her heart. Elliott was upstairs now. Was he packing? Perhaps he found his cramped New York apartment preferable to this house of lies.

Lena poured herself a glass of wine and eased down in a chair. A few flames flickered low, the fading embers glowing orange as a sunset. Lena wished she had on a sweater but didn't want to go upstairs because Elliott was there. They both needed their space.

Clomps down the steps weren't him, she knew that before Abby huffed into the room. She approached Lena, her hands tucked into the pockets of her nubby fleece jacket. "Everything okay? El looks like someone just kicked his kitten."

"Then I guess everything isn't okay," Lena answered.

Abby regarded her for a long moment then said, "That wine looks great. Think I'll join you." Abby went to the kitchen. Lena heard the back door open, then close, the clink of glass against bottle, then Abby's clogs thunking against the hardwood floor as she returned carrying the chardonnay, a glass, and a thick log for the fireplace. She heaved the log onto the glowing ash and wedged a chunk of fat lighter she'd found on the hearth underneath it. The fire shwooshed to life.

"Thought that might cut the chill." Abby poured herself some wine. "Did you and Elliott have a . . ." she hesitated, measuring her words. "Disagreement?"

"No." Lena sipped, hoping the wine might infuse her with the bravery she longed to feel. Abby kicked off her shoes and stretched her broad feet across the coffee table. Firelight reflected in the bowl of her glass.

"You carry quite a load, Le-Le. Wish you'd let me help."

"I betrayed Mitch." The words hung in the air like stubborn smoke. Saying it a second time was no easier.

Abby didn't say anything.

"It was two years ago. I took an oil and acrylics class at the university. I'd wanted to go for years but always talked myself out of it. I missed painting, though. It felt like a part of me that I kept locked in a box." She had wondered if it was still alive. "I was in a bad place. Smothered. That may sound dramatic but that's how it was. It started out as boredom, but then it got . . . darker. Besides keeping house and getting dinner ready for Mitch and Becca, I had no way to fill my hours. After a while, I stopped trying." She remembered the clock ticking. Three hours till Becca comes home. One hour before time to start dinner. Ten minutes before Mitch comes through the door. Three hours before time for bed. Twelve hours before she'd do it all over again. Tick. Tick.

"How were things with you and Mitch then?"

It was painful for Lena to consider the death of her marriage. Nothing sudden, but five years of steady decline. Habits had hardened. Mitch's rituals, like cleaning his ears with a Q-tip that he left on the sink, or flossing then studying each millimeter of the string as though looking for treasure, changed from minor annoyance to maddening. Worse was his panicking over every little health issue, becoming needier when she lost patience with him. The more he pulled on her, the stronger the drive to pull away.

Her habits became entrenched, too. Starting projects that she'd never finish. Expensive changes to the house like the granite countertops, new teak cabinets, and the garden tub in their bath: changes she made out of sheer boredom, to hell with the cost. Sex became a monthly exercise of sweat and tolerance. Things in bed were never creative, more like following a recipe: first do this, then this, etc, but after thirty years Lena grew to dread it.

"You and Mitch were together since you were seventeen. I can't imagine being with anybody that long," Abby said.

"I hungered for a change. Any change." The hunger became starvation. Lena had felt herself on the edge of a terrifying and familiar precipice: the black hole that swallowed her after Becca was born.

Abby lifted the bottle and refilled Lena's glass.

"I took the class. I was scared to death."

"Was Mitch supportive?" Abby asked.

"Of course he was." She could have told him she wanted to go to the moon and he'd support it. If he felt threatened by the disruption to their lives, he never voiced it.

"The class was intense," Lena said. "One of our first projects was to paint a self-portrait. I wanted to do it right. It had to be . . . perfect."

"That's my sister," Abby said with a smirk. "Never second best at anything."

Lena considered the truth in those words. It had been what their father expected. How she craved his approval, those fleeting smiles and nods, between drinks. God help her, she'd put the same burden of perfection on her own children.

"Did you create a masterpiece?" Abby's voice held a hint of sarcasm.

"No. It was . . . difficult for me." Lena's mind flashed on Becca at her last piano recital, frozen on the bench, unable to play. Lena had not comforted her, something she regretted to this day.

"When the class ended I asked to take the project home," she said to Abby. "But Royce wanted me to stay. To try again. So I did. And that was how it all started.

"The class was okay but I loved the studio time. Royce let me come early and stay late. I felt that was the time I could fully and completely breathe. He understood that." Nobody else had.

"Sounds like a kind of epiphany."

"I was living two lives. I hated being home. I loved being at the studio. I loved being with him. Royce." She stopped her story here, wanting to gauge Abby's reaction. Abby gripped the wine glass against her chest, her face soft.

Lena continued. "One day when Mitch came home—it was raining. He came home and hung his raincoat on the hook, adjusting the folds so that it hung just right, and he put his umbrella in the stand like he always did, the curve of the handle pointing left, and I wanted to hurl his raincoat on the floor and toss his umbrella out into the garage just to shake up our life. It was like I couldn't stand it for another single moment." She had wondered if she was going crazy, because the house was suffocating her, and the husband she had loved drifted farther and farther from her heart.

"And that's when you left?"

"For just a few days at first. I told Mitch I needed some time to myself. Mitch just stared at me like I was on the verge of a breakdown or something. His eyes held many questions but he didn't ask a single one." She had hoarded these memories for two years; it was hard to give them voice.

"I went to a hotel." She had gotten a room at a bed-and-breakfast downtown, but barely tossed her suitcase on the bed before she left to take a long walk on one of the riverfront trails. The sky had been gauzy gray with clouds pushing in. When the rain started, she kept moving, pounding down the path, as if she could walk forever if it kept her from going back to that coffin of a home. But instead, she made the call that changed all their lives.

"Royce met me there." She would never forget that first night. So awkward at first, Lena floundering and scared but Royce confident and amazed. He loved touch, read her body like it was Braille, every inch to be discovered. Later, cocooned in the four-poster bed with its Irish linens, they watched the rain through the window's rippled glass.

"Telling Mitch the truth was the hardest thing I've ever done. He looked like something had burst inside him. I moved out the following Friday. He called it a 'trial separation.' He thought it was some phase I'd work through."

"And Becca?" Abby asked.

Lena closed her eyes, remembering how she gave her daughter the news: "I'll have a place downtown, Becca. You can come see me on the weekends. I think it's best that you live here with your father so you won't have to change schools." It sounded so easy. *Here, daughter, you stay here. You don't really have a compartment in my new life.*

Lena said, "I thought I was doing the right thing for all of us, leaving Becca with Mitch. But when I told her she gave me this look—this completely blank look—as though she had no feelings at all about it. About me. She didn't get hurt or mad. She said, 'Okay,' and went upstairs to her room. I thought maybe she was expecting it. I thought maybe she was fine." But she had not been. She was so very far from fine.

Why hadn't Lena seen the signs then? The changes in her daughter's body she had attributed to puberty, the baby fat melting away, her limbs growing long as vines. Becca's self-consciousness, hiding in layers of clothes, all girls felt that way. It would change as she matured, as she discovered boys.

"I rented a loft," Lena said. "Bought new furniture. Royce didn't move in, but he was there every night. My separation lasted five weeks."

"Five weeks?" Abby jerked forward. "What the hell happened?"

"My life got hijacked." She had never said it like that but it was how she felt. One moment life was a new adventure. The next, a struggle for air.

"Royce found the lump," she said. "I hadn't been good about self-exams and Mitch—there wasn't much intimacy there. Royce insisted I get a mammogram and I had no intention to argue, it scared me to death. Dr. Jordan got me in the next morning, followed by the biopsy. And then I was summoned to his office."

It had rained again. One of those dark, engorged days, the sky roiling with clouds and then the heavens opened up. She couldn't find a place to park and didn't have an umbrella so she arrived at Dr. Jordan's waiting room drenched and terrified. "When I got to the appointment, Mitch was there. Dr. Jordan had called him, too."

He'd accompanied her to Brad Jordan's office. She remembered little of their conversation after the word "cancer" started ricocheting in her brain. She watched as Mitch took notes, asked questions, looked at the films that showed the mass like a white spider spreading inside her. Mitch took her hand and squeezed it. "It will be alright, Lena," he said, as if that were true.

Brad's nurse handed her a bunch of instructions and appointment slips saying where she would see the oncologist. Her numb fingers tried to grip the papers but they fluttered to the floor and Mitch gathered them up, slipping them into his appointment book. "I'll make sure she gets where she needs to," he said.

"Mitch drove me home," she said to Abby. "Not the apartment, but our house. He made me a cup of tea. My hand shook so hard I broke a cup."

"Are you going to tell the boys? Becca?" he had asked.

"I suppose." How would she, though? How would she say aloud, "I have cancer," to her youngest? She'd have to practice letting that word into her vocabulary.

"What about Royce?" Abby asked.

"Later I called, left a message on his cell that I needed to talk. That was one of many messages Royce didn't return. He told me later—much later—that he couldn't handle it."

"What a cowardly son of a bitch," Abby said, her voice venomous. "The least he could have done is offered you some support."

Lena smiled over the wine glass. Her big sister, defending her.

"Right before the surgery, I drove by the art studio and saw his van. Just parked there, like it always was. I wanted to throw up. I couldn't make myself go inside." His rejection had hurt as much as the cancer.

"You never got to say goodbye."

"Not then. But the other day. He called, wanted to see me, so we met for coffee."

"How'd that go?"

She shrugged. "I guess it answered some questions. But I'm not the person I was when I was with him. Not anymore."

Abby took a sip of wine and lowered it to the table. "It's weird to say this, but I'm grateful to Royce. He found the lump. If he hadn't . . ."

"I might not be here."

"That scares the hell out of me," Abby said.

It didn't scare Lena, not anymore. Had she died from the cancer, she wouldn't be living the nightmare of losing Mitch.

"I'm also grateful to Royce for waking you up. Hell, I'm even glad you had good sex. That may sound crass but you know me," Abby said.

Lena lifted her brows.

"What matters is that you and Mitch survived the affair. Things were good between you at the end, right?"

"Cancer changed everything. All I wanted was home. And Mitch was always, always home to me." But it wasn't as simple as that. She had seen something new in Mitch, blooming like that stubborn foxglove in the yard. He looked at her differently, studied her face like it was uncharted land. Touched her with more gentleness, fingers skimming her skin like a breath, asking her, "Does this feel okay?" and listening, really listening, when she said, "There, that's where I like it."

"And now you've lost home," Abby said. "I'm so sorry, Le-Le."

"It's worse than that. Everything—every little thing—is wrong in my life." She stared into the fire, yellow ribbons of shifting light.

"It will get better," Abby said.

"You don't know that. I sure as hell don't." A black knot of rage gripped her.

"No, I suppose I don't."

"Becca lived through all of it," Lena continued. "First the separation, then I came back and we had the cancer to deal with. She got lost and I didn't notice."

"Is that why she's so angry?"

"I think for her, the wrong parent died."

"She needs her mother. She may not know it but she does."

"Yes," Lena answered. Her most important job was to be Becca's mother. To get her well again.

"I want to help you with her. For as long as I'm here," Abby said.

"Thank you."

"Besides, it'll be good practice for when I get Esteban."

"How long can you stay?" Lena realized how much she didn't want Abby to leave. She'd come to expect Abby's clomping footsteps through the house, her booming voice filling every room, even the smell of burned coffee.

"Glad you're not ready to be rid of me." Abby lifted her glass. "I'm meeting with the lawyer again tomorrow. We'll see what he says."

CHAPTER 23

Tonya, dressed once more in her warrior suit, sat at her desk proofing the deposition she'd found in her email inbox. Heeding Ruth's advice, she had printed them out to edit, red pencil sharpened to a perfect point. The document had many errors and some of the statements made by the witness, as recorded, made not a lick of sense. She dreaded having to go back to the recordings but saw no other option if she was to prove to Ruth she did, in fact, have "an eye for details."

Her cell phone rang. She knew from the "Need You Now" ringtone it was John. She did not want another argument like this morning, when he showed her a flyer for a fancy new Toyota he wanted to buy with the money they'd get from the Hastings. He'd been to the car dealer without Tonya, and got huffy when she mentioned another minivan would suit her better. Maybe he was calling to apologize.

"Hey," she said.

"The Nissan Rogue," he said. "That's the car for us. I just test drove one. Smooth as satin."

"Shouldn't you be at work?"

"I'm going in late. Honestly, the way things are going, maybe I should just quit. The more time I'm there the more depressed I feel."

"Quit and do what?"

"Maybe take a few months off to get my head together. Once we get the settlement money, maybe I can start my own firm. I'd be the boss, I wouldn't have to put up with crap from anyone else."

Settlement money. Like it was his to spend. "We'll talk about it when I get home." She clicked off.

Marion was on the phone, too, with Dan-the-Man. He'd called twice and it wasn't even ten o'clock. Just as she hung up the phone, Janet rushed into the room, her blond hair hanging like drapes around her face. She had on a black shrug over a teal dress; her boobs bulged like pale jellyfish over the top. "Is Arthur—I mean, Mr. Jamison—available?"

"He's talking to a client," Tonya said. Behind Janet, Marion cupped her own breasts and jiggled them.

"I was supposed to get this to him." Janet wagged a file at her. Janet's nails were bright cherry red, like her lipstick.

"You can leave it with me if you'd like," Tonya said.

"The thing is—this is confidential," Janet said.

"Much of his correspondence is." Tonya faked a smile. They worked in a law firm; confidentiality came with the territory. "I'll put it right in his hands."

Marion straightened her back and tugged down the neckline of her cotton sweater, flashing a lacy pink bra, just as Ruth entered from the door behind her.

"Ruth!" Tonya hurried to snatch her attention. "Janet has a confidential file for Mr. Jamison."

Ruth approached her desk, her movements smooth and contained. Ruth always glided into a room like she was on invisible skates. She wore a brown suit, cream top buttoned to her chin, dark hair clipped back, every strand in place. Marion smoothed down her sweater and pretended to start on her inbox.

"He wanted me to give it to him." Janet emphasized the "me" as she held up the file. After Ruth regarded her for a moment, she grabbed the folder from Janet's hand and shoved it in Mr. Jamison's mailbox. Without a word, she exited.

"Guess that settles that," Marion said.

Janet flipped her hair back as she walked out.

"Things might get interesting around here." Marion peeled the wrapper from a fun-size Snickers bar. By the end of the day, she'd eat twelve of them and then marvel at the empty bag.

"What do you mean?" Tonya asked.

"Turf fight between the old bitch and the new bitch. We should sell tickets." She held up another piece of candy, offering it to Tonya. Tonya shook her head.

"I think Ruth can handle Janet."

"Did you hear Janet call him 'Arthur'?" Marion asked. "Think maybe they've got a thing going on?"

"No!" Tonya clutched her collar as disturbing images of a naked, turkey-necked Arthur Jamison and an ample-breasted Janet Price flooded her brain.

"I wouldn't put it past Janet. Maybe that's how she got the raise."

Tonya looked over at the closed door to Mr. Jamison's office. At last year's Christmas party she'd met his wife, Joy, a plump, smiley woman with a strand of pearls hanging over her olive green dress. She carried a small album of grandchildren photos in her purse and showed them to Tonya with obvious pride. Mr. Jamison kept Joy's picture behind his desk.

"I don't think Ruthless is too pleased about Janet's little raise. Makes me want to rethink my whole push-up bra plan." Marion looked down at her breasts; the lacy pink number must have been new.

Tonya said, "It seemed to work on Mr. J."

"Maybe. But do you think he's the most powerful person in this office? Think about it. Who actually rules this roost?"

She had a point. Mr. Jamison solicited Ruth's opinion on most things. His partner, Mr. Patel, depended on Ruth to keep the entire firm running like a machine. Ruth might not make all the major decisions, but she was in on the discussion. Without her, the place would grind to a halt.

Tonya glanced down at her warrior outfit. Ruth wouldn't wear such a bold color, though Janet might. Tonya might have to rethink her wardrobe.

• • •

Two hours later, Tonya adjusted the ear buds that were plugged into the digital recorder, pressed rewind, and listened again to what the witness had said. His voice wasn't pleasant though it was expressive, climbing up and down the scale as he defended his defunct factory that had sickened some of its workers. Mr. Patel, the senior law partner, loved litigation like this.

Tonya had spent two hours going over the witness statement and comparing it to the typed deposition. It had been tedious, boring, and productive. She struck through two lines of testimony, inserted her comments, and clicked off the machine. It was time to take her findings to Ruth.

Five minutes later, she stood in the doorway to Ruth's office, her mouth tasting minty because she had just brushed her teeth. Something about visiting Ruth's lair prompted good oral hygiene.

"Ruth? Got a second?" Tonya wished she didn't sound so hesitant. Janet never did. Even if Janet was flat-out wrong about something, she talked with complete confidence.

Ruth looked up from the computer, regarding her for a long moment. "Is there a problem?"

"Uhm. I think so." She cursed herself. Ruth hated indecision. What Ruth loved about the law, she often claimed, was that there was so little vague about it. She liked a world of black and white.

"You think so?" Her drawn eyebrows shot up her forehead.

Tonya straightened, pulling her shoulders back, forcing herself to meet Ruth's eye. She held up the stack of papers and gestured at the chair beside her. "Can I sit?"

Ruth nodded, clicking off the file she had been working on. Tonya cleared her throat. What if she was wrong? No, she wasn't. She had checked three times.

"I was reviewing the depositions from yesterday," she began. "You know, you told me to print them before editing and I did that. I saw something I wanted to show you."

"You found a typing error?" Ruth asked.

"No. Well, I thought it was at first. See, here on page seven, Mr. Patel asks the witness about the amount of money in the foreign accounts. Mr. Wagner—that's the witness—says he has seventy-three thousand dollars."

Ruth nodded. "We're suing him for unsafe labor practices. We have two plaintiffs suffering from COPD after asbestos exposure. The plant has closed, of course."

"Yes." Tonya flipped through the pages. "Only here, when Mr. Patel references the money again, Mr. Wagner says, 'the free seventy three is not accessible to me.' I read that over and over because it didn't make any sense."

Ruth looked at the blue-highlighted text. "It is strange. But a deposition can be stressful on the person being questioned. People sometimes stumble over their words."

Tonya flipped back through the pages. "I found other errors on this transcript, so I thought maybe Janet had typed the wrong word or something."

"Janet? Janet did the deposition?"

Tonya nodded. "Mr. Wagner talked very fast. I could see how she might—"

Ruth waved a hand, dismissing the excuse. "Go on."

"I listened to the recordings of the deposition to make the corrections." She was proud of this proof that she was "going the extra mile," like Dr. Allaway would have done.

Tonya said, "Mr. Wagner didn't say 'free seventy-three', he said 'three seventy-three.'"

"Are you sure?"

"Definitely. He changed what he said was the amount of his overseas account by three hundred thousand. He sort of stuttered after that, shifting to a discussion of the value of the plant itself, which he says will never sell because of the asbestos. I think he was trying to cover up what he'd divulged."

Ruth snatched up the pages, comparing the text that Tonya had high-lighted with a pale blue marker. "Well damn," Ruth said.

Tonya had never heard her curse before. She suppressed a smile, eager to tell Marion.

"You know what this means?" Ruth asked.

"That Mr. Wagner is hiding assets. I guess that's easier to do if you keep money overseas."

"It is. But since we know it's there, we'll just have to dig a little more." She straightened the sheets of paper. "This is great work, Tonya."

Tonya blinked, embarrassed by the praise from such an unlikely source. Ruth must have noticed because she actually smiled at her.

"I mean it. You found a problem and then you researched it. That's taking an extra step. I haven't seen you do something like that before." Ruth watched her like a cat eyeing a lizard. Curious for now, but capable of pouncing. "Want to explain this change in you?"

Tonya smoothed her skirt and tried to summon courage. Ruth could advise her about her situation. Or, Ruth could decide she was a moron for getting herself into it. She looked at the clean surface of Ruth's desk, the arranged folders on the credenza behind her. The lone photograph of a groomed poodle in the window sill. Ruth's life lacked the clutter that Tonya's had.

"The wreck. It's made me re-evaluate some things. I want to put more focus on my career."

Ruth steepled her fingers, trim pale tips clicking together. "Your career as an administrative assistant?"

"No. I want to become a paralegal." There, she'd said it. She sucked in a deep breath and continued: "Janet was able to work and go to school, so I think I can do that, too. I want to have more challenging assignments. I want to know I can provide for my little boy and give him a home and save for his college even if I'm on my own, even if I don't take the money from the lawsuit. I want . . ." Oh hell. Why had she said all that? Once the words started coming out she couldn't seem to stop them, and now they lay splattered across Ruth's pristine desk.

Ruth rocked back in the chair, narrowing her eyes, and Tonya had a panicked thought of rushing from her office, maybe even hiding under her own desk. She didn't though. They sat in a cool, unsettling silence, except for the steady ding of emails coming into Ruth's computer.

Tonya drew a deep breath, felt her lungs push against her ribs, and released it like Dr. Allaway had taught her to do. She said, "I'm sorry, Ruth.

What I meant to say is, I think I have more I can offer this firm. And I'm hoping that with your help, I can prove it."

• • •

SANDY TOOK A SIP OF iced tea and grimaced as Sean placed the seven wooden tiles on the board, the first covering the "triple word score" square: b-r-a-i-n-e-d.

"Brain is a verb?" Sandy asked, shuffling her own scrabble letters on the rack. Sarah McLachlan's voice poured like warm honey through the stereo speakers. They used to listen to Lady Gaga when they played, but that put them in a partying mood.

"Look it up!" Sean tossed her the dictionary. Miss Saigon hopped up on the coffee table, causing it to quake, letters nearly bouncing out of the plastic ridges.

"I could brain you for scoring that high," Sandy said. "Guess it is a verb."

This was a more sedate Scrabble game than they were used to, since they'd had to forgo the "hit of tequila for every double or triple word scored" rule. Sandy gripped the sweating tumbler of sweet tea.

Miss Saigon batted at the letter "B" until she loosened it from the board and flipped it off the table.

"Rained. Only twenty-eight points. Thanks, Miss Saigon."

"A conspiracy of females." Sean replaced the letter and scooped up the beast. "Glad y'all are getting along better."

"I've grown to admire Miss Saigon. She's got herself a perfect little life here in my house."

Sean positioned the cat like an infant and cooed into her face. "We should get you a kitten. A little yellow tabby. Adam says they make the nicest cats."

"Me? Seriously?" She played d-a-m-n-e-d for eighteen points. "Like I need something else to take care of?"

He ignored her. "We could name her Evita. Miss Saigon would love to have a little sister, wouldn't you, Doll?"

"No. And by that I mean, NO. We do not need another cat."

Sean twisted his lips into an exaggerated pout as he played w-a-r-m-s, the S, on a double word space, also attached to z-a-p. Another forty-eight points. The guy was a freakin' Scrabble wizard; you'd think it would take him less than fifteen years to finish college. "I want you to have company. Don't want you to ever be all by your lonesome."

Sometimes being all by her lonesome sounded like heaven to Sandy, like on days when Sean came in from work at one A.M. and felt the need to listen to Kiss CDs before going to bed. "I like the freedom of not being tied down. Animals have to be fed and walked and tended to. I do enough of that at work."

"Animals make a home a home," Sean retorted.

She pointed at Miss Saigon who, paws in the air, nose pressed into Sean's t-shirt, snored. "You mean, animals make themselves at home." She couldn't imagine another creature living in their house. Sean's cat produced enough hair to stuff a mattress, and Sandy was the one who did the vacuuming. Besides, she wasn't sure she'd even stay in Columbia. Once her probation was over and her nursing license fully reinstated, she might choose to start over in Atlanta, or Charleston, or even Canada.

A bell preceded the front door opening and Adam's head popping in. "I brought pizza. May I enter?"

"Come on in." Sandy realized she was hungry, but then she thought how great pizza went with beer, and wasn't sure how well ginger ale would measure up. Maybe she should excuse herself, take a drive or something, so the guys could share a couple of Coronas with their meal.

"Ohhhhh, Scrabble. Can I play?" Adam asked.

"You can take my seat. Sean's killing me," she answered.

Sean held up a hand. "Nope. You see this through to the end, dear cousin. We'll give Adam the mean of our scores and he can draw his letters."

"After we eat," Adam said. "It's white pizza with sundried tomatoes and asparagus."

"That sounds sort of horrible," Sandy said.

"Stretch a little. It's much better than pepperoni. I also brought us this." He opened a bag and pulled out a six pack. "Un-beer. I hope that's okay."

Sandy reached for one of the alcohol-free lagers and studied the label. "Hell yeah, it's okay. Let's eat."

The beer tasted slightly different than her favorite. It would take a few minutes for her body to miss the alcohol buzz. The pizza went down easier if she imagined it some new haute cuisine rather than her favorite comfort food. Adam's presence always enlivened a room. She laughed at his jokes and tried to imagine herself living somewhere else.

The traffic in Atlanta would drive her to madness. Charleston had its charm, and its endless stretches of beach, but summer there was like a hot rag draped over your face, and Sandy no longer had the physique for strapless sundresses. Could she return to Charlotte? She still had friends there—maybe—and the city was large enough that she wouldn't have to run into Donald. No, Charlotte would be a step backwards.

Sean was telling Adam his "new kitten for Sandy" idea, and Adam was ready to pile them all in his car to visit shelters.

"No," she said, popping a grilled asparagus in her mouth.

Maybe somewhere north: Virginia or DC or even New England, which she and Donald had visited that luscious green summer when she'd been pregnant. They had gone to every lighthouse they could find and stayed at quaint inns in villages like Boothbay Harbor, Pemaquid, and Castine. Later, they'd picked wild blueberries and cruised along Casco Bay, with Donald taking enough pictures to fill an album.

"What about an aquarium?" Adam asked. "Beautiful betta fish. All those fluttery fins. Like water rainbows."

"Aren't they killers?" she said. "Don't they, like, slaughter each other? Do I need that kind of drama?"

Adam laughed and opened another non-beer.

Sandy slid her plate away, her mind full of New England breezes. A niggle of sadness tugged at her, but there was also joy there, too, a small bright flash of it, at the glimpse of Donald's smile, at the feel of his hand on her swollen belly. Sandy realized with amazement that it was the first time she felt something other than sorrow at remembering that time. She could remember Donald without zeroing in on his betrayal. How had it happened?

"A kitten then," Sean said definitively. "I'll bring one home and you'll fall in love and that will be that."

Sandy's cell phone rang. She didn't recognize the number. "I already have a two-legged pet," she muttered to Sean, carrying the phone into the kitchen.

"Hello?"

"Sandy? This is Becca. Do you remember me?"

"Of course I do," Sandy answered, stunned that the kid had actually called her. "How are you doing?"

"Okay."

"Hmmm. You sound like maybe you don't feel okay."

"I shouldn't be bothering you," Becca said, like she planned to hang up.

"No, it's fine. I'm glad you did," Sandy said.

"I had a session with Dr. Owens. I'm waiting for Mom to pick me up."

"That's good. Dr. Owens knows what she's doing."

"I guess." Becca's voice was hesitant.

"Was it a hard session?" Sandy asked.

"They're all a little hard."

"I suppose they are." Sandy's therapy in rehab had been that way. She dreaded every entrance into Dr. Flanders's office and sometimes when she left, she'd want to crawl into bed from sheer emotional exhaustion.

"I met this girl in the waiting room. She was weird," Becca said.

"Weird how?"

"Skinny. But that wasn't all. She had strange hair growing all over her arms and neck and face. I asked Dr. Owens about it but she said she couldn't discuss other patients."

"What color was the hair?" Sandy asked.

"That was what was weird. It was white. The hair on her head and eyebrows was brown."

"I'll bet that did look strange." Sandy had seen it once before on an anorexic girl in intensive care. She had looked like a mythical creature: a fairy or nymph, except for the machines beeping around her.

"I thought maybe you would know what was wrong with her, since you're a nurse."

"It's called lanugo."

"Lanugo," Becca repeated slowly.

"When people with eating disorders lose all of their body fat, they sometimes grow this layer of soft fur. Our bodies are wired to do that for warmth. Premature babies are often born with lanugo."

"She looked like she was part albino ape."

They were tube-feeding the girl Sandy had worked on. When she regained enough strength, she tried to tear the sustenance from her body, fighting so hard to die. While they'd gotten her stabilized so she could move down to psych, Sandy didn't have much hope for her long-term survival. The disease had her in its grip and wasn't letting go.

"Did the girl seem self-conscious?" Sandy asked.

"Not at all. She was proud of herself."

Sandy wasn't sure how to proceed here. She wasn't Becca's nurse or counselor. She shouldn't have given the kid her phone number but she had.

"She said she weighed ninety-two pounds but that she'd been down to seventy-three," Becca said. "She acted like they should give her a trophy or something."

Trophy was an interesting choice of words. Did Becca now understand the self-deception? How the drive to lose more, more, more, could become a fatal competition? That the trophy was sometimes death?

"She talked about puking and stuff," Becca continued. "Like it was something to be proud of." She grew silent. Sandy heard swallowing, then Becca spoke again, quieter now. "I know how that girl was thinking. You do feel proud when you've contained your calories. And especially when you get on the scale and a few pounds are gone. You work so hard and it feels good."

"After a while it doesn't feel good, does it?" Sandy prayed she was saying the right things. She had no real business offering advice to this kid, not with her so screwed up herself. She should tell Becca to talk about this with Dr. Owens and end this call.

"Sometimes you get so hungry. You don't mean to. And then you've made a big mistake. You've eaten and eaten and you feel fat and bloated and all you want is to be empty."

Sandy understood this. Twice before rehab, she'd tried to quit using, but had failed both attempts. The slip from the wagon felt good at first, the drugs taking hold, warm pharmaceutical light filling her up. Until the drugs wore off and blackness descended.

"But then empty feels worst of all." Sandy hoped this was the right path. "Doesn't it?"

"I don't—" Becca's voice was so soft, Sandy could scarcely hear it. "I don't want to be her."

"You don't want to be like the girl you met," Sandy echoed.

"She scares me."

Scared was good. Scared might give Becca the drive she'd need to recover from the monster. "You're not her, Becca. You're not her." Sandy wanted to keep saying it, let it be a mantra for the troubled kid.

"I keep thinking about how my dad used to drive me to school," Becca said, changing the subject. "I'd read the crossword puzzle out loud. He knew most of the answers."

"Your dad was a smart guy."

"We haven't done that in a long time. I stopped asking him to drive me to school after Kayla got her license. But what if I'd asked him to take me that morning? Maybe I could have stopped the wreck. Or done CPR sooner. I could have kept him from . . ." her voice trailed off.

"I don't think you could have, even if you'd been in the car with him. His heart—there was a lot of damage."

Becca didn't say anything.

"You were a good daughter. But you could not have saved him." She used her firm, no-nonsense tone.

More silence. In the living room, Sean and Adam had the classifieds spread out, undoubtedly looking for a pet for her. Sean looked up and smirked.

"Becca?"

"Okay. Bye, Sandy."

CHAPTER 24

Lena sat across from her unexpected visitors. Sims sometimes came over like this, but Bill Tanner, sans clerical collar, showing up right behind him had been a surprise. "Wasn't sure I'd find you at home," he said. People didn't just stop by like that anymore. They did when she was a child, especially on a lazy weekend afternoon. A friend of her mother's would knock on the door and say, "Brought y'all some zucchini," then stay for a few hours for sweet tea and gossip. Her mother always kept the house neat as a pin, just in case, and Lena had followed that tradition.

"I asked him to come," Sims said, which alarmed her. Had something else happened? "Sims?" she asked.

He placed a folder on the kitchen table, not meeting her eye.

"Somebody better tell me what's going on," she said.

Bill held up a stack of envelopes. "I've received a ton of memorials in Mitch's name. I wanted to talk to you and Sims about how to use the money."

"Oh." She exhaled. Mitch had so many friends and colleagues. How should they spend the donations?

"There's the church organ fund," Bill said. "And we have the homeless outreach program. There's enough money here to sponsor that for a year."

"What do you think, Sims?" she asked.

Sims seemed lost in thought. He fidgeted with the glass salt shaker, spinning it so that it rumbled annoyingly against the table. She almost yanked it from him. "That's not the only reason you're here," she said.

He twirled the shaker again and let it go. It toppled over, dusting the table with salt.

"What is it? Just tell me," she said, as though needing a band-aid tugged off.

"I've been going over Dad's finances. Things aren't as—solid—as I'd hoped."

"We knew that."

"When his business fell off, Dad had to make some changes."

"What kind of changes?"

"For starters, he took out a second mortgage on the house. Damn place was almost paid for. Now we owe over three hundred thousand."

"Three hundred thousand." Speaking the words made them no more real. "He didn't . . . he never told me."

"Didn't tell me either." Sims's voice was edged with anger.

"What about our bank accounts?"

"You have enough in checking to cover bills for two months."

"And savings?"

"About six thousand."

Six thousand was nothing. Six thousand would barely get them through Christmas. Lena turned to look out the window as the news took root. Mitch's garden. The expanse of lawn, now a dusty brown. This had been her home for thirty years but she would lose it. She was losing everything.

She saw Sims looking at Bill, who said, "Tell her the rest. She needs to know."

"What?" she demanded.

"It's about Dad's accident. The other vehicle—a mother and kid were injured."

Of course she knew that. She remembered the relief she felt when she'd heard they would be okay. "The paramedics said they weren't badly injured."

"Right. But you know how it is. Whiplash and the like. People claim pain and suffering, go to one of those shyster TV lawyers."

Bill leaned back, crossing his arms, but didn't speak.

"They won't settle with our insurance company," Sims said. "They smell money to be made. They could go after Dad's personal assets."

"Personal assets?" It was preposterous. What did they have to go after?

"We may need our own lawyer to fight this thing. But the bottom line is Dad caused the crash. He was the one ticketed." He gripped the shaker again, knuckles paling.

"But we don't have anything. How can we pay—" She pressed her hands against the table, needing to be grounded by the solid wood.

"We'll have to settle. Maybe throw some money at them to see if they'll go away."

Hadn't he heard her? "Money from where? The life insurance? That's Becca's college money." And what she counted on to cover the mortgage and bills until she found a job.

"Yeah, about that." Sims shot an awkward glance at Bill.

"There is life insurance, isn't there?" she asked, dread mounting. "He didn't—"

"It's there, but Dad renegotiated his policy around the same time he refinanced the house."

"How much?"

"He's got twenty-five thousand on his policy."

How could Mitch have done this to her? To them?

"Mom," Sims said. "It'll be okay."

"How will it be okay? How can you say that? Nothing is okay." Where would she and Becca go? An apartment? A trailer? Fear spread its icy fingers through her gut. She stood, her hands still on the table, and glared at the two men.

"So now I know," she said. "I have a lot to think about. You can show yourselves out." She left the room. Upstairs, she splashed cold water on her face and stared at her reflection in the mirror. Was this her penance? Maybe she deserved it, but Becca didn't. Mitch should have told her how bad things were. They would have reduced expenses. She would have gotten a job. Maybe they would have moved somewhere smaller.

It felt like walking on a tightrope against a fierce wind; it was impossible to find balance. It wasn't just her—she had Becca to worry about, too. How could she make things right?

When she returned downstairs she found Bill Tanner alone at the table. He offered an apologetic smile. "Just wanted to make sure you're alright."

"I'm a long way from alright." She reached for the coffee she'd poured earlier. It had chilled, but she didn't care.

"I know this feels like too much," Bill said. "But God—"

"Don't go there, Bill. I am not in the mood for one of those 'God doesn't give us more than we can handle' talks. I don't believe it, and quite frankly, I'll throttle you if you start."

He flinched, running a hand over the stack of memorials. Brown spots peppered his skin.

"My husband worked hard his whole life. He was a good man. And now—he's gone. Snatched up? Why? What the hell is the point?" Anger unwound itself inside her, frightening but strangely energizing.

She clutched her coffee cup, a piece of emerald green pottery she and Mitch had bought during a weekend trip to North Carolina. He had chosen a blue one, but broke the handle by overstuffing the dishwasher. He had always done that, cramming pots around plates, bowls around cups, even when the dishes didn't get as clean that way. They had bought a larger dishwasher when they did the kitchen renovation she now knew they couldn't afford.

Bill started to speak but didn't. His eyes wouldn't meet hers.

"And now I find out Mitch kept all this from me," she blurted out. "He's gone, and I'm left with this . . . mess." She had trusted Mitch wholly, completely. Had given herself to him from that fragile place of surviving cancer, and he had lied to her. Lied.

"Maybe he wanted to protect you."

"Or maybe he didn't trust me enough to tell me. Did he think I'd leave him if I knew? Damn it, Bill. I thought we were stronger than that." Her hand bound itself to the cup, squeezing, wanting to hurl it. She felt him watching, wondering if he was assessing her for one of the five stages of grief. *Well guess what, reverend. I've reached the "my life has gone all to hell" stage.*

Lena carried her mug to the sink, rinsed it, and placed it in the dishwasher they couldn't afford. Out the window, Abby's rental car pulled into the drive. Elliott had criticized her choice of the mammoth, "gas-guzzling, to-hell-with-the-planet" vehicle, but when Abby said, "I'm used to getting shot at. Forgive me if I want lots of metal around me," it had shut him up.

She noticed Abby slamming the door with more force than necessary. What had her so upset? She had gone to see the attorney who was helping with the adoption; Lena hoped she hadn't gotten bad news. There'd been enough of that today. Abby stomped up the steps and threw open the door, her face crimson, her eyes so wide that Lena could see a rim of white around the irises. "What's happened?" Lena asked, guiding her to a chair. "Are you ill?"

Abby's gaze searched the room like a trapped bird.

Bill hurried to the sink for a glass of water for her.

"Bill, this is my sister, Abby," Lena said, keeping her voice calm. "Abby, what happened?"

Abby's lip trembled. This was very un-Abby. Was she having a heart attack?

"It's . . . not going to happen. Esteban. I'm not . . . I'm not getting him." She lowered her head, grinding her hands into her eyes to erase tears, quaking to stifle the sobs she was too proud to release.

"Oh, no," Lena said.

Bill looked confused but he didn't ask questions, just let Abby feel the tremors of this change in her plan.

"Abby?" Bill's voice was gentle. "Take a deep breath, okay? I know you're very upset but take a deep, slow breath."

Lena realized he was trying to keep her sister from hyperventilating.

"That's good," he said. "Now try another."

Abby looked at him, terrified, but complied. Lena dropped into the seat beside her as the news sunk in. Abby loved that little boy. Had already invested her heart. And now?

"Who's Esteban?" Bill asked, returning to his chair.

Lena told him all of it, Abby filling in a few details: "He's a beautiful boy. And he's doing well now that he's getting physical therapy and help with his speech. I can't let him stay in that orphanage . . . I can't!"

"I can see you're quite attached to him," Bill said. "Can you tell me what the lawyer said?"

"The adoption agency didn't follow the rules. You don't know what it's like down there—so much corruption. Yes, I've paid bribes. I did everything I was told to do. But there's this thing called the "Hague Process" that the agency didn't follow so they voided my application." She spoke in a staccato ramble, ticking off the details.

"Can you start the process over?" Lena asked.

"There's no time. I'm fifty-five this year, which makes me ineligible." She shook her head. "I've got to get back down there. I have to do something."

What did that mean? Would Abby kidnap the child?

"Hold on a second," Bill said, lifting a finger. "Tell me about the agency you used."

Abby told him. Since she'd been living in Peru, a local church-run agency had said she qualified to adopt. It would be quicker than an international process, they told her, especially because she had local references. Others in her situation had done it; she'd met the children they'd adopted. She thought it would be fine. She had already paid twenty-eight thousand Nuevo Sol, which was about ten thousand dollars, and now it felt like her whole world had been ripped away. Lena knew how that felt. She reached Abby's hand.

Bill listened, his forefinger pressed against his top lip. When Abby finished, he regarded her for a long moment and said, "Abby, do you mind if I look into this?"

Lena raised her brows at the minister. Maybe Bill and his God could help Abby. At least someone might get a happy ending to all this.

• • •

THE SUN HUNG LOW on the horizon. Joe tried to ignore the growl of hunger in his gut as he eyed the line leading up to the Methodist church soup kitchen. The clatter and talking inside was enough to tell him the supper wasn't half bad, but he didn't dare go in, because Cyphus Lawter might be eating, and

Joe was doing all he could to avoid that man. So he'd find something else for his supper. As he trudged uptown, he detoured down an alley behind a string of restaurants. His Dumpster-diving days were over, but sometimes there'd be bags of fresh garbage stacked behind kitchen doors that he could pick through. Luck was with him; a man tossed a box of fruit outside the fancy dessert place: two bruised bananas, a clump of grapes, and three apples. Joe stuffed his pockets and kept moving.

The apples had a few mushy spots he munched around as he headed towards his nest. It hadn't been a bad day. Not too cold or too windy. He'd spent the afternoon up by the river, listening to the gurgle and rush of the current. The voices had quieted, no Satan, but no word from the Lord. Joe hoped the Lord hadn't left him again, because of what had happened with Cyphus. Because Joe had let the devil inside loose. He would have killed Lawter if Rag Doll hadn't stopped him. And now Lawter aimed to kill Joe, which was why Joe was being careful.

Now that he thought about it, a week had passed with no sign of Cyphus. Maybe he'd gotten busted. Maybe he'd pissed off a dealer and run off. He was like that, terrorizing the town then disappearing for months on end. Maybe Joe didn't need to be so cautious; his problem might have taken care of itself. Joe picked up speed as he headed toward the church.

Reverend Bill's car was still in the lot and he could see the pastor in the churchyard talking to someone, maybe somebody from the church who needed prayer or guidance. Joe slowed his stride, not wanting to interrupt. Reverend Bill spotted him, though, and motioned him over. Maybe he had work for Joe to do.

As he approached, he recognized the large presence looming beside the pastor and trepidation filled his chest. Cyphus Lawter. Not here. Not on this holy ground. Joe hurried through the gate and caught the pastor's smile in his direction. "There you are, Joe," he said.

"Reverend." Joe felt queasy. Lawter had on dungarees, his hands in his pockets, rocking back on his heels like he deserved to be in a conversation with Reverend Bill.

"This fella came to see you," the pastor said, his voice kindly.

"Yes, sir."

Lawter's mouth slid back in an icy smile. "I been waiting on you Joe. Had a nice little chat with the reverend here."

Joe's hands made fists at his side. What did Lawter have in mind? What if Joe hadn't got here? Lawter might have hurt the Reverend. Stolen from him. Left him bleeding in the graveyard.

"You okay?" Reverend Bill studied Joe's face as if looking for some answer that wasn't there.

"I'll leave you two to your business, then." Reverend Bill gave him another long look before exiting the graveyard. As Joe watched the pastor slide into the blue car and drive away, a wave of relief washed over him. Reverend Bill was safe, for now.

"You ain't an easy man to find, Joe Booker. But I got my ways." Lawter plucked up a stick and twisted it in his hand. "Got yourself a nice little squat here. The reverend there looking out for you. Nice man, ain't he?"

Joe felt the devil building inside like hot lava at the idea of Cyphus Lawter in this Holy place. He wanted to pummel the man, to finish what he started in the park. Not here, though. Not so close to the Lord's house.

Lawter chewed on the stem of the twig. "You and me got some stuff to settle. Can't do it right now cause I got some people waiting. A little transaction in the works."

Drugs. That beast of a man brought drugs to the churchyard.

"But now that I know where to find you—" Lawter smiled.

"You won't find me here again." Joe trembled at the meaning of his own words. He could no longer stay at the church, not with Lawter knowing. He wouldn't bring that kind of evil here.

"But I will find you. And once I'm done with you, I might make this my nest," Lawter said. "Got all them rich people come here every Sunday. Got that nice reverend nearby. Maybe he'll say a prayer for me. Or maybe . . ." Lawter flicked the stick to the ground, backed through the gate, and trotted away.

Joe stumbled over to Mr. Pinckney's grave, a heaviness like the headstone sinking onto him. He had to leave and never return. He'd been wrong to stay this long, wrong to leave a trail Lawter could follow. Wrong to bring that kind of evil to Reverend Bill. What about Lawter's other threats? What if he came back here? What would he do?

Joe touched the shiny granite tombstone that had been his home, had brought him peace, for so long. He shook his head.

There'd be no peace for him now.

CHAPTER 25

S andy ventured into the break room, relieved to find it unoccupied, so damn tired of being "on." On for nursing report, for rounds with the chief of staff and three new residents who followed him around like goslings, for the wife of a new admit, a red-faced woman who sought constant reassurance, "Are you sure that machine is supposed to make that noise?"

Sandy was running out of nice. After pouring a cup of coffee, she dropped into a chair and stared into her mug. She used to drink two Starbucks lattés a day. Now she was up to five mugs of crap coffee and maybe she was changing one addiction for another, but at least she hadn't picked up smoking. Yet.

"There you are. Didn't you hear my page?" Marie Hempshall stood with her back to the door, arms folded across her ample chest.

"Is there a problem?"

"You bloody well know there's a problem. Come with me."

"Come with you where?" Sandy rose slowly, not wanting to overreact to Marie's dramatic tone.

"The medical director's office." Marie led her out the door and down the hall, slowing at the nurse's station and giving a pointed look at the med cart parked there. Other staff had clustered around it: Pete Borden. The pharmacy tech. And a man and woman from security, who stepped behind her.

"What's going on, Marie?" Panic echoed in her voice. The officers came close enough to brush her arms.

"I think you know."

Sandy looked at Pete who fanned out his hands as if to say, "You got me." The security officers nudged her forward. Deep shit, that's what this was. She was in deep shit and she had no clue why. Something to do with the med cart? Crap.

Marie held open the door to the Medical Director's conference room, the two security guards entering and taking seats. Sandy positioned herself as close to the door as she could.

"I think you need to tell me what this is about." Sandy tried to summon indignation when all she felt was terror.

Marie said to one of the officers, "Do you want to take over from here?"

Sandy had seen the man before; he had silver hair that made a widow's peak over an oily forehead. "Please take a seat, Ms. Albright," he said.

She obeyed, deciding it best not to argue with security.

"I understand you are restricted from access to Schedule Two medications. Is that correct?" he asked.

"Yes."

"Did you approach the pharmacy cart today when you were on rounds?"

"No."

"Are you sure? Records indicate that you were in room 517 and then 523. The cart was parked just outside room 521."

"I wasn't administering meds," she said.

"No, but Pete was," Marie interjected. "He and the pharmacy tech had loaded the cart. When they reached 523, the medication cup holding two Oxycodone tablets was missing."

Sandy swallowed. "I didn't take them."

"That's your answer?" Marie glared at Sandy like she expected a confession.

"That's my answer. I'm in recovery. I haven't used in almost four months." Stupid tremor in her voice. So stupid.

Marie said to the man, "Sandy admitted to me that this is her drug of choice. And as you know, she has a provisional nursing license that will be revoked if she has a single drug infraction."

Sandy slammed her hand against the shiny table. "I didn't take them! You can't just accuse me of this."

He lifted a finger. "Let's take it down a notch, Ms. Albright."

"I can't believe this," Marie said. "I thought—" Her mouth drooped in disappointment, as though she gave a damn about Sandy.

"Let's have the cup." Sandy stood. "Marie loves for me to pee in a cup so she can check it. Now's your chance, I'm ready to give you a sample."

"Very well." Ever-prepared Marie pulled a small white package from her pocket and ripped it open. "Dr. McKenzie has a private toilet, we'll use that."

So that was why they'd come in here. Sandy took the collection cup into the small bathroom. She tried to shut the door but Marie's foot came through the opening. Sandy closed her eyes, swallowing her humiliation as her boss backed against the wall to watch her urinate.

Sandy's bladder seized up. She was so screwed. Marie turned the faucet on. "This might help."

Sandy focused on the running water and tried not to imagine her future

236

going down the drain. At last, she was able to produce the urine sample. "Here." She gave the cup to Marie.

They returned to the conference room, Marie placing the specimen on a napkin and inserting her test card. Sandy's humiliation mounted as three sets of eyes riveted themselves to her piss. It felt like having a public mammogram. Marie clucked her tongue as she removed the tester.

"Positive?" security guy two asked.

'No," Sandy said. "Tell him, Marie. Tell him I tested clean."

"She hasn't taken the drug. Yet."

"Ms. Albright, will you consent to a search?" the older guy asked.

"And if I don't?"

Marie didn't reply.

"If I don't I'm fired," Sandy clarified, feeling queasy. "I can't believe this."

"Officer Nichols?" the man turned to the other officer.

When Officer Nichols stood, she came up to Sandy's armpits. She had a jowly face and long dark hair with red highlights. "Stretch out your arms," she said.

Sandy squirmed against her touch, jerked when the foreign hands reached into her pockets and patted her breasts and buttocks. How could this be happening?

"See? Nothing. I've got nothing on me except that used tissue you're holding," she said to Officer Nichols.

"What about her locker?" Marie directed this question to the man who shook his head.

"You've searched my things? Christ! Don't I have rights?" Fear waned, replaced by raw, grating anger at this violation.

"Your locker is hospital property." Marie took a seat, hands on table, fingers steepling. "Whatever you did with the drugs, it's best that you tell us," Marie said.

Sandy shook her head. No matter what she said, or did, she'd already been convicted. Still, they had no proof, and she didn't need to be subjected to anymore of this bullshit. She glanced at the officers. "I think we're done here."

Officer Nichols looked at her colleague who shrugged. "I guess you're free to go," he said.

"Wait a minute!" Marie blurted out. "She took the drugs. We can't have her working here if she's putting my floor at risk."

Sandy tore down the hall like a tornado, blew past her gathered colleagues and slammed the door to the locker room. "Damn it!" she spat out.

Her locker was ajar; her belongings strewn all over the bench. She found her purse on the bench, wallet, makeup case, and car keys scattered beside it. She collected everything and left the room. She knew exactly where she needed to go next.

When she reached the seventh floor PT department, she didn't stop at the reception window, but moved straight through the treatment areas to the staff offices. Nathan Capers sat in his cubicle, one leg up on the desk, cell phone in his hairy hand. He looked up at her and at the bundle of her belongings in her arms. He clicked off the phone.

She didn't say a word. Nathan smiled, and it filled her with edgy hope. "I'll fix you up," he said.

And he did.

The staff elevator was empty. The pills lay in a cozy pile in the bottom of a plastic bag she'd shoved in her pocket. She thought about taking one right there between floors, but opted to wait. She'd stop for a bottle of wine on the way home—Sean was working, so she'd have the house to herself—and take the oxy with a glass of pinot because that was her very favorite recipe. She willed the elevator to hurry down so she could make this final escape.

Her purse, jacket, and an extra pair of crocs made an untidy bundle in her arms. The elevator stopped and someone entered. Crap.

Dr. Owens looked at her and smiled. "Hey there. Sandy, right?"

"Right," Sandy shifted her load and one of her crocs plopped to the floor.

Dr. Owens picked it up. "Quite a load you have there."

Sandy gathered her jacket closer and thought about the pills. The elevator pinged as the door closed.

"I wanted to thank you for your help with Becca Hastings. She's been good about keeping appointments," Dr. Owens said.

Good for her, Sandy thought, willing the elevator to pick up its pace.

"She mentioned you last session. Said she'd talked to you on the phone."

Sandy closed her eyes. So what if she'd given a patient her phone number? So what if that violated hospital policy about professional boundaries? Just add it to the ways-Sandy-screwed-up list.

Dr. Owens pressed the stop button on the elevator. "What's going on? Did you clean out your locker?"

Sandy looked down at her feet. The security officer had squeezed her ankles and searched in each shoe for the lost pills. She was lucky to escape without a cavity search.

"Sandy?" Dr. Owens's voice was insistent.

"Yes. I screwed up. Four months ago. And I'll never be free of it."

"Did you hurt someone?"

"Myself mostly."

"Yourself?"

"I'm an addict." The word felt sharp and pointed on her tongue, but so very right.

Dr. Owens pointed to the bundle in her arms. "You're leaving. Quit? Or get canned?"

"Neither. Yet." Sandy didn't understand the soft expression on the doctor's face. Hadn't she heard what Sandy said? *I'm an addict.*

"Are you in recovery?"

"Yes." So far she was, but the pills in her pocket beckoned.

"How long?"

"Twelve of the longest weeks of my miserable life." She blurted out the rest, how she'd been caught, gone to rehab, returned to work where her sins hung over her like a guillotine blade.

Dr. Owens didn't interrupt, didn't press the "start" button, listening to every single word. Sandy didn't even know why she was telling it, but couldn't stop, the whole story spread out in that cold steel elevator. "I can't keep working here. This place is a black hole. I've been sucked in too many times."

"That's an apt description."

Sandy eyed the panel of buttons beside the door. "Don't you think we should get this thing moving?"

"There are five elevators, Sandy. And they don't use this one for patients." She stepped closer. "Why did you give Becca your phone number?"

She leaned against the wall, cold steel pressing against her spine, remembering Becca's unsteady voice, how scared she was when she talked about the girl with lanugo. "Because that kid looked so lost. Patients like her—you throw whatever life rings you have and hope she grabs onto one."

"She grabbed onto you. You got her talking about her dad's death which is good. Real good. But next time, tell her to use the emergency number I gave her."

"I will." Sandy decided she liked Dr. Owens. She was smart and didn't seem to be full of shit like the others at this hospital.

"Do you like Intensive Care nursing? Maybe it isn't the best thing for you."

"I don't know what's the right thing. Guess that's what I need to figure out." Except the right thing was in her pocket: little disks of white that would make this pain go away.

"I hear you. Your recovery has to be priority one. Everything else is yards behind that."

Dr. Owens started the elevator again. "Good luck, Sandy. With whatever you decide."

Sandy flashed a shell of a smile. She needed a helluva lot more than luck. "Thanks."

CHAPTER 26

Becca walked through the garden to the sasanqua tree. The pink blooms had browned, though a few hung lush and rosy, nestled between dark green leaves. She picked one and tucked it behind her ear, a stupid thing, the petals would fall off before she made it into the house. Dylan would be here in an hour so they could go running together. There were many ways it could go wrong. One: he could meet her mother. Ugh. Or brother, double ugh. Two: She was so out of shape she might only be able to run a block. She'd be humiliated. Three: When Dylan saw her in her workout clothes, he might be repulsed. Becca slipped a finger under the rubber band encircling her wrist and snapped it. No negative thinking!

She rounded the yard, her hand skimming the tops of the azaleas and Chinese fringe bushes, the bare sticks where hydrangeas had colored the yard all summer. She'd miss all this when they had to move.

A van pulled into their driveway, dirty white, with no markings, but vaguely familiar. As she approached, something uncomfortable unfurled in her stomach. Royce Macy climbed out.

"Hey, Becca." He waved like they were old friends. He wore a flannel shirt over a turtleneck that looked seriously dorky, his hair tied back in an unraveling pony tail. "Nice flower."

She pulled the bloom from her ear as she stopped at the fence. "Mom's not here."

"When will she be back?"

She didn't answer. He'd parked in the spot where Dad used to park. She felt a little nauseous.

"Maybe you can you come and help me with something?" Without waiting for an answer, he circled to the back of the van. She didn't want to help but maybe she'd be rid of him sooner if she complied. The doors groaned when he jerked them open.

"This is your mom's stuff." He handed her a box full of canvases then pulled out a second box. "She left it at school."

"When?" Becca asked. Had Mom returned to classes? Had she deceived Becca once again?

"A year and a half ago." He plopped his box on one of the back steps leading to the kitchen. "I hope she'll get back to painting. Might help if she has this stuff."

Bringing the supplies had just been an excuse to come over. How dare he?

He pulled out a canvas and handed it to her. Colors swirled: reds, blues, purples. "She's got talent. Have to give her that."

That picture didn't look like proof of talent. She preferred the pictures of flowers and trees that Mom used to paint, or the one of Spats that hung in her bedroom. As she dropped the painting back in the box, she noticed another canvas: a picture of a woman with long brown hair sitting by a fire. Her long, elegant fingers interlocked on her knees; a half smile played on her lips. Under the figure, in small, cursive letters, was written "Future Becca."

Seriously? There was some resemblance, the shape of the jaw maybe, but this person was older and prettier and no way it could be Becca. Why had Mom painted it?

"Your mom coming home soon?"

She shoved the picture to the side inside the box and lifted it, hoping he'd get the hint and leave.

"Maybe I could wait for her?" He was not entitled to this conversation. He had never been a step-parent. He'd never been anything to her.

"I think you'd better leave."

His smile flattened. The other box rested at his feet, its contents a jumble as though tossed inside with little care. "Is she doing okay?"

"Actually, she's none of your business."

"Ouch." He wrinkled his nose as though stung and took a step towards the van. "Okay. I'll get out of your hair."

With that, Royce strode over to his van and drove away.

• • •

AN HOUR LATER, BECCA slid on her red jog bra, then swapped it for the blue one, and finally, the black one. Black was slimming. Her running capris were also black, but she donned bright green anklet socks for color before rooting around in her closet for her Nikes. Once she unearthed them, she stood, finding herself eye to eye with The Box.

She'd opened it once since Dad died, and that was for restocking. The Oreos package, still sealed. The two Snickers bars and quarter pound of M&Ms. The tube of Pringles—not her favorite chip, but they fit in the narrow cardboard space. All these treasures awaited her, yet she hadn't touched them.

When Dr. Owens asked about binging, Becca hadn't mentioned The Box. Maybe she would, one day, but then she'd have to give it up. Not yet. Maybe never. She replaced the lid and placed it inside an old gym bag.

Back in her room, she smoothed her hair back and secured it in a scrunchy, wishing it matched the neon socks. She glanced at the clock: another half hour before Dylan arrived. She decided to drink a half-glass of juice before the run for energy. Her first venture out in weeks, she'd need all the help she could get.

She was relieved to find the kitchen empty. Maybe she'd escape without twenty-thousand questions about her new running partner.

"Hey, squirt." Elliott entered so quietly she wondered if he was a ninja.

"Hey." She poured the juice, a little more than half a glass.

"That's not all you're having for breakfast."

She closed her eyes, fighting off a strong drive to bellow "Leave me the hell alone!" because saying that would confirm Elliott's—and everyone else's—belief she was off her rocker. But Christ, why did everyone have to interrogate her about what she put in her mouth?

"I had breakfast a while ago. I didn't just wake up." She smirked at his pajama bottoms. He'd been on his cell phone when she went to bed, and she'd heard his muted laughter as she drifted off to sleep.

"Touché." He stumbled to the cabinet for a bowl, then another for the cereal, which he doused with milk. He seemed too old for Cheerios, but Mom bought the box for him, as though she didn't remember he was no longer eight years old.

He sat at the table, plunging his spoon into the bowl. She sat across from him, positioning herself to look out the window for Dylan. She shouldn't have agreed to this run with him, she was too out of shape, but he'd been persistent. What if she didn't even make it to the park? She'd be humiliated.

"You're finally going to be rid of me," Elliott said.

"You're going back to New York?"

"Yep. Tomorrow. Should be back in time for a gig." He slurped from the spoon.

"Does Mom know?"

"She's the one who made me get the ticket. I don't feel right about leaving y'all, though."

She was pretty sure this was the first time he'd used the word "y'all" since arriving. New York had erased southern-speak from his vocabulary, but some was sneaking back in.

"We'll be okay," she said. Still, it would be strange not to hear him clattering around in the kitchen, or strumming his guitar, or chatting on the cell phone behind a closed door.

He pushed the cereal bowl away, propping his elbows on the table. "Are you sure?"

"Would people please stop asking me that?" She tried to sound more annoyed than she felt.

"I know you're tired of us worrying." He reached over and coiled his fingers around her hand. "I know you think I meddle too much. But you're my baby sister and I love you. Sorry, but I can't help being scared that something's going to happen to you."

"I . . . don't want you to be scared about me." She didn't pull her hand away. She studied his perfectly trimmed nails, felt the calluses on his fingertips, wanted to hold him here, in the kitchen, so he wouldn't fly back to New York to a life that she wasn't a part of, even if he was a huge pain in her ass. When Elliott left, it wouldn't be long before Abby'd go, too. Then it would just be her and Mom and a whole lot of house.

Elliott lifted their joined hands and kissed hers. "My friend Chloe—the woman who's an anorexic—she wasn't as brave as you are about getting help, not until she was really sick. Dad would be proud of you."

She swallowed a lump the size of a volleyball that rose in her throat. "I wish he was here," she said.

"Me, too." Elliott unwound his hand from hers to wipe his eyes. "Anyway, I loaded Skype on the desktop so we can talk more often. Plus I can keep an eye on you."

"Yeah, right." She rolled her eyes, but there was this little tug of relief to think she could see him on the computer.

Keys clattered against the back door. Not Dylan. Sims shoved himself into the kitchen, dropped the Bronco fob onto the counter, waved a vague hello before heading straight for the coffee pot. "What's with the boxes?" Sims pointed to the stuff Royce had brought.

"Someone dropped them off for Mom," she said. "They're from when she was in school." She had taken the portrait from the box and stashed it in her room, though she wasn't sure why. Maybe she'd shove it in the closet beside The Box. Then again, maybe she'd hang it on the wall beside Spats.

Sims shrugged, sipped his coffee, and looked at his brother. "You're still in pajamas." Sims had on golf clothes: ugly plaid pants, a red shirt, uglier shoes.

"Always the sharp eye," Elliott replied, returning to his cereal. Becca winced at the soggy mess in his bowl.

"I talked to Mom. She said Bill Tanner's coming over," Sims said.

"Mom summoned the priest?" Elliott asked. "Something we should know?"

"Aunt Abby got some troubling news about the adoption thing. Bill's trying to help. He knows somebody who knows somebody who handles that kind of stuff. Or something like that."

"Good," Becca said. Reverend Bill could maybe help her aunt. Let them all fuss over someone other than Becca for a change.

"Coffee tastes like crap." Sims drifted over to the sink and dumped it. "You're heading back to New York?"

"Yep. Mom insisted. She thought the idea of me helping with the realty firm was as ridiculous as you did."

"She didn't think that. Neither did I." Sims spoke quietly.

Elliott narrowed his eyes like he half-expected Sims to burst out laughing. Sims didn't. "That's . . . weird for you to say," Elliott commented.

"Mom wants you to stick with music. I think she feels like she never gave her art a real shot so she's living vicariously through you."

"Great. No pressure or anything." Elliott leaned back against the counter beside his brother. "What do you think?"

Sims offered a one-shouldered shrug. "I'd like it if you stuck around, but you should do what makes you happy. That's what Dad would want."

Silence stretched like a blanket over them. Becca eyed the door.

"I've got a conference in New York this spring," Sims said.

"Maybe you can stay with me."

"Maybe I'll stay in a hotel that doesn't have roaches," Sims said.

"Maybe I'll bunk with you," Elliott added, and they both laughed. Becca didn't understand how her brothers had come to this point of peace after days of conflict, but it was always like this with them. They goaded, harassed, and insulted each other, and a day later they were side by side in the kitchen, like two fingers on the same hand.

A gentle rap at the door had her springing from the chair to answer it.

"Ready?" Dylan asked. He wore running shorts with a blue sweatshirt that brought out his eyes. Two new pimples dotted his forehead, but his long curls made them easy to overlook.

"Sure." Becca grabbed her running jacket as she tried to sidle out the door but Elliott grabbed the knob.

"Who are you?" Elliott asked.

"I'm Dylan Dreher, sir," Dylan said.

"Sir?" Elliott elbowed Sims, who joined him in the doorway. "He called me sir."

"Welcome to adulthood." Sims extended a hand to a puzzled-looking Dylan. Becca wanted to pull her friend away before the brothers began their interrogation.

"I'm Sims, this is Elliott," Sims said.

"They're my brothers," Becca added. "Come on, let's go."

"Nice meeting you." Dylan eyed Becca, looking as nervous as Spats when they took him to the vet.

"You're a friend of Becca's?" Elliott crossed his arms.

Becca grabbed Dylan's arm and tugged him down the steps. "We're going running. Bye."

She half-dragged him to the side of the house, away from the door and kitchen window. "Sorry. They're a pain."

"At least they give a shit. I could have a crack dealer come to our back door and my brother would show him to my room."

So Dylan's father loved porn and his big brother didn't give a shit. Becca couldn't imagine that kind of indifference in her house. Maybe indifference was better than constant meddling, but she doubted it.

By the dogwood, she began her stretches, legs apart, hands wrapped around each ankle to loosen her hamstrings. She became excruciatingly aware of Dylan's gaze on her. Had he noticed her bulbous ass when she bent over? The bulge under her ribs since Dr. Owens had her eating like a starved pig?

He looked away. "Sorry. You're smart to do that."

"Don't you stretch before you run?"

"Not like that," he said. "But I think I got a good warm-up on the bike getting here."

"Then let's start. I usually head towards the school." She began at a jog, Dylan right beside her, his long legs moving with surprising grace. Becca matched her breathing to the rhythm of her feet hitting the sidewalk. Inhale four steps, exhale four steps. The sky had brightened to a vivid blue, clouds like dollops of cake frosting high above them. A breeze cooled her skin, yet she could feel sweat seeping from her pores and slithering down her arms and face.

When they took the right turn, the bulldog behind the yellow house greeted them with a low bark. Dylan jumped to the side.

"He can't climb the fence. Besides, he's a big baby," Becca answered, pausing to scratch his ear between pickets.

The bulldog gave her hand a lick.

"There's a Doberman in the next block," she warned, "but he's behind a six-foot enclosure."

"Good to know," Dylan said.

Becca picked up speed, five steps to each intake of breath. She was flying, Dylan matching her pace, his hands balled chest level, his back lean and straight. He saw her looking and winked. He didn't pant like she did. Dylan wasn't perspiring, even though water dribbled off her chin. Her feet began to ache, the sidewalk harder than it used to be. Her heart pounded in her chest like it wanted to break out, but she kept going. Flying. Dylan right beside her.

Until she reached the middle school, when a cramp squeezed her right side like pliers. She slowed, pressing her hand under her ribs.

"You okay?" Dylan asked.

"Stupid cramp."

"Let's take a break," he said, slowing to a fast walk.

She swallowed her embarrassment, digging her hand deeper into her flesh. "I'm out of shape," she confessed. "Sorry."

"Don't be sorry. You have to ease back into running."

"I just want to be normal again." She said it without thinking.

"You're the most normal person I know," he said.

"Shows what you know. I am *not* normal." Becca spotted a bench under a gigantic live oak tree. Maybe if she sat for a moment, the cramp might release. Dropping onto the worn wooden seat reminded her of another bench, the cramp that twisted her insides, her panic that she might die. Waking up in a hospital room with a new diagnosis. She wiped the sweat from her face. Strands of her stupid brown hair were plastered against her forehead.

"Why do you do that?" His words went upwards, towards the tree limbs. "I say something nice and you say I don't know what I'm talking about."

"I didn't mean—"

"If you don't want me around, just say so." Dylan's face had reddened like a stoplight.

"I do." She sounded needy. Pathetic. He'd be smart to flee. "Sorry. I'm— I'm pretty screwed up these days."

"You are good at saying shitty things about yourself."

"Well, at least I'm good at something." She didn't mean to sound flippant. His wince, his turning away, made fear flutter in her stomach.

"I just—" Her voice hitched. She couldn't bear it if he walked away, even if it was what she deserved. "I'm supposed to work on that."

"Work on what?" he asked.

"Saying shitty stuff about myself." The cramp relented. She stretched out her legs and looked at her neon green socks. "That's what my therapist says." There. She'd said it. She was messed up and seeing a shrink and now he knew. He'd be polite, because that was his way, but he'd find an excuse to disappear. Who could blame him?

"Who are you seeing?" he asked.

"Huh?" The question rattled her. "Dr. Owens. Her office is on Forest."

"Don't know her." He sat beside her on the bench. "I used to see Miriam Aster. Her office was downtown. She was nice."

She stared. Dylan had a shrink?

"I had this stupid problem—it's embarrassing." He shook his head like it was too shameful to speak about.

"I doubt it was stupid."

"It was a long time ago. I was eight. Mom dragged me there till I was ten. Though honestly, it was fun to have someone to talk to. I kept going even after I got over my problem."

"You did?"

"We played games, stupid stuff, but I liked her. And I'll tell you why I went but you have to promise never—*never*—to tell anyone."

"I promise."

He held up his little finger. "Pinkie swear?"

"What are we, fifth graders?" She retorted, but he didn't lower his hand, so she linked pinkies with him and hoped he didn't notice her cuticles bitten raw.

"I was a bed-wetter." He dropped his hand and stared down at it. "There. I said it. I got over it before I was ten, but it was awful. You can imagine my brother—"

Now she really hated his brother, enough to knee him in the groin, to sic *her* brothers on the douchebag.

She drew a deep breath. "I have eating problems." She couldn't make herself say bulimia or anorexia. "It messed up my body some, so that's why I'm seeing Dr. Owens. There. I said it," she said, repeating his words, then adding, "but I'm not over it yet."

She closed her eyes. When she opened them, he'd be gone. She knew this, but still she'd said it. A chill spread in her chest, icy tentacles tingling her arms and legs.

Fingers wound themselves around hers. Her eyelids flicked open. He was there. He smiled, lifting her hand and kissing it. His lips were warm like spring sunshine.

"I'm glad you told me," he said. And so was she.

• • •

LENA STOOD IN THE CORNER of the backyard, her easel beside the naked dogwood tree. Withered leaves lay at her feet. The yard needed to be raked, the patio swept, the table and chairs wiped clean. She and Mitch used to love fall, to sip coffee in the cool air, to watch the colors fade from brilliant gold to brown. Spats would stretch across Mitch's lap, and Mitch would tell Lena where he'd plant the pansies that would bloom much of the winter, asking if she preferred purple or white. (The answer was always purple). He'd mention piling leaves on the mulch pile behind the garage. "We've got lots of worms this year. Should be healthy soil for spring." The absence of that voice threaded each and every day.

She used a pencil to sketch the lines of the house, the jutted angles of roof, the wide windows, and the steps leading to the back door. (She remembered the time Elliott tried to climb down those steps wearing his in-line skates, how he'd sprawled across the cement with skinned knees and nose and elbows.) She traced the outline of the screened porch they'd added after Becca was born. (Mitch had bought a rocking chair to rock her to sleep those days when Lena couldn't.) She added the silhouette of the magnolia tree that grew outside their bedroom window. The tree was a hundred years old. Plump ivory blossoms filled its limbs every spring. (Five-year-old Becca had shimmied up it, then grown too terrified to come down. Sims climbed after her, coaxing her descent limb-by-limb.)

The oils she'd gathered in her wooden basket would have to be mixed with care to get the exact shade of brick and roof. When they left this house, when she and Becca moved to something she could afford, the painting would be all she'd have left of it.

The notion of leaving clawed inside her; something else to grieve. How different it would be from the last time she moved, when she'd fled this home and Mitch and Becca, sure there was something better waiting for her. Now there was nothing better, there was only an uncertain future, a troubled daughter, and a countless number of Mitch-less days.

Lena steadied her pencil against the canvas. She had to move forward. She'd find a new home to share with Becca. They would live a different life but she would make it a good one. She had to.

She had called Phillip and arranged to meet with him tomorrow to discuss her taking over Mitch's half of the partnership. Phillip would tutor her for the licensing exam, and she'd work under him for the first year. Their first project would be doing something with the strip mall Phillip had purchased near where the Wal-Mart wasn't being built. So much of the firm's money was tied up in it; they had to find a buyer or lease the units. She'd make Phillip take her to the site so she could see it and be involved in the planning. She would not trust him on his own as Mitch had.

Someone stood in the kitchen window. Probably Abby. Bill had called her first thing that morning. She'd been on the phone since then, speaking in a fast, animated Spanish. Maybe Bill had found a way to get Esteban. Someone in Lena's family deserved good news.

The back door swung open and Abby emerged. She grabbed a chair from the patio and carried it to the corner of the yard where Lena was, huffing as she dropped into it. "Hope you don't mind," she said. "But I want to talk with you."

Lena shook her head. She continued to sketch the arcing lines of the birdbath beside the porch, the one Mitch had given her for Mother's Day two years before. Would she take it with her? No, it was too heavy. Besides, it should remain in this yard; the birds counted on it through each season.

"Bill Tanner has been a godsend," Abby said. "The Episcopal church has a mission in Peru, and he went to school with the priest assigned there. He's pulling some strings, trying to help me get Esteban."

"That's wonderful."

"It's still a long shot, but there is hope at least. I've got to get down there and make sure the paperwork gets processed before my birthday. The clock is ticking."

"When do you leave?"

"Just booked my ticket. I'm heading out tomorrow."

Lena lowered her pencil. A rush of sadness swept through her: another person leaving. She should be used to it by now.

"My flight leaves at seven A.M. An ungodly hour, I know. I'll have a cab take me."

"No you won't." Tears welled in Lena's eyes. She had been brave when Elliott left, smiled and waved him through security, blew him a kiss on the other side, letting herself face the full impact in the privacy of her car.

"I don't see why you need to get up before dawn to be my taxi service," Abby said.

What did it matter? Lena awoke at all hours of the night, snatching a few elusive hours of sleep. "I'll take you," she said, her voice hitching. Embarrassed, she stepped closer to the canvas.

"Le-Le?" Abby stood and came to her. "You're crying. I'm sorry, I . . . "

"It's okay. I get emotional these days."

"Of course you do. Of course. My God."

Lena looked back at the birdbath. Joe always freshened the water when he came, though they'd never asked him to. Last winter he'd had to chip through ice to clean it. When they moved, would they have a yard for Joe to tend?

"I won't stay gone, Le-Le. I've booked a round trip ticket. I'm coming back for a little while, hopefully with Esteban. I don't know when. I want to make sure you and Becca have your feet under you."

Lena started to say that was absurd, of course they'd be fine, but she saw no need to lie. "Are you going to live in South America?"

"That's the million dollar question. Bill suggested moving Esteban out of the country. Maybe coming back to the US. Somewhere with strong schools and no coca trade. My agency's national office has a vacancy in DC. Maybe I'll move there."

"Hard to picture you in Washington. Wearing suits and pantyhose." Lena smiled, imagining her sister wobbling on two-inch heels, briefcase in hand, cursing with every step.

"I've adjusted to other foreign countries," Abby replied with a smirk. "But hell, I may go ahead and retire. I have the years in. Maybe work part-time. Do something sane for a change."

"You can retire?" This surprised Lena, though it made sense. Abby had been with the same federal agency for over thirty years.

"One more thing," Abby said. "I wanted to do something in Mitch's memory. And I didn't want to contribute to the church organ fund or plant a stupid tree. I wanted to do something more personal."

"There's no need—"

"I'd say there's a hell of a need. I've given this a lot of thought, and I don't want you to argue with me. In memory of Mitch, I'm paying off the second mortgage on your house. I've already talked to the bank. I've got a cashier's check ready to go. Don't argue with me; it's done."

Lena stared, wondering if maybe her sister had gone insane. Abby lived like a vagabond, how could she afford such a thing? "I don't understand."

"I've been a federal employee for eons. I make good money but I can't spend it down there. It's just piling up in the bank. I can't imagine a better investment than your house. I wish I could pay all of it, but you have savings enough to cover the first mortgage for a while. You and Becca have enough to worry about, where you live shouldn't be one of them."

"It's . . . it's too much. I can't accept it." Lena groped in her pocket for Mitch's stone and squeezed.

"It's not enough, as far as I'm concerned. And this is a gift to Mitch, so you can't refuse it. You can take that off your worry list." Abby had that confident, insistent tone that made her impossible to argue with.

Lena studied the faint lines on her canvas. The house, hers. The magnolia tree and birdbath and patio. The porch and rocking chair and garden and thirty years of memories.

Hers.

CHAPTER 27

J oe searched for Cyphus Lawter over three days. He'd looked in the parks,
under bridges, behind the abandoned Piggly Wiggly, but there was no sign
of him anywhere. While Joe could no longer stay at the church, he stopped
by twice a day, making sure Lawter hadn't carried out his threat. No sign of
him there, either, but it brought little relief.

Rag Doll said Joe might not find him. That the man stole crack from
some gangbangers who were hunting him down, and Lawter was good at
hiding. That was okay, though, because Joe was good at searching, and he
would not rest until this deed was done.

The Lord would be ashamed of what Joe planned to do, but Cyphus Lawter wasn't going to hurt anybody else, especially a man as good and holy as
Reverend Bill. If taking care of Lawter put Joe back in jail, so be it. He'd pray
that maybe the Lord might forgive him one day.

Sundown came on fast, turning the sky gunmetal gray. A breeze stirred
up leaves and sand as he left the old quarry on the east end of town, the last
place he knew to look, but Lawter hadn't been there. Maybe Joe would go
through the park once more before he found a place to sleep for the night.

A police car slowed at the park entrance. They'd do rounds through the
park at sundown to make sure nobody bedded there. Joe stopped at the water
fountain, tilting his head to watch the car inch on by.

When he reached the north lawn, the sun had sunk low and tree shadows
stretched long over the grass. He fastened the top button of his coat.

"Joe Booker." The low, gravelly voice sent a chill along Joe's spine. He
turned to meet Cyphus Lawter dead in the eye.

"Hear you been looking for me," Lawter added.

Joe didn't answer. Cyphus stepped closer. He wore a green army jacket
with bulging pockets, and held his right arm stiffly at his side. Hiding something, Joe was sure. A gun? A knife?

Joe swallowed, trying to pull up courage from deep inside.

"Well, looks like you found me, Joe." Cyphus flashed a soulless smile. Joe
thought about all the people Lawter had hurt. The old man at the bus station.

Rag Doll. He thought about Reverend Bill and his churchgoers, and pictured the damage Lawter might do.

Lawter raised his arm, a steel pipe gripped in his hand.

"Joe!" Rag Doll's voice caught him off guard.

Cyphus slammed the pipe down. Joe sidestepped him, catching the force of the blow on his shoulder. He closed his mind to the flare of pain.

"Run Joe!" She stood by a live oak tree, wearing that stupid hat, gesturing wildly. Joe wasn't going to run.

Lawter came at him again with the might of a grizzly. Joe grabbed his wrist before the pipe made contact, but holding on took every ounce of strength he had, and the burn in his shoulder started to spread. Cyphus breathed foul breath on Joe's face as his eyes glowed wide and feral.

Joe's arm quaked; sweat streamed down his face but he held on. If he could twist Lawter's hand, he'd have to drop the pipe, but it was like trying to bend a maple tree.

Tree. The live oak they fought beneath had a wide expanse of roots like tiny mountains coming out of the ground. Joe scanned down. Behind Cyphus's feet was a fat knuckle of root so Joe leaned in. Cyphus stepped back, tripped, and toppled to the ground.

Joe fell atop him, grabbing the pipe, but Cyphus wasn't letting go. One elbow jab into Joe's jaw and Cyphus shimmied out from under him, pulling the pipe from Joe's grasp and heaving his bulk on top of him.

"No!" Rag Doll yelled. "Police! Help him!"

There'd be no police to help. Cyphus had gotten the best of him. It was over. Joe's mind flashed on Reverend Bill's kindly smile, on Wortham Pinckney's headstone, on Mama's face. Maybe he'd see her again. His gaze trailed to Rag Doll. Her tears surprised him.

A cold breeze swept over them as Lawter swung the pipe.

"Leave him alone!" Rag Doll rushed him, kicking Cyphus hard in the ribs. Lawter shifted, off-balance, and Joe took advantage, bucking till Lawter fell. Joe snagged the pipe from his hand. He squeezed the cold, cold metal and lifted it high. He swung the pipe. Once. Twice. Three times.

"Joe! That's enough!" Rag Doll pawed at his arm, trying to stop him.

He almost swung again, but then he saw the dark spread of blood under Lawter's head. The darker emptiness in his open, unblinking eyes.

Joe dropped the pipe. It was done. Cyphus Lawter would hurt nobody else.

Another chilly wind blew by, snatching up leaves that twirled around them. Joe's breath came in fast pants, puffing out clouds, as he tried to calm himself. A yellow maple leaf drifted down to land on Lawter's half-open mouth like a hand quieting him.

Rag Doll pinched its stem and plucked it from the body.

The sound of muted voices came from behind them. Rag Doll stood and squinted toward the noise. "It's the police," she whispered.

He nodded.

"You gotta run." She grabbed at his arm.

"Too late."

"No it ain't." She grabbed the pipe and wrapped the end he'd held in the hem of her skirt. Pushing Joe to the side, she grabbed Cyphus's hand, curled two of his fingers, and scratched the flesh on her neck with his dirty nails.

She'd gone crazy, he was sure of it. "What are you doing?" he whispered.

She tore the front of her top as the footsteps drew closer.

"It should have been me that done it. Go hide in them bushes until you can sneak away." She shoved him towards the shrubs—the same ones where Cyphus Lawter had attacked her. "Do as I say," she growled. "I mean it, Joe."

What followed was the strangest bit of confusion Joe had ever seen. When the police approached, Rag Doll yelled, "Over here!" like she wanted them to find the body. Flashlight beams swept the grass and focused on her, huddled beside Lawter's corpse.

"He almost killed me!" she cried, holding the pipe. "He come after me with this and tried to beat my head in! If he hadn't tripped, he'd a done it!"

The officers checked out the body and radioed for help. When they asked Rag Doll questions, she interrupted them, screaming: "I told the police Cyphus Lawter tried to rape me. I told them he was coming back, that he aimed to kill me, but y'all didn't do nothing. You didn't do nothing and he almost beat my brains out!"

"Calm down, Rag Doll. You say that's Cyphus Lawter?" an officer asked, as though familiar with both names.

"That's what I said alright." Rag Doll went on, her loud voice droning out all other sounds until the wail of approaching sirens pierced the night.

It was all the distraction Joe needed. He crawled behind the row of bushes to the end, then heaved his aching, sore body over the wooden fence.

He was going home.

• • •

TONYA SAT ON THE FAUX leather sofa ignoring the SpongeBob cartoon that had Byron chuckling on the floor. She gripped the schedule in her hand. Business Law I was held Saturday mornings. Civil Litigation would be her class on Tuesday evenings. Ruth had said she could leave work early on Tuesdays to have a little time with Byron before heading to the university. If she could handle the schedule, she would complete her Certified Paralegal certificate in one year.

It was Ruth who had helped her with the decision to settle the lawsuit. From Ruth's office, Tonya had called the insurance company and told them she accepted the latest offer of nineteen thousand dollars.

That morning, when Tonya picked up the check, she'd set aside nine thousand to purchase a used minivan and then paid four thousand for spring semester tuition.

John knew none of this.

Nor did he know that she'd paid off her Visa bill and put the rest of the money in savings. Tonya would have to work hard to add to that account to cover tuition for the final semester, but she was determined to complete the degree without debt. What worried her most of all was the studying that would be required. She and Ruth discussed this, too. She would bring her lunch to work and use the hour every day to catch up on her reading. She'd use another hour after Byron went to bed, and Sundays would be devoted to schoolwork (except for a few hours on Sunday afternoons when she liked to take Byron to the park). John played no role in her planning, though she had, reluctantly, recruited her mother. Curious that Mom had called just as she left the university, chatting at first, then growing somber, saying, "I never meant for you to think I loved you less than Buddy." Tonya had replied, "I know, Mom," even though she did feel less loved, but what good did it do dredging up history? Tonya told Mom about returning to school and asked about babysitting; Mom had agreed. "You've never asked me to before," she said. "I thought maybe you didn't think we'd take good care of him." So standing Tuesday night and Saturday morning visits to Grandma's might be in Byron's future. It all depended on how things went with John.

SpongeBob ended and Tonya flicked off the TV. Byron came to her and crawled up in her lap. Out the window, the lawn lay small and brown as a slice of wheat toast. The dogwood tree had lost all its leaves; the camellia's green branches held no blooms. John would be home soon. John would be home and she would tell him all of it. He could decide for himself if he was part of the plan.

Byron pulled up, his knees on her thighs, his pink face inches from hers. "I love you, peanut," she said.

• • •

THE PLASTIC CRACKLED UNDER Lena's feet. She unrolled the painter's tape, securing the sheeting to the legs of the desk and the base of the bookcase. She placed the easel close to the window and switched on two lamps, leaving much of the room still in shadow. It would temper what she painted, but that was okay. In fact, it was important.

She uncapped her oils and dotted her palette with primary colors for blending, adding other shades like coral, teal, and crimson, the hues that always pulled at her eyes. By the door she had stacked a jumble of canvases she'd grabbed from the garage. She selected a large one and clipped it to the easel. She glanced around Mitch's office: the unscratched wood floors, the alphabetized books, the monster desk and cracked leather chair he'd gotten from his father—this room was Mitch. She could almost catch his scent, as though wood and leather had soaked him in. She closed her eyes to let the emotions have their way.

The feeling passed as quickly as it had started. This mourning had so many edges to it, but she'd learned over the days that fighting it gave it strength. Better to surrender. Always surprising to come out on the other side.

She lifted a brush, dabbed it in the crimson, and approached the canvas. How to start? There was always this hint of panic when beginning, self-doubt nudging her away from it, and she had to stand strong and not submit. She touched the brush to the canvas. Feather-like strokes, almost in a circle but not quite. Two larger splotches in the center, more defined. Between them, an amethyst curve like a mountain stream pouring between boulders.

With the finer ox-bristle brush, she made delicate, precise strokes of black and umber. Symmetrical figures emerged around the edges of red. What were they? Almost numbers but not quite. Little faux Chinese characters, faint and small in the wide expanse of white.

She blurred purple and blue, making a broad sweep at the bottom of the canvas. She loved the color. Indigo. She brought the brush upward, bursting through the little figures.

Her hand began to quake. Why? What was it? She touched the color again, trying to recall something that was just out of her grasp. What did it remind her of? The azurite pin Mitch had given her last year.

There had been that tall art student, in her flowing skirts and hand-beaded jewelry, who had commented on the azurite stone, some Wiccan-sounding nonsense about how indigo "turns one inward. It is for reflection and insight." And inspiration, she had said. Great things come "out of the blue."

Lena played with the color, trying different shapes and textures. Muting it with white for a paler hue. A smidge of black. All these remarkable shades of blue.

"Are you going to make this your studio?" Becca's voice startled her.

"Hey." She lowered the brush and turned to face her youngest. "Maybe."

Becca climbed onto the desktop, gathering her legs against her chest. She wore a Gamecocks t-shirt with a hole over the "G." Mitch caught it at a basketball game when Becca was ten.

"Can't sleep?" Lena asked.

"Not much." Becca studied the stack of real estate books beside her on the desk. "These are Dad's books."

"Yep. I've been studying them."

"Why?"

She moved closer to her daughter. "Because that's going to be my job. I'm taking the realtor exam. I'll apprentice under Phillip and take over your Dad's office at the firm." She'd read the manual a half-dozen times; the laws were complex but not impossible.

Becca shook her head. "Hard to picture you selling strip malls and gas stations."

"Yeah, it's hard for me too," she confessed. "I've read about how important 'staging' a property is—making it look as good as it can, especially in the current market. Sometimes a coat of paint can make all the difference. Maybe my artistic eye will come in handy." When Phillip drove her to the strip mall he'd purchased, Lena had insisted on entering every door. She was glad she had. She found interior walls of glass brick, hidden under layers of grime. Black and white tile and an art deco mural. She imagined a fifties-style restaurant, an espresso bar, and upscale consignment shop. It was a long shot, and the economy had to turn around, but maybe she could make it happen.

Lena returned to the stack of canvases, sorting through them. Most were aborted efforts she should have tossed.

"What's that one?" Becca pointed at the half-done painting in Lena's hand. *That one.* Lena brought it to the desk. "Remember the morning of the accident? I had decided to paint again."

Becca nodded.

"This is what I was working on. An exercise. Just trying to get back into it."

Becca traced the outline of pink. "A flower?"

"Foxglove. One in Mitch's garden that kept right on blooming long past the time it should have died back. So it was my starting point, anyway. I didn't get very far before the call came." A claw gripped under her sternum as she remembered. Almost not answering the phone but its incessant ringing annoyed her. Not understanding the police officer telling her that Mitch was on his way to Mercy General Hospital. Throwing on clothes, tripping on her way to the car, thinking, "My fault, my fault, my fault" and not knowing why. She didn't remember the drive or parking, but she soon found herself surrounded by white coats tossing a new vocabulary her way. "Myocardial infarction" and "anoxia" and "absent brain stem reflexes." Thus began her descent.

"They called me out of class," Becca said in a whisper. "I was late getting to poetry so I thought I was in trouble. The principal was in the hall. He told me."

Lena wished that she had been the one to tell Becca, to gather her in her arms, to reassure her that they would survive this.

"I didn't believe he'd die. Not really. Not until—" Becca pulled her legs in closer, two garnet humps in the t-shirt.

"I didn't either. Not at first. After all we'd been through, it seemed absurd that he would leave us like that."

Becca tilted her head as though seeing the painting from another angle. "It's nice. You should finish it."

"Not now. I can't." Lena placed the canvas on the floor.

Becca rested her head on her knee and watched as Lena returned to her new project. Lena dabbed the brush in lavender paint and made an arc at the top of the painting. Too pale. She darkened the tint.

"Does painting help you feel better?"

"Sometimes."

"Can you paint out your sadness?"

If only she could. "No. But I can sort out how I feel, or it makes me feel things I've tried not to." This was a strange thing to confide in her daughter, but something about the shadows and Becca's unexpected presence made speaking it important. Lena crossed to the painting that hung across from Mitch's desk. She had painted it when Becca was three: pigtails and a ruffly denim skirt and pudgy hands gripping a GI Joe doll. A crooked smile playing on her lips.

"Like this one," Lena said. "Mitch's Kitten."

"Ugh," Becca muttered.

"This was an important piece for me. I hadn't painted in a while. I was coming out of a dark place. After you were born, I had post-partum depression and it took me a long time to recover. I saw a therapist like Dr. Owens." Lena could feel Becca's stare, this last secret unfolding.

"It was bad for a while, Becca. I couldn't find a way to be happy. To connect with you or the boys or Mitch. It was like living in a cave without color or light." The shame still weighed on her like an oversized coat. "You were sick," Mitch would say, "and that's nothing to be ashamed about." But she had seen the strain on her family, the unattended baseball games, the tiny arms lifted up that she couldn't reach for.

"But the therapy, and medication, helped," Lena said. "One morning I woke up. I mean I really woke up. I went to your room and you were sitting up in your bed, holding that GI Joe. You smiled at me. I sat on your bed and you handed me your stuffed dog and we played together. You giggled so much you almost forgot to breathe and that had me laughing, too. The shadow lifted. I started this painting that day."

"You got depressed because you had me?" Becca asked.

"Not at all," she said firmly. "I got depressed because that gene runs in our family. The hormonal changes after the pregnancy triggered it." She stepped closer, looking Becca in the eye to make sure she understood. "Seeing the therapist helped, but you are the one who pulled me out of it. You and that GI Joe."

"It's in your family?"

"I think Dad was depressed. That might explain why he drank so much. Mom definitely had it. I've had two bad episodes—and I'm lucky that's all."

Becca's gaze on her was like probing fingers. Lena moved to the window. The faintest swath of pink stretched through gauzy clouds, the beginning of sunrise.

"When was the second time?" Becca asked.

Lena swallowed. "Right before I went back to school. I felt like I was suffocating."

Becca's legs slid out from under the shirt and she stood. She approached the painting on the wall. "How come nobody told me?"

"Mitch wanted to protect you. He was always overprotective, but I was worse. I'm sorry that I let you down."

Becca didn't say anything. Lena let the silence lie across the room as she returned to her project. She swirled the oxtail brush in crimson and smeared it into the white, trying to replicate the color out the window.

"How long do I have to see Dr. Owens?" Becca asked.

"I suppose that's something the three of us will have to decide. Do you think therapy is helping?" she asked.

"I guess. But sometimes I leave with more questions than answers."

"I think that's how it works."

Silence descended again. Lena played with the paler colors on her canvas. "Elliott said a young man showed up to run with you Saturday."

"Elliott should mind his own damn business."

"Is he someone in your class?"

Becca let out an exaggerated sigh. "Yes. His name is Dylan."

"Want to tell me about him?"

"No." Becca sounded like a slamming door. "Are we going to move?"

The question surprised Lena. "Do you want to?"

"No, but I know we're having money problems. Maybe we can't afford to live here."

"We are having money problems, but that's for me to worry about. Not you. Besides, things aren't so bad now. The insurance company finally reached a settlement with the woman who was in the accident with Mitch. And your Aunt Abby paid off the second mortgage. A very generous gift." She still couldn't believe it. "I'm not saying things are perfect. I've got to make a go of this real estate thing, but you don't need to worry."

Fingers of light filtered through the window and brightened the canvas. The pink dots looked too pale. Lena dipped the brush in crimson, creating a sharper hue, like a recently healed wound.

"I didn't think Aunt Abby had money. I mean—she dresses like she doesn't," Becca said.

Lena smiled. "She's a federal employee and she's squirreled away most of her earnings. She's actually ready to retire and live on her pension. At least, that's her plan if she's able to adopt Esteban."

She looked around the heavy room. There was so much house here. Lena and Becca would take up a fraction of it. Would the absence of Mitch fill the rest? This wasn't what she wanted, nor would Mitch.

Becca picked at a toenail she had painted navy blue. Abby was so good with her. She had a rare confidence that cut through Becca's defenses. Lena was working harder at her relationship with Becca, but for Abby, it came naturally.

Lena set down her brush. "What if . . . " she eyed her daughter. "What if Abby and Esteban came here to live? We have plenty of space. Abby has no real home except Columbia, and we could help her with him. He could go to school here and learn English." As she spoke the words, they took shape. A little boy running around the back yard. A new swing set and sand box. Elliott's room painted blue, with soccer balls (didn't they love "futbol" in South America?) along the chair rail.

Becca's head shot up. "Here?"

"Why not?" They'd use a shelf in the den to hold Legos and Lincoln logs, another supporting a library of children's books. She stepped closer to her daughter to get a better handle on her reaction. "This would have to be a decision we make together. Your vote is just as important as mine. It's a big step. You may have to help with Esteban when I'm at work."

She approached her daughter. "I'm hitting you with a lot all at once. Give this Abby/Esteban idea some thought. We don't have to decide until we know for sure if she's getting him."

Becca stood and crossed to the window. Lena joined her. Dawn had brightened the yard, sunrays falling on the tangle of vinca vines around the patio, the pink drooping blossoms on the sasanqua, the bright red berries on the nandina. Mitch had made sure the garden had color year round.

"Might be fun to have a little boy around," Becca said.

CHAPTER 28

The river roared. Rain from the past few weeks had made it swell, turned it forceful and fast, like a thundering serpent. White froth boiled up as the rapids shot between rocks that protruded like smooth gray teeth. Tree limbs that had fallen into the water and ridden the current made a murky pile of sodden debris, but the water moved too fast for beavers to claim it.

Sandy pulled out the Ziploc baggie, opened it, and studied the pills awaiting her. She'd survived three days, unable to let them go. She had held them, sniffed them, come so close—but she had not taken a single one. Yet.

As she stood at the familiar overlook, tiny drops of spray chilled her skin. She lifted the collar of her jacket, yet she relished the cold, the way the trees quivered and swayed, the way her flesh felt raw. The way this place reminded her of Jesse.

How many times had she met him here? Jesse liked to take walks. Actually, Jesse liked to take hikes but Sandy would have none of that so they settled for a mile or two on this much-traveled trail. She checked her phone to see if he'd replied to her text, knowing he wouldn't. After the debacle at her house, he probably wanted to stay as far away from her as he could get. Hell, she wanted to stay away from herself, if that were possible.

She had met Jesse a year and a half ago at a pharmacy rep event: heavy hors d'oeuvres, robust cabernet generously poured, and a hive of doctors bragging about golf scores and investment portfolios. Jesse had positioned himself by the fruit tray and when he reached for a strawberry, his eyeglasses tumbled into the caramel dip.

He pinched the nose bridge to lift them from the golden goo. "That was smooth," he said, licking the rimless frames. "Kind of tasty."

She laughed. "You're not a doctor."

Dimples dented his cocoa skin. "Why do you say that? Don't I look smug enough? I can do smug. Just get me talking about my action figure collection."

Caught mid-sip, Sandy laughed out wine.

"Ah. So we're both too classy for this party. I'm Jesse Riniere, by the way." He extended a hand, long, tapered fingers enfolding hers.

"Sandy Albright." The wine on top of the valium she'd taken had her buzzing and flirtatious. They left the party and walked a few blocks to a jazz club where the owner welcomed Jesse by name. They drank more wine, followed by coffee and a meandering stroll back to their cars. She gave Jesse her number.

She'd given up on him calling back when he phoned over a week later. "I've been out of town," he said, and asked her out to dinner. She almost didn't agree because it worried her how much she wanted to. When he picked her up, he suggested a walk before dinner and brought her here, to the riverfront trail. They talked, then they didn't, their silence punctuated by footfall on leaves and chattering squirrels. When they reached this overlook, he kissed her. It had filled her with a strange mix of fear and hope.

This was the rhythm of their relationship. Their sex was raw and fast, two bodies diving into each other then parting. And Jesse would disappear. A week, two, an occasional phone call. She didn't question him about it. She settled for what they had, finding safety in not expecting more. There could be no betrayal where there was no commitment.

And what did she have now? No Jesse. She'd texted him, but he hadn't answered. Why would he? What did she have to offer him? She had no job. She lived a miserable, pathetic life. In her hand lay the pills her body screamed for. The solution to her desolation: pale blue circles of bliss. She just needed to swallow them. So easy.

So damn easy.

She drew a breath deep enough to reach her toes. No.

She lifted the bag, tilted it, and watched the pills plop into the current. She thought, perhaps, recovery was this: bearing the unbearable moment. The relief overwhelmed her. A little stronger than her regret.

When her cell phone rang it wasn't Jesse. "Is this Sandy Albright?" the voice was familiar.

"Yes."

"I'm Lillian Owens. You've been a tough lady to track down."

"Has something happened to Becca?"

"No. She's okay. Though of course, she has a long road ahead of her."

"Then why—"

"My nurse is going out on maternity leave. I was wondering if you'd be interested in filling in for her."

Sandy gripped the phone, dumbfounded. Dr. Owens continued: "My private practice is small. Me, an RN, a nutritionist and a part-time psychologist. We stay busy as hell. So many women—and some men too, we're finding out—have eating disorders. We'll never run out of clients."

"I suppose not."

"It would be temp work, though it might become permanent. This is Nancy's third kid, I half expect her to decide to stay home. So if you like us, and we find you to be a good fit, then it could be a permanent job."

"You remember the part where I said I'm an addict, right?"

"Yep. And I heard you say you were in recovery. That still true?"

Sandy looked down at the water. "Yes."

"I'm in recovery, too. Not from drugs, but from anorexia when I was a teen. Having walked that road helps me in my work. I think your recovery helped Becca."

Sandy thought of a thousand reasons to say no. A thousand reasons why she'd be the worst person on planet earth to do this kind of nursing.

"I'll expect you to be honest with me if you have a slip," Dr. Owens said. "You have to work your program like I work mine. And it might help that we don't keep much of a pharmacy. So . . . ."

"Nothing to tempt me," Sandy filled in. "Can I give it some thought?"

"Sure. But call me no later than tomorrow, okay?" Dr. Owens clicked off.

Sandy stared at the phone, disbelieving. Could she do that kind of work? It would challenge and exhaust her, but there were a lot of Beccas out there and what if she could help a few?

"I thought I was hallucinating when I got your text." It was Jesse's baritone voice. She turned around to find him a few safe feet away, in his leather jacket and garnet Carolina scarf.

"I wasn't sure you'd want to meet me. I wouldn't blame you if you didn't."

He didn't answer, but came to stand beside her and stared out at the river.

"I think I quit my job," she said.

He glanced at her and then turned back to the water. "Okay."

"They accused me of stealing drugs. I didn't do it, but they treated me like scum. Did the urine sample thing, searched me, my locker, and my purse. It was so humiliating." Bile crawled up her throat at the memory. "I bought some pills. Almost used, but didn't."

"You still have them?"

"Fed them to the river."

"Good."

A mockingbird sailed by, landing on a branch hanging over the river. It let out a series of high-pitched screeches, pissed off at the world. It sounded a little like Marie Hempshall.

"So what now?" Jesse asked.

Was he asking about her job? Or their relationship? Either way, the answer was the same. "I'm not sure."

"Guess you can let Sean support you for a while."

She laughed at that. "Yeah that'll work."

"You've hated that job for a while."

"I hated my life for a while," she corrected. A shadow swept over his face; she realized she'd hurt him. "Most of my life, anyway. But the job sucking me dry hasn't helped."

"You're a great nurse. I'm not just saying that. I've heard the cardiac crew say it. And they're stingy with compliments."

"That's nice to hear, I guess."

The mockingbird altered its cry to a gentle trilling warble, perhaps mimicking the river on a quieter day. One lived near the hospital that could imitate a siren.

"Did you resign from the hospital?" he asked.

"Not officially. Why? I should crawl back?"

He flashed a dimpled grin. "I was thinking more along the lines of doing it with flare. Maybe you could write 'I quit' on that beautiful rear of yours and moon Marie H."

She laughed. "Maybe I could spell it out in urine sample cups glued to Marie's desk."

"Or we could hire one of those sky-writing planes. 'F-you, Mercy General.'" He drew the letters in the air.

She turned back to the river. A stronger breeze nudged the tree limbs. The mockingbird complained. "I keep thinking about the things I've lost. My marriage. The child I miscarried."

Jesse looked strange, his eyes wide and curious. He didn't say anything.

"My sponsor thinks I'm finally grieving. That using drugs kept me from doing that for two years. Maybe she's right."

Jesse wiped at sweat that had collected on his top lip, and Sandy couldn't figure out why he'd be perspiring in this cool weather.

"But maybe I am getting to the other side of it," Sandy continued. "I used to not think that was possible." She turned to look into his eyes. She had never laid herself so naked before him, but he needed to know the truth.

He didn't say anything. Tears filled his eyes.

"Jesse?"

He held up a finger and cleared his throat. "You and me, we do this dance. We swoop into each other's lives, then we swoop out. I thought I liked it that way, you know? Then you went to rehab, and there were weeks that stretched on and on with not seeing you, then I got scared to see you. I know I let you down. I let myself down." He was stumbling over his words, so un-Jesse-like.

"But then I couldn't not see you. When I went to your house, I half expected you to slam the door in my face." His smile was nervous, uncertain. "You didn't. But you have new rules. No drugs around you. I can't even have the smell on me."

Sandy stepped back, annoyed at Jesse and at herself. There were new rules, and she had to follow them or risk relapse. Risking relapse was risking everything.

"I can do it," Jesse said. "I can follow the rules. But not if we're doing the same dance. You keep me at arm's length, Sandy. I get too close, you shut down. You hurry me out the door. We've played it real safe, doing the once-a-week thing, but it's not enough for me."

She glared at him, trying to figure out what he was saying. *She* was the one who kept things shallow? *She* was the one who kept the wall up? "I can't believe you're saying that. You're the one who goes days and days without calling."

"I've been doing what you wanted me to do, whether you admit it or not. You have not invited me into your life. Hell, this is only the second time you even mentioned your marriage or the child you lost. All I'm saying is, if we're going to do this thing, I want—I need—more."

She stumbled back from him, the truth ricocheting in her brain. She had held him at bay. She wanted nobody close. She had lived on her own little island, floating on oxy and valium, but it didn't work anymore, and now she had this man who wanted into her world. What would he find there? Hell, she didn't know how to answer that question for herself, much less for him.

"Getting ready to bolt, aren't you?" He flicked a tongue over his lip and narrowed his eyes. "Always the easy way, isn't it?"

"No. It's not easy. It sucks, to be honest. And no, I'm not bolting. I'm standing still, here, with you." She said it definitively. "If you want to try this Sandy-Jesse thing, then I'm in. But you need to know I'm one screwed up person. You get closer, you're going to see that for yourself."

He smiled and came towards her, his arms snaking around her, his chin rubbing the top of her head. "I don't think you are. You're just a little prickly. That's okay though. It keeps me on my toes."

CHAPTER 29

Lena climbed down the steps to the back yard, sketchpad and drawing pencils gripped in her hand. The sun, angled mid-horizon, washed the yard with yellow light. She surveyed the garden, which had gone all to hell in the months since Mitch's death, her gaze resting on the hydrangea bush by the fence. It had grown too tall, leggy stalks with blooms much darker than last year. Funny how they'd morphed from lilac to indigo.

Nothing stayed the same.

Becca was on her phone in the kitchen, the ice machine on the fridge groaning as it clunked ice into her glass. Was she talking to Kayla or Dylan? The sudden burst of laughter made her think Kayla. Dylan conversations had a quieter, private tone. Dylan visits to the house required fifteen extra minutes of dressing and grooming, with the occasional panicked "Have you seen my red jacket?" or "Can I wear your brown boots?" For these moments of normal teenage angst, Lena felt profoundly grateful.

Her last appointment for the day had been at three, a restaurateur looking for a site to expand his small chain. She'd been pleased he could see the potential in the old dime store building on Taylor. Others, like Phillip, doubted that part of downtown would ever revitalize, but Lena felt it happening, like a baby bird about to hatch. Matching new tenants with building owners had become the most interesting part of her job. It allowed her to rescue something old and watch it become something new. Phillip accused her of over-romanticizing but she cared little about what he thought. He had his strengths, she had hers.

She flipped a few pages in her sketch pad—aborted efforts she should throw away—but stopped when she reached a drawing of the foxglove. She carried the pad to the edge of the yard where the foxglove plant had started to bloom again. She wasn't sure if she should paint it, or uproot the thing and toss it in the trash. No, she shouldn't blame the flower. It had been one of Mitch's favorites.

She opened the case and selected a graphite pencil and a pressed charcoal crayon, the one from school that Royce had returned to her. She didn't need color at this phase of the project. She plopped down on the ground, the grass thick and itchy, and studied the earlier sketch. Maybe if she tilted the stem a little to destabilize it, it would have more tension. For the background, maybe she'd add a pale charcoal tone to accentuate the arc of fuchsia blossoms. No, she wanted a closer perspective, to sketch every vein, to capture the spray of brown freckles within the drooping petals. This would add a dynamic the sketch had lacked. "Not static, but movement. Movement in the stillness of the painting," Royce had instructed.

At the base of the plant was a clump of dark, moist soil that had given birth to the flower. Mitch had planted it a few years ago. He had dug into the earth, added compost and mulch, applied fertilizer at the right time. He'd watered and babied it and, when it bloomed that first time, brought Lena and Becca out to admire it.

She reached for the stone that hung from her neck: the one from Mitch's pocket. She'd taken it to a jewelry artist, a woman she'd met in school. "It's a pebble, nothing special," Lena had stammered, "but it's important." When the artist called a week later, Lena wasn't sure what to expect, but the necklace was perfect. Silver threads wrapped the stone; three faceted onyx beads clustered in the middle like eggs in a nest. One for each of their children, Lena had decided.

As she surveyed the sketch, she ran her thumb along the smooth edge of the stone, something she did a hundred times a day, and smiled.

Her Mitch.

• • •

"TEND THE GARDEN," The Lord said.

The voice was an urgent whisper in Joe's ear, louder than the truck dieseling down Gervais Street. Joe had been sure he'd never hear that voice again. He'd killed Cyphus. He'd broken the most important commandment, and the Lord knew it. Joe had lived with that cold truth for how many nights?

"Tend the garden."

What garden? The graveyard? Joe glanced around his squat. No, this wasn't what the Lord was talking about. He had to figure it out—maybe the Lord was giving him one more chance, despite what he'd done. A chance he did not deserve.

Rag Doll had gone to jail but dang if she didn't hit the streets just a few months after. "I told them it was self-defense," Rag Doll explained. "That Cyphus was such a sorry son of a bitch I think they were glad he was dead."

"You gonna have a trial?" Joe had asked, because he couldn't let her take it that far.

"Nope. They believed me. I can be right convincing when I need to be," she had answered, and he knew it to be true.

"Joe," the voice spoke again.

He had one chore to do before taking on the Lord's assignment. The statue stood twice as tall as Joe, sleek white with an angel standing on top like a praying sentry. The brass plate that read "Mitchell Hastings" gleamed in the morning light. Joe pulled a napkin from his pocket and buffed the letters, even though there was no trace of dirt on them. Mr. Mitch's resting place would shine clean as long as Joe was around.

Mr. Mitch's name brought one garden to mind: a wide expanse of grass with scattered trees surrounded by all kinds of flowers. A tall fence nearly hidden by fluttery purple and pink blooms that Mr. Mitch had called hydrangeas. A cement area with long trails of vines and pale yellow lilies all around. Mr. Mitch took such pride in his yard, but months had passed. Who was tending to it now?

The Lord just told him who.

He did the walk to Mr. Mitch's house as fast as he could, cramming crackers into his mouth to fuel his steps. He hadn't been over to Mr. Mitch's house since he died. He'd seen the widow, though, going to church on Sundays with Miss Becca.

That tall woman, Miss Abby, had visited him in the graveyard, asking if he was okay, if he needed money, if he had a place to stay. He'd appreciated the kindness but didn't much care for the prying. He was fine, he told her, and maybe he was, if the Lord had come back to him.

When he arrived at the brick house where Mr. Mitch's family lived, he didn't ring the bell but slipped through the gate into the back yard. Maybe he'd have the garden looking tidy like Mr. Mitch liked before anyone knew he'd come.

He could see why the Lord sent him. The vines by the cement area had grown into a thick woody tangle. The bright flowers by the fence didn't have the luster they used to. The patch of lawn needed de-thatching and all the shrubs needed to be trimmed a good six inches. This would take several days but no matter, he had nothing but time. Time and the Lord's instructions.

He started on the vines, tugging and chopping and thinning and working up a good, cool sweat as the sun rose higher in the sky. Before he tackled the shrubs, he needed to get the clippers from the tool shed, so Joe opened the door and stepped into the cluttered little room.

It saddened him to see the film of dust on Mr. Mitch's tools. The neglected rakes hung on their racks; the shovels stood in the corner as though waiting for strong hands to put them to use. He snatched up a rag from the box Mr. Mitch kept under his table saw and went to work cleaning the tools and shelves. A broom behind the door took care of the floor and the thready cobwebs hanging from the lone light bulb. Once the shed looked tidier, he grabbed a pair of gloves and clippers and returned to the yard.

He was no longer alone. Mr. Mitch's wife, Mrs. Hastings, sat at the table with the tall woman, Miss Abby. Each had a cup of coffee. Joe eased the tools back into the shed, closed the door, and tried to figure out how to sneak from the yard without being spotted.

"Joe? I thought that was you. Come say hi." Miss Abby waved him over.

He wiped his hands on his britches and wished he could climb over the fence.

"Come on now. Don't be shy." Miss Abby had a way of speaking that made her hard to defy. Joe limped over, his gaze fixed on the gate.

"I see you've been hard at work," Mrs. Hastings said. "I appreciate it. I've let the yard go all to hell."

"You've been plenty busy, Le-Le. But you're right, we have to do something with this mess. Thank God Joe came by."

"Uhm. I'll be—"

"Having a cold glass of water." Miss Abby stood and hurried up the steps. "I'll be back in a second."

The remnants of vines made an untidy heap close to the table. He shouldn't have left the mess there; he scraped up the vines to take out to the street.

"Leave it there, Joe," Mrs. Hastings said. A chain hung from her neck, and attached to it was a small glittery stone like the one he'd found in the park. The one he'd left on Mr. Pinckney's headstone months ago, a thank you to the Lord for all he'd done.

"Just leave it for a moment," Mrs. Hastings said.

He didn't know what to do instead. He couldn't leave, not with Miss Abby bringing him water, and he couldn't work, because Mrs. Hastings didn't want him to. He stared at a spot of purple paint on the cement, wondering how he'd clean it up.

Miss Abby returned with the water, which he drank in four long swallows. "I think he wants to get back to work," Miss Abby said.

"Because we've left him such a mess," Mrs. Hastings replied.

Joe nodded his thanks for the refreshment and returned to the shrubbery. He clipped tall, spindly branches, and uprooted wild grape vines woven between the azaleas, glad to see the small, bright green leaves of new growth deep in the shrub. He approached the hydrangea bush by the fence. It had grown too tall, a wild, unkempt thing, but to trim it would mean cutting the blossoms.

He heard a voice, an odd, light sound, like a chuckle. Not the Lord. Not the devil. He turned to find a little boy standing there, half as tall as the bush, with black hair cut straight across his forehead and skin the color of dried leaves. The child looked up at him with eyes as dark as nighttime.

"Hey." Joe squatted down, ignoring the tweak of pain in his knees.

The boy pointed at one of the flowers.

"You like that?" Joe cut the bloom and handed it to the little boy.

The child squeezed the stalk with long-fingered hands. "Bonito."

"That means pretty." Miss Abby appeared, lifting the boy into her arms. "Joe, this is my son, Esteban."

The child looked nothing like Miss Abby, but rested his head against her chest, the flower clutched close to his chin, like those arms were where he belonged.

"Bath time," Miss Abby said. "Ring the bell before you leave, Joe. I have something for you."

Joe nodded and returned to his work. He'd leave the giant bush alone for now, let the beautiful flowers have their way. Next he'd tackle the grass, scatter fertilizer across the speckled patch of green so it could grow thick and lush, a soft place for a running little boy to land, a beautiful stretch of yard like Mr. Mitch liked it.

Mr. Mitch's garden would thrive, as long as Joe Booker walked the earth. The Lord told him to tend it, and that's exactly what he'd do.